A Doubter's Almanac

A Doubter's Almanac

Ethan Canin

BLOOMSBURY

LONDON · OXFORD · NEW YORK · NEW DELHI · SYDNEY

Bloomsbury Publishing
An imprint of Bloomsbury Publishing Plc

50 Bedford Square   1385 Broadway
London   New York
WC1B 3DP   NY 10018
UK   USA

www.bloomsbury.com

First published in Great Britain 2016

Grateful acknowledgement is made to the Mathematical Association of America
for permission to include the Professor Gamble problem from p. 49 of *The Contest Problem
Book VII* by Harold B. Reiter as well as the modified answer to said problem, copyright
© 2000 by the Mathematical Association of America. Reprinted by permission.

British Library Cataloguing-in-Publication Data
A catalogue record for this book is available from the British Library.

ISBN: HB: 978-1-4088-7964-1
TPB: 978-1-4088-7965-8
ePub: 978-1-4088-7962-7

2 4 6 8 10 9 7 5 3 1

Text design by Simon M. Sullivan
Printed and bound in Great Britain by CPI Group (UK) Ltd, Croydon CR0 4YY

To find out more about our authors and books visit www.bloomsbury.com.
Here you will find extracts, author interviews, details of forthcoming events
and the option to sign up for our newsletters.

For Barbara, Amiela, Ayla, and Misha,
and for my parents, Stuart and Virginia

Contents

PART TWO

Restatement

Conjecture

PART ONE

Induction

A Late Arrival

FROM THE KITCHEN window, Milo Andret watched the bridge over the creek, and when he saw Earl Biettermann's white Citroën race across the span he hurried out the door and picked up a short hoe. Biettermann was driving too fast. *Reckless* was the word for it—but that's the way he'd always been. Arrogant. Heedless. Lucky to stumble onto the right roads, the right career, the right woman. Lucky even to be alive. For any other driver, the route from the bridge to the cabin would take five minutes: Andret figured it would take Biettermann three.

Outside under the trees, he crossed as quickly as he could toward the garden, his feet today somehow obeying his commands. Next to the strawberries he lowered himself into the folding chair and used the coiled hose to dash a few palmfuls of water onto his shirt and hair. The sun was high. He ought to be sweating.

He heard the car throw gravel as it made the turn into the driveway. Then the engine shut off. A fan came on the way it did in French cars. Biettermann probably loved that fan. One door slam. Andret waited.

Then, a second.

He let them knock at the door to the cabin. His name called: "Professor! Professor!" This was an affectation. Then steps on the cluttered path to the back of the house, where he was bent low over the plants, pulling strenuously at the roots of a marauding false grape.

"Professor Andret!"

He turned to offer his greeting, squinting, wiping the spigot water from his brow. A shock: Earl Biettermann was in a wheelchair. He realized he'd heard something about that. From her, maybe?

He couldn't remember.

She was here, though—that was the important thing—and now she was guiding her husband in a wheelchair, pushing him in front of her across the bumpy ground like an offering. It could have been awful: but he saw immediately that it wasn't going to be.

He also realized with a start that she'd been the one driving.

Impossible

MILO ANDRET GREW up in northern Michigan, near Cheboygan, on the western edge of Lake Huron, where the offshore waters were fathomless and dark. The color of the lake there was closer to the stormy Atlantic hues of Lake Superior than to the tranquil, layered turquoise of Lake Michigan, which lapped at the tourist beaches on the far side of the state. Milo's father had been an officer in the navy during the Second World War, a destroyer's navigator driven by the hope of one day commanding his own ship; but at the age of twenty-four, after an incident in the Solomon Sea, he'd abandoned his ambitions. The incident had occurred in November 1943, just a year before Milo was born. Coming north out of the straits near Bougainville Island, the destroyer had been hit by a string of Japanese torpedoes, and in the wake of the explosions the ship's life rafts had drifted into unknown waters. Milo's father and another sailor had managed to get aboard one of the rafts, and before nightfall they'd picked up two more men. A week later, though, when a British cruiser finally sighted them off of Papua New Guinea, all but Milo's father had been eaten by sharks.

By the time Milo was born, his father had been discharged back to Cheboygan, where he'd found work as a science teacher at Near Isle

High School. It was a position from which, for the next thirty-nine years, he would neither be offered a promotion nor seek one.

Milo's mother had been the first female summa cum laude chemistry major in the history of Michigan State University; but she too was willing to forsake her ambitions. She raised Milo until he was old enough to go to school, and then she found a job as a secretary in the sheriff's department in Alpena, the county seat. In Alpena, she typed reports, brewed coffee, and made mild banter with a generally courteous group of men several years her senior, more than one of whom could neither read nor write.

This was most of what Milo knew of the lives of his parents.

After school his father graded homework in his office, and after work his mother sometimes stepped out for a drink with a few of the other secretaries from her building. On most afternoons, Milo walked up the hill from the bus stop to an empty house. By now it was the mid-1950s.

In those days Cheboygan was already something of a resort town, although Milo didn't realize this fact until he was older. For most of his childhood, he knew only the deep woods that ran behind their property—350 acres of sugar maple, beech, and evergreen that had managed to remain unlogged during the huge timber harvests that had denuded much of the rest of the state. He spent a good part of his days inside this forest. The soil there was padded with a layer of decaying leaves and needles whose scents mingled to form a cool spice in his nose. He didn't notice the smell when he was in it so much as feel its absence when he wasn't. School, home, any building he had to spend time in—they all left him with the feeling that something had been cleaned away.

The shaded hollows of his particular tract were populated by raccoons, skunks, opossum, and owls, and by the occasional fox or porcupine. The small meadows were ringed with ancient birches that crashed to the ground when the younger trees crowded them out, their fallen, crisscrossed trunks making shelters and bridges for him to discover. The woods were in transition, his father had told him.

When a great tree came down, the report could be heard for miles, a shifting crescendo of rustling and snapping as the trunk yanked away the limbs around it, culminating finally in a muffled thud like a sledgehammer striking moss. Whenever this occurred, Milo would set out to find the corpse. He had an intricate memory of the landscape's light and shade and could tell instantly when even a small piece of it had been altered. Something in his brain picked up disturbance acutely.

How many hours he spent in those woods! He was an only child and from early in his life had invented solitary games—long treks into the landscape with certain self-imposed rules (two right turns to every left, exactly a thousand steps from departure to return, the winding brook crossed only where it bent to the west). These games passed the most precious part of the day for him, the too-short interlude between the time the school bus released him at the bottom of the hill and six o'clock, when his mother came out to the edge of the woods holding the lid of a garbage can and banged it three times with a broom handle to call him for dinner.

The Andrets lived fifteen miles from the beaches on Lake Huron; but it might as well have been a hundred. His father stayed to the land in a part of the state where everyone else was drawn to the water. This was no doubt attributable to his experience in the Solomon Sea, but Milo was too young to understand something like that. On weekends his father went hunting with his friends or tinkered around the house, or if the weather was poor he sat in a chair by the fire and worked puzzles from a magazine. In the Andret family, there was never any question of shared recreation—no canoe trips, no bicycle rides, no walks together at the shore. Such dalliances were from another universe. There were no pets, either, and no games other than a couple of boxes of playing cards and an old chess set of Philippine ivory that had been brought back from the navy. If Mr. Andret was at home, he was either grading schoolwork or performing household repairs, walking around with a tool belt and setting a ladder against the eaves. He would finish one job and move on to the next, never alerting anyone to what he was doing. If his mother was there, she was in the kitchen, at the small table by the window, with a glass and a book. If Milo wasn't at school, he was in the woods.

The Andret house was an old-fashioned, darkly painted, thoroughly ornamented Victorian that had been built by a prosperous farmer at the turn of the century, as though it would one day sit on the main square of a town. It was three stories high with a steeply raftered roof whose scalloped tiles radiated a statuesque formality. But to Milo there was always something disappointing about this formality. From the time he was young it had seemed forlorn to him, like a woman in a ball gown sitting at a bus stop. (This wasn't his own phrase; it was his wife's, uttered many years later, when she first crested the hill.) The walls were an evening blue, both inside and out, and the exterior trim was a deep maroon. Everything a shade too dark. There was a sidewalk in front, but it ended at the property stake. A brass mailbox stood on a post at the head of the driveway, and an exactingly painted garage looked out from buttressed eaves at the rear. The property boasted all the details of a fine residence in a fine little town, except for the town itself, which had never appeared.

The Andrets' house was the only one for miles.

EVEN AT A young age, Milo understood that he was in large part a replica of his father, this solitary, middle-aged man who shared their house with them but who appeared to will himself away from anyone even when he was at home. When Mr. Andret wasn't grading schoolwork, he was walking unceasingly through his dominion, mending all sorts of breakage and deterioration that were apparent only to him.

Like his father, Milo himself learned at a young age to carve wood. Very fine objects, in fact. But also like his father, he never showed anyone what he'd made. He whittled ornate whistles that he rarely blew, detailed animal figurines that he abandoned in the undergrowth, and intricate talismans of celestial design, which he hid in the dimples of maple burls or inside the crevices of the twisted roots that emerged from the forest's peat like tangles of surfacing snakes. For his finer work, he used a magnifying glass.

One day while whittling a whistle from a tiny piece of tamarack, he turned the magnifying glass a certain way and watched a scalding yellow dot lift a curl of smoke out of the bark.

Did others know about this?

He turned the lens the same way again and held it still. When the wood began to smolder, he wet his thumb and rubbed out the ember. Then he whittled away the imperfection and carefully burned a tiny star into the spot. After that, he began burning this tiny star into everything he made, as a signature. It wasn't that he felt any particular pride in his work but rather that the miniaturized sun itself, inverted and shimmering as he guided its bead across the grain, seemed like a force that had been revealed only to him. The smoke lifted off and vanished: something from nothing. Magic. He was aware that other similar powers might exist in the universe. That morning, when he left the newly carved whistle in a bed of ferns, he felt that he was performing an act of humility before some unnameable entity.

ONE NIGHT, DURING the summer of his thirteenth year, a windstorm swept down the straits, and he was awakened in bed by a crashing from the woods. The next morning, at the edge of a ravine, he came across a stump that was as wide across as a tractor tire. It was a beech tree, broken off at the level of his waist. The rest of the tree lay several yards away, neatly divided into three, as though the immense thing had been scissored up, carried off to a safe distance, and placed down for his inspection. He took a seat on the rim of the broken base. For the whole morning he sat there, contemplating what had presented itself to him, until an inspiration arrived.

He spent the rest of the summer executing his idea.

Over the long days of July, then the shorter ones of August and September, he hardly came in from the forest. He found that he could work for ten or even twelve hours at a stretch, so that by the time fall arrived, he realized that he'd produced something miraculous. It was a single, continuous loop of wooden chain, more than twenty-five feet long, carved out of the top of the stump and resting above it on hundreds of tiny spurs that had been whittled down to the thickness of finishing nails. The chain coiled in a tightening spiral toward the center of the tree, then doubled back and coiled out again toward the rim, returning to the spot where the last link closed around the first. He'd carved a twist into each of the links, which produced a startling effect: if he ran his finger all the way around the surface of any single one of them, the finger would circle not once but *twice* around the twisted link before returning to its starting point. This strange fact felt like another secret to him.

Finally, one peat-scented evening in the warm October of 1957, he understood that he had finished. He had needed his creation to be perfect, and now it was. One last time, he ran his hands over the length of it, feeling for flaws. Then he severed the spurs and meticulously sanded away their nubs. At last, he lifted the whole thing into his arms, doubling it around and around his shoulders until the slack was gone. It felt like a living thing now, yet it was as smooth and heavy as stone. When he breathed, it tightened around his chest. Standing in the quietly darkening woods, as the lights began to come on in the distant house, he felt like an escape artist, preparing a feat.

THAT NIGHT, BEFORE he went home, he stowed the chain in the trunk of a maple. The maple had been struck by lightning, and inside it was a cavity that he'd smoothed with a rasp, adding a meticulously carved cover piece that he'd cut with a wire saw and blended into the ridges of a burl. He'd carved the screw threads of the cover in reverse, so that even if his hiding place was discovered, his chain would be safe: nobody would think to unscrew a cover backward.

In his mind, this was the end of it. He would no more have shown his parents what he'd made than he would have asked what his father was fixing on the ladder or his mother reading at the table. Once, as a child, he'd come across his mother crying at the back of the kitchen, holding an old newspaper in her hands; but he'd never asked her what had been the matter. Since that day, silence had become their standard. He felt affection for his parents, and he understood that they felt affection for him. But the three of them hardly questioned one another, and they almost never revealed to one another anything of importance.

On the day he finished closing the chain inside the tree, however, he realized that he'd passed a milestone in his life: he'd long wanted to produce something worthy of concealing.

As IT TURNED out, though, he did show the chain to somebody: a teacher. Mr. Farragut was the shop instructor at Near Isle High, and a year later, as he was lecturing on the industrial applications of ferrous metals, nonferrous metals, open-grain woods, and closed-grain woods, he mentioned that nobody, for example, would ever choose to make a chain from wood.

"Where'd you get this thing?" he said the next afternoon as Milo pulled the beechwood creation in long loops from a burlap sack.

"Made it."

Mr. Farragut chuckled, then caught Milo's expression and quieted. He bent forward to examine one of the links.

Milo knew what he was looking for. "There isn't any," he said.

"Any what?"

"Glue."

After several more minutes of inspection, Mr. Farragut finally said, "I see that, son. What's your name again?"

"Milo Andret."

"Well, Milo, I don't see offhand how this was done. And I hate to say it, but I certainly don't believe you made it yourself." He pushed the coiled loops back across the table. Then he added, not unkindly, "And I have to say, I doubt your friends will, either."

. . .

THIS WASN'T A problem. Milo didn't have friends.

It wasn't that people didn't like him. In fact, plenty of them *did*. On a fairly regular basis they would approach. But there was something about him that dependably turned them away—as a young boy he'd become aware of this unchangeable fact—some glancing force that never failed to deflect their attempts at friendship. And it wasn't that he didn't like other people himself. He did, generally speaking.

He just couldn't figure out what to say to anyone.

The wooden chain came back home with him. He coiled it into its waxed burlap sack and stowed it again inside the trunk of the maple.

HE DID HAVE one friend, actually. Perhaps not a friend, but there was something different about a certain kid at school. Vene Wheelwright was the son of the lighthouse keeper at Cheboygan Point. He was an unusual boy. Self-reliant, like Milo. Quick to leave school at the end of the day, also like Milo. Slight of build—again like Milo—and adept in the woods, like just about every other boy around Cheboygan. But unlike Milo, Vene had a fire inside him. He was an ordinary-looking young man, sharp boned and rabbitish, but wherever he went, people gathered. Though he didn't talk much, he always knew what to say. Vene was a great climber and would in a moment break free from a ring of classmates to scale the high schoolyard fence and sit gleefully at the top. Once, Milo watched him pull himself up the courtyard flagpole by its wire halyard until he was hanging by the crook of one elbow from the small globe at its peak. With the other arm, he was waving.

Vene and Milo sometimes spoke, though usually not more than a few words. They didn't have any classes together, but whenever they passed in the hall, Vene would say something like "How's it moving, Milo," and offer his hand, which Milo would shake, saying something in return like "It's moving along, Vene. How's it moving on your side?"

What amazed Milo, though, was that Vene always seemed happy to see him.

Once, on a bike ride that Vene took one Sunday morning after church, he pedaled all the way out to Milo's house. Mrs. Andret called Milo in from the woods, then baked cookies for the two of them. She hovered over the visitor, the way everyone hovered over him, and encouraged him to stay. After the cookies, Vene and Milo went back out to the woods, where over the course of the afternoon they walked together comfortably, almost without speaking. They whittled lances from hickory saplings. They treed a raccoon. They climbed a beech tree by crossing to its crutch from the limbs of a maple. It was a frightening traverse for Milo—although not apparently for Vene— and when the two of them were on the ground again, walking home, Milo felt a kind of calm that he'd never felt in the presence of another person. When he was with Vene, there was no pressure for either of them to say anything. This solved Milo's great problem.

"A strange name" was all Mrs. Andret said later that afternoon as they watched Vene pedal away down the slope. She sat down again at the table and stirred her drink, but Milo could see that she maintained her gaze out the window until the bike had disappeared at the bend.

To be fair, Vene was happy to see *everyone*. But still, the fact that he was pleased to see Milo generally astonished him. Milo expected Vene's affection to fade. It was another mystery to him, in fact, that it never did. Vene was reliably welcoming to him for all the time they knew each other.

Still, he wasn't exactly a friend. They saw each other in school, and they spoke whenever they passed, and they shook hands in the halls the way they did and once in a while even ate together in the cafeteria. But Vene didn't ever come to the house again.

It always seemed that he would have, though, if Milo had asked.

. . .

Milo himself was never truly pleased to see anyone, not even Vene.

This was just the world as he knew it.

His childhood was neither happy nor unhappy, and the thought of either would hardly have occurred to him. He lived in his woods like an animal, aware only of the hierarchy of necessary information— the nearness of evening or dawn, the overwarm humidity that meant a thunderstorm, the wintertime reversal of the prevailing breeze and the descent of a padded quiet from the southwest that meant, between October and May, the onset of snow. He kept a handful of books in an old metal tackle box in the crook of a stump and had built several shelters where he could read them even in a downpour. He liked Jack London and Willa Cather and Mark Twain, along with the occasional biography of a ballplayer or crime boss. He was unaware of the distinction between a young man's books and an adult's books, and in those days would read either one with equal pleasure.

The remainder of his world was as solitary as the woods. Now and then, his mother gave dinner parties, but he didn't take much notice of them, eating his own portion silently and keeping his eyes averted, much as his father did. At school there were the ordinary problems with bullies, and he was knocked around a bit—not badly—once or twice a year, always in the fall. Then left alone. It was a ritual that seemed to establish whatever needed to be established at Near Isle High School. It happened to plenty of other kids, too. His father expected him to fight back, but he couldn't bring himself to do it. Instead, he would go into the forest afterward by himself, the way a maimed animal might seek familiar shelter. Here is where his humiliation would transform itself. He'd pick up a fallen limb, then stride along, swinging it against the rows of trunks until it shattered. Then he would do the same thing with the fragment that remained, and with the one that remained after that, until finally he was swinging nothing but his own stinging hand, clamped around a shard. When he left the woods he felt absolved.

His mother, if she'd known of his solitary ritual, would have preferred it to fighting. But his father believed in the primacy of reputation. He would have been disgraced.

With the exception of these minor, fall-semester humiliations, however—which rarely resulted in anything worse than torn pants or a few welts on his cheeks, or sometimes a trail of blood drops across his shirt—the tough kids at school left him alone. They perhaps respected the fact that his father was a teacher there. For this, Milo felt a note of gratitude.

Welcome to the World

THEN ONE YEAR something different occurred.

This was December 1958. The sunless winter had painted the coast an unshadowed gray. On the news, integration was being delivered by bus to the public schools and another Pioneer rocket had failed to circle the moon. Not long before Thanksgiving, a local Great Lakes freighter, the SS *Carl D. Bradley,* had gone down in a gale off Gull Island, drowning most of the men aboard. A dozen kids from Near Isle High School had lost their fathers.

At school, services were held in the classrooms, sometimes instead of classes, and in the weeks that followed, a quiet descended on the building. It was like something Milo might have sensed in the woods, the approach of weather. Walking in the hallway one afternoon after the last bell, he was stopped by an upperclassman, one of the innumerable Polish kids whose fathers manned the freighters or worked in the quarries where their tumblehome hulls were loaded with calcite. Milo wasn't unaccustomed to being approached by schoolmates he didn't know. This one tapped him on the shoulder and said in a soft voice, "You carved some kind of chain?"

Milo leaned forward to hear. "I guess so."

"What you do that for?"

Milo thought about it. "I don't know. Wanted to see if I could, I guess."

The boy's face was blank. At the periphery now, a group of other boys had appeared, milling in the background.

"It take you a long time?"

"Couple of months," said Milo. "How'd you hear about it?"

"Mr. F told me you wanted to hand it over."

"How's that?"

The boy, who was so skinny his shirt bagged over his belt, whispered something.

Milo leaned in closer. "What?" he said.

"I said, what you think I got here?" The boy reached above his head to pull the light cord. Milo looked up at where he was reaching.

When the hall turned over, he remembered noticing that there was no light cord at all, only the rows of pine boards on the ceiling, punctuated by rusting nail heads. After that, there were only the blows.

THE SCHOOL NURSE shaved his temple. When she pulled away the pad of gauze, it dripped blood onto the tray. "That's *mine*?" Milo said.

He hadn't seen a mirror.

"Nasty little punks," she answered. "What'd you do to deserve this?"

"I really don't know. I made something."

"Like what?"

Milo shrugged. "A chain."

"You hit one of them with it?"

He eked out a laugh.

She looked at him, her manner easing. "Well," she said, taking his elbow, "they did a number on you, anyway."

She wiped his wounds with iodine. He tried not to show her how much it burned. Then she lifted his shirt and examined his ribs. The boy who'd done it had lifted Milo's shirt, too, had yanked the tails up over his head, then tripped him backward, so that when the punching started he was on the floor inside a sack, his arms pinned in beside him. He winced as the nurse eased the collar up over his head. Before moving to his back, she brought him a mirror. Up and down his spine were clumps of bright red rectangles.

"Steel-toed," she said.

"WHY WAS HE asking about a chain?" said his mother, turning from the sink of dishes.

"I guess they wanted it." He shrugged. "It was something I made."

At this point, they asked him to show it to them. He went out to the woods, and when he returned, they both admired it in their reserved way, which meant that his mother regarded it for a long moment with a smile on her lips, and his father picked it up and inspected several of the links. His father had had a drink that night, too, which he rarely did.

The chain lay on the table now. Milo gazed at it as his mother went back to her washing. He could resurrect every link in his mind, the change in color at each turn of grain.

With a clank, his father set down his glass. He went to the closet, and when he came back to the table he was putting on his hunting coat. "People punch *up*," he said. "They punch the ones who are better than them. Nobody likes a kid who does something well. That's what happened."

This was a compliment. Milo was aware of it.

In the mirror above the mantel now, he regarded his own face. From the work of the nurse, his hair was ragged across the brow, and on one temple was a gauze bandage that was weeping a dark stain. His neck was crisscrossed with scabs that in the low light looked like caterpillars crawling on his skin. He couldn't keep his eyes off them.

He was a different person. He could sense it. When the kicks had started, he'd thrashed away from them and tried to kick back, but then, when they'd moved from his spine to his skull, he'd just curled up and let himself surrender. That's when he'd felt himself rising. The thing was, there had been pleasure in it.

This was something he could never tell anyone.

"Next time," his father was saying, "you hit 'em. Before they get the jump. That's how you do it. You hit 'em with whatever you have in your hand."

"You do no such thing, Milo." His mother held a soapy plate in her hands. "He has a better way of dealing with his problems."

"The bridge of the nose is good. Butt 'em with your forehead right there, between the eyes."

"He has—"

"You hit 'em with a bat, Milo. You kick 'em in the nuts. You smash a book into their face—you do whatever the hell you have to. You move *fast*. Do you hear? You show 'em what you're made of, or they follow you around the rest of your life. That's the deal. Do you understand?"

"Henry," said his mother, "what you're telling him—"

"Do you understand?"

"Yes," said Milo.

His father stood, nearly toppling his chair. Then, coming around the table, he leaned down to whisper in Milo's ear.

"What was that?" said his mother.

"I was talking to my son."

"Well, what did you say to him?"

At the threshold, he said, "If I'd wanted you to hear, I would have said it loud enough."

The door rattled on its hinges.

When the sound of his footsteps was gone, his mother sat down beside him. She finished the drink that was on the table, then reached over and laid her hand on his arm. After a moment, she withdrew it and returned to the sink. The faucet sprayed noisily, and the pots and pans rattled against the basin.

"Well," she said after a time, "what did he say?"

"I don't know," Milo answered. "I didn't hear."

SOONER THAN HE would have imagined, though, his wounds had healed. He was different now, he knew, but he also knew that he probably didn't appear any different to the other kids at school. People paid no more or less attention to him than they had before. Not long after the incident, Vene had stopped him in the cafeteria with a couple of friends and offered to help him find the attackers; but Milo had put him off, saying he didn't remember what they looked like and that all the Polish kids were pretty much the same, anyway. There were hundreds of them at Near Isle.

The truth, though, was that he'd learned something. As he'd felt himself giving in to the blows, he'd understood that he was entirely alone in the world. He lived in it alone, and at that moment, alone, he might actually depart it.

The truth was that this had comforted him. That's what he'd learned.

Vene didn't mention the incident again, and before long, even Milo had stopped thinking about it. His life renarrowed. Every morning, he walked down the long hill to the bus, and every afternoon he returned, climbing the slope toward the dark house, dropping his books in the kitchen and heading out again into the woods. At night in his room, before climbing into bed, he did a few minutes of homework.

Strangely, though, he would never have said that he was lonely.

Whenever his mother had a free moment, she was reading a novel—and, of course, his father was a teacher—but Milo, unlike many such solitary souls, wasn't a particularly good student. He enjoyed the books he chose for himself, but he found the ones assigned to him a chore, like sickling the tall grass that grew up between the house and the garage or sweeping the floor of his father's shed. He had passing grades in social studies, citizenship, shop, and history.

Once in an art course he'd been told by a teacher that he possessed talent; but the subject held no interest for him. As a courtesy to his father, he made good grades in science, but that was the extent of it. Math bored him.

HE HAD, OF course, heard what his father had said to him. What he'd whispered in his ear was "Welcome to the world."

Singularity Theory

ONE SATURDAY IN June, his mother banged the garbage-can lid at dinnertime, but when he came in from the woods he found his parents sitting in the Plymouth. His father beckoned him into the backseat. As soon as he got in, they drove away. His father was dressed in a flannel shirt and a fedora. When they stopped, they were in downtown Cheboygan. The Andrets rarely came here. His father paid to park at the pier, even though it would have cost nothing to park a block away. Already this was strange. So was the fedora. The day was warm. Along the boardwalk, a bicycle cab was bumping across the planks and a cotton-candy salesman was spinning cones. The sun was low already, and where the dark lake was disturbed by watercraft it winked with painful brightness, as though the moving vessels were sprinkling glass behind them. Today was his parents' anniversary, he discovered. He could see that there had been some kind of disagreement, though. His mother fidgeted with a picnic basket.

At the public pier, they rented a boat. Now, this was stupendous. A bright blue wooden dinghy, fifteen or sixteen feet long, with a plank seat at the oarlocks and a high-backed bench in the rear, shaded by a canopy. It looked like the king's skiff in a royal amusement ride. Warily, his father examined it. Then he took off his hat, held it to the side, and jumped down into the hull. The vessel shifted, its keel striking the still surface with a sound like a pan slapping a table, before it steadied against the dock. He took his position at the oars, then waited with a hard expression while Milo and his mother climbed in under the canopy. The picnic basket was placed on the floor. In a moment they'd set out for the northern point of the harbor, a short distance across the inlet, his father's rhythmic stroke swiftly shortening the stretch of water that had now begun to reflect the purplish gold of the sunset. The oarlocks creaked, and the slatted seatback pressed and eased against Milo's spine. Beyond the breakwater lay open lake. As they crossed the far end of the timber-roofed pier, the church bells chimed eight o'clock.

ALMOST FIFTEEN YEARS later, at his interview for graduate school at the University of California, Berkeley, the famous Dr. Hans Borland, of the Borland invariant, asked Milo how he'd first become interested in mathematics.

"I was out on the water with my parents," Milo began. Something had changed in him, and he'd found in his twenties that he could tell stories, even long ones, with surprising ease. Nonetheless, he'd remained as alone in the world as he'd always been and could still neither predict nor understand the behavior of others. He remembered Dr. Borland leaning forward. A glimpse of shrewd irises above gold-stemmed trifocals.

"It was evening," Milo said. "We'd gotten a late start. This was in Lake Huron. The northern part."

"Lake Huron," said Dr. Borland, peering over his spectacles. "An underappreciated body of water."

Someone laughed.

"My father took no pleasure in boats," said Milo.

"A disadvantage on the Great Lakes, is it not?"

"He had his reasons."

Milo waited for something more. If they asked, he would tell the story about the Solomon Sea.

"Go on with what you were saying, young man," said another professor, from the back of the room. "What happened on the lake?"

"It was mid-November," said Milo. "Practically winter in our part of the state. My father had rowed us out past the harbor, but he hadn't accounted for the currents or the dark." He paused now, enjoying the quiet. "By the time the sun set, we were still a good ways out. Then the wind came up. It built a sea. Three- or four-foot swells. It was a small boat. We were coming down pretty hard into the troughs. My father's left arm is stronger than his right—we're a family of lefties—and we got turned around."

"Ah," said Professor Borland. "Interesting—and you too are a lefty?"

"Yes, I am."

"Go on."

"So, in the dark, he began rowing us"—here he paused—"away from land. The hills north of town block the light, so when you're out that deep you can't really see much. Lake Huron might as well be an ocean. My father's a good navigator, but he must have been keeping track by some other landmark—maybe the lights from the salmon boats up to the northeast. I figured he knew he was rowing us deeper, so I didn't say anything. Not for a while, anyway. But eventually I realized he didn't know that he was bringing us the wrong way—out to sea."

"And how did *you* know that?" said Dr. Borland, leaning forward now.

"I've always been able to do it."

"Do what?"

"Maintain awareness of my coordinates. Know where I am."

"Day or night?"

"Either one. Doesn't matter. I don't think it depends on sight."

"And what does your father do?"

"He rowed us a quarter mile further out—"

"I mean, what's his job? What does he do for work? I assume he's still living."

"He teaches high school. At the school I went to. Chemistry and physics."

"Which might explain such a skill in the boy," said Dr. Borland, briefly turning to the other faculty. A couple of them nodded. "Although you might have expected the old man himself to have positional aptitude. Which he obviously hasn't."

Milo could see that the story had impressed his questioners, and he decided not to offer anything more. He chose not to mention his mother, for example, who could always give directions in the car without consulting a map. Or her brother, who made a living in Las Vegas playing blackjack from a memory system.

There were other problems with the story, as well. The November part of it, for one. This was far from the truth. As was the wind. They'd indeed gotten lost in the moonless night, but it had been in June, in warm weather, on a calm lake. In fact, the summertime wind on that part of Lake Huron almost always calmed at dusk, rather than grew stronger. And by November, when the salmon were in the rivers, the fishing boats were in dry dock. But he was sure that none of these men would know such facts. The water in reality had been as smooth as oil, and the air had been a warmish, comforting presence on his skin. His mother had nonetheless grown worried as dark fell over the shore, and his father had responded with grimness and silence, pulling strenuously at the oars until, by Milo's estimation, they were a half mile out to sea, under a black planetarium sky. That's when Milo had finally led them home.

"In actual fact," said Dr. Borland, turning his head again to the others, "very few can do this sort of intrinsic, spatial mapping." There were murmurs, and he returned his gaze to Milo. "And this marked the beginning of your interest in mathematics?"

"I suppose it did."

"And you led your parents home that night because you could picture the plane of the earth and had accounted for all your movements on it."

"I could, Professor. I did."

In fact, he'd long been able to picture the world, all of its six directions, his exact place in any three-dimensional topography. Perhaps the skill had evolved from his years in the pathless woods. For as long as he could remember, his surroundings had been forming themselves into an inverted, low-sloping bowl, a hemisphere of smoothly shifting coordinates in which his position at the center was continually being recalibrated. That part was true. The other details just made the story more memorable.

"Amazing," said Dr. Borland, peering at him again over the tops of his glasses.

"I would call it the bowl of the earth, actually, Professor Borland. Not a plane. An upside-down bowl. A spherical cap, as one of you might say."

"I stand corrected."

Now there was laughter. Borland silenced it with a finger. "Tell us, young man," he said, "how do you pronounce your name?"

"Milo, sir. Like *silo*."

"And the surname?"

"Andret," he said. He glanced down. "Like *bandit,* but with the *r* there."

"Ah," said the professor, turning briefly to his colleagues. "The Midwest."

There was laughter again, looser this time, but Borland once more silenced it with a finger. He turned to the room. "Some of you might have noticed," he said drily, "that this candidate did not take the usual exams. On the recommendation of a colleague from the great state of Michigan"—here he bowed, slightly mockingly, in Milo's direction—"I had him sent a few problems instead, which I chose myself." He turned to the audience. "Let me tell you, gentlemen, these were not your standard questions from the graduate record exam." Now he turned to Milo. "Do you know how you did on them, young man?"

"No, sir, I don't."

"Suffice it to say—" Now he removed his glasses. "Suffice it to say,

I see a great deal of potential in you." He looked up. "This is a name, gentlemen—Milo Andret—that you'll all be wise to remember."

There was some coughing. Then silence. Milo could discern little meaning from it. Almost a decade before, as a freshman at Michigan State, he'd earned a perfect score in linear algebra, better than all of the graduate students in the class, without doing a single evening of homework. But for the five years since his degree, he'd been working at a Gulf station in Lansing.

"Young man," said Dr. Borland, "your qualification exam was remarkable." He removed his glasses and peered down at him. "Truly remarkable."

Milo was silent. He'd had a smattering of Cs in the humanities and one D, in sociology.

"And you spent your twenties working in a filling station?"

"It was a service station, really. I did plenty of engine work. I wanted to get a little experience." His father had suggested he might be asked such a question.

"Well, you've had an exceptional, if not a bit erratic, record in college," Professor Borland said. "Let us hope the experience has matured you." He quieted the murmuring. "Let us also hope that we haven't wasted too much time in finding you. I'm sure you'll fit in very well with the mathematics program at the University of California, Berkeley. Which we consider, by the way"—here he snapped away his gaze—"to be the best on the planet."

Deduction

Nature Never Lies

IN GRADUATE SCHOOL, Dr. Borland was assigned as his adviser. At the time, Hans Borland was the most famous mathematician in the country. His office was the size of a living room, its walls cut by a band of California sunlight that flamed the plaster and jeweled the long, floral-patterned Persian carpet on the floor, as though real flower petals had been sewn into the wool. Milo had never seen colonial furniture. Nor glass-fronted bookshelves with beveled panes. Against the spines of the professor's books, the light fanned itself into straight-sided rainbows. A long window framed the perfect green grass below the bell tower, and in the distance, under high clouds, the bay shimmered like a sheet of mercury.

The man himself was distinguished in every way. A pressed shirt striped in contrary nap and a thrust-knotted tie. The stately trifocals. He seemed to have aged since the interview, though, and he wandered tensely about the room as he spoke—table to window, window back to table—as if trying to dispel a physical urge. In a carved bow-backed chair in the center of the rug, Milo sat warily.

"I could do the same thing myself, you know," Borland was saying, lowering himself finally into the chair behind the desk. "Once could, at least. I recognized you immediately."

"You recognized *me*?"

"As myself, you know. *You*—a young Hans Borland."

"Well—thank you, Professor."

"The way we both have of locating ourselves in the world. It's a rare thing to witness." Once he was seated, his movements seemed to liquefy. "And two lefties, on top of it all." He lifted that hand, and with the other one reached across the desk to proffer a stoppered decanter. "Dry sherry?"

"No, no. No thank you."

The professor poured a glass for himself, then pulled a sheaf of folders from a drawer and waved them over the blotter. "We turned down several hundred applicants with better records than yours, I should add. From far-better departments, too, obviously." He tilted the sherry to his lips, closing his eyes. "Why? Because I had the feeling we should take a gamble on you, Mr. Andret." The eyes opened and found their way over the lip of the crystal. "I'll lay it on the line, young man: your exam was remarkable. Probably the best I've ever seen. No, *certainly* the best. I glimpse the possibility of greatness in you, Andret. My father was a chemistry teacher, too, you know, just like yours. Were you aware of that? East Scranton High School. What do you know about topology?"

Milo felt heat on his cheeks. "Professor?"

"What do you know about the field of topology?"

"I've read some Fréchet. And maybe some Euler. And a little Hausdorff."

Borland stared at him. "That's like an English Ph.D. saying he's read some Shakespeare and a little Melville, and maybe a bit of Tolstoy."

Milo flushed.

"And what did you learn from your little bit of Hausdorff?"

"I suppose I haven't read it carefully enough, Professor."

"That's right, you haven't." The old man swept the folders back across his desk. "But let me tell you something—topology is your future, young man. I'll have my secretary put a reading list in your box. Go home and study it."

. . .

CALIFORNIA. IT SWEPT him in. The drums in the parks. The racks of
clothes for sale on the street corners. The ocean light billowing all the
time in the sky like a sheet snapping on a line.

In North Oakland he found an apartment. A basement flat lit by
two windows high apart on the wall, through which the constant
milling commerce of Grove Street cast its shadows. A clicking stam-
pede of pants and skirts and boots and heels that jettisoned cigarettes
and coffee cups and sandwich wrappers at all hours of the day and
night. Every morning he lifted the glass and cleared away what had
gathered in the wells. The caretaker of a filthy, fishless aquarium. Yet
at the same time there was an aspect to the outlook that was akin to
the maple and beech forest of his childhood. The sense of a con-
strained world that nonetheless suggested a borderless one. His first
weeks, he spent hours staring through the high frames of glass. Constant sameness. Constant newness. The swift legs of pedestrians scis-
soring a wobbling flame of sun.

It was a way to think.

He'd had a rocky start in the department. He was still drawn to
numbers, of course. This part was unwavering. Number theory. The
charismatic singularity of primes and semi-primes. The inevitability
of numeric functions and their astounding analytic capture of the
world—the V-shaped cadres of flying geese he'd watched as a boy,
the fragmenting clouds yielding to disorder high above the two glass-
paned graphs through which he now gazed hour upon hour. It was as
though the numerals had been expressly fabricated, like more-perfect
words, to elucidate the details of creation. He wanted to say this to
someone. Instead, he sat in his thrift-store chair and watched the
passing legs: steps, random crossings, the probability of flows. Mathematics not only described it all but could in large terms predict it. In
his bed sometimes he wondered absently if it could be developed to
alter it.

He was interested in other fields besides topology. Commutative algebra, for one: the work of Gauss and Cayley and Lasker. But whenever he spoke with Hans Borland about it, the old man seemed irritated.

"Topology's the one for you, Andret," the professor said brusquely, the next time they met. "I guarantee it. Forget algebra. Forget Gauss. Lasker was just a chess player with airs. Topology's a perfect suit to your gifts, man. That sense we both have of the world. The rest's a waste of your time." He exhaled tiredly. "And talent." A glass of sherry stood on the polished desk. He raised his left hand again, dramatically, as though it affirmed his conclusion. "Should have been a topologist myself."

"You still can be, Professor."

"A wasted thought." He sipped from the narrow glass, then set it down carefully, as if balancing an egg. "Have you read Bott and Kuratowski and the rest on the list?"

"Yes."

"And what did you find there to work on?"

"I guess I haven't settled on anything. Nothing specific yet, anyway."

"Well," he sniffed, "focus yourself. Settle on something."

Now AND THEN, one or another of the graduate students in his department would stop by for an assignment or to discuss a problem. The conversation would begin optimistically; then it would falter, as conversations had all his life. Milo watched his colleagues walk back up the stairs of his apartment into the hectic brightness of the day. Satchels swinging at their sides. The spring-loaded door whooshing and slapping.

He needed something to fill the hours. Borland's admonition breathed steadily in his ear. Startling. He'd somehow not fully appreciated that a graduate student was obligated to write a dissertation. How insanely idiotic to be unaware of a requirement like that. He needed something to unbind his thinking.

One day in Evans Library, he noticed that a girl was watching him. She was sitting at a desk by the window, and he was standing all the way across the room at the shelves along the far wall, looking at a book about Tycho Brahe, the great sixteenth-century astronomer. When he glanced over again, the girl was still looking in his direction. Dark hair and a man's button-down shirt. That's all he could see. He shifted his gaze.

Brahe had used a quatrant to define the orbits of the planets. Milo flipped a page and found a drawing of the instrument itself, which looked like a mariner's sextant but was many times larger. Onto the palm of his hand, he sketched the spoked arms and the notched, chordal circumference.

When he walked back out of the stacks, she was gone.

That afternoon, at a lumberyard near the bay, he bought some cheap lengths of maple from a scrap pile. In a trash can behind the five-and-dime he found a sheaf of balsa. From there it was straight-forward. A couple of weeks later, the arc and axis had emerged from the maple, and the calibrated rim from the balsa. It was scrupulous work—but so was a wooden chain and so was a mathematical proof. Puny assaults on the heavens.

Distractions, too. He was well aware that he needed to distract himself.

THAT SEMESTER HE was taking algebraic geometry, Lie groups, and special topics in number theory. Six problem sets per week, each calculation illustrated, each solution rederived for accuracy. Again: distractions. He was also teaching two sections of undergraduate calculus. And all the while, the carefully angled quatrant stood alongside the door of his apartment, steadily emerging from its parts. Turning back to his desk with its piles of student quizzes to mark, he imagined himself in a world where the workings of the heavens remained a mystery, a world in which observation alone might propel forward the lot of man.

This astral machine was going to lead him to a discovery. That's what he told himself. Not directly, but along an obliquity. The sun's otherwise imperceptible climb across the equinoxes. His daily, progressive readings on the notched scales. The enterprise touching him, unexpectedly, with a remembered calm. This would free him.

Alone in a city that ran like an unclean river outside his window, he found, for the first time in his life, that he desired friendship. This, too, might free his thinking.

"WELL?" BORLAND SAID, offering the decanter.

"Okay, sure."

A bright November afternoon. In the distance, a pale-blue Frisbee rose above the frame of the window, hovered like a flying saucer, and descended into shouts.

Borland filled a glass with sherry and slid it across the desk, then cast his glance where Milo had been looking. The Frisbee showed itself again. "An imperfect set of parabolic coordinates," he said. "More aerodynamics than quadratics. Still, one of the benefits of the view."

"Along with the Dopplerized shouts," said Milo.

Borland chuckled, leaning back with his glass. He seemed to be enjoying the conversation. "Christian Doppler was a mathematician more than a physicist," he said. "Son of a bricklayer, you know."

"Is that right?"

His eyes found Milo's. "Yes, it's right."

Something had soured the man.

"I just meant I didn't know that about him."

"Doppler's work wasn't particularly impressive," Borland said flatly. "Not compared to his reputation."

"I don't know much of his history."

"Evidently."

"But I'd like to. I'd like to read more of it."

"Nature never lies," Borland said, leaning forward to refill his glass. "That's what history tells us."

"I see."

"Men lie."

"Okay." Milo sipped the sherry. It puckered his cheeks.

"Do you know Lars Hongren, the number theoretician?"

Milo searched his memory. "I might."

"You *might*?"

"Remind me."

Borland leveled his eyes. "Never pretend to knowledge, Andret. Never do it. Learning is to be hungered for, not treated as currency."

"I'm sorry."

"Have you heard of Hongren then?"

"No."

"Of course you haven't. Lars Hongren was the most brilliant student we'd ever seen here. That's who he was. That's it, and that's all." He took a drink. "He was working on a new approach to the Catalan-Mersenne problem."

"The double Mersennes are all primes," Andret offered.

Borland waved him away with his hand. "He was closing in on a solution. Extremely talented young man. His dissertation was drumming up plenty of excitement. I'd phoned Stanford and Princeton about him. And then?"

Milo met his professor's gaze. "Yes?"

"And then, I discovered what he'd been doing."

Milo waited.

"Even recalling it disgusts me." Borland closed his eyes. "I trusted the man at his word. Without checking on him. Suffice it to say that now Lars Hongren works in a bank somewhere, stapling together loans."

The old man opened his eyes and let a silence settle.

"A sad story," Milo finally offered.

"An *important* story. Lars Hongren stole his research, young man. He *stole* it. He lied to all of us. If you ask me, it should be a much-sadder story. He should be in prison. I tried to put him there, you know. But your country doesn't deem it a crime."

"Is that right?"

Borland leaned forward. "Look," he said. "You have a talent, Andret. A significant one. Maybe like Hongren's. Maybe like mine— that's perfectly okay to say, by the way, if it's *true*. Do you agree with me?"

"I can't say."

"This is what I'm trying to tell you, Andret. I *can* say. You've been chosen by God, young man. By humankind. By the cosmic order. By whatever you think runs this place, to translate a language. Topology is God's rules, Andret. That's what I'm telling you. And you've been called upon to translate them." He tapped the desk. "Your talent is *that major*."

"Thank you, Professor. I'm grateful."

Borland looked across the desk again, this time blinking. He poured himself another sherry. "If you're *grateful*," he said, chuckling once more and turning back to his work, "then perhaps you misunderstand."

Poets

ONE MORNING, WHILE thumbing a journal in the common room of Evans Hall, he came across a problem: the Malosz conjecture. In the early part of the century, Kamil Malosz had written to a friend wondering whether certain equations might have solutions in complex projective spaces; and over the years the question had evolved into a deeper and deeper problem. No mathematician had ever been able to find a solution. In *Zentralblatt für Mathematik,* Milo discovered a long history of attempts.

But that was what he was searching for, he realized: something that would earn Hans Borland's respect.

Later in the afternoon, when he knelt to the quatrant, practicalities began to enter his mind. Even if he didn't ever *solve* the problem, Borland could not fail to notice the attempt. He could just take on a small part of it, even, as he'd seen in *Zentralblatt* that other mathematicians had done. And the work itself might easily widen from there, into a dissertation, perhaps. Even a career.

At the time, most of his classmates hoped to find jobs at Xerox in Palo Alto or at IBM in White Plains or at one of the industry-funded think tanks that were popping up now along the coast; but to Milo, such ambitions were impure. He was not a practical person, but that day he decided he needed to be practical. The Malosz conjecture. His mind came to rest.

In his office, Professor Borland said, "Might as well start at the top."

"How do you mean?"

"Submanifolds of complex projective spaces—it's a famously difficult problem, young man."

"Yes, I read about how difficult it is."

"Ha! You read about it!" Borland seemed to be in a lighter mood today. He fiddled with the ascot at his neck. At that moment, somehow, they both turned to the window, where against the pewter-colored bay the sun abruptly turned the bridge's suspension cables into a pair of shining silver parabolas.

"Ah," said the old man. "Perhaps we've just witnessed a sign."

"It did look like it."

Borland turned. "Young man," he said, his voice hard again, "plenty of ships have gone down on those rocks, I have to tell you. Men have died trying to outsmart Kamil Malosz." He lowered his glasses and gazed across the desk at Milo, his eyes stony; but the lips below them expressed a tinge of wryness. Milo was incapable of deciding whether the old man meant him well or ill.

ONE AFTERNOON AT the mathematics library he returned from drinking a soda on the steps and found someone sitting in his chair. He circled the table and approached from the other end: it was the same girl who'd been watching him before.

"No," she said.

"No what?"

"No. You're not confused."

"Did I—"

"You have a minute?"

"For what?"

"For me."

"Well—"

"To talk."

Dark, sleepless eyes. A man's shirt again, her black hair tucked into the collar. "That depends," he answered.

"On what?"

"On what you want to talk about."

THEY MET AT the Lime Rose, a basement café she knew, not far from campus. He arrived early. She'd arrived earlier.

"Borland's impressed with you," she said, the moment he took the seat across from her. The shoulders of her sweater were dusted with rain. At the small table, her face was prettier than he remembered. The same sleepless eyes, but filled now with either sadness or willingness. She had an odd name: Cle Wells.

"How do you know Borland?" he said.

"Everybody knows Borland. Everybody in the math world."

"And you're in the math world?"

"Not exactly, but I know plenty of people who are. My dad, for one."

"Oh?"

"A professor. Of analysis."

"Here?"

"No. But he knows Hans Borland."

Milo swallowed. "Okay, then what did he say?"

"That he's telling people you have promise."

Milo laughed.

"He's not exactly famous for his generosity, you know." She raised her chin at him. "You know that, right?"

"I'm aware of that rumor."

"Then why'd you laugh?"

"Because I already know what he thinks of me."

She lifted her coffee to her lips, smirking. "Well, then, indeed."

"I just don't know whether he's right."

"You don't know whether he's right about *you*?"

"No, in fact—I don't."

She set down the cup. "Well," she said. "He is."

"And how might *you* know?"

She looked out the window. "That's a little mystery, too, isn't it?"

"I don't believe you know any more about it than I do."

"Well, that's where you're wrong."

"One of us is, anyway."

She looked back at him.

"Wrong," he said. "Clearly."

"Okay then." From her bag she produced a pack of Camels. "The Malosz conjecture," she said, tapping out a cigarette. "Submanifolds, right? In some kind of weird mathematical space. Famously difficult." There was a pause while she rummaged for matches. "Killingly difficult."

"All right," he said. "That's a way to put it. So what?"

"So that's just the beginning."

"Of?"

"Of what I already know about you."

She blew the smoke over his head, and he ducked to let it pass.

"By the way," she said, looking straight across at him. "I hope you don't think I'm trying to seduce you."

THE FINISHED QUATRANT was the size of a kitchen table, its four thickly carved spokes exactly dividing its circumference. One cloudless night late in the winter, he waited for the last coat of lacquer to dry and then lifted the whole structure onto a tripod at the center of the apartment. From there, its outlook bisected the windows.

Just before sunrise, he climbed from bed. Chilly air flowed underneath the door as he sat down and began tallying the sun's path across the two trapezoidal illuminations of sky. Afterward, he went hurriedly to the library, where he worked his way through a backlogged pile of problem sets.

The next day, he stayed home again, irritatedly dispatching class-work as he recorded another set of coordinates, carefully tracking the low winter orbit that was evolving along his tiny patch of cosmos.

HE WAS A teaching assistant in two different classes that semester: Differential Equations, which was populated by math majors and engineers, and Calculus for Poets, which was populated by girls. Or at least it included quite a few of them. Differential Equations had none.

Late in the year, he handed back one of the midterms. Professor Rosewater was known for writing grueling exams: there were plenty of Ds and Cs and only a few Bs. One student, a lackadaisical young man from the back row whom Milo had taken for a loafer, had scored 100 percent.

The name on the booklet was Earl Biettermann.

He saved Earl Biettermann's test for last. He'd already asked the math-department secretaries about him. At the rear of the classroom, the young man sat sprawled in a chair, his scuffed motorcycle boots crossed at the ankles.

"You're a mathematics major," Milo said, slipping his exam booklet onto the desk.

"So?"

"So what are you doing in a class like this? You're taking PDEs and real analysis."

"And?"

Milo felt a prick of anger. "So, why are you taking Calculus for Poets?"

"Because I happen to be a poet," said Biettermann.

"THAT'S SOMETHING EARL would say," Cle Wells said, again at the Lime Rose. "That's definitely something he would say."

"You know everybody, I guess."

"I guess everybody knows Earl."

"The commutative property."

She wrinkled her nose. "I would call it the associative."

"Well, no," he said. "*I* don't know him, and I don't really *want* to know him—so it's not associative."

At this she smiled. She reached across and tapped him on the end of the nose, a gesture she might have made with a child. "Well," she said. "It'll be associative *soon enough*."

The Newton of North Oakland

By FALL SEMESTER of his second year, he had his habits. Berkeley had grown familiar to him by now—the stand-up sandwich counters and the head shops, the cars and buses and all the milling crowds. He spent evenings in the library at Evans, working on the Malosz conjecture. A good part of this time was spent poring over papers by other mathematicians. A professor in Kyoto. A graduate student at McGill in Canada. An amateur topologist in Kiev. None of their papers mentioned the Malosz specifically, but he could see what they were doing. They were positioning themselves around its edges.

By now he'd spoken again to Borland, and the problem had become the official topic of his dissertation.

At Evans, the topology journals arrived wrapped in paper, like purchases from an expensive department store. At the circulation desk, the librarian handed them across the counter to him. As he opened the covers he imagined his competitors doing the very same thing at other libraries around the world. Not just the rivals he knew about but the ones he could only imagine: graduate students in Bombay and Moscow and Taipei. Men as focused as he was—or more focused—on unearthing the bones of the universe.

Sitting in the warm quiet of the reading room, he would scan the journals, then settle himself into his work. Into the precise, incremental logic of geometries. Sometimes he succeeded. Sometimes the hours themselves became numbers, in turn fractionating into other numbers. Minutes. Weeks. Onward he pushed. At this early point, the problem didn't seem impossible. It was like a great mountain that he was still seeing from a distance.

On the way home one night after a successful evening of work, he found himself stopping at the bar at the end of his block, a dark, windowless place called the Shed. Only a sawhorse marked it from the sidewalk. He climbed down the steep stairs and took a seat at a table in back. Caught off guard when the bartender approached him, he stumblingly ordered a dry sherry. He'd never bought a drink in his life.

Whatever the man brought back, though, it wasn't a dry sherry.

A few minutes later, moving to a stool by the cash register, he ordered another.

THERE WERE BEGINNING to be rumors. Cle reported them. He was an eccentric. A savant from the woods. Isaac Newton in North Oakland. "That kind of thing, anyway," she said, stirring a hot chocolate with the tip of her finger. Another café, another afternoon. "Your name's around," she said. "I keep hearing it."

Later, as they were buttoning their coats to leave, she said, "I flattered you, didn't I?"

He reddened. "Hardly."

She smiled, then reached up and tapped him with her finger on the lips. "Yes," she said. "Hardly."

THE NEXT TIME he saw Earl Biettermann, they were in a car together. Biettermann was driving. Milo sat in the rear, watching the hair swing from Biettermann's cap when he dipped into the curves. He was driving too fast. The road was wet from a storm and glinted like ice. But this was California, and warm air was whipping through the windows. They were in the hills, on the way home from a party above campus. An old stick-shift GTO without a muffler. Biettermann sluiced into the curves like a skier, accelerating as he came into the straightaways. Milo was in the backseat, pressed against the door alongside a line of girls he didn't know. Cle was in front of him, next to Earl. Milo's gut tightened. It tightened again when the car upshifted. Biettermann wasn't looking at the road. He kept turning his eyes to Cle, who was throwing back her chin beside him and laughing.

"You didn't like that," Cle said the next day when he found her at the Lime Rose. He shouldn't have gone in, but he did. He should have been at the library.

"Didn't like what?" he said.

"The way Earl was driving." She looked across the table at him.

"Actually," he said, "I didn't notice."

She smiled. "Ah," she said. "I could see that you didn't."

SHE WAS RIGHT about the rumors. Before long, he overheard someone in the lounge call him a savant.

People knew about the quatrant, but nobody had seen it, and nobody seemed to know about his real work. Nobody saw him alone in the stacks reading Akira Kobayashi's abstruse deductions on the Hirzebruch-Riemann-Roch theorem. As he made his way through the paper, his face grew hot. Kobayashi was preparing an assault on the Malosz. That much was clear. Milo looked up at the heads of the other graduate students, bent to their work in the carrels around him like rows of oil derricks. Later, he tried to make his way through Marat Timofeyev's densely reasoned preprint on algebraic isotopy. Another assault.

His rivals were all unseen. At any time, any one of them could render all his work useless.

And yet the talk about him persisted. His untrained brilliance. His rogue ambitions. The quatrant was the subject of steady questions from his undergraduates, who were eager for the diversion, and sometimes even from his peers, who nodded with pursed lips when he answered, turning away to exhale smoke. All of them were competing for the attention of the faculty. Dissertation topics were discussed like the movements of armies.

He'd become known by now as Hans Borland's protégé.

It wasn't from Borland himself that he gathered this information but from another comment he overheard one evening in the department lounge. He didn't even recognize the graduate student who said it. Again, the sideways turn. The exhaled cigarette.

HER FATHER WAS a professor at Carleton College. She told him this the first morning she woke up in his bed.

"Never heard of it," he said.

"That's because you're basically an illiterate."

"Well, thank you."

"It's in Northfield, Minnesota. Kids ride tractors to class."

He looked over at her.

"It's a half hour from Minneapolis, you idiot. It's an excellent school. You can't get away with the things you can out here."

"You think I'm illiterate?"

"Yes, basically. You really are an idiot, you know. Socially speaking. That's one of the things I like about you."

"About me? That I'm an idiot?"

"You're charming," she said. "But it's an idiot's charm."

She kissed him on the mouth. Her tongue had a flavor—the brandied hot chocolate that had been resting by the bedpost since the night before, when they'd come in after a walk from the Lime Rose. As soon as they'd gotten into the apartment, she'd set the cup on the floor, pulled the band out of her hair, and kissed him. "That you even have trouble with the concept"—she said now, pulling back—"this actually proves the concept."

"It's kind of thrilling to be called an idiot," he said. He tried to kiss her again, but she sat up against the headboard and pulled the sheets to her shoulders. He looked at her hidden there in his bed. "It's not good that your father's a mathematics professor," he said.

"Why?"

"Because you'll compare."

"You to *him*?" She laughed, in a way he didn't like. He'd noticed that about her already, how quickly she could turn. "My father's an asshole," she said.

Those words actually made him look away.

"Then maybe I shouldn't mind the comparison," he finally said.

"Maybe you *should*."

Later in the morning, when he returned from the store with doughnuts and coffee, she was out of bed at last, wearing nothing but his Detroit Tigers T-shirt, kneeling on the floor examining the adjustments on the quatrant. "You didn't move it," he said. "Did you?"

"I wouldn't dare." She was peering along one of the slots. "It's really incredible, isn't it?"

"Not bad for an idiot."

"No, not bad."

"It's a distraction. That's why I made it."

"No, it's stupendous. Have you shown it to anyone?"

"Just you."

"Really? Just me? You know, I was kidding when I called you an idiot."

"Half kidding," he said.

"Okay, that's about right. Half kidding."

She rose and came to him then. Truthfully, a bother was still inside him, but he was powerless to hold on to it. She took the doughnuts from his hand, walked him to the bed, and leaned in against him.

The night before, of course, he'd been a virgin.

"Is that the truth?" she asked later, as they lay back on the pillows, messily eating the doughnuts. "I'm the only one?"

It took him several moments to realize she was referring to being shown the quatrant.

.   .   .

LATER THAT WEEK, a house he didn't recognize. Big rooms full of tacked-up posters. Velvet couches. He was following her in the hallways. The starry waterfall of San Francisco shivering in the glass. He was hoping to lead her into one of the bedrooms, but he was always a step behind. A dog on a chain.

She was stopping in front of every knickknack. Abalone-shell ashtrays. Incense pots. In the dark stairway he followed the swaying bangles on the bottom of her sweater. Along the back wall of the slope-roofed attic, a dozen other grad-student types were scattered on the cushions and mattresses.

Was that Earl?

It was. He was on a mat beneath the far window, his narrow head resting back. He sat that way during Milo's section meetings— exactly that way: in the last row, his long hair against the wall behind him, his boots crossed. Sticky little smile on his lips.

When Cle walked up to him, Biettermann tried to kiss her. "Isaac Newton," she said when she turned, gesturing with her hand. Milo moved up behind her. "I'd like you to meet Gottfried Leibniz."

It wasn't funny. She was nervous.

"A pleasure, Gottfried," said Biettermann.

Milo could think of nothing to say.

Biettermann tilted his head and peered into Milo's eyes, then offered his hand: the soul shake. He looked stoned. "Earl Biettermann," he said. "From your calculus section, in case you forgot."

"I didn't forget. Is this where you write your poetry, Earl?"

CLE WAS THE one who gave it to him. Not ten minutes later, after Biettermann was gone. A tiny square on her palm. A little Mickey Mouse in bright blue and red. No bigger than his pinkie nail.

"Open up," she said.

He was alone with her.

"Come on," she said, nuzzling him. "Open the hatch." She went up on her toes and kissed him.

The bite of smoke. The linger.

"Come on," she said, moving it to his lips. "Open."

A NORMAL DOSE for Berkeley in those days: probably 250 micrograms. Lysergic acid diethylamide. You could buy it in the public parks. Milo's mood was expansive. His experience was nil. Cle stretched out on the mattress and pulled him down beside her. The gold-bangled sweater, the lemon soap. Biettermann was gone. Time difficult to locate. In his eye, the line of her knees and hips, a black horizon with hills. Everything he'd ever wanted.

Nothing was happening.

The ceiling: stamped tin. Victorian curlicues in repetition, repeating squares within repeating squares. Here was something now, a wave rolling across his vision—his concentration unraveling. Okay, there it was—a long, looping pull. The band downstairs rumbling the floor. Biettermann again now, at the far end of the room. Then gone. A black light vivifying the posters like a hidden sun.

Then he plunged.

At the bottom he found himself. Silence. He was inside something. A shimmering construction. It began to rumble like a buried engine. Immediately: his bearings. He was aware that his mind would burn but that it would survive the fire. All he had to do was climb. A slippery wall of flame steadily increasing its slope. Hanging on to the mattress now: he turned. She was beside him, mummified. Wrapped in gold. The gold smoldered, then began to burn. She was curling away in smoke. He gave in, dropped farther, was aware of a hovering border, stretching and respiring, billowing around him. A tent in the wind. Yellow and orange. The border now a point, now falling away. Gathering slope and velocity until he was stranded at its tip. A man on a boulder in an ocean.

He reached but couldn't touch her. Then he knew he hadn't even moved. There was no history to his actions. They disappeared into a maw. The surface of a dark pond that swallowed without a ripple, then grew into waves. The waves cannibalized themselves. Then grew again.

An unseen dimension prodding a boundary.

He was aware then of other shapes, floating away before he saw them. Volumeless interiors. Infolding crenellations. A circle—the two-dimensional cut of a sphere; then the sphere itself—the three-dimensional cut of its encasing sheen. It oscillated. The sheen itself encased. Unseen shapes consuming unseen shapes. Superbounded by complexities darting at the edge of his vision. Animals breathing on the far side of a wall.

He reached again for her hand.

"It was mathematical," he said the next day. They were in a bar. "That was the interesting part. What I saw was mathematical."

She laughed. "It was an acid trip, Andret."

"No. It was the Malosz conjecture. I'm sure of it."

"Every artist has thought that kind of thing."

"I saw mathematical ideas."

"That's just what you remember." She poured a beer. "Because of who you are. If you'd been like the rest of us, you'd be talking about the colors. That's what I remember."

He saw them again—the melting yellows and blue-reds.

But he also knew he'd understood something. Something geometrical. It was gone now, though. It was behind something.

One night, he lit two candles and in their flickering light read all the quatrant's numbers from the month. Then the ones from the previous month. His hands shook as he scanned back through the pages and pages. Something stood up inside him. There was a shape there.

He imagined Brahe himself, four centuries before, in a Copenhagen attic, seeing the same shape.

He began to shun sleep and took to calculating at night, followed by classwork, so that he could record data during the day.

There was a time in history when the pattern of numbers he saw on his columned pages would have upended the world.

HIS APARTMENT WAS a half-hour walk from school, but even so, there were occasional knocks on the door: undergraduates asking to see the quatrant. Sometimes they'd just kneel on the sidewalk and look down through the window. He took to closing the shades. Their cheap fabric admitted a gloom of yellow light.

Cle had her own knock—three short, three long, three short. "Morse code for SOS."

"Why SOS?" he said.

"Because you're my savior."

He laughed. They both knew it was the reverse.

He should have been devoting more time to the Malosz—Borland would be expecting some evidence of progress. But between classes and teaching and the quatrant and now Cle—she arrived every other afternoon with a cup of tea and a book—he had no chance. His intention was to work, but she would do something—touch one of her calves, unspool her hair from its bun—and they would move frantically to the bed, pulling at each other. They'd stay there until one of them grew hungry. Then they'd go upstairs to the Indian restaurant across the street. The spices turned her lips bright red. He almost couldn't eat.

All the while, he could feel Borland waiting.

One afternoon she was pounding on the door. She rushed in, threw it closed behind her, and pulled down the shades. A Turkish coffee was in her hand, the blue ceramic cup shaking on its saucer. "It's from that Middle Eastern place on the corner," she whispered breathlessly. "I was going to bring it right back." She lifted one of the shades and dropped it again. "But they came after me. I think he's out there."

"Who is?"

"The waiter."

He regarded her. "Did you just steal a cup of coffee, Cle?"

"Screw you, Andret." She peeked out from behind the shade again.

Then it happened: he was confused. For a moment, there seemed to be two thoughts entering his mind at once. It was a moment—half a moment—of misperception. She seemed to be very far away, her voice coming from some other room.

Then it cleared.

"All right," he said. He took the cup and pulled out a chair for her. "Partners in crime, then. What do you think of that?"

"You're not the type."

"I'm not? What about this?" From the closet he pulled out a pint of whiskey that he'd bought that morning. He'd wrapped it as a Christmas gift for Borland; but now he tore apart the wrapping and fortified the coffee. He needed calm. "To something different," he said. When she'd drunk it down, he poured a shot for himself.

AT CHRISTMAS, HE took the bus home to Cheboygan. The road leading up to the house was piled with snow, and all along the hill the rows of spruces hung low with their winter weight. In Berkeley, he'd boarded the bus in a T-shirt. Now he moved morosely through the old rooms in his flannels, looking out the windows while his mother sat at the reading table and his father tinkered outside. He read his coursework; he slept long hours in his bed; sometimes he went out to the woods, though he felt separated from them now. He would open the thin Pelado and Harkness text on characteristic classes that Hans Borland had lent him, then sit at the radiator flipping the pages in his lap, thinking of Cle.

Calling felt like weakness.

Only when he was asleep did he not pine for her. His nights were fitful, disturbed by dreams of plunging. Every morning shortly after dawn, regardless of whether it had snowed during the night, his father would put on his boots and go out to salt the walks. Then came the hollow wallop of the drifts falling to the hedges as the old man worked his way around the garage eaves with a broom. Milo would turn to the wall and try to sleep, thinking of the soft shelf of heat where he'd curled his legs behind Cle's just a few nights before.

She'd gone home to see her family in Minnesota. No more than a narrow sliver of land separated them now, but something other than the map made it insurmountable. He'd called her on his first night home and she'd seemed distant, an intermittent stream of laughter emerging on the line from somewhere in the house. She had sisters. He waited for her to call back, but she didn't. He gave in and tried again two nights later, but the sister who answered the phone hesitated for a moment, then told him she'd gone out. He vowed not to call again till the week was up.

He wondered what Earl Biettermann was doing over the break.

Time was interminable. He knew he ought to be working on the Malosz, but watching his mother with her novels and his father with his tools—he was starting another one of his projects—leadened him. It took a certain energy to lift his mind to the plane on which it could bring force to bear on a problem. Now this energy had deserted him.

One morning, a few days before the vacation ended, his father brought him outside to the garage. Laboriously, the old man bent down, turned the cross-shaped metal latch, and raised the creaking door. Inside, the family's old powder-blue Valiant had been cleaned and polished.

"Yes?" said Milo.

"We're getting a new one," said his father. "Delivered tomorrow."

"I don't understand."

"The Plymouth. It's yours."

Milo didn't know what to say. He walked around to the driver's window and looked in at the familiar seats. A pair of keys on the dashboard, tied together with string. He stepped over and shook his father's hand.

The old man said, "In this kind of weather, use thirty-weight oil. Forty in the summer if it's hot."

"I will. Thank you."

"Your mother's inside. It was her idea. She'll want to know if you like it."

"I do. I like it very much."

That evening he called Cle again. This time her sister handed over the phone. He told her about the new car. She told him about her vacation. The Wells family owned a toboggan, and the sisters had taken it into the hills around Northfield, then cooked supper over a fire. They'd roasted a goose for Christmas and spent the rest of the days in Minneapolis, ice-skating on a lake and shopping.

There was a silence.

Finally she said, "Don't you want to know whether I got you anything?"

"Do I?"

"Well, I might have."

This knocked down the wall inside him. He told her he would drive across the Upper Peninsula and pick her up in the Valiant at her front door and bring her back to school.

"I already have my plane ticket, silly."

"I'll drive underneath the plane."

She laughed.

"Really," he said.

"That's silly. I told you."

"When do you leave?"

"Day after tomorrow."

"Which flight?"

"Why do you want to know?"

"So I can make sure God protects it."

"He doesn't do individual flights."

A silence. Then she said, "Actually, that was kind of sweet."

Two days later at the American Airlines terminal in Minneapolis, he ran up the corridor waving a bright orange hunter's hat. At the gate, the passengers were already lining up to board.

"Lord," she said. "Am I dreaming?"

"No, *I* am." He took her valise. "The car's outside, Cle. Come on, I almost burned it out getting here. I'll drive you all the way to your door."

She looked around. "You'll have to get rid of the hat, though."

IT WAS A three-day trip that took them five. The roads were good, but snow stretched knee-high to the horizon. They stopped three times in the first hundred miles and tore at each other's clothes—at the back of both rest stops between Minneapolis and Albert Lea, where she hung her Catholic-school sweater in the window and climbed past him into the backseat, and the third time on a picnic table beside a creek culvert that passed under the highway, his pants pulled down and her skirt pulled up, the whole thing hidden from the cars but not the trucks. Big rigs blared their horns as they passed. It was still broad daylight.

When they reached Albert Lea a lazy snow was filtering down. They turned west, then south onto 60 at Worthington, the clouds breaking up finally near Sioux City, where they came out onto the Missouri River under a clear sky at nightfall.

A huge barge lit from bow to stern was making its way up the dark waterway. "Our own private constellation," he said.

"Floating toward us through the heavens."

They got out of the car and stared. She cradled herself in the crook of his shoulder. They must have stood there for an hour in the windless night, silently watching as the lights moved up the river past them. Then the landscape turned black again. It might have been the happiest hour he'd ever spent.

Onward. It was twenty-five degrees out, and after a dinner of Ritz crackers and a can of Spam from a country gas station, they spent the night on a side road near Onawa, curled around each other in the backseat beneath their coats and a wool blanket that he'd found folded around a tin of chocolate bars in the trunk. In the morning she nudged him awake. She pointed through the gap she'd rubbed in the frost: a herd of elk was filing slowly past the car.

"It's a sign," she said. "Thank you."

"For what?"

"For picking me up. You seem to have figured out what a girl wants."

"I have?"

"Some of it, at least. I guess you're actually not an idiot. Not a complete one, anyway."

In the rising light they ate the chocolate bars and stepped a few yards from the car to drink from a shallow stream whose icy coat he broke with the heel of his boot. At midday, near Ogallala, she pulled a tiny bottle from her bag. She split its contents between the two Styrofoam coffee cups that had been rolling around on the floor since their gas-station stop the night before and offered one across the seat.

"What is it?" he said.

"Irish coffee."

"Where's the coffee?"

"Already in our stomachs."

He kept one hand on the wheel as he sipped. It was Tennessee whiskey. The feeling he had then, with the empty road rolling ahead of them through the white fields and the warmth of the liquor easing through his veins—it cracked open the world. Near Julesburg he turned to look at her and found her gazing back at him, her lips not quite closed.

"That was your present," she said.

"What was?"

She held up the cup.

He steered them off at the next exit and on a dirt road behind a farmer's field left the engine running. She slid over on top of him, but when he tried to enter her she pushed him aside and rolled to the passenger seat. She dropped the backrest and pulled his hand between her legs. He moved over onto her, but she pushed him away. "Kiss me like you mean it," she said. She rubbed her mouth against him. "Go slow."

He did. Warm air blasted from the heaters. She placed her hand over his, pushed it down between her legs, and showed him. She began to sigh. She lifted his other hand onto her breasts. She spread her legs wide and guided down his head. She was whispering. She arched her back, shivered, and pulled him over on top of her.

On they drove. Just east of the Wyoming border they stopped to eat. At an insanely bright truck stop they shared an order of barley soup under the gaze of a sturdy middle-aged waitress who returned with a full plate of warm bread and set it down next to their bowl. What they couldn't finish they slid into their pockets.

When they were done eating, he gave Cle the car keys and walked back to use the bathroom. He washed at the sink and in the chipped mirror examined his face. His features had never pleased him, and he looked no different now except for the unusually dark beginnings of a beard. His forehead was still too broad, his entire face far softer than he wished it.

Still, he'd changed again. He could sense it.

When he got back out to the car, the trunk was open and she was in the front seat with the burlap sack on her lap.

"My *God,*" she said. "What *is* this?"

"A chain." He closed the trunk and went around to take his place at the wheel. "What does it look like?"

"My God, Milo. Where'd you get something like this?"

"I made it."

"You *made* it?"

"Yes."

"With your own hands?"

"Yes."

"It must have taken years."

"A couple of months."

"And it's all wood?"

"Yes."

"Here," she said, "let me see those hands." She reached across the seat and took them. She rubbed the skin on his palms, touched each squarish yellow callus, ran her nails up between the indented joints that beneath her ministrations presented themselves to him as though for the first time; sitting there with her, he saw his fingers not just as straight, utile extensions of his will but as the varied isthmuses of form that they actually were, narrowing and widening, hiding and exhibiting their wrinkles. In the pearly light of the High Plains afternoon she brought them one at a time to her lips and kissed them. Then she lifted both his hands and for a long moment held them there against her cheeks.

At last she let them drop and he started the car and drove them on toward California.

Devil's Fork

BACK IN BERKELEY, he took his usual seat at Evans Library and looked down at the stack of journals whose tables of contents had long ago become litanies of worry for him. In any week, there were at least a dozen publications that might arrive with someone else's breakthrough on the Malosz.

He placed his arm over the cover of *Acta Mathematica* and for a few minutes tried to focus his mind. Finally he gave in and opened to the first page. Fortunately, there was nothing there to upset him, as there wasn't in any of the rest of the pile. He set it all aside.

His habit then was to close his eyes. He had a particular gift for logical cartography and all his life had been able to leave his thoughts whenever he broke for the night and then return to them the next day at the exact location where he'd quit, as though his internal mappings—in his mind, he was currently unfolding three-dimensional knots and refolding them antichirally—were an illustrated book in which he'd simply turned down the corner of a page.

But this time something different occurred. A darting little flicker on the screen of his cognition. For several moments he couldn't re-summon the previous night's picture. The blankness lasted almost no time at all.

He'd been getting too little sleep.

. . .

ONE NIGHT IN a deadening rain, Biettermann offered him a lift home from the mathematics building. Just the two of them this time in the rumbling old GTO, red taillights wobbling against the slick asphalt all the way up College Avenue. The car slid between lanes, moving headlong through traffic. Horns faded behind them.

"Can't you get this thing to go any faster?" said Milo.

Biettermann snorted.

Biettermann made him edgy but in truth there was something he liked about him, too. The long hair straggling over such eager eyes. Want played on Earl's features the way it played on an animal's. He was leaning up close to the windshield, one hand on the wheel, the other drumming the shifter. The brainy people that Milo knew—he remembered Earl's perfect calculus exam—didn't behave like the guy next to him. They didn't drive as though a checkered flag had been dropped. The tires screeched, and the GTO shot through a gap in the traffic; then they were out in front, racing south toward Oakland, the wipers revealing an astigmatic world in brief half circles of clarity.

"I was kidding about faster," Milo said. "Maybe be a little careful."

"I know you were kidding, man. I laughed."

At a red light in front of the new BART station, the rain was slackening, the wipers painting ever-renewing Venn sets onto the glass.

"Actually, Andret," Biettermann said, "you're the one who should be careful."

"Me? Of what?"

"Of *her.*"

They peeled out again.

"You're talking about Cle."

"I am."

"I am completely careful with her, Earl."

"I don't mean it like that."

"Then how do you mean it?"

They caught another red. This far south, the streets were quieter, the wipers squeaking against the glass. Earl looked straight ahead. "Not careful *with* her, Milo. Careful *of* her."

"What are you talking about?"

"She's dangerous, my friend."

"All right."

"Me," Biettermann said, "I *like* dangerous." He turned now and regarded Milo, not unsympathetically. "But *you* don't."

"You're right, Earl. I don't."

When the light changed, Earl pulled away more reasonably. At Milo's corner, he said, "And why's that?"

"And why's what?"

"Why don't you like dangerous? What are you afraid of?"

It was an interesting question, the kind of question mathematicians enjoyed posing to one another: an inquiry into the apparently obvious. Milo thought about it. "I don't know," he said. "I'd have to think about it."

In front of his building they shook hands—the soul shake again—and Milo slid out into the drizzle. As he unlocked the apartment door he heard the squeal of the GTO. In the chilly basement, he set down his things, then put on water for tea and called her. No answer. When the water boiled, he added a finger of whiskey and set the cup on the night table. Then he called again. Still no answer.

Lying under the covers as the rain ticked against the windows, he thought about Earl's question. In every single drop on the glass he could see the incrementally rotated orb of the solitary streetlight that was shining down from the post across the way. This in itself was a puzzle. The world, if you let yourself consider it, was a puzzle in every plane of focus. Why *was* he so afraid of it?

Then the corollary: Why *did* he want to live?

Shortly before sleep, the answer came, at least to the corollary: he wanted to live so that he could solve a great problem.

.   .   .

ONE DAY, HE was in a teahouse with Cle when Biettermann walked in and gave her a kiss. This time, she didn't deflect it. Then Biettermann sat down, and the three of them spent the morning chatting in the cramped chairs. From next door, old Jefferson Airplane vibrated the table. Biettermann nodded his chin to the beat, his hair bouncing over his eyes. "The pleasure we get from counting," he mumbled, "without knowing we're counting."

"What's that?" said Cle.

He glanced up. "Music."

She laughed.

Milo shook his head. "Leibniz said that, Earl."

"Indeed he did, my friend. Indeed he did." He nodded at Milo. "Round one to you, I guess."

Milo looked away.

For the rest of the morning, they sat in the rattan chairs talking about nothing. It was an activity Milo despised, but he wasn't about to leave. At one point, Biettermann used an unfamiliar word. Then a few minutes later, just before he finally left for a class, he used it again.

As soon as he was gone, Milo said, "What the hell did that mean?"

"What did what mean?" said Cle.

"That pompous little word he kept bringing out."

"Entheogen?"

He wrote it on a napkin.

"Look it up, Andret." She winked at him.

"All right, I will."

"Wait a second," she said, leaning closer. "Wait a minute—that bothered you, too, didn't it? Not to know a word that *he* knew."

"I'm interested in knowledge."

"Of course you are."

Silence.

Now she was smiling. "And while you're at it," she said, "here's another one for you. *Theodicy.* That's another word Leibniz used. As long as you have the dictionary out, you might as well look 'em both up." She sipped her tea. "He wrote a whole book about it, as a matter of fact."

"All right," he said. "I will. I like to learn."

She leaned toward him, her hand grazing his leg. "By the way," she said, "I like to learn, too." She rubbed her lips along his cheek and stopped at his ear. "And in case you're confused," she whispered, "Earl's got it backwards. *He's* Leibniz. *You're* Newton."

THEN, ONE CHILLY night in December, a night during which he'd been forced to sit at a different desk—the room he normally worked in was being recarpeted—he became aware, briefly, of the presence of something. Some force or even some being just behind him. A charge in the air. For a moment he had the sensation that a net was about to be tightened around his arms. He fought it. By an act of discipline he was able not to turn his head.

OF COURSE THERE was nothing there. But now and again the idea would materialize without warning—a feeling on his shoulders.

He refused to turn.

If he did, if he gave in to the urge, he saw nothing, of course. Just the blank rows of study carrels and the line of storefronts down Euclid, colored by lights. They stretched to vanishing in the darkness.

He would face forward again and close his eyes. For a change of scene, he'd begun spending time in the main library instead of Evans. Still, there could be other mathematics students around. If Milo Andret's eyes were open, the other students would notice. Milo Andret worked with his eyes *closed.* He was Hans Borland's protégé. The savant.

At this point he was usually done for the evening.

Occasionally he would drop all pretense and just walk over to one of the big windows and stare out toward the bay. The air from that direction smelled of fog and turned the streetlights into rows of yellow moons. Sometimes this was enough; but usually, he would need to leave. To calm himself he would take a longer route home. The couples with their dogs. The rows of wooden bungalows lit by porch lamps. The orange-rind scent of the trees. All of it gathered by the steady beat of his step. At the apartment he would go immediately to his notebook, which was dense now with figures. In such straightforward work he could forget himself.

And thankfully, the night itself never failed to wash him. In the morning he would wake early and begin recording again. In the tradition of Copernicus or Leonardo, he was extrapolating from nothing but his own data. His perfect two-windowed view of the universe. Figures upon figures.

In their incremental intervals, he was certain now of what he was seeing: the recognizable proof of a harmony. The numbers in their perfect columns bearing him forward.

NOT LONG AFTER: another row of panes in Earl's palm. It was early afternoon when he let Cle slip one onto his tongue. Hours later, when he came out from its hold, she was gone. So was Earl. It was different this time—there'd been no mathematics, no visit from his sources.

Still, he'd understood something.

The way she'd been visiting his apartment lately: every other afternoon.

Around him the room was dark. Thin coronas of light flaring the perimeters of the shades. Bodies on the rugs and couches. The upswell of the drug making him queasy. He recognized a girl from somewhere, rose and walked over and touched her on the shoulder.

By the time they were outside, they were arm in arm. The curve of her hips. His brain undone and the drug still not finished with him: colors swooping in his eye. Yellows from a line of hollyhocks, blocks away. The silver-green glitter of the bay. His focus leaping.

Cle. This new girl next to him, her voice falling and rising. Block after block while the colors struck from a distance. Night had fallen before they tired, somewhere below the hills of Albany. A tiny bar, dark and quiet. Colors gone at last but the drug still skirmishing at the edges. A longshoreman's place—iron stools and a jukebox. A hint of threat. Vodka for her, bourbon for him: a double.

Its woody bite touched his throat and brought back the world.

ALONE, LATER, HE woke in a strange bed. The room bright: morning. Gray snakes of incense twisting on the ceiling. Clothes on the floor—his own. Jeans, boots. A fringed leather jacket on a peg by the door. He looked away: not the kind of thing Cle wore.

Whoever she was, she'd left. The tossed sheets. The dent in the pillow. He looked around for a note. Then, through the window, he searched for a street sign.

It was infinitely strange not to know where he was.

He remembered nothing: this was the odd part. A hole in the world, starting in the bar. The street. The stairs. The heat of her beneath him. But before that, nothing.

He must be in the flats, he realized, somewhere near Gilman. He gathered his things and left.

Block after block of low houses, dogs barking behind chain-link. The vistas obscured. Finally, at a corner park, he caught sight of the water, and the world snapped back into place. Turning toward home, he tried to piece together what had happened.

The Orrery

THE THOUGHT EITHER woke him or came to him as he woke. The dark of night. He rose and checked the log-book again, inserted the month's coordinates. Then he calculated.

Neatly, he wrote:

1. *The orbit of every planet is an ellipse with the Sun at one of the two foci.*

$$r = \frac{p}{1 + \varepsilon \cos\theta},$$

Underneath this:

2. *A line joining a planet and the Sun sweeps out equal areas during equal intervals of time.*

$$\frac{d}{dt}\left(\frac{1}{2}r^2\theta\right) = 0,$$

And, below this:

3. *The square of the orbital period of a planet is directly proportional to the cube of the semi-major axis of its orbit.*

$$P^2 \propto a^3$$

There they were, summoned by nothing but his own devotion. The *Epitome Astronomiae Copernicanae*. Working blindly, he'd re-derived what the great Johannes Kepler had first deduced three and a half centuries before.

The laws of planetary motion.

WHEN HE ARRIVED at his teaching sections the following Monday, his students were already reading the article. The front page of the *Daily Cal*. He'd had no warning. The illustration was the famous seventeenth-century portrait of Kepler himself, a simultaneous artistic study, Milo had always thought, of both malleability and relentlessness. The byline leapt from the page.

Cle had said nothing about it.

All day, people greeted him. Professors. Other graduate students.

That evening, Hans Borland reached across the desk with the decanter. "Dry sherry?"

"Please," Milo responded, pulling a glass from the row and sliding it across. "Might as well celebrate." Then, an unmitigated lie: "I've been making progress on the dissertation."

Borland fiddled with his cuff link. "Progress?"

"Yes."

"That's funny. Because I read today that you're wasting your time."

"Well—"

"With your antique sextant."

"It's a quadrant, Professor. Derived from a mariner's sextant, yes."

"I know what a quadrant is, Andret." He looked stonily across the blotter. "It's a fool's stab at attention. What's it got to do with the Malosz conjecture?"

"It's a hobby, sir. I became interested in the work of Tycho Brahe."

Borland's expression froze. "The Borland invariant," he said. "I was eighteen years old when I came up with it. And not even a month after my birthday, are you aware of that? I was at Caltech, already doing graduate work." He glanced over. "And a year after that, I was on faculty."

"As you know, Professor, I got a late start." A pathetic remark.

Borland ignored it. "Tycho Brahe"—he reached for a stack of folders—"Tycho Brahe thought the earth was the center of the solar system."

"He was a genius."

"He was no genius at all, Andret. He got it wrong."

"Nobody gets it entirely right."

"Pardon?"

"Or almost nobody. Kepler, maybe."

"Listen to me, Andret. Stop talking nonsense. It's the excuse of the lame, and it's fouling this campus. It's fouling this whole country of yours, for that matter. You are *not* lame, Andret. Do you hear?"

"I try not to be, anyway."

"Poppycock, Andret. Listen to me. Are you *listening* to me?"

Borland seemed to actually be waiting for an answer.

"Yes, I am," said Milo.

"You have to go against the times. You have to always go against the times. Do you know what that means? What do you think Kepler was doing? What do you think Galileo was doing? It is where discovery comes from, Andret. Not from going this way and that with the crowd."

"Yes, I know, but—"

"Now get back to work. All you've done is rederive an ancient calculation. You have a talent and you have a discipline, and I can see that you're wasting both." He dropped the folders back onto the desk. "Don't make me wonder if we've made a mistake with you."

. . .

"Well," she said. "Did you like the article?"

It had been days. He'd been at work, trying to change things. "You're with Biettermann," he said without looking up.

"What?"

Now he lifted his head.

She exhaled smoke. "And what if I am?"

"Well, for one, you could have told me."

She lit another cigarette. "Stop acting like a bourgeois."

"There's nothing bourgeois about it."

"Stop caring about your parents' morality, Andret. You're above that."

He looked away. It was unclear if she even knew about what he'd done. He still couldn't remember the girl's name.

"And stop being so ugly," she said.

"Thank you. Glad to know what you think."

"Andret, do you really want to hear what I think?"

"No."

"I think you're incredible."

"Bullshit."

She looked into the distance. "I want to save you," she said. "I think that's what it is. Save you from your own brilliance." She tapped out another cigarette. "Or maybe *for* it."

"What?"

"You heard me."

"I don't need to be saved, Cle. That's ridiculous."

Awake now for almost two full days, scribbling notes into the tiny cardboard pad that he'd been carrying since the meeting with Borland. To meals. To class. To every single place he went. He'd made his way deeper into the problem. Walking alone along the water one evening, he watched the cargo ships creeping south beneath the bridge. Tiny blinking cities of light on the water. Starry bottles drifting sideways in the black. Incredibly, this was where he'd stumbled upon a crack. A narrow one. A thought had reached back. Encasing sheens. Volumeless shapes. He sent his mind deliberately away, then allowed it back. The crack remained. It was real.

The Malosz was not insurmountable. It could be solved in the higher dimensions.

This is where the answer first made itself known to him, in the muddy-smelling dark on a garbage-strewn dock above the tidal flats in Emeryville. Tinge of rot in the air. Wintertime headlights streaming ceaselessly from the west, dividing north and south at the shore. Complex white curves incising themselves against a black-paper rendering of the world. The trudging ships below. It would be provable in another dimension. This was the route. His rivals would never think of it because it was so deeply counterintuitive. But the more he considered it, the more clearly he knew—this path would be orders of magnitude simpler.

He'd found it.

From a tar-soaked piling, he flicked his cigarette into the smelly sand. Pinched a drink from the flask in his back pocket and headed home to sleep.

"EARL AND I are mortals," she said.

A doughnut store this time. Shattuck Avenue.

"Bullshit."

"Mortals hang out with mortals, Andret. Do mortal things."

"Bullshit, Cle."

"We talk. We walk. Sometimes we trip. We don't bother with conundrums the human mind has never breached."

"You're sleeping with him."

"Maybe I am."

"What? Cle?"

"I said maybe I am."

"I'm begging you."

"Don't beg."

"Please, Cle."

"I said don't."

"Then fuck you."

"Brilliant. Thank you." She looked out the yellowed window, dragged on her cigarette. "If you want to fuck me, you know, you still can. Anytime you want." The smoke lingered. "You can always do that."

"Thanks."

Silence.

"You don't think I know what you did, Andret?"

"I'm sorry."

"Don't be. It doesn't matter."

"Yes, it does. I'm sorry." He'd been waiting to say it. "I'm sorry, Cle."

He took her hand. It was someone else's hand.

"You think I care, Andret? I don't. I don't give a damn about her."

"I don't either. I'm begging you."

"Look at me, Andret. Only mortals beg. You're not to do it." She reached and pulled his face close, held it there. "Not you, Andret. Stop following other people's rules. You're beyond them."

THAT NIGHT, ANOTHER party: Biettermann again. Alligator smile. A girl beside him and a bumping crowd.

Biettermann said, "China White."

The girl lifted her fist. A blue dragon, twisting across her knuckles.

"China *what*?" said Milo.

Biettermann laughed. The girl, too. Biettermann grabbed her mouth and kissed the full lips. The girl looked at Milo. Kissed Biettermann and looked at Milo. He turned away. When he turned back, she was still looking. Her mouth still on Biettermann's. She nodded, tilted her hand toward him and opened it. The dragon's fire curling into her palm.

Then, stepping from behind her: Cle.

Biettermann kissed *her,* then, too, right in front of him. His arm around both of them. Cle closed her eyes.

Milo stared.

All three of them looked at him now.

"White," said Biettermann. "China *White.*"

They all laughed.

Then Biettermann opened his palm: a syringe. "You ready to travel, my friend?"

LATER, HE WONDERED why he'd refused. He could have at least stayed near her. Instead, he'd gone off by himself, walked home, and spent the rest of the evening in the bar near his apartment.

A month and two weeks. That's how long it was before he saw her again. On his calendar he checked off the days.

China White

THERE WERE AT least two ways to solve any problem: from the beginning, which was the usual approach; and from the end, which was not. Likewise, every theorem could be proved either directly, using incremental logic, or indirectly, by conjecturing the negative of the hypothesis and demonstrating a contradiction. Thus there were at least four permutations to choose from.

This was how he began.

A pad. A room. A tiny view. Not numbers but geometry. One couldn't draw a fourth dimension. This was a mathematical dictum, and of course he challenged it, but after days of trying to negate it he at last accepted its truth. Yet one could extrapolate.

At night he experimented. With his eyes closed he built a one-dimensional world and imprisoned himself within it. From there he imagined the second dimension—the unfathomable impingement of a greater universe. Then, after days of this, he imprisoned himself in two dimensions and imagined a third. The fracturing of experiential knowledge. It was forceful work. It was physical work. It required him to bind his thinking. He could maintain the fiction for only minutes at a time. The effort left him hungry.

In a way it was akin to idiocy—Cle was right. But he understood at the same time the radical difficulty of what he was attempting. The weight of discipline required to unlearn the world and refabricate it from principles.

Intuition mattered, too. There was no going forward without intuition.

At last he relented in his experiments and took to the problem itself, attacking first from the ordinary dimensions. This was merely underwork to confirm his approach. It was work that Akira Kobayashi was obviously embarked upon, too, in Kyoto. A month later, he was aware—though unsuccessful in articulating the particulars—that this route would lead nowhere. At the bottom of his own labyrinth of reasoning he glimpsed an infinite loop, a multibranched chain closed only by its own first tenets. A logical dead end. The realization flooded him with relief. Kobayashi was not a threat.

Marat Timofeyev, on the other hand, in Kiev, seemed to be attempting the problem from the negation of the hypothesis, working apagogically—the path that Andret now turned to. Timofeyev's steady papers on complex manifolds, his meticulous proofs of midlying conjectures: this was a man laying a foundation. But soon Andret grew sanguine about Timofeyev, too. Unless his rival's papers were diversionary, he was creeping forward by inches on a journey that was many miles long. A careerist, he realized one night in Evans Library as he unwrapped a new set of journals. A man interested only in a professorship.

At the realization, he allowed himself a weekend's rest. A bottle of bourbon. In his apartment he sipped it from a coffee cup.

He didn't call Cle. He didn't want to go over a cliff.

Then he went back to work. His first task was to leapfrog what Timofeyev had done. He began by assuming the result, by starting from the proven conjecture and filling backward. If this was true, then so must have been that; for that to have been true, then so must have been this. The individual steps were simple, each requiring the smallest of conclusions. But the complexity of them all together was exhausting. It was as though in the morning he built a house of 1,000 cards, all in his mind, and in the afternoon he chose a single one to remove. Then the next morning, he would build a house of 999 cards. This was what Timofeyev had been doing, but in reverse. One morning, he realized that in this manner it would take years to reach a proof.

He also realized that his own stumbling had disappeared. The blink-outs. He hadn't had one in weeks.

He bought another bottle of bourbon and set it on the desk. A sip or two seemed to align his thinking. During one stretch of mental projection, he fleetingly envisioned a course all the way to the finish—it laid itself out before him like a rock skipping across a pond. Then was gone.

He was able to reconstruct the particulars only long enough to realize that such a route, momentarily discernible as it was, would soon be overwhelmed by calculation. With growing confidence, he moved to his original insight—that the higher dimensions, despite their unseeable complexity, would yield the answer.

This was the correct path, he sensed with finality one night as he walked again on the Emeryville flats, where before him on the dark bay the ships cast their crawling illumination against the night. This was the path on which he would stake his future.

HE'D FOUND HIS approach now. He was quite aware of it.

But he could no longer work in the library, the quiet there speeding up his thoughts to where they raced beyond him. He'd taken to working in the coffeehouses instead and even a sandwich shop near his apartment, where the noise buffered his thinking. The brain needed to work at a certain speed. And alone. The parts of him that were Milo Andret needed to go away.

One rainy night, waiting for sleep, he was startled by the phone. 1:23 a.m. He sat up in bed.

"Andret—"

It was Cle. This was ruination.

He couldn't make out the words. He didn't want to say anything, but he couldn't hang up. He set the receiver on the sheet. Now she said nothing at all. The only sound he heard was music. More voices. He forced his own silence. A clock leaf flipped down.

Finally, he said, "What did you want?"

No answer. Behind her, brief voices again through the noise: a party.

"I'm going to hang up now," he said. "I don't want to. But I'm going to hang up."

That he didn't—that he didn't set the phone back in the cradle, that he laid it on the pillow instead, beside his ear, where it kept up its whispering—that he didn't hang it up because he'd had an intuition became a point of comfort to him that would buoy him many years later, when he was stricken all the time with doubt.

Five clock-flips later, she said, clearly enough, "Help."

SHE WAS LIGHT. No weight at all. Running. Her body limp across his chest. A crowd. Voices.

At Durant the squeal of a cop car and a veer from the curb. Now they were in the back, her pale face tilted up. Speeding through the night. The twirling strobe cracking the world.

The steel gurney. The double doors. The gray mask pushed against her mouth.

"WHAT'D YOU DO?" he asked when they finally allowed him in. It was the next afternoon. He'd gone home in the early morning and picked flowers outside his apartment with a flashlight. Since daybreak he'd been waiting in the lobby.

A tube ran from her nose.

"Could have been laced," she said.

"What could have been?"

She looked around. "How do I know?"

"Where'd you get it?"

She nodded off.

"Cle, where'd you get it?"

"Where do you think?"

"What was it?"

"Won't—" She nodded off again.

"Won't what?"

He pinched her hand. She looked bleached. The name bracelet on her wrist was stained with either blood or puke. An IV was taped into the crook of her arm.

"Thanks," she mumbled. Her hand tilted toward the flowers. "Taking care of me—"

"You're welcome."

She might have smiled. Her arm twitched. He covered it with the blanket. She was asleep, but he said it anyway. "Looks like I wasn't the one who needed to be saved."

IN A ROOM at the end of the hall he found Biettermann, sitting up against the headboard reading *Rolling Stone*. A dripping noise. Andret pulled back the curtain. The tubing had been removed from Biettermann's nose, but the white tape still clung there.

"What was it, Earl?"

"How do I know?"

"Nice."

"Thanks, brother."

Milo came around the bed. The dripping sound was the IV emptying onto the floor. "Interesting approach to treatment, Earl."

Biettermann smiled wanly. "Ah, a joke."

"You could both have died."

"Ah, yes—you're right." He shook the magazine to turn a page. Then he looked into it and pretended to read. His eyelids closed.

"Well, I happen to care about her," said Milo.

"That's sweet."

"What'd you give her?"

"What'd *I* give her? I didn't give her anything." He shook the magazine, but the page wouldn't turn. Andret leaned down and lifted the sheet. The other wrist was handcuffed to the bed rail.

"Jesus Christ, Earl. What'd you do?"

"Evidently something."

"You don't even remember, do you?"

"Listen, Andret. I buy the best."

"What are you talking about?"

"I take care of my friends. I took care of *your* friend."

"What'd you give her?"

"Why don't you go ask her?"

"I just did."

"And?"

"She doesn't know."

Biettermann snorted.

"She doesn't."

"Listen, Andret. She *begged*. I don't push anything on anybody. She's not the Snow White you think she is. And you're not Prince Charming."

"Wrong fairy tale."

"Doesn't change the point. You think you're going to save her with a kiss?"

"I couldn't have. She wasn't breathing."

"Then how come you didn't carry *me* away, too? How come you didn't come back up for *me*?"

"I'd say you're lucky I called an ambulance."

"Well, somebody called the cops, too." Biettermann looked at him. "That was you, wasn't it?"

"It should have been."

"Listen, Andret, we're not junkies. This stuff gives me ideas."

"What stuff, Earl?"

"I don't want to talk about it." He leaned forward and shook the magazine. Then he said, "But when you're ready to try it out, you just let me know."

. . .

IN MARCH, THREE weeks before spring break began, he left school. A bag of sandwiches and a tank of gas. Bells ringing from the towers and a silver light in the hills. North on 80, a flask propped beside him. He stopped at the same places they'd stopped on the way out—Reno, Elko, Salt Lake, Rock Springs—and walked alone on the same paths they'd walked together. Napped in the same truck stops. Huddled in the same clear cold with the same rumbling big rigs. In his mind he was going to demolish her. In the back of the car where he'd once slept curled into her warmth, he dozed with a peacoat pulled across his chest.

He was going to think about her and think about her until she disappeared.

On a ruined trail near Rawlins he followed the path they'd followed that winter, blinking his eyes into the stiff wind. On the banks of a river east of Cheyenne, where hand in hand they'd sat on a boulder tossing rocks onto the snow-dusted ice, he sat tossing them into the rushing current. Each one splashed and vanished. She vanished alongside, down into the black. On his third night on the road, just past the Nebraska border, he pulled in at the same bright diner, where the same middle-aged waitress refilled his barley soup but didn't come back with the bread.

When he finished, he found his way to the bathroom. Took a long pull from the flask. Before the same chipped mirror he examined his face. It had been hardened. It had been turned to stone.

Something had been removed, too. What remained was ambition.

He took another pull. Back in the dining room, the waitress was already wiping the table. He stood off to the side until she looked up at him and smiled. "Where's your friend?" she said. "You leave her somewhere?"

He lifted the jacket off the chairback and worked his arms into the sleeves. "California. Things didn't work out."

She swept the utensils into her palm. "You'll find another."

"I don't know."

"Well, *I* do," she said, leaning to push in the chair. "You'll find another."

He arrived in Cheboygan just as his parents were sitting down to Sunday dinner. His mother's hand went to her mouth. His father reached to the china cabinet for another plate.

Almost a month remained before the university returned from break. The next morning, the phone rang. It was the registrar's office. His sections had gone untaught. The police had been sent to his address. Did he wish to withdraw? Four days later, a certified letter, asking the same question. His fellowship money was on the line. Finally, a call from the dean. His father fielded it.

He did his work out in the woods. Frozen days. Bright snow. His thirty-second year on earth—late, in fact, for a mathematician. Wool coat. Spiral notebook. Flask. He'd brought the chain home with him, and on his first day in the woods he set it back in the maple where it belonged. After that, a month spent nearly entirely outside, in one of his old shelters under the trees. He wasn't hungry, and he barely needed sleep.

He was going to make her sorry.

"You look terrible" was the first thing Hans Borland said when he walked back into his office. One day still remained of the break. The campus was quiet, the students just beginning to filter in.

"Kamil Malosz and I have been in battle," said Andret.

"Good, good. I can see it." Instead of sherry, the professor pulled a bottle of whiskey from the cabinet and cleared off his desk. Two glasses, filled to the top. "And have you defeated him?"

Andret gulped the whiskey, then laid his notebook beside the glass. "Yes," he said. "I believe I have."

Contraposition

Fine Hall

PRINCETON UNIVERSITY. MILO arrived on a day of hail—billions of
white spheres the size of gumballs bouncing off the lawns and streets
of central New Jersey as he carried his new briefcase across the quad.
A miracle. Blue sky. Hot as a clothes dryer. And suddenly hail was
bouncing up from the walk in a skittering dance higher than his
belt—corn in a popper. Within a few seconds the brim of his fedora
had filled with it.

Then, just like that, it stopped.

He'd bought the hat—a Borsalino—along with the dark suit, for
the commencement of his position. Borland's advice: Don't look like
the rest of them. *Go against the times.* And this was what he was doing,
striding among the long-haired students, leaning down now and
then to pick up tiny melting fragments of the universe. Around him,
the dowdy-looking faculty toed back kickstands and resumed their
rides. The undergraduate boys emerged from under the eaves to boot
a Hacky Sack again in the electric brightness of the storm's wake.

Dr. Milo Andret, Ph.D.

He'd had time to think. The life he'd been living—the quatrant,
the deadbeat parties, Cle's obtuse, demanding visions—it was all behind him now. From this point on he would live by different rules.
He'd sold the Valiant and tossed away the old clothes. Now he wore

a bespoke suit and an astringent cologne. The world parting as he stepped. He wouldn't miss a molecule of what he'd been through.

The briefcase had been a gift from Borland on the occasion of his dissertation defense, which had been a triumph. As he reached Fine Hall, he set it down, removed the hat, and poured the hail from the brim into his palm. Little messages from the stratosphere, crenellated oblongs from the heavens.

In the departmental office he found a trio of secretaries—a pair of blondes in sweaters typing at the desks up front and a darker one in back, her head down. He held out his palm.

One of the blondes said, "You brought us candy."

"Wish I had," he answered. "To tell the truth, it's hail. Heavenly mothballs. You don't get this kind of thing in Berkeley. It's amazing, really."

"Relatively speaking, I guess," said the other blonde, not looking up from her typewriter. The first one laughed brassily.

"Well, it might be if you looked at it," said the dark one in back, still not lifting her head.

"Might be," said one of the blondes, glancing up at the wall clock. "But I was hoping it was candy."

A hush. It was a Friday afternoon, just a few minutes before five— he glanced up at the clock himself now for the first time. It seemed that everyone else in the building had left for the day. "Well," he said, "I was just hoping to get the key to my office. I'm Milo Andret. The new hire. I just got here." He dropped the melting remnants into the trash can.

The two blondes went on typing. One of them looked at the clock again.

"Well," said the dark one in back, "if nobody's going to help Professor Andret, then I will."

"I'm not a professor," he said a few minutes later, after she'd ridden up with him in the elevator and unlocked the door to his office. It was a nice-sized room with two windows over a curving footpath and a view of a sports field truncated by evergreens. Princeton had recruited him heavily. Still: it was more than he'd expected. "I'm an *assistant* professor," he said.

"Me, too," she said, brushing the hair from her eyes. "I mean, I'm an assistant secretary."

A FEW MONTHS before, within hours of showing the proof to Borland, rumors of the achievement had begun to spread. Soon after, the paper had been accepted by the *Annals*. Publication in October: an unheard-of turnaround. At thirty-two years old, he'd found a solution to one of the great problems in the history of mathematics. The article would arrive next month in libraries around the world: the Malosz conjecture, thanks to Milo Andret, had become the Malosz *theorem*.

He thought briefly of Kobayashi and Timofeyev.

On his first day on campus, he walked around unrecognized. The pressed suit. The fedora. He had the feeling that he was someone else, that he'd been handed a disguise. Even in the mathematics department, only the dark-haired secretary, whose name was Helena Pierce, paid him any notice.

That Monday, his first day at work, she showed him around the building. The semester didn't start until the following week, but his mailbox was already filled with letters. "A lot of departmental duties, I guess," he offered.

"Yes," she said. "Or no, actually." She blushed. "Probably not that many, at least not now. Chairman Hay tries to give the junior faculty time for their work." She brushed the hair from her eyes again, then pointed to the slots on either side of his name. "Not that you're junior." The blush deepened. "In title, maybe. I read about the Malosz theory, I confess. Congratulations, Professor Andret."

"Assistant Professor Andret."

She ignored the flirtation. "These are your colleagues' mailboxes," she said. "The other new faculty are here, and here, and here. Not as full as yours—well, I guess you can see that."

Now she paused, as though she'd overstepped.

"Thank you," he replied. He lifted out a handful of envelopes. Several of them were hand-addressed. He lifted out a second batch. Even before he'd left Berkeley, he'd been invited to dozens of seminars.

"I noticed you get a lot of correspondence, Professor. More than some of the senior faculty receives."

"Book-of-the-Month Club flyers."

She blushed again.

"The other faculty probably pay their bills on time, too," he said, glancing at her. She was a little formal, but she was pretty enough—long necked and pale. A girl from a Flemish painting. The wine color of her blouse brought out her eyes.

He shifted his attention back to the envelopes.

"Well," she said carefully, "I was going to tell you—there's a piece about you in the department newsletter. It's very nice, obviously."

"There is?"

"About the Malosz theory. It's quite impressive. But of course you already know that. All right, I'll be quiet now."

"Perhaps I don't already know that," he answered, turning to smile at her.

LATER THAT EVENING, in the Downtown Club, a white-tablecloth establishment near Bank Street where he'd convinced her to stop for a drink, she broke a pause in the conversation by asking him about his research. "Just tell me a thing or two about topology," she said. "For my own education. I like to learn a little at work."

"Of course, of course." From a far room came the sounds of a string quartet. He pulled the pewter ring from the rolled napkin beside him and set it at the center of the table. Then he bowed slightly and leaned in. "An introductory lecture on the subject of topology," he said, "by Assistant Professor Milo Andret, on the occasion of his stupendously lucky hire."

She blushed.

"This napkin ring," he said, lifting it between them, "is the same to me as my coffee cup." He poked his thumb through the napkin ring and then slid the pinkie of the same hand through the handle of the coffee cup. "See," he said, holding them up together. "They're both loops that I can stick a finger through. It's just that the coffee cup has a little bleb attached to *its* loop, to hold the coffee. Whereas the napkin ring is nothing *but* the loop."

"I see."

"As a contrary example, the coffee cup is fundamentally different from the highball glass." He picked up his bourbon with the other hand, turned it around in the air, and drained it. "There's no handle on a glass of bourbon to put your pinkie through. In fact," he said, "a coffee cup and a highball glass could hardly be *more* different, topologically speaking."

"Yes," she said. "Topologically speaking."

There was something about her.

"What I'm saying with all this is that the coffee cup and the napkin ring are *topologically* equivalent. One is nothing but a loop, and the other can be quickly reduced to a loop. Another way to think about it is that if the napkin ring were made of clay, you could squeeze it and pinch it until it became the coffee cup. You see?" He made the motion with his fingers of pinching off a little bowl from the side of the napkin ring, so that it became a cup, and then tilted it to his mouth. "You wouldn't have to make any holes in it, or cut it, or use any glue. You couldn't do that with the bourbon glass, though, right? You couldn't make it into a coffee cup with a handle on it no matter how hard you tried. Do you see what I mean?"

"Because you couldn't make the handle?"

"Exactly. Not without punching a hole somewhere for my finger to go through."

"Yes, I can see that, I suppose."

He took out the pile of letters now from his briefcase. There was a rubber band around them, which he pulled off and placed onto her hand. "To a topologist," he said, "the rubber band is the primal object. That is because our field deals with what we call *continuous deformations.* You can stretch or twist a rubber band in any way you wish, to any degree you like, just as I did with the napkin ring; but you can't ever cut it, or glue it, or make any holes in it." He smiled at her, bowing slightly. "That's it," he said. "Those are the rules of topology."

"I'm sure it's more complicated than that."

"Perhaps by degree."

Now there was a silence. The sound of the string quartet grew louder. Helena Pierce appeared to be thinking, sipping absently at her water. "And I couldn't make the napkin ring into the bourbon glass, either," she said, "unless I glued it together, right? There wouldn't be a bottom unless I could glue it closed somewhere."

"Precisely. You and I are peers now."

She tittered.

"I'm a napkin ring, too, by the way," he said. "And so are you."

A flush pinked her cheeks.

"I mean," he said, "all human beings *are napkin rings,* topologically speaking. We have that in common, too."

It was at this point that his second bourbon was delivered. He accepted it and nodded at the waitress for another. Technically, a human being wasn't a napkin ring but a double torus; but this was too complicated to explain at the moment. He took a satisfying gulp of the woody liquid. She was still blushing. He said, "Would you consider helping me with my mail?"

"Of course, Professor."

From the pile, he lifted off the first envelope.

" 'Dear Professor Andret,' " he read, leaning toward her again and lowering his voice. " 'You please excuse our not very good English. However, I am to select and ask for deliver this year the our first lecture named from Leonardo Fibonacci, guest of the Department of Maths in the University of Pisa, Pisa, Italy. The date will be the year next at city of Pisa, or April or May, your choose.' "

He read the remainder to himself. "Not from the department of Englishes," he said finally.

"No. But it's lovely."

"I think they invited me to speak somewhere."

"Yes, Professor. In Tuscany."

The waitress arrived again. Milo saluted his new drink before handing back the old one.

"Should I accept?" he said.

"I would think so."

"Perhaps. But it would be much more pleasant if I could convince another napkin ring to come along."

Now she turned the color of her blouse.

"I take that back," he said. "In retrospect, I don't believe I meant to say that."

"Of course not, Professor."

"Let's go on now."

"Okay."

On the table between them stood her own untouched bourbon, and to his surprise now she picked it up and tried it. But she sipped like a girl taking medicine from a spoon. Her first mouthful didn't even uncover the ice cubes. It was charming, actually. She tried again, pursing her lips this time, and before long he realized he'd have to finish it for her.

LATER THAT NIGHT, at the door to her building, she turned and said, "Thank you for introducing me to all that, Professor Andret. I learned quite a lot."

"*Assistant* Professor Andret."

"Well, thank you."

"You're welcome, Assistant Secretary Pierce."

Her building was a narrow townhouse set behind a huge sycamore. She stood a couple of steps above him on the brick stairway, searching for keys in her purse.

"Here," he said, reaching. "Let me get the door."

He didn't exactly fall, but when he righted himself she was holding him by the elbow.

"Are you all right?"

"Perfectly."

"Are you sure?"

"Of course I'm sure. However, Assistant Professor Andret regret not delivery today lecture to Downtown Club for Pisa this evening— as I choice, you're welcome."

She laughed.

He bent to retrieve his hat, and when he straightened he found himself standing against her again. She moved up one stair.

"All right, Assistant Secretary. Maybe is true that Assistant Professor Leonardo Fibonacci he self—maybe I could just sit down for a second, Helena. I think I need some water."

"All right. You can come up. But just for a minute."

As they climbed the stairs to her apartment, she kept turning around, saying, "Are you really sure you're all right?"

"Yes," he said, pulling himself up the banister behind her. The staircase went on and on. "But your railing's loose." He rattled it, although now it seemed perfectly tight. "Heisenberg," he mumbled.

Her apartment was on the top floor. When they finally reached it, he removed the fedora and held it against his chest, like a minister at the home of a parishioner. As soon as she'd succeeded in opening the locks, he followed her inside and hung it on the hook.

"Here," she said, pulling out a chair from the small table. "Sit down. That was a long climb. I'll get some water."

"Water is my enemy," he said solemnly.

This silenced her. He had no idea what he'd meant. But he knew she wouldn't ask for an explanation. At this point, he could have spoken about Hilbert manifolds and she wouldn't have asked for an explanation. In the scant kitchen she pulled a glass from the cupboard and rummaged in the freezer until she found an ice tray, then had trouble freeing the cubes from it. He ignored the chair she'd pulled out and sat down on the couch instead. In front of him on the coffee table was an art book. The first few pages were oil paintings—nonsense art or maybe abstract landscapes. He set it down and looked around. The apartment itself was singularly tiny. A couple framed prints propped on the mantel above a bricked-in fireplace. A desk crowded into the hall. Underneath it he noticed some kind of un-combed terrier shivering on a mat. He hated dogs. Through a half-closed doorway, he saw the bed: a single.

"Well," he said. "What were we saying?"

She came in from the kitchen, handed him the water, and took a seat at a miniature stool—to his surprise, it slid out from the wall like a subway bench. The couch he was on was short but deep, and at the far end of it he felt himself sinking into the cushions. After a few moments, he moved to the center. He spilled some water but moved on top of it. From her spot on the wall, she was saying something about the secretaries in the department, her legs crossed at the thigh and her hands clasped over her knees. He realized that she was afraid to let a silence fall. He himself could think of nothing he'd appreciate more.

Next to the door of the bedroom his eye fell on a crucifix. It hung on a chain from a hook above the light switch.

Well.

He felt a burst of sourness. The illogic of religion had always galled him. It occurred to him that the whole evening was going to be a waste.

At that moment, however, she went to the cabinet and returned with a bottle of wine.

"Would you like me to open that?" he said, struggling up from the couch. At the table he took a closer look at the cross. It was a dime-store thing. The hook was an old nail. This was better. He turned and focused on the wine label, wiping off the dust. It was burgundy.

He'd never actually tasted burgundy.

"All right," she answered at last, although he'd already ripped off the foil and pushed the opener into the cork. "Go ahead and open it. I doubt it's very good. But it's more my speed than what you ordered for me in the bar." She sat down on the subway seat. A moment later she rose again and went to the record player in the corner. After a short pause, the air was decorated by the first notes of a piano sonata.

In the morning, he let himself out early. The sun hadn't even risen as he closed the apartment door and stepped into his shoes in the hallway. Though he knew nobody else in the town of Princeton, New Jersey, he hurried home with the hat pulled low over his face. At the edge of her neighborhood, he turned and made for the woods. He shouldn't have taken the crucifix, but it was in his hand now. In the cool shade of the first stand of trees, as dawn was coming through the boughs, he leaned down quickly and dropped it into the mat of rotting leaves.

Occam's Razor

AT THE FIRST meeting of the faculty that year, Knudson Hay, the chairman of the department, introduced all the incoming assistant professors, who were seated in a line of folding chairs across the front wall of his sizable office. Milo's chair stood in the middle of the group. When his name was called, he nodded briefly, as had everyone before him. But then, from somewhere in the rear, a voice called out, "Congratulations, Andret."

When he looked up, he couldn't discern the speaker. But he noticed that a few of his first-year colleagues had reddened.

THERE WAS A pause, then in the background the clearing of a throat. The phone had rung while he was fixing dinner. It was six in the evening. He recognized the formality of the old man's tone.

"Listen, Andret," Hans Borland said neatly, "I was calling to inform you of something. First, how's that friend of yours?"

"I don't know who you mean."

"The Wells girl. Jim Wells's daughter. Cleopatra."

"Oh, that—well, that's over, Professor."

"I'm sorry."

"Don't be." Through the window, he watched a girl walk past in shorts. "I've moved on."

"I'm sorry to hear it, all the same." He paused. "Listen, Andret, I recommended you for this position, you know that, right?"

"I know, Professor. I'm grateful."

"Comport yourself with dignity there, will you? Do what you're capable of. It will reflect nicely on both of us."

"I will."

"Are you carrying the briefcase?"

Down the hall he could see it, overturned beside his bed, a sheaf of student assignments spilling from the pocket. "I have it right next to me," he said.

"And you're managing your affairs as we discussed?"

"Yes."

"You're a professor, now. Not a graduate student. People notice."

"I'm an assistant professor."

"Well, yes. For the time being."

Borland coughed then, rather harshly, and covered the mouthpiece. When he came back on, he cleared his throat again. "The Malosz theorem," he began. "If I'm not mistaken, Andret, you believe it was a fluke. You consider yourself undeserving."

Andret felt the truth of the words.

"Perhaps you feel like a fraud," the old man went on. "This is entirely natural. Believe me, I've seen it plenty of times before. Lars Hongren was a fraud." He paused. "You, Milo Andret, are *not* a fraud."

Outside the window, the girl in the shorts disappeared around the corner, and at that moment exactly, the evening turned into night. Andret became aware of his own figure in the glass, of the twisted white catenary of the phone cord bridging the darkness from his cluttered desk, crossing the bookshelves, and arriving at the pale moon of his face.

"Yes, I see," said Borland. "Well, listen now, Andret. You have a limited amount of time. That's what I called to tell you. To *warn* you about. I'd hazard ten years, on the odds. Then things will begin to cloud over. I was at the doctor's yesterday. I'm sixty-two years old now, did you know that? I guess one can't expect a clean slate forever."

Milo heard the clink of a glass.

"Is everything all right, Professor?"

"Well—thankfully—yes, it is. But I did have a scare. I jog five kilometers every day, you know. Have for more than twenty years."

"You've nearly run around the world, then."

The old man laughed. "At the equator, that's correct. At Berkeley's latitude, I'm actually on my second lap. But I mention it because it's set me to thinking. How old are you now, Andret? May I ask?"

"Thirty-two."

"Well, you have five or ten years then, in all probability, and then perhaps a standard deviation. Two at the outside."

"Yes, sir."

"To finish your work."

"I understand."

"Your *life's* work, Andret. You need to start something new. Something as great as what you've already done. Preferably, *greater*."

Andret paused. "I'm already working on something."

He could hear the old man breathing.

"What I'm trying to tell you," Borland said, "is that the Malosz theorem was merely the beginning of what Milo Andret can do. Of what he *will* do."

Andret couldn't speak.

"Just the beginning," Borland repeated.

"Yes, I heard you."

He hadn't intended to sound so sharp.

"I see," said the professor. After a time, he added, rather clumsily, "Well, that's all I wanted to say. Goodbye then, Milo."

．   ．   ．

AT THE OFFICE now, he had difficulty facing Helena Pierce. He quickly discovered that she had the same difficulty facing him.

By the end of his first month, they hadn't even spoken again. Was she angry? He didn't know. Wounded? Was it a triviality to her? He had no idea. Could it have been the crucifix? No—if that was what was bothering her, she would have mentioned something. It could have been that she was merely shy. Certainly she was inexperienced, and more than likely she'd been drunk. They'd both been.

Whenever he appeared in the mathematics offices now, she was there at her desk, but always at the rear, her head lowered over her typewriter. It was as though she could sense him through the two concrete walls, the carpeted anteroom, and the pair of frosted-glass doors that led from the hallway. When he entered, the blonde secretaries in front continued their noisy laughter and their cheeky asides, but Helena Pierce no longer rose to defend him.

HE COULD WORK on something related to the Malosz, as plenty of other mathematicians would have done in his situation. But Hans Borland was right: there would need to be something greater.

That winter, as he perused the journals, his attention landed on the work of a man named Ulrich Abendroth, a midcentury Austrian who at nineteen had proposed an eminent problem. Abendroth's precociousness itself had been the stuff of legend: at sixteen he'd been appointed to the faculty of both Cambridge and the École Polytechnique; at eighteen he'd fathered two sets of twins with two different women on two sides of the English Channel; and at twenty, a month after he'd proposed his conjecture, he'd been found dead in a coffeehouse. His problem had entered the canon with a flourish of intrigue. In fact, if mathematicians had believed in any sort of superstition, they might even have considered it cursed. It was famously difficult—

very likely as difficult as the Malosz—and in the years since its appearance it had resisted every advance.

All of this sat fine with Andret. He *was,* in fact, superstitious—but in reverse: what was supposed to be cursed attracted him.

The central puzzle of the Abendroth conjecture concerned a subset of Whitehead's CW-complexes that were infinite yet finite-dimensional. Clear enough. Though it was considered part of algebraic topology, Andret had a feeling that its solution—if it was going to be solved at all—would come not through equation but through the ability to visualize strange and unearthly shapes.

At this he was quite adept.

In those days, as it happened, the broader discipline of topology was at the apex of its ascendance. The field had become prominent at the turn of the century with the publication of "Analysis Situs," and in the following decades it had only grown in eminence, not just among mathematicians but among scholars of every branch of the natural sciences. The years leading up to his arrival at Princeton had charted themselves perfectly for the wave of new thinkers who were beginning to populate the upper levels of the universities. These men were no longer bound by symbology but instead spent their days constructing complicated hypothetical shapes that had never before been seen—nor likely imagined—by the human mind. Topologists built undrawable figures in their imaginations, then twisted and folded them. They devoted their time to inventing a cosmology in which the world as it was known—the world of earth and sea and sky—was no more than the three-dimensional rendering of an infinitely higher-dimensional space, much as a two-dimensional movie screen might appear to hold a three-dimensional tableau. In the new paradigm, sensory experience counted for nothing. Pure mathematical ingenuity—the ability to ignore common understanding, to construct a world solely from derived principles—had begun to supersede empiricism.

The field itself required a particular mode of thinking. Not merely the standard mathematical skills but a visual dexterity that could retain complex constructions in the mind for long periods of time, transforming certain parameters while leaving others intact. It was a strenuous and disobliging intellectual endeavor, a sea change of thought in which the brain performed multidimensional mapping. There were topologists who could build architectural structures in their imaginations, then turn them over, then flip them inside out, then spin them around, then open them up and go inside them.

Andret's own gift for such internal rendering seemed to him to be a derivative of the old positional sense that had once located him in the woods. And not only did it guide him now when he pictured objects in his mind, but also when he drew them with his pencil. He found that he could begin any topological rendering at the upper corner of a sheet of paper and proceed diagonally down to its opposite. No matter how complex the figure, no matter how many layerings of foreground and middleground and background interceded, he could steadily bring to life an entire theoretical construction, with all its dapplings and stipplings, depicting shadow and volume and transformation, in a single, angled pass. It was an astonishing aptitude, really. As far as he knew, nobody else in the department possessed it.

He'd been equally capable of it during his years at Berkeley, of course, but he'd rarely had the opportunity to use it; none of his peers and none of the faculty had even been aware he could do it—not even Borland—and Andret himself had been no more impressed by it than he would have been on any given morning to see his unexceptional face in the mirror.

At Princeton, on the other hand, midway through the semester, he'd been approached at an outdoor café by one of the endowed professors and asked to produce a fully rotated rendering of a Steiner surface, which was formed from the smoothed union of three hyperbolic paraboloids. Andret had complied immediately, sliding a cocktail napkin to the center of the table and using the pen from his jacket pocket to move without hesitation from the top left of the paper to the bottom right. When he'd finished, the professor said, simply, "Remarkable." For a few moments, the two of them exchanged pleasantries. Then the professor left, taking the napkin with him.

Yet equally remarkable was the fact that until this point in his life Andret had felt little desire to avail himself of such a talent. He never drew the world around him. Not trees. Not landscapes. Not the human figure. Never the land and never the lake or the woods he'd grown up with. Never the faces he knew. As a child he hadn't entertained the slightest feeling toward art, and as an adult he'd remained entirely unmoved by the world of the visual. Princeton had an art museum. He would never have considered spending an afternoon there.

By the middle of the winter, he'd narrowed his search to the Abendroth and two other possibilities. One was the Goldbach conjecture, a problem in number theory that had been around since Goldbach first posed it to Euler. Its statement was simple—*Every even integer greater than 2 can be expressed as the sum of two primes*—yet a dozen generations of mathematicians had worked on it without finding a proof.

The first Kurtman hypothesis, on the other hand, was the product of a man who was still on the faculty at the Free University of Berlin. Andret had only learned of its existence when he'd stumbled upon Dietrich Kurtman's face on the cover of a copy of *Der Spiegel* that was sitting on a coffee table in the department offices.

A mathematician on the cover of an international magazine. He'd felt his bile rise.

But in the end, he concluded, both the Goldbach and the first Kurtman were problems of number theory. He liked numbers, but he wasn't a number theorist. He was a topologist. Hans Borland had seen it in him.

He would need to be disciplined now. He would need to make the wise choice.

Late in January, at the depth of the winter's cold, he put away his notes on the Goldbach and the first Kurtman. He cleaned his office. Into a drawer he brushed everything from his side table, then taped together a file box. On the cover of the box he printed the words ABENDROTH CONJECTURE: 1977–19——. He had a feeling that Ulrich Abendroth had proposed a problem that might not be solved for decades; but he pulled the table alongside his desk anyway and set the file box on top of it.

Rise Over Run

Sitting in his warm office, he would begin by layering figures in his mind. When he reached the end of a construction, he would bring out the pad from his drawer, center it on the stained leather blotter, and draw what he'd imagined. He produced these drawings of the Abendroth not so much because he would need the references later but because the act of depicting a figure fixed it permanently in his memory. That was how his brain worked.

Now and then, at the monthly departmental cocktail hours that he'd begun to look forward to, he was asked to display his artistic skill. Usually it was the wife of a colleague who asked. There she would be, some mild beauty with a colored drink in her hand, pointing out the window at the bright spectacle of trees and spired rooftops that formed the view from the high floors of the mathematics building. Would he consider drawing the scene for her? Well, perhaps he would. The bejeweled fourth finger. The thickly lashed eyes. If he'd had the proper number of drinks himself, he'd comply, the picture emerging from the envelope, or the napkin, or the index card, as though a cover were being lifted from the corner of a photograph. He knew that these drawings would be shown later, at the back of the party or on the car ride home, and that eventually they might be folded into albums or framed on office walls, some emblem of an admiration he neither deserved nor fully comprehended. He sensed this admiration around him, and although he didn't exactly understand it, it did bring him pleasure.

Sometimes, in fact, he thought that his hunger for such pleasure was the only thing that drove him forward.

To his own mind, in truth, his actual gift seemed closer to a form of idiocy. Cle had been right. It was as though he didn't see the object he was drawing but the entire array of space instead—all things that were the object and all things that were not the object—with equal emphasis. It was symptomatic of something he'd noticed in himself since childhood—an inability to take normal heed of his senses, the way other people did as they instinctually navigated a course of being. In this way, it was like mathematics itself: the supremacy of axiom over experience. He wondered why others didn't see this.

It was an expression, he knew in his heart, of confusion.

ON THE DAYS when work on the Abendroth went badly, or on the occasional one when he was afraid to face it at all, he would walk down to Nassau Street in the center of town and stroll among the businesses. There was a drugstore there, Brandt's, that he liked because it reminded him of something that he might have found in Cheboygan. Brandt's used a pulley to deliver orders through an opening in the wall at the back of the store. When a prescription was ready, a bell sounded, and a black iron basket the size of a bird cage glided out from a hole above the pharmacy counter, carrying a white paper bag that had been stapled closed. The basket paused with each pull of the cable above an aisle that displayed support hose and fold-up walkers and yellowing plastic humidifiers, descending in arm-long increments until it arrived alongside the cash register at the front. At Brandt's, he saw few patrons from the university. These kinds of places, the dusty old spots on the rear streets of the downtown, were populated by a second phalanx of Princeton citizenry, a population of secretaries and maintenance men and low-level city workers who provided the bulwark for the professors and the professional class that had been appearing here for generations. The professors were all singletons of a sort, men and women like himself, arriving without history or ancestry, making their marks on their fields—or failing to—and then sending their children onward, or moving on themselves. They were outsiders to the drama—Andret found this fact comforting.

One winter day, as he was leaving through the double-glassed atrium of Brandt's, he held open the door for a woman coming in. She was a member of this second phalanx of citizenry, a secretary or a travel agent or a store clerk, dressed in a brown wool coat and a winter hat, with a dark wool scarf wrapped over her face. Her shoulders were dappled with snow. She stepped in hurriedly. It was as she was stamping her feet and unwrapping the scarf that he recognized her.

Something struck him in his heart.

He couldn't think of what to say, so he continued out the door into the cold. Outside, he quickly crossed the street, wrapping his own scarf over his face. There was a lunch counter on the other side of the avenue, and he took a seat at the front. The snow was swarming and the windows of Brandt's were white with fog, but he could still see her. She'd stopped near the register.

It was Helena Pierce.

He leaned forward and wiped the glass. She turned toward him then and rewrapped her scarf. Was it really who he thought it was? He looked closer but still couldn't decide.

It was the strangest thing: he could have seen her anytime just by walking into the departmental offices; but out here in town he felt disturbed. He wondered if she felt the same way. With his gloved hand he rubbed again at the window.

Then, as though she sensed him all the way from the other side of the street, she stepped toward the door. She took off her hat and pointed her gaze directly across at him. She didn't lower her eyes.

After a moment, he raised his hand and waved.

She made no response.

When she turned again and moved toward the rear of the store, he realized that, whoever it was, it wasn't Helena.

Instead of returning to his office, though, he stopped for the afternoon at Clip's, a dark-paneled pub that catered to cops and road crews. Sitting at the bar with his bourbon, he gazed out at the sidewalk, at all the shoppers and clerks and bookbag-lugging students hurrying through the snow. At five o'clock the crowd thickened, and at the dinner hour it quieted. He stayed there until long after the streetlights had come on. A couple of times in their yellowish glow he thought he saw Helena again, moving toward him across the slushy sidewalk. But each time the figure drew closer, he realized that it was someone else.

EACH FACULTY MEETING began with Knudson Hay straightening his tie and neatening the stack of papers in front of him, then noting attendance and reading the agenda. Then, within moments, the proceedings would degenerate into wrangling. Andret's senior colleagues seemed to disagree over every imaginable issue, from whether the honor code allowed an undergraduate to remove an exam book from the classroom to which drinks would be served at the fall-semester mixer. Each item was approached like an affair of state. Some of the voices were decorous and level while others sounded like curses in a foreign street. At the center of it all, Hay kept his hand on a copy of *Robert's Rules of Order*.

There seemed to be no question too small to generate a half hour of steady opposition. Would a third, lower-level calculus course be added? Should there be a bench in every hallway or only in those that ended at a ladies' restroom? By some kind of self-imposed discipline, the new hires sat in metal folding chairs in the center of the grand room, generally unwilling to speak, while the tenured professors arrayed themselves among the leather armchairs at the perimeter. Obviously there were factions and alliances, but Andret couldn't parse them. Along with the rest of the new faculty, he sat silently.

Midway through the semester, there was a deliberation about whether to plant an oak tree or a sycamore tree in the mathematics quad, in honor of a recently deceased emeritus chair who had been an accomplished cabinetmaker. The conversation went back and forth among the senior faculty while Knudson Hay took notes at his desk in the center. This was the pattern on most questions, at the conclusion of which the group would generally vote.

Finally Andret could contain himself no longer. "Why not a beech?" he blurted. "There's no tree as magnificent as a beech."

For a moment, nobody spoke. Then, to Andret's surprise, Knudson Hay said, "Well then, a beech it shall be."

IT WAS TRUE: he'd sometimes thought he'd seen her other places, as well. Standing in a group of pedestrians once, under a traffic signal where he'd been waiting for the light; in the parking lot of the dry cleaner's another afternoon when he was running to his car in the rain; even outside on the front walk of his own building one spring evening, when he opened the windows for the first time after winter and saw a woman walking away from him following a small dog on a leash.

But he couldn't say with certainty whether any of them had actually been Helena Pierce.

What he felt when he saw her each time, he couldn't discern. Shame? Disappointment? Longing? He was aware of something attempting to make itself known inside him, but he couldn't decide what it was.

"YOU LOOK NERVOUS," said a voice behind him. "You have done something wrong?"

Andret turned, laughing falsely. "Is it so obvious?"

"No, is not exactly obvious."

She was pretty. Short chestnut hair and a tight skirt. Vaguely Eastern features. He'd positioned himself next to the sangria bowl, and now he held the ladle over her glass. It was the first mixer of the new semester.

"Thank you," she said. "And I see you have chosen strategic place to fish, Professor Andret." She glanced down as he filled her drink.

"Have I?"

"I would expect no less. Certainly not from man who defeated Kamil Malosz." She took a sip and frowned. "But why this dirty water you are fishing in?"

Twenty minutes later, he and Olga Petrinova were walking in two different directions across the campus—she insisted on taking her own car. And ten minutes after that they were sitting side by side at a plywood bar upstairs from a defunct auction-house on the outskirts of town. In front of them were two double bourbons, no ice.

She was a visiting scholar from St. Petersburg State University, newly arrived after the thawing of Soviet relations. Even her work was fashionable: hyperbolic and elliptic geometries. She drank the bourbon like water.

After her second one, she stopped calling him Professor.

After her third, he felt a knee against his thigh.

He excused himself. In the bathroom, he looked into the tiny mirror and saw the same face he'd always seen—long and stolid, wide at the temples, the nose overly defined, the dark eyes made prominent by the thickness of their ridges. Young for his age, a face flawed by overreaching. It had always slightly shamed him.

Since the Malosz theorem, though, it seemed to have gathered a new charisma.

He tightened the knot of his tie, the bourbon gently separating him from his thoughts. He checked the mirror again, decided the knot was better loose, and walked back out to the bar, loosening it.

.   .   .

THAT SEMESTER HE was assigned to teach the midlevel introductory class in calculus. Three days a week he found himself at a dusty green chalkboard expounding in front of a lecture hall full of first-year students. These were not the mathematics majors or the electrical engineers; and these were not the poets from Professor Rosewater's class at Berkeley; these were the doctors and the accountants and the bankers, the young men—Andret could see few female faces—with enough intelligence to make it to the top but without nearly enough brainpower to change anything. He realized he was envious.

That year, having accepted every lecture invitation in his mailbox, he'd discovered himself to be an able speaker; but this audience of submissive-looking teenagers didn't seem to care. Looking out at their vaguely distracted faces, he suspected that whatever would induce them to their historical destiny hadn't yet arrived on the scene. Sometimes he would lower his voice to a whisper—a trick he'd learned while on the lecture circuit—or pause for several long moments, waiting for their attention to return.

He always had a drink or two before he taught, and now and then his mind would bring him back to his own undergraduate days in East Lansing. By the time he was a sophomore, he was already taking upper-level courses, sitting at the back of the room considering the differences between himself and the boys he'd gone to school with in Cheboygan, most of whom were by then a good way through their second or third tours in Vietnam. He himself had been kept out of the draft by collapsed arches in his feet—he still sometimes wondered if the doctor had exaggerated his condition—and then in Berkeley had been given another five years of reprieve. Now the war was over, and the draft, too, and when he looked out over his classes, the seriousness of those times seemed no more relevant to the students in front of him than some ancient Assyrian epic. In East Lansing in the sixties, the men—future or past soldiers, nearly all of them—had worn ties to class, and there was a gravity to the tone that he hadn't found since. Not even in graduate school at Berkeley, the thought of which, as he stood before his class one day recalling the incense that burned in the back corner of the Lime Rose, deflated him. On the other side of the podium, in the rows of sloping, newly upholstered seats, sat the sons of attorneys and financiers. They rested their sneakers on the chairbacks, passed notes across the aisles, and opened sodas loudly as he spoke. A few of them fiddled with skate-boards.

AT THE BACK of his mailbox one morning, a sealed envelope with his name on it.

I was buying a humidifier for the office. (I never shop there myself, the prices are ridiculous.) If you need anything related to the depart-ment I'm available and hope you will ask. I'm not ashamed about what happened but I'm not proud on the other hand, and it's better if we just ignore whatever it was and pretend it didn't occur. (Of course I mean better for both of us.)

Dogs and Horses

THERE WAS NO denying it: time had passed, yet he'd made almost no progress on the Abendroth. He wouldn't be able to overpower it the way he'd overpowered the Malosz.

Tactic rather than force: that's what he would need.

At first consideration, the problem appeared almost facile; but the essentials quickly hid themselves. He'd begun to conceive of the proof as a fortified castle pierced by ten thousand brightly painted doors, each of which was designed to deceive him. All ten thousand would open—this wasn't the issue—but so far, none of them had allowed him entrance.

Perhaps none ever would.

After a year and a half of effort, he realized that it made sense to limit his aspirations. Perhaps it would help to give up on a solution altogether and focus instead on merely locating the proper vulnerability.

He also understood with a dull sense of foreboding why so many gifted men had been circling the problem for most of a century. The work to all of them must have seemed a seductive lover. By now he'd grown accustomed to waking in the middle of the night with some electrifying premonition, to hurrying through the dark to the mathematics building, to laboring alone in the predawn hours while the radiators clanged around him, as though being hammered by Ulrich Abendroth's own imperious ghost. But over the course of the pale, tree-obscured sunrises, which turned his office from blue-gray to dusky orange to a brightly nauseating yellow, his thrilling premonitions uniformly faded. He could find no passage in.

ONE AFTERNOON NEAR the end of his second year at Princeton, there was a knock at his office. He ignored the interruption; but a moment later it came again. When he opened the door, a woman said, "Oh! You're here then."

"Forgive me," said Andret.

She was well dressed, almost prim—his own age or slightly younger. Dark red heels and a somewhat-dowdy outfit of a related color. Although he never trusted his memory of people, he was fairly sure he'd never seen her before. "I must have been lost in my work," he said.

"I'd give anything for that."

He looked again. A rather pretty face. Maybe a little rebellion in the eyes. No: they'd certainly never met. "Would you?" he said.

"You must be busy. I just wanted to see if I could make an appointment. But I can come back another time."

For a woman who'd arrived uninvited she seemed insistently timid. Yet on the other hand she made no move to leave. In fact, she appeared to keep herself before him by some calm demonstration of will, like a mystic holding a finger in a flame.

He lifted a box of work off the visitor's chair and gestured her in. "The problem," he said, taking the seat at his desk, "is that I might be even busier the next time. You'd have to estimate *those* odds, too. What may I do for you?"

"You're absolutely sure?"

"No." He shook his head. "Nothing is absolutely sure." He smiled. "But now's as good as ever."

She sat down across from him and returned his gaze. Her name was Annabelle Detmeyer, and she was an associate professor in history. "My husband, Yevgeny Detmeyer"—she paused—"my husband is the chair of economics and the co-chair in political science."

"Ah. A double threat."

She laughed, pleasingly. Her laugh wasn't so dowdy.

"How can I help you?"

"I just wanted to learn what a mathematician does," she said. "It's so different from what I do, and I'd heard so much about you. I read an article about the Malosz theorem, and I was intrigued. I actually tried to read it. The proof itself, I mean." She laughed. "I got about a half a sentence in."

"Well, history might be beyond me, too."

"Your work is quite mysterious to someone in a field like mine. That's all. I was just wondering what a person like you does all day. As a historian, I know what I do."

"Which is what?"

"Travel and search out sources and make notes. I teach. I write. At the moment I'm stuck in a little skirmish over Sigismund the Third, of Poland. But I don't imagine you spend your days fretting over anything quite like that." She rose. "Well, you're obviously busy. I can come back another time."

Beneath the dowdy clothes, he glimpsed a body that, like the laugh, wasn't dowdy in the least. "No, no," he said. "In fact, I welcome the interruption, and I'll almost certainly be busier next time. As it so happens, I was just trying to figure out the same thing myself."

"The same thing?"

He leaned back in his chair. "What someone like me does all day," he said.

SHE WAS A farm girl. Had spent her childhood on a cattle ranch half a day's drive from a library and now found it ceaselessly amusing to be teaching seventeenth-century history in the Ivy League.

In a way, then, she was like him.

She told him all of this the next afternoon, when they met for a drink on the patio of a place on Chambers Street. She ordered a glass of wine. Spring had appeared. They sat along the sidewalk, where bikes and baby strollers and students on roller skates ambled past. The peak of the afternoon in the peak of the season. As they talked, she greeted a number of professors who stopped at the table to talk. Most of them looked quite senior—cuff links and bow ties—and all of them forwarded their regards to her husband.

When another of them had walked away, Andret lifted his bourbon and examined her over the top of it. "Your husband is evidently quite an important man," he said.

"Yes, indeed he is." She glanced to the side, then brushed at her hair. Then she took a swallow of wine.

"Ah, yes," said Andret. They were silent for a few moments, during which the air seemed to grow warmer. "Why don't we go someplace a little less public," he finally suggested.

ONE DAY, ALMOST three years along in the task, he happened upon a paper by Paul Erdős. There was an older theorem of combinatorial topology that Erdős and a colleague named George Breville had proven rather magnificently, but also rather whimsically, by modeling their analysis on a children's game. The game was called Kutyák és Lovak, or, loosely translated, Apples and Oranges. Erdős had played it as a young boy in Budapest.

In the game, one child named an object—a lemon, say, which was sour—and the other child countered with an object that possessed some antithetical quality: a cube of sugar, say, which was sweet. The first child then had to do the same for the cube of sugar, but in relation to another quality—it was orthogonal, for example, while a sheet of paper was flat. And so on, until one of them accidentally named an item that shared one of the previously named qualities with the lemon. The game, as Erdős and Breville pointed out, was simple enough for children; but if one began with multiple objects and multiple players, it became more difficult. There were other permutations, too. If after a certain number of moves, for example, the players were allowed to secretly change direction, so that one group might be racing away from the lemon at the same time that the other group raced toward it, it became devilishly complex. This last incarnation was the drinking game that Erdős and his friends had played for bar money at university.

The paper was printed toward the rear of the *Journal of Combinatorics,* spring 1978. Andret read it late on a Monday afternoon. He stared at the poorly printed page in the small lounge where the department shelved its literature. A steeple bell chimed the hour; but he hardly heard. Someone entered the room, poured a cup of coffee, and left. Andret turned back the page and reread the paragraph.

Erdős had cited a method he'd developed to discern the probability that one of his opponents had changed direction in the game. Andret closed his eyes for a moment, then went back and read the paragraph again.

This was it. This was the way to breach the Abendroth.

He shut the journal, set it back in its place on the shelf, and looked around, as though he'd been caught at something.

Another Roof, Another Proof

NOW HE BEGAN a search. The instructive theoretical instance was the prize he sought. When he arrived at the office, he would clear the desk of yesterday's notes, then spend the morning in thought—it might take three or four hours to assemble a single figure in his mind. In the afternoons, he would sketch, committing what he'd composed to memory. At first he tried to conceive of a figure that might invalidate the approach he'd picked up from Erdős; but then, as such figures one by one proved assailable, he began to work on examples that might support it. At home on his bed table, he kept a pen and paper, in case something came to him at night.

For months, he pushed on. The proof might require another three years of work, maybe four—but so what? To solve two great problems in a lifetime would bring him to the pinnacle of his profession. He asked one of the secretaries to buy a half-dozen cartons of laboratory notebooks. When they arrived, he numbered their bindings, then filled the pages with variations on certain theoretical shapes—3-manifolds parsed into every sort of Heegaard Splitting and torus decomposition that he could imagine.

Then he began, slowly and at first by negation, to bridge the moat around the problem. It was tedious work, but the moat needed to be crossed before he could scale the walls. In a day he could fill an entire pad with drawings. As he worked, he felt warmed through his body, down to his hands and feet, as though it were vigorous physical exercise he was performing and not a motionless feat of endurance, sitting still at his desk for hours. He kept a window open for air. Sometimes he grew breathless nonetheless, as first he sensed himself moving to the edge of the moat, then starting across it. On he went. Into numbered file boxes he laid numbered notebooks, which in turn he stacked in numbered sequence along the bare walls of the office. He didn't need his own drawings in order to think, as did some of his lesser colleagues; but he knew that he would need them later for reference—a year from now, five years from now—when he went over the wall into the castle.

IN OLGA PETRINOVA's basement apartment, the radiator was set so low that she kept a sweater on indoors. But underneath the sweater was always a dress, pleasingly stretched, and underneath the dress a queerly sewn, Bolshevik-style undergarment that he grew to crave. Between the knees and breasts it was a thick gray wool, but around the hems ran lacy sinuations of black silk that might have come from a shop in Paris.

The revived state of his work made him ravenous.

Afternoons, he visited. At the door, which was down a flight of stairs, she would greet him with her hands on her hips, her breasts thrust forward through the sweater in a way that was both flirtatious and accusatory. Was this only in his mind? At the small thrift-store table by the refrigerator they would drink a pair of bourbons, then slide the chairs across the room to wait for the sun. Her hands smelled of fennel, and there was something not quite real about the color of her hair, but her bony beauty never failed to catch him. By 2:30 or so, when the sun and the bourbon had warmed her enough, she would narrow her eyes.

In bed she liked to talk, a little before and a little after, both of which were courtesies that the drink allowed him. Before she would let him touch her, she would converse with him solemnly for a few minutes, about Soviet politics or academic mathematics, the way other women might talk about the roses or the house. She seemed to regard these moments as a test of her character. As she talked, Andret would make gentle, two-fingered tugs all the way around the hem of her dress to expose the lacy parts of her undersuit, like a child pulling candles from the rim of a birthday cake. Then he would begin kissing the frills. This she found beguiling. During sex she would quiet, moving suddenly on top of him like a lion over its prey. Her eyes stayed wide. Andret liked to keep his own closed; but whenever he opened them, there she would be, staring down at him, her black pupils gyroscopically inert. Again: leonine. He couldn't help thinking that her gaze, even as she bent over him and strained her shoulders like a collared beast, was in fact an indictment.

The act itself was fervent. Like a brisk tennis game or a summer track meet, something performed in daylight between competitors. The cheap mattress bounced. She liked to do it more than once, and he was usually able to comply. Bourbon was his gasoline. Between sessions, he poured it at the counter while she lay panting on the sheets. Sweat burnished her body. The lean neck. The surprisingly full breasts. He would down another glass and return. The competition would continue in the relentless searching of her eyes, which never rested. Sometimes there was even a third time, in which those eyes, even as they sharpened with arousal, then fogged with it, continued their accusation: he was a cad; he was really just using her; he cared little for anybody.

He was aware, of course, that all of this was true.

ANNABELLE DETMEYER, ON the other hand, would greet him at the servants' door of the Detmeyer estate, humid eyed and already wrapped in some easy-to-remove vestment. In the kitchen a meal would be waiting. Some sumptuous-smelling casserole warming in an iron pot beside a pair of parsley-garnished bowls. Heated bread beneath a square of linen. The Detmeyers had two girls, five and nine, but the house had a half-dozen bedrooms on the second floor alone and an entire top story above that. Behind the property ran a tract of forest preserve. He used the preserve for cover, entering it behind a parking lot in town and emerging like a spy at its near end, across from the tamarack that hid the back door of the Detmeyer garage. Annabelle preferred his visits in the morning, just after the girls had left for school. Except for the few feet of lawn between the woods and the first branches of the tamarack, it was an entirely cloaked journey; but he wore an overcoat anyway, and a pair of dark glasses. Her husband traveled nearly every week.

Bookshelves lined the walls of the house, not only in the library and study but in the living room and kitchen and all the bathrooms. To Andret's mind, this gave the whole downstairs the appearance of a rambling, geometric painting, in which the colored spines of thousands of books formed unintentional refuges of color— predominantly green here, predominantly maroon there—the way random patterns tended to do. In the mathematics section of the study, in fact—Yevgeny Detmeyer taught quantitative economics— there were treatises on exactly such patterns. Andret amused himself with the titles.

About mathematics Annabelle herself knew nothing. She liked bourbon, though, and after their first meeting in town they'd been drinking it regularly at the house. With the children in school they could lounge together on the plush European mattresses upstairs. There were three guest bedrooms on that floor alone, but to his surprise she preferred the master suite, despite the bowl of cuff links on the dresser there. He indulged her preference. The room took up the full width of the house and on two sides looked out on nothing but forest, which allowed him to rise when they were done and gaze out the window like a baron.

His mind in those moments was suffused with calm, the work gone for a few moments of a day. He found Annabelle a refuge and partook of this refuge on every weekday morning that he could.

She was strongheaded and not particularly bright—for Princeton, anyway—but unfailingly generous.

As a lover she was somewhat demure—maybe this was her prairie upbringing—and like Olga, she required conversation. With Annabelle, though, it was always about him. His work. His plans. The detailed narration of his endeavors, both professional and quotidian. In this way she reminded him of Cle Wells, constantly fitting him to an ambition that seemed somehow to have become her own.

In bed, she liked to start out prone. He would begin by kissing her spine through her dress as he answered queries about his life, moving slowly to the neighboring regions—her smooth shoulder blades, the moist rise of her neck, the hot sides of her breasts as he released them from the fabric. Her skin smelled of mint. As he moved, she continued to question him, her eyes closing finally as he began to answer only in grunts, her hand reaching for his hair. When she was sufficiently aroused a hush would finally settle and then with a sigh she would roll over gently onto her back, like a doe turning in leaves.

How he loved that bed! Yevgeny Detmeyer, as it turned out, spent an inordinate amount of time abroad, in Tokyo and Zurich and London and Berlin and Zagreb. He was an extroverted and unstoppable public personality, a highly regarded macroeconomist, and an avidly sought consultant on international politics. And as Andret discovered one afternoon while thumbing through the *Princetonian* in the man's own kitchen, he was also regularly mentioned as a candidate for the Nobel Prize.

The Nobel Prize!

That was Princeton for you. The fact revved his libido.

One day near lunchtime, from the side window of the bedroom, he watched the two Detmeyer girls clomp up the porch steps with their bookbags. Annabelle sat up in bed and gasped at the sound: she'd forgotten that they'd been let out early from a field trip. As she rummaged in the closet for an outfit, he made for the door, pulling on his clothes and hurrying down the back set of stairs.

After that, she wouldn't see him past eleven in the morning. But this wasn't a problem. In fact it made things simpler. He learned that day that if he took a diagonal through the woods and came out of the trees alongside the soccer fields, he had time to stop at Clip's for a pick-me-up and still be at Olga Petrinova's before the afternoon sun came through the window.

Time and Chance

In keeping with the fickle nature of the work, however, his optimism soon began to wane. On most mornings, he woke with a vivid idea of the day's endeavor, but he'd also begun to recognize that his new state of hope was also a state of agitation. And the agitation wearied him.

He'd been at Princeton now longer than he'd been at Berkeley. At the mixers every September, the new hires were already in the habit of asking him to draw their portraits, a practice that had grown to become something of a welcoming rite into the department of mathematics. He'd taken to performing it as a kind of joke: he'd look at the face of whichever new assistant professor had approached him, then look down at the paper, then back up at the face, then back down at the paper, drawing steadily until at last he presented the recipient with a perfect rendering, depending on the man's subject, of Descartes, or Pascal, or Grothendieck. The likenesses were framed in half-a-dozen offices around Fine Hall.

On and on he worked. He walked around campus worrying the lessons of the Erdős paper like a man fingering a wound in his side. It seemed possible now that the paper's conclusion would be no more crucial to his final push against the Abendroth than any of a dozen others he'd read. Yet still it battered him. He was certain there was a clue there, even if he'd not been able to name it. That was the nature of mathematics. You mined a hunch until the hunch was proved either right or wrong. So far, he'd proved it neither.

In the meantime, he'd befriended a man at Clip's. DeWitt Tread was a former member of the mathematics department who'd either been denied tenure or resigned it and now worked as a fabricator for the School of Engineering. This mattered nothing to Andret. What mattered, at least at the start, was that Tread liked to drink. He was from an aristocratic East Coast family and had the facial features of a white-wigged colonial governor, but his life had been one long rowdy procession of drugs and booze and shady business deals that had left him with two teeth broken at the front of his mouth. Like Andret, he wore suits at Clip's; but Tread's, unlike Andret's, were worn to a shine. He owned a huge, ruined house in Princeton Junction and filled it with all kinds of junk that he was always either buying or selling. Most nights, he closed the bar. They began spending time together.

The thing was, Andret could talk to Tread about the Abendroth. There were probably no more than a dozen people in the world who were even capable of understanding the question that the problem necessitated solving; yet Tread, a nodding drunk who had to pay for his drinks before the bartender would pour them, turned out to be one of them. It was preposterous. A derelict in a workingman's dive a half mile from Andret's office. Yes, a mathematician; yes, a former member of the department; yes, a man reputed to have an Erdős number of 2—which, in a manner of speaking, gave Andret an Erdős number of 3—but still, a disheveled, nearly wordless man who'd sat down next to him by chance one day in a cocktail lounge.

At Clip's, Andret would begin a summary of his day's work, sometimes drawing shapes on the tiny napkins, and Tread would listen, noting any unwarranted assumptions that might have been made. All this over doubles, no ice. Andret's tab. Tread could outdrink him 2:1, but Andret paid because he found his friend's analysis so helpful. Sometimes acutely so. Reading a mathematical paper was difficult under any circumstances, but analyzing at speed another mathematician's thoughts was next to impossible. Yet Tread could do it. He was, Andret sometimes thought, a genius.

He also appeared to have no instinct at all for his own advancement. Mathematicians were always celebrating their efforts as communal—and great collaborators like Erdős were beloved all over the world—but Andret himself had never wished to take part in any type of cooperation. He was going to vanquish Ulrich Abendroth entirely on his own. And when he did, he was going to share the credit with nobody.

As Andret talked about the problem, Tread would slump in the stool next to him, his lips parted to show one of the broken teeth, and stare at the rail of the bar. He appeared not to be listening at all. But if even the tiniest increment of mathematical rigor was evaded, he'd look up immediately, his veiny eyes brandishing a glitter. He didn't even have to speak; his expression alone—combined with the fact that Andret, too, possessed an inborn sensor for even the most trivial lapse of logic—was enough to point out the error that, by the following meeting, Andret would have carefully readdressed.

Yet Tread never spoke of collaboration. He never spoke of working on a paper together.

The other thing about him was that by the time they next saw each other—usually a day or two later—Tread would have forgotten everything that had been discussed. This was another quality of his that Andret appreciated.

ONE SPRING DAY, Knudson Hay called him at home and asked him to come down to the office. It was late afternoon and Andret had no desire to return to campus, but in the end he agreed. When he arrived at Fine Hall, Hay went straight to the cabinet and poured out two scotches on the rocks. Andret had already spent a couple of hours at Clip's. "How's the work going?" Hay began.

"Another day, another dollar. Might we have discussed this on the phone?"

"I've found that some things are better addressed in person, Andret. Please sit down." Hay's face tightened and he cast his eyes to the door. "I'm sorry to have to say this, so please listen well. I'd prefer only having to say it once." He appeared for several moments to be composing his next sentence. Then, in a level voice, he said, "I hope you're not entertaining Professor Petrinova."

Andret stared back, revealing nothing.

"You must understand," Hay went on, "the State Department will have my head. Her husband is a colonel in the Soviet Air Force. Are you aware of that?"

"Yes, I am."

"Are you entertaining her?"

"Am I what?"

"Are you *entertaining* her?"

Andret rattled his ice cubes. He liked his scotch neat. "What's the matter?" he said. "You worried she's KGB?"

"Olga Petrinova is a guest of the mathematics department, may I remind you—not to mention the Department of State. For the record, I'm warning you about her. Are you entertaining her?"

"I thought you were only going to ask me once."

"For the record, Milo—I'm warning you."

"Well, I'd prefer only having to answer you once," Andret said. "So please listen well." He was drunk, he realized, in a thick and irritated way. He plucked the ice cubes from his glass and dropped them into the trash. Then he downed the rest of the scotch. "Yes," he said when he sat again. "I'm fucking her. Not the best I've ever had, but pretty damn good. Pretty *entertaining,* actually."

"Jesus," said Hay, working his jaw.

"Don't tell me you're surprised."

"I *am* surprised. I'm not even sure what to say."

In truth, though, Andret was the one who'd been surprised: she hadn't told him she was married.

You Can't Comb the Hair on a Coconut

BY THE BEGINNING of his fifth year on the problem, his energy was clearly flagging. His morning drink generally tired him now rather than revitalized him, and on the days when he taught he'd begun napping at home after lunch. Now and then on such afternoons, he didn't return to the office at all but went to find DeWitt Tread.

What remained to be discovered on the proof was still formidable —indeed, daunting. He considered himself flexible in his attack now—his approach had moved from pure visualization to a mix of visualization and figuring—but what he couldn't deny was that a certain sameness had entered his work. The methodical approach itself, somehow, had become an end. The hours of thought. The incremental charting and drawing. As though by performing them both, even for brief periods, he could systematically check off the set of steps that would in time deliver a solution. Like a man moving a load of gravel with a wheelbarrow. He knew this was absurd. He knew that fortune of the kind he sought was chimerical and couldn't be plundered by method alone. Brilliance. Luck. A moment of godly imagination. He would need all these things but like every mortal could do nothing to summon them. He could only hope, as he sat silently at his desk, that one of them might one day make a wary visit. He was aware that he'd set course for a shore that he might never reach.

Intuition—that's what he needed. His intuition had always served him.

Occasionally, his mind went back to Tycho Brahe and that period of history in which every reasonable expedition in the sciences seemed to produce a discovery of note. How unfair it all seemed. He knew that Hans Borland would never have tolerated such brooding, but he couldn't help indulging in a comfort: he'd been born in the wrong century.

At the same time, and almost without him noticing, his office had begun to grow dark. First in a curious way, then in a bothersome one. He realized that the hemlock outside his window had thickened. He raised the blinds one morning and saw that its branches reached higher now than the ceiling of his office. He bought a lamp. Then a second one. But the electric light failed to achieve the necessary feeling. The stacked boxes were obscuring the lower half of his view, and the room itself had taken on the smell of their contents, the thousands of pages of hand-drawn hypotheticals, lying dormant through the humid summers. In one corner, his notes had reached the ceiling.

HE WAS INTERRUPTED in his work one evening by another knock on his office door. When he opened it a crack, Hay was standing there with a purposeful look on his face. Andret was aware of having mistreated him the last time they'd spoken, but the details were hazy. "Ah," he said, opening the door wider. "Chairman Hay—another personal visit."

"I hesitate to say this," Hay answered, taking off his glasses. He massaged the bridge of his nose. "But I need to ask a favor."

"Of course I'll do you a favor, Knudson."

Hay put his glasses back on. "Are you feeling all right, Milo?"

"I think I am. Yes."

"The Pentagon needs some help from us."

"Pardon?"

"The Pentagon. They want war simulations. A bomber-fighter

engagement. They asked us to game it out on paper before they commit resources. Rather high-stakes risk/reward is what it is, and they need a strong statistical-algebraic mind. They've been very kind to us over my years here."

"A little *jeux de hasard* then."

"Exactly."

"And a little quid pro quo."

"Perhaps so. But I'd like you to do it, Milo. They need it soon. It's not your field, but you've got the talent and you're fast. You could have it done in two days. Your father was a military man, was he not?"

"Yes. Navy." Andret thought for a moment. "You're testing me, Knudson, aren't you?"

"Why would I be testing you? I'm just asking you for a favor. I need someone in the department to do it. I'm sure some of your colleagues would have objections. And you might, too, for all I know. And it goes without saying that you're free to say no."

"Am I?"

"Of course you are."

"In that case," Andret said, "I'll say yes."

HE WALKED HOME the next afternoon with a pamphlet sealed inside an envelope marked CLASSIFIED. They were simulation models. Secret ones. A bomber with limited ammunition engages a fighter that attacks with a single salvo of rockets. Game theory. He spent an evening reviewing the writings of von Neumann and Morgenstern, then set aside the Abendroth. This felt like taking off his boots after a long hike.

In his mind, he visualized the possibilities, then fractured them. For the pursued bomber he postulated the different scenarios: steady firing, intermittent firing, distant attack, close attack. To his great surprise the act of simulation brought him joy. He worked through until morning.

It was the kind of pleasure he'd not experienced since boyhood.

Two days later, in Hay's office, he placed a dozen typed pages onto the desk. In the interim he'd hardly slept. Hay picked up the top sheet and ran his finger over the opening paragraph, reading it half aloud, the way he did when he was thinking.

1. Preliminaries. The game considered has pay-off

$$V(x, p) = A(x)\, \underline{\underline{\o}}(x, p)$$

where

$$\underline{\underline{\o}}(x, p) = e^{-\int_o^x p(y)r(y)dy}$$

The remainder he perused in silence. When he'd finished, he rose, walked to the cabinet, and poured two scotches, neat. "Thank you, Andret," he said. "You did it."

"Looks like I might have."

"You look good, too, by the way. I haven't seen you look this good in a while. Tired, naturally—but happy. You look like you've enjoyed something finally. Am I right?"

"Consider it a favor," Andret replied.

Walking home that afternoon, though, he repeated Hay's words in his mind. *You've enjoyed something finally.* He *had,* hadn't he? For the first time in years, he'd enjoyed something in mathematics again.

IN THE SPRING, during a trip to Palo Alto, a reporter from *The New York Times* was sent his way. He was appearing in the Distinguished Lecture Series at Stanford, and she approached him after his talk. The *Times,* he noticed, liked to cover mathematics the way it covered state fairs or stock-car racing—as a wink to its readership. And it usually sent human-interest correspondents on the stories. But this reporter, a severe-looking young woman in a gray-striped pants suit, appeared to have been genuinely intrigued by what he'd said. She requested an interview.

Her name was Thelma Nastrum, and when she walked into the hotel bar that evening to ask him her questions, she didn't look nearly as severe as she had at the lecture, nor quite as young. She'd changed out of the pants suit.

"A beautiful name," he said as soon as the waiter had left. "Like a flower. A subtle, midwestern flower."

"A fast-moving Scandinavian weed," she answered. Out came her pad and pen, and she took a long swallow of her martini. "So," she said. "What do mathematicians do all day?"

"Evidently that's a popular query," he answered. "What we do is *think*."

She stirred her cocktail, then picked out the olive and sucked it into her mouth.

"And drink," he added.

She made a note. "Imbibing," she said. "While deriving."

He liked her.

After a few minutes of questions, she asked if he thought he might possibly win the Nobel Prize for his work on the Malosz conjecture. She picked up her pad, smiled, and said, "I interviewed your colleague last fall. Yevgeny Detmeyer."

Andret composed his face.

"When he won the Nobel," she added.

"Yes, yes, I know. I'm well aware." He signaled to the waiter again, pointing at their glasses. "There *is* no Nobel in mathematics," he said, as tersely as Hans Borland might have uttered the words. He was irritated to realize he was already drunk. But he also wanted to salvage the evening.

"Oh, I didn't know," she answered. "Why not?"

"Some say because the lover of Alfred Nobel's wife was a mathematician."

"Ahh, yes—well, that would be a good enough explanation, wouldn't it?" She made a note on her pad. "But certainly there's an equivalent. What's the most coveted prize in mathematics?"

"The Fields Medal."

"Well, okay then—I'd imagine you'd have a good shot at the Fields Medal for your proof of the Malosz theorem. Do you think you'll win it?"

"It's not an unlikely proposition."

"Ah," she said, "a double negative." The waiter arrived, and she launched impressively into another martini. When she raised the tetrahedral glass, it divided her smile into three.

"Indeed," he said. "From a mathematician, however, a double negative is an acceptable proposition."

"Two negatives make a positive, am I correct?"

Andret smiled. "You are indeed correct. At least for operations in which the identity element is *one*."

In her reporter's pad she noted this as well. Then she excused herself to use the restroom. When she returned, her sweater was draped over her arm. He watched her hang it over the chairback. She was a few years older than he'd thought, but she was still in excellent shape.

Later, in the hotel room, she told him that she'd already been to bed with two Pulitzer Prize winners. "But never a Fields Medal," she said.

He rose to freshen his glass. "I haven't won it yet."

"Well," she said, "neither had they."

THE PROBLEM STARTED, blinkingly, that fall. Walking to work one morning, he passed near a streetlamp whose cover had come unlatched. When he looked up, its bulb suddenly exploded into a halo of brightly flaming stars. He blinked. When he looked again, it was back to normal.

Later that day, he glanced out his office window and saw the fender of a bike do the same sort of thing. It transformed for a moment into a burning, multipointed polygon that flared and retracted. Then it was normal again.

"SIT DOWN, ANDRET."

"No telephone again?"

"I'm afraid not," said Hay. "Not for what I need to speak with you about this time, my friend."

My friend. Andret took a seat across from the desk and accepted a scotch. Again Hay skipped the ice.

"I've forgiven you for your behavior with Mrs. Petrinova, by the way," Hay began, twisting the cap back onto the bottle and returning it to the drawer. "Well, not with Mrs. Petrinova, of course, but for your behavior with me when I spoke to you about her. That's behind us." He pursed his lips tersely and picked a bit of lint from his sleeve. "Last *year,* Milo—when we spoke in my office."

"What do you need, Knudson?"

"I'm a practical man. I don't stew. I do what's best for the department."

"Yes, I know."

"I did you a favor with Mrs. Petrinova."

"And I did the Pentagon work for you in return. That makes us even."

"Indeed you did, Milo. Indeed you did." He picked at another spot of lint, then folded his hands. "The reason I've asked you here is to tell you that the department's been given an endowment. A very nice one." He leaned forward. "You might even say an *obscenely* nice one. For a newly named chair. The Hyun Chair in Experimental Mathematics. It would be an entirely new subdepartment—still under my direction, of course, but *new.* Man-Sik Hyun runs the Hyun Electrics Company, in Seoul, South Korea. And now in Camden, New Jersey, as well. Geometer, himself." He smiled efficiently. "He wanted to call it the Hyun Electrics Chair, actually. But someone from endowment explained the problem."

Andret chuckled.

Hay gestured to the glasses. "Refill?"

"Please."

"And you're one of those up for consideration, Milo."

"I don't have tenure."

"You'd get it."

"I've solved *one* problem in my career, Knudson."

Hay raised his glass. "But what a problem it was, Milo."

"Well, thank you."

"In any case, it's a circumstance I can take care of. They give me that kind of latitude here. I'm talking about early tenure and promotion, you realize. The chair of a subdepartment and a major new endowment."

Andret sat up.

Hay lowered his voice. "What are you working on these days?"

"Still the damned Abendroth conjecture."

Hay leaned back, letting out a whistle. "Well, you certainly can't be accused of giving up on anything."

"No, I can't."

"Tell me, though, are you close?"

"Close to what, Knudson?"

"Don't be coy. Dr. Hyun would like to see something solved with his name attached to it. Something big and famous." He raised his glass. "Like Abendroth's last conjecture."

Andret gazed evenly at him. "I might be," he said.

"A year?"

"Perhaps."

Hay studied him. "I should tell you," he continued, topping off the drinks. "There are those in the department who are against it."

"Okay."

"They find you—let's see, how do I put it?" He looked down at the stack of papers on his desk. "Abrasive. Arrogant. I've heard both those words."

"What do you want me to say?"

"I don't want you to say anything, Andret. I'm just letting you know. These are the difficulties I face in making a decision. You could help me out, you know."

"How could I do that?"

Hay set down his drink and neatened his pile of papers. "You could begin," he said, "by behaving a little more civilly."

. . .

LATER THAT WEEK, a note in his mailbox. A pink office slip this time, folded over, with Helena Pierce's initials on the front. The square alongside PHONE MESSAGE had been checked. The caller: *Professor Earl Biettermann.*

So the son of a bitch was a professor now. It was strange that he hadn't heard.

He unfolded the sheet and read the Selectric's dark type:

```
Sad news. Hans Borland has passed away.
Asked that you be notified.
```

Jesus. Even now he heard the old man's sour voice. He set his arm against the mailboxes and felt the same mean game of jousts between them, as though even in death his teacher had managed to deliver one last blow with the pike. He shook his head and turned to the wall.

Behind him, the office door creaked. He was still looking at the wall when a hand tapped his shoulder. "Professor Andret?"

She hadn't addressed him kindly in years.

"I'm okay."

"Professor Andret—"

"Really—I'm fine."

The footsteps retreated. A moment later, a box of tissues. He accepted one.

"I know he must have been important to you."

"He was, he was. He was—I can't really figure it." His own words surprised him. "Oh," he said, turning. "Oh, Helena."

"I've been looking for you all morning, Professor Andret, to be honest. Since the call came in." There seemed to be tears in her eyes. "Professor Biettermann told me how upset it would make you. But I guess Professor Borland had asked him to give you the news, if it happened. I know he was sick for a while, but it still must have been such a shock to hear it like this. I'm so sorry, Milo."

He looked more closely at her: yes, those were tears in her eyes. "He's the reason I'm here," he said softly.

She nodded at him, her hands on her mouth.

"His voice is the one that tells me to keep going."

"Oh, Milo, I'm so sorry. I should never have just left a note. I should have come and found you. I'm really so sorry about all of it." She laid her hand on his arm.

He touched it there and looked up again: yes, he could see it—she *was* sorry. He didn't in any way deserve it; but there it was.

LATE THAT VERY afternoon, his phone rang at home. This time Hay's voice was curt. "We need you down here right now, Andret. It's important."

When he pushed open the frosted-glass door of the chairman's office, a line of startled faces looked up at him. It was the nine most senior members of the department, arranged around the elegant oak meeting table.

Hay rose from the chair at the end. "I thought you'd have knocked. But thanks for coming on such short notice."

At the news of Borland's death, Andret had spent the day at Clip's, where they'd somehow run out of bourbon and had served him rye instead. Now he felt darkened. Darkened and wrapped, like a man in a sack. Hay had spoken, but it took a moment for him to understand that the faces in the room were awaiting a response. The sheen on the windows broke into a row of angled prisms. "Well, I didn't," he said, turning away.

A silence. Some of the heads glanced around.

"Knock," he clarified, directing his gaze to the carpet.

"Well," said Hay. He cleared his throat. "This is an unusual circumstance, but some of the department wanted to speak to you in person. I'll be frank—as you know, you've been nominated for the Man-Sik Hyun Chair in Experimental Mathematics. Which of course would be bestowed with tenure. And a subchairmanship. Did you have anything you wished to say?"

"Wished to say?"

"To the committee, Milo."

He looked up. "I'll do a top-notch job, gentlemen." He nodded at the faces. Then, gravely: "I'm a damn good mathematician, and I appreciate the opportunity."

Hay smiled. Andret folded his hands. When he glanced at the windows again they were just windows. He turned his gaze then to the familiar Eastern European features in the room. His colleagues at the table looked like the survivors of a sunken Lithuanian ferry, with the exception of Hay, who looked like the captain of the Nordic vessel that had rescued them. The Department of Broken Englishes— that's how they were known around campus. A startlingly uniform wall of bulbous Semitic features, threadbare sport coats, and colorless ties. He was gripped with the abrupt, sour understanding that he hated them all.

Then, as he stood there trying to shake the feeling, he suddenly understood the obvious: that *they* hated *him,* too, just as savagely. Faces emerged from the book-cluttered background. Small-time tyrants and shameless throne coveters. Second-rate strivers: every single one of them. And all of them out to destroy him. The conviction gathered strength. Out of his mouth came "Vile looks won't stop me."

"Pardon?"

"You're all nothing. A fancy fucking table of nothing."

Someone laughed aloud. Then the room went silent. The windows shot another flicker of color.

"Let's try to ignore that," said Hay. "Please, everyone."

"It's exactly what I was talking about," said a voice.

"Look, Andret," Hay said, "I'll keep it specific. What are you working on now? Can you tell the committee?"

Andret turned his eyes to the carpet again. The premonition receded. He blinked. "Abendroth's last conjecture. You know what I'm working on, Knudson."

"I'm asking for the sake of the committee. There was some question about it. And how far are you from a solution?"

"That's an ignorant question."

"He's right," someone said.

"I mean, in your rough estimation." Hay chuckled as though he were enjoying the exchange. He opened his hands. "Milo—what we discussed right here, a couple of days ago. How far are you from a proof?"

Andret looked up again. The room remained the room. But now there were adjustments in the faces. Nods. Turnings. The details less decipherable. He began to think that perhaps he was standing before friend and not foe. It was possible that he'd misjudged. Enrico Petti, a geometer, appeared to be the one who'd laughed, then spoken up in his defense. Riney Burtsfield shot his gaze around angrily, but his malice was obviously directed at Hay. Raul Shortkopf, one of the department's minor despots, tapped his nanoid fingers clumsily as he performed a compulsive computation. Hay himself continued to smile.

"Roughly," Hay said again. "Tell us what you think *roughly,* Professor Andret."

"A year," he responded. Then, "Maybe two."

Someone whistled.

"Thank you," Hay said. "That's the information we needed. We appreciate your time."

A hand on his elbow. He was being guided out. At the threshold, it released him. In the hallway, hidden from the others, he covered his eyes. When he uncovered them, the world was again unremarkable. The dark floor. The overpinned corkboard. He took a step. The pearled window of the mail room. He realized that Hay was still there behind him. When he turned, his chairman leaned forward from the doorway and whispered, "I'll let you know what happens, Milo."

Words came from inside the room. Someone said, "The biggest pig eats the best apples."

Andret looked Hay straight in the eye. "I don't give a rat's ass about any of you," he said. "None of it matters to me one goddamn bit."

Hay appeared startled. But then his expression changed. "That's where we differ, Milo," he said. "To *me,* it does matter. It matters quite a lot." And he wearily pulled shut the door.

"I DON'T KNOW," she replied, the line echoing. "It's a long way."

"It would mean a lot."

A pause. Classical music playing in the background. He pictured the narrow bed.

"We'd get separate rooms, right?"

"Yes, of course. Separate rooms."

"I mean, *if* I agreed to come."

"Yes, *if* you did. I'm being considered for a promotion, you know."

"Yes, I heard. That's wonderful. Congratulations."

"Thank you."

"Well—" she said, "—I still don't know."

"Separate rows on the plane."

A small laugh.

"Helena."

"I'll consider it."

"Will you? I'll agree to whatever you want. *Really.* And it goes without saying that I'll pay for everything."

"I'll be back in time for work on Monday?"

"You can stay as long as you like. I'll pay for a couple of more days out there if you want. I mean for you, alone. You could make it a vacation. I'll talk to Knudson. All I ask is for you to come to the service, that's it. Do you have people in California?"

"I don't know. I might."

"Please, Helena," he said. "*Please.* There's nobody else I can ask."

Regression to the Mean

BERKELEY. THE VERY same place as on the day he'd left. Nearly six entire years, disappeared into a perfect, metaphysical maw. The same shouting street huckster in the same red bandanna. The same black-lipped dog leaping for a Frisbee. On Telegraph, a line of hippies against a storefront, their tire-tread sandals stretched across the concrete. Helena took his elbow, and they stepped around the legs. She was wearing a pleated skirt. "Is this where we're planning to spend our time?" she said.

He led her up Bancroft. A few hours remained before the service. On College, a cab. At his old corner he paid the driver to wait, and they walked up the ramshackle block. At last he stopped and looked down into the familiar windows. Behind the two dark panes, he could make out the edge of a thinly tassled rug. Suddenly he saw Cle Wells step from the shower in his T-shirt.

"What?" said Helena.

"Oh, God."

"Is this it? Is this where you lived?" She leaned sideways to look up at the building.

"It's all different."

He led her back to the cab. This time they got out in Rockridge. The coffee shops, the sandwich places, all of it entirely the same. The same chai tea special taped to the window of the Lime Rose. The same pale-skinned counter boy who used to serve them their Turkish coffee.

Why was he still thinking about her?

He needed a drink.

At a corner market, while Helena used the bathroom, he downed a mini. Then he took her arm and they headed up Claremont toward the hills. The houses were larger here, blue gums and eucalyptuses arching the roofs. Lemon trees in the well-kept yards, the lemons hanging like earrings. And towering above them all were the stately sycamores, holding out their marble boughs. "Hans Borland used to live up here," he said. "In one of these mansions with a view of the bay."

"What was he like?"

"I don't actually know. I could never really figure. I couldn't decide whether he was my friend or my enemy."

"He was your friend," she said. "He championed you."

"Did he?"

"Yes."

Her step quickened. She might have been blushing. Andret caught up. The street rose more steeply now, and they ascended in silence, her heels picking a path. The pleated skirt swishing. She wasn't as pretty as Olga or as welcoming as Annabelle, but there was something else about her. Her arms swung steadily.

Near the summit, a stone terrace opened onto a view. They sat across from each other on a crumbling wall. "Tell me about *you*," he said.

She blushed again. "Oh, I don't know."

"Come on, tell me. What do you like to do?"

"The usual things."

"Like what?"

"Like garden. I take care of the roses behind my building. I guess I paint a little, too."

"What kind of painting?"

"Landscapes, mostly. Not very good ones. Really, most of what I do is help my middle sister with her kids. I work hard in the department, though. I enjoy working hard at everything. The garden, too." She seemed to be more comfortable with him now and even smiled. "I take care of twenty-five roses and a rare kind of peony."

"Do you like it?"

She looked up at him. "I like working hard, if that's what you mean. I love being an ant."

He was startled.

"Interesting," he said. "It's an appealing thought, though, isn't it?"

"What is?"

"Being an ant. Giving up on all the rest." He leaned down to tie his shoe. As he sat up again, he recognized his mistake. "And what about you?" he said. "Do you want your own children?"

She was looking out at the view now. From this high up they could see the spires of both bridges.

"Yes, I do," she finally said. His gaze went to where hers was turned, toward the clumped buildings of San Francisco and the twisting black stripe of the freeway. The gray clay water. The faint slashes of ships. This was the sight that had given him his first breakthrough on the Malosz, a thousand years ago. His dissertation defense. Borland's nodding head—the approbation so rarely given. The job at Princeton. He closed his eyes.

"And what about you?" she said.

"What about me?"

"Do *you* want them?"

He looked at her. "Oh," he said. "Kids—God no." Then he added, "That would be cruel."

AT THE SERVICE there seemed to be lines of bereavement on her face—as though she were the one who'd lost the great figure in her life. In the narrow pew next to him she dabbed steadily at her eyes.

An impressive crowd. Hundreds of mourners filling the long

wooden benches. What looked like the entire mathematics department spread across a dozen roped rows before the pulpit. It was all puzzling—Borland was a major figure but also a damning and truculent man. Yet there seemed to be such genuine sorrow in the church. In Helena, too.

Andret was suspicious. Plenty of these people had to be feeling relief.

His own feelings shrank from him. He'd had a couple of drinks at the hotel, but by now their velvety wrap had withered to a scrim of irked melancholy. The pain that had been circling him had landed. A point in the center of his skull. He rubbed at it. For a moment, the mosaic floor wobbled. He closed his eyes. The thought occurred to him that the dean here must already be searching for Borland's replacement; well, he wouldn't take it. Princeton still owed him tenure, no matter how much it bruised the envious ones. And there was the possibility of the Hyun chair, too, if he hadn't damaged it too badly.

Still.

The spectacle of the extended eulogies and the sea of bereaved faces continued to confound him. What were all these people truly feeling? Purposelessness sunk him into the pew. What was actually in the minds of all these scholarly-looking charlatans? Of all these meager men in their poorly knotted ties? Of these lugubrious women in their mournful dresses? He centered his wing tips in front of his knees and tapped them on the floor. The tiles bulged again. Then settled. The world teetered. Helena's gloved hand entered his vision. A lacy black animal in repose across her lap. He reached to grasp it.

At that moment, his glance fell on what he'd been searching for.

AT THE RECEPTION, he excused himself and left Helena at the front bar. At the rear one, he ordered a pair of bourbons, then took a position behind the milling crowd. Yes, he was right: there she was, next to the grand piano, gazing out the windows at Vine Street. Someone who didn't know her the way he did might not even have recognized her: hair expensively done, dark linen dress, pearls at her throat. But he saw that like the city itself she'd not actually changed at all.

He wondered if she'd come to see *him*.

When he reached her, he whispered from several feet away, "The kind of event where one *expects* to meet up with ghosts."

She turned. "Milo?"

"Gottfried Leibniz, actually. Arriving with a gift."

She took the glass and kissed him on the cheek. "No—Leibniz is with *me*. I told you that." She laughed. "But I'm happy to see the gift." Then she reached and kissed him on the mouth.

"Well," he said.

A bit of puffiness around her eyes, but yes: otherwise still the same. She pointed at a man standing a long way off, near the door.

"Ah," said Andret. "He lives."

Biettermann looked older, too, and as superficially changed as Cle. Tanned skin. Dark tie pushed to the throat. But even from across the room the arrogance still glowed like a pilot light. Cle pulled Milo by the arm. When they neared, Earl turned, a quick gust of apprehension stiffening his features. He changed it into a smile.

Andret gave him the soul shake. Two men in similarly expensive suits, but Biettermann now with wisps of gray in his slickly combed hair. "Touché," Andret said drily.

"Touché, brother," answered Biettermann, equally drily.

Cle stood between them, smiling.

THAT EVENING IN the hotel lobby, Andret coached Helena. She was to avoid saying anything about herself; he would provide the particulars. They were friends only. She was in the physics department, pursuing graduate work. No—Biettermann might question her: she was in the department of art history. Next to him on the plush couch of the atrium, she giggled. He'd brought her a glass of Chablis.

"Why would I be studying art history?" she said.

"As a matter of fact, you might actually consider it. It'd be good for you. You told me you like to paint, didn't you?" He downed his drink. "And Earl won't know the first thing about it."

A moment later, his old friends were at the curb. An elegant European car. Deep leather seats. Shaded windows. As always, Biettermann drove pugnaciously. Switched lanes and pulled up close to the traffic on the crowded streets. All of it beneath a steady winter rain.

At the restaurant, a doorman guided them through the entranceway under an ivory-handled umbrella. In the palely flickering foyer, the maître d' took their coats. "Professor Milo Andret," he said, bowing. "An honor for us."

This was Biettermann's doing. The sarcasm was evident.

At the table, his old nemesis lost no time in launching into the details of his career. He was dressed in a different suit now, this one even more elegantly cut. Cle's wrists sparkled with rows of bangles. They might have been diamonds. Andret made a point not to look. Next to him, Helena had on the same dress she'd worn to the memorial, but at least she'd done something with her hair. It was up in a bun. Biettermann droned on. At Berkeley he'd finished in mathematics and been accepted into all the top programs—Harvard, Stanford, MIT, Princeton—before undergoing a change of heart.

The waiter arrived with wine, a Vega Sicilia. Biettermann tasted it and sent it back. A different bottle appeared. Then the appetizers— clams Casino, bruschetta, a layered arrangement of sugared dates. Biettermann looked like he'd been taken apart by a machine and reassembled. Tan hands. Glowing teeth. Andret didn't mind staring. Beside him he could hear Helena whispering over the tiny plates that steamed with garlic and pepper. Biettermann grabbed the new wine from the waiter and poured it around the table, looking pleased. A '71 Château Latour. Cle took over the story. They'd been married at the Cape, four years earlier—"a small wedding," she added, when Andret glanced. Then they'd moved to Manhattan, where Earl's father had set him up at Dean Witter.

Andret spit his wine. "The *brokerage* firm?"

"Not even a year there," said Cle. "Now he steers the whole ship at Piper Jaffray Hopwood."

"What's that?"

"Investment specialists. Sophisticated ones. Earl runs arbitrage. They *bribed* him away from Dean Witter, Milo." She opened her purse and handed him a card with a Park Avenue address. "Made him top animal in five months."

"Arbitrage?" Andret said. He set down his glass. "Is that an entheogen?"

Cle laughed aloud.

"Actually," said Earl, "it might be."

"No more poetry, then?"

To Andret's satisfaction, Cle guffawed.

Andret turned to her. "And what about *you*?" he said.

"Me?" she answered. "Me what?"

"What have you been doing with yourself all this time?"

"Oh, well, I haven't done anything since Berkeley."

"That's not true, dear."

"Of course it is."

"You went to grad school, for one. Now you're on the board of the foundation. And don't forget—"

"Oh, Lord," she said. "Grad school was dreadful. I never finished my dissertation." She looked around, stopping at Helena. "In fact, I never started it."

Helena smiled meekly.

In the silence that followed, Biettermann said, "Actually, it *is* a kind of poetry."

"What is?" asked Helena.

"My work. The arbitrage. It really is a kind of poetry, as long as my friend here was asking. Futurist, if I had to label it. Although also formalist. With definite rules of prosody." He smiled at his own wit. "What we do is game the risk of other entities. Companies. Organizations. Nations. Without assuming proportionate risk ourselves. That's essentially the rhyme and meter. One takes as one's subject what one finds in the world." He turned. "And I run just one division of arbitrage," he said to his wife. "Not the whole ship, dear. But yes, in fact"—here he raised his glass—"finance is indeed an entheogen. A modern-day entheogen, carried home from the jungle."

"Fascinating," said Helena.

"The fattest pig eats the best apples," said Andret.

"Indeed," said Cle.

"Wait just a moment," Andret said to Earl. "I thought you were supposed to be a professor."

Biettermann stared.

Cle burst out laughing. A short, rising aria that ended in a swallowed cough.

"That's what your phone message said anyway—Professor Earl Biettermann. The message you left with my secretary."

Helena flinched.

"I was joking, Andret." He refilled their glasses. "I guess you didn't get it. You never were quick with a joke." Then he raised his wine. "Anyway, here's to Hans Borland. A great mathematician. A great teacher. A great man."

"To Hans Borland," said Helena weakly.

"I see," said Andret. "You were joking. Funny."

"Oh, please, Milo," said Cle.

"Look," said Biettermann, "as a matter of fact, I employ professors now on a regular basis. Have several of them working for me at this very moment. They couldn't pull the ejection cord fast enough from the *academy*." He drew out the word. "Physics and mathematics and philosophy. Any field that employs sound logic—that's my rule. To be honest, Andret, you might consider it. We do groundbreaking work."

"I'm sure you do."

"Geared derivatives. An unplayed field."

"Sounds brilliantly interesting."

"It is," said Cle. "That's why it has a French name." She finished off her wine and poured herself another. "Château Latour. Lazard

Frères. *Arbitrage.* Anything interesting involves a French word, haven't you noticed? Here's to everything that Hans Borland taught the two of you. *Tout de quel.*"

"Enough now," said Biettermann.

Helena dropped her eyes. Cle snickered.

"No negative cash flow at any probabilistic state," Biettermann whispered now, leaning forward and tilting his head toward Andret, "and a positive cash flow in at least one."

Andret turned the stem of his wineglass in his fingers. "In other words," he said, "risk-free profit."

"You've got to put into the bowl what the dog wants to eat, my friend."

"Yes, I guess you do, my friend, don't you?"

"You could do it, too, Milo," said Cle. "You could mint money at what Earl does."

"No thanks."

"Honey," said Biettermann, "remember that even in my branch of arbitrage, you have to enjoy risk. You have to *thrive* on it. Finance is *based* on it, for God's sake. Milo here dislikes risk. We all know that."

"And I don't get jokes, either. You've said that before, Biettermann. It gets old."

"Like the two of us, my friend?"

"Are we friends?"

"My, my," said Cle. But she twisted her glass slowly in the candle-light, the way Andret had done a moment earlier. "Can we talk about something else now?" She picked up the expensive-looking cigarette case that her husband had set on the table. "Look at this," she said, turning to Helena. "Isn't the carving exquisite?"

"Oh, yes, it is, Mrs. Biettermann. It's really lovely."

"You recognize the artist, perhaps?" Cle held it up to the light. "It looks like a Fra Angelico, maybe? Or a Giotto? Or maybe it's a Dürer?"

"Give me that," said Andret.

"It's a Maitani, in fact," said Cle, turning a flirtatious smile to him.

She held it out as Milo stared at her. Then she turned to Helena. "The frieze from the grand Duomo di Orvieto. In Umbria. A brutish vision, don't you think?" She lowered her voice. "But it's hard to take your eyes off it, isn't it?"

"I'll be the judge of that," said Andret. When he took it from her hand, he saw that it had been made from a single slab of silver. Tiny, intricately carved figures writhed in violent copulation, their flesh torn by wounds. "It's just hell," he said. He dropped it back onto the table as though it hadn't fascinated him in the least. "That's all they painted in those days."

"This is carved, Milo," said Biettermann.

Cle set down her wine now and focused her eyes on Helena. "Do you enjoy risk, too?" she said. "Is there much risk in the history of art?"

Helena blinked. A clam steamed on her fork. Andret saw the humiliation confounding her. "This whole evening is ridiculous," he said.

"Look, Milo," said Biettermann. "Let's change the subject then. How about it?" He shot his cuffs and ceremoniously refilled the glasses. "I've read your proof of the Malosz theorem," he said. "It's very, *very* good."

"Okay, then, well—thank you, Earl."

"I still keep up with research mathematics, you know. Yours is a spectacular piece of work. An unexpected approach to a famously evasive problem." He raised his glass. "It's brilliant, in fact. The most brilliant mathematical leap in a decade. No, not just in a decade—in our entire lives, perhaps."

"I'm honored."

"Well, don't be," said Cle, picking up the case again and tapping out a cigarette. "Earl's trying to disprove it."

"What?" said Andret.

"He works on your proof every night, Milo. It's an obsession of his."

"Cle, dear—please."

"Well, you *do,* sweetheart. Might as well stand up to the facts. Even though there's not a chance in hell you'll find anything wrong with it."

"What's this about, please, dear?"

"Are you really trying to challenge my work, Biettermann?"

His old nemesis set down his fork. "All's fair in love and war," he said finally.

"At last then," said Andret, "a little poetry. Thank you." He rose, took Helena's arm, and tossed his glass of wine across Biettermann's suit.

Back at the hotel, he twisted himself into a rage. He was grateful for Helena's presence, grateful that she'd gone along with the charade, grateful that she'd left the dinner with him and stormed out beside him into the night. He wanted to show his appreciation. He truly did. But his brain was unspooling. In the cab he'd been spun by all the glinting raindrops on the glass. Inside the hotel lobby now, his eye fell on a brass urn that immediately bulged into a spheroid. The spheroid elongated. At the elevator, he kept his gaze to the carpet. But the elevator wouldn't come. He stepped forward and kicked the planter. Dirt covered the floor. The metal doors began to emit winks of light.

He lit a cigarette and sucked at it.

"What are you doing?"

"Calming myself."

She pointed. "You're already smoking one."

"Fuck that."

"You're not supposed to do that in here, Milo."

"The hell I'm not."

She took his sleeve and whispered something. Oh, that mouth. He leaned in. That luscious hair. At last, the elevator. More sensation. The lurch of ascent on cables. The spinning, weather-pattern burls gyrating in the wall panels. The columns of smoke sewing themselves into uncurling maps. He reached his nose up into one of them. At her floor, they exited, and at the door to her room he crushed out his cigarettes into the rug. When he raised his head again he felt a gust of warmth from her skin. He closed his eyes and began kissing her neck. She stepped back and worked her key into the lock.

"Please," he moaned.

"You're drunk."

"I'm not drunk."

He moved down, grasping at the buttons of her dress.

"Milo," she said. "I've done my best to care about you." She pushed him away. "But you don't let me. You're dead drunk."

"I'm not drunk, Helena. I'm lost. Help me."

She twisted free and squeezed through a crack in the door. It swung shut.

"Please help me!" he wailed as he rattled the knob. "Fuck you!" he shouted, sliding to the carpet. "Let me in!"

Silence.

He yanked off his shoe and began pounding the wall with it. "Open the goddamn door, Helena!"

From down the hall a man yelled, "Shut up already!"

"Fuck you," Andret shouted back. "And fuck Helena Pierce!" He started in with the shoe again. "Fuck all of you!"

"I'm calling the cops," came the voice.

"Shut up and call them then!"

That's when he heard the bolt unlock behind him. Helena leaned out, thrust her hands under his shoulders, and pulled him into the room.

Welcome to the Future

"Well, wouldn't you like to know whether you got it?"

Hay hadn't offered drinks. "Why don't you call me about it tomorrow?" Andret said, reaching for the doorknob.

"Okay, Milo, fine—yes, you did. You got it. Congratulations." Hay smiled perfunctorily. "These are the appointment letters right here, one from me and one from the dean. You certainly don't make it easy, you know."

"My job isn't to make it easy."

Hay tilted his head. "That's your sense of humor," he said thoughtfully. "Isn't it?"

"It's my sense of truth."

"The Hyun Chair in Experimental Mathematics, Milo. Tenure in the finest department in the country. A subchairmanship. Not a bad day, even for a man who doesn't give a damn. Congratulations again, my friend. But still, you really do need to be more careful."

"Of what?"

Hay leaned forward, squinting now, as though trying to see something that Andret wouldn't show him. Finally, he said, "I understand that you were at Hans Borland's memorial."

"What if I was?"

The appraising gaze continued.

"What?" said Andret.

"I'm not exactly *sure*," Hay said slowly. "Are you *actually* belligerent? Or do you truly not understand the way you appear to your colleagues? I mean, to the whole world. I heard that you didn't say hello to a single member of the department in Berkeley. Not to a single one of your old professors. Were you even aware of that?"

"They're no friends of mine."

"Perhaps not. But you know that *I* am, don't you? I'm your *friend*, Milo. You must understand that."

Andret reached. "Can I see the letters?"

Hay pulled them back. "You're lucky I recognize your brilliance, Milo. You're lucky I can handle it. And you're lucky I understand that the rest is just the price. I go out of my way to protect you, you know. I'm your ally. And not everybody thinks I should be."

"Just show me the letters, please."

"Yes, yes. All right—and there's a third one here, too." He slipped a business card into an envelope. "This fellow's an acquaintance of mine, Milo. Dr. William Brink."

Andret peeked at the card, then burst out laughing.

"It's nothing to laugh at. Bill's a psychiatrist. A very good one."

"Dr. Brink, the shrink."

"You might at least consider calling him."

"I don't need a shrink."

"Then what exactly *do* you need?"

"I'm not going to answer that, Knudson." He thought for a moment. Then he added, "But it does rhyme with *Brink*."

His difficulty had begun to surface more regularly now. Not just the star in the streetlamp or the bulging urn in the lobby, but other more complex, transitory shapes. As he went about his day, his eye would light on some ordinary entity—a metal mailbox or a kite in the sky or a brick chimney spilling smoke—and his brain would instantly fling itself into weird geometries. The mailbox, melted like toffee, would become a teacup; the kite, a two-ended, bulbous vase; the chimney, an undulating trapezoid. He could never predict it. Once, as he was walking home, a line of geese transformed itself into a sliding, anfractuous matrix of single-sided, single-edged spirals, the distant black curves burrowing into themselves like the blades of a windmill. Then, in another moment, the whole scene turned back to normal again. He blinked.

And soon he'd noticed something else, as well: that whenever one of his visions occurred, he'd be struck soon after with the old sensation that someone was watching him from behind. And later in the day, he would suffer from a particular headache—as though his skull had shrunk until it was just slightly too small for his brain. Still later, a queer residue of feeling would center itself at some odd spot in his body. Sometimes he would feel it in his fingers, which would seem to have inverted themselves, often in a shifting manner. His pinkie would now be his thumb, for example—for the most transitory fraction of a second—or his knuckles would now be attached on the wrong side of his palm. It was as though a telephone operator had patched a cord into the wrong line; then, while trying to correct the mistake, had moved it fleetingly—but to another false position— before at last yanking it out. Yet this wasn't exactly it, either. The feelings—actually, they were more like the *memories* of feelings— never lasted long enough to summon. In this sense, they were very much like his visions. And if he drank a glass of water before the next bourbon, they would generally subside. Certainly he'd be fine by the next morning.

He never mentioned his problem to anybody, though. Not to Helena, certainly, who on the plane trip back from California had sat rigidly in her seat three rows ahead of him and paid for her own cab ride home from the airport; not to Knudson Hay, who, peering in closely, would now and then inquire about his health; not to Annabelle, who would no doubt have pressed him for details; not to Olga, who wouldn't have cared at all; and never to a doctor, of course. For Andret was not in the habit of seeing doctors.

. . .

THE CALL CAME one morning in the fall of his thirty-eighth year, not long after his birthday. He was slouching at his desk in Fine Hall, preparing a class as well as trying to bring to a point a spate of recent ideas on the Abendroth. He was in a vulgar mood, frustrated in his attempts to sustain order in his life. He wanted to be at Clip's, but it had become difficult to prepare a lecture in a bar. Hay had mentioned his teaching—there had been complaints. He hadn't had a drink since the night before, and when the phone rang he spilled coffee all over his sleeve.

A foreign accent. French maybe. "Professor Andray?"

"No. Andret."

"Professor Meelo Andray?"

"*My*-lo An-*dret*. Who *is* this, please? I'm working."

"Congratulations, Professor Andray. I have an important news."

He pulled his feet together and sat up in the chair.

AT CLIP'S, HE closed the side door and crossed to the rear, where one of the tables was hidden behind a pillar. Sure enough, he could see the back of DeWitt Tread's suit at the bar. But he knew his friend could sit for an entire night without turning away from his glass.

It was a Friday evening. Hay had obviously been surprised by the invitation; but he'd accepted, and now Andret was here for a warm-up. He ordered a double. At exactly the appointed hour, Hay entered, glancing around. He was well dressed, of course. Andret raised a hand and beckoned him to the table.

"Well, well," Hay said, sliding into the chair across from him. "This should be fun. To what do I owe the pleasure?"

"What are you looking for from your life?" said Andret.

"What am I looking for from my *what*?" Hay shimmied out of his jacket and hung it on the peg. "How about I start with a drink?"

"Of course. Sorry."

The waitress arrived and took their order. To Andret, she said, "Another?"

While they waited, Hay started in on a story. As he rambled on, Andret glanced toward the bar, where DeWitt Tread was talking to the man next to him. The other man was of the same ilk as Tread—a maniacal-looking academic in a pilling sport coat—and even from a distance it was clear that the two of them were not much better than bums. Andret was shaken. Was this what he himself looked like when he was here? Tread's head bobbed when he spoke and sunk slowly toward his chest when he listened. As Andret watched, the bartender leaned over and plucked a bill from Tread's shirt pocket, then poured.

Hay was looking expectantly across at him. "Well?" he said.

"Well what?"

"You asked me what I was looking for from my life." He tapped the table. "Now tell me what you're looking for from yours."

"I've been thinking about that a little, Knudson. I had some news recently, and I guess it's made me philosophical."

Hay raised his eyebrows. "May I ask what kind of news?"

"Nothing I can reveal at the moment."

"About the Abendroth conjecture, perhaps?"

"I said I really can't say. Not now, anyway."

Hay sipped his drink. "I guess I don't know what to think then."

"Of what?"

"Of you, Milo. Sometimes you're perfectly discreet and charming. Like tonight, for example."

"Thank you, Knudson."

"Other times, you insult everyone in the department."

"*I* do?"

"Yes, Milo, you *do*—with the things you let yourself blurt out."

"I speak the truth, that's all."

"Well, the truth isn't always what needs to be spoken."

Andret thought about this.

"Look, Milo, it appears to be good news that you've heard, am I right about that much, at least?"

"I don't know. I haven't thought it all the way through. It might be."

"But look at you—you can't stop smiling."

"Is that right?" Milo touched his own face. Yes, Hay was right—it felt different. He must indeed have been smiling.

HE NEEDED A signature on some arcane departmental form and finally found Hay in his satellite office, a small, chilly room in the warrens of Fine Hall where Hay worked on his own mathematics. Andret knocked, then pushed the door partway open.

His chairman stood at the far wall, concentrating on something on the desk. From beyond him came the clicking sound of a small machine, like a bicycle with a chipped gear tooth. "Absolutely remarkable," Hay said, without turning. After a moment, he added, "Come in and take a look, Milo."

"At what?"

"It's a TI-99. Come have a peek."

Andret stepped over. "It's a 99/8," Hay said proudly. "The public can't even get them yet. Not the 8 anyway. Not for a while."

Andret knew what he was looking at. He'd seen computers before, but large ones, in the engineering department.

"This little machine in front of you is the most powerful portable ever built," Hay said. "At least for civilian use. Fifteen megabytes of silicon memory. I imagine there's a general over at the Pentagon who's got more"—he lowered his bifocals—"but I'm not even sure about *that*. And it's damn spectacular for a mathematics department."

The computers Andret had seen in the engineering building ran the length of the room, their tape spools stuttering behind mirrored panels. This one now was the size of a cereal box. The keyboard looked like one of the slanted beige Selectrics that the secretaries used in the office. From the rear, a cable ran to a TV box on a pedestal. Hay tapped a few keys, and a row of blue letters flickered onto the screen.

"So what?" said Andret. "I've seen computers before."

"Not this small. Not this powerful. And it sits right here on my desk. I could have one in my house if I wanted. This thing is going to change *everything*."

"Don't be so sure, Knudson."

"My God, Andret. What are you talking about? Don't be a fool, man. It's already got a language on it called Pascal—a bit ironic, no? And I can put any other languages on it I want, any time I need to. That's the beauty of it. I've already ordered Fortran and C and Simula." He smiled mischievously. Then he rummaged in a bag on the desk until he found a thick envelope, covered with stamps. "An old friend of mine at Cambridge just sent me this."

"And what might that be, Knudson?"

"It happens to be a prototype of the most powerful programming language the world has ever seen, Milo. They're calling it C++."

"Sounds like the grades I give around here."

Hay chuckled perfunctorily. "Listen, Milo—once I get it down, I'll be able to run any simulation I can think of." He looked sideways over his glasses. "And soon, I might add, so will any other mathematician." He smiled now—victoriously, it seemed. "And if you're not worried about *that,* my friend—well, you damn well ought to be."

"I'm not a fool, Knudson. I know these things have potential."

"*Potential?* Are you kidding me? All of us need to get a jump on this *right now,* before we're lost in action. Before our whole sorry generation is a casualty of a little box of silicon."

Andret ran his hand over the dull plastic of the case. "They're curiosities, Knudson, I'll give you that much. But I can assure you that there are plenty of things they won't ever be able to do. And fortunately for our *whole sorry generation,* abstract mathematics is one of them. Frankly, I prefer the old way."

Hay glanced at him. Then he opened a cabinet under the counter, from where the chipped-gear clicking grew louder. "Come on, Andret. Stop sounding so goddamn arrogant. Step over here."

Behind the door was some kind of printer: a pen plotter. A roll of paper was creeping forward, pausing for a pair of styluses that darted in from the sides, depositing ink. From the outfeed slot, a long, multicolored graph was inching its way along the shelf. A trapezoidal plane in red crossing a second-degree algebraic curve in blue, the intersection of the two shapes highlighted in a perfect wet-brown hyperbola that was drying to purple where it curled from the roller.

"Welcome to the future, Milo."

Andret straightened. "I didn't realize—I hadn't known they'd actually gotten this far." He drew himself to his full height, which slightly exceeded Hay's. "But for the record, Knudson, I'm still not worried in the least."

Order of Operations

HE'D LOST CRUCIAL time.

He sent one of the secretaries to the library, but all the manuals on Pascal had already been checked out; so he had her call the publisher and order one directly. Three days later, he tore the package from the mailbox and hurried down the hall to his office. At the desk he poured coffee into his bourbon and turned on all the lights. Then he closed the shades.

By morning he'd deduced that the actual technique was elementary. Remarkably so. Programming was both highly logical and perfectly systematic. In other words: trivial. Shortly after daylight, when the cathode-ray terminals opened in the School of Engineering, he hastened over in a chilly rain, and by the next day he'd raced through the entire book. The engineering terminals were crude appliances, several times the size of Hay's TI-99, and every one of them was marred by dead spots on the screen or keys that stuck; but the mother computer to which they were tethered—he could see it looming behind the mirrored glass like a sinister cop—was monstrously powerful: a glimpse of the approaching giant. That night, he didn't rise from his chair until the janitor tapped him on the shoulder.

The next morning, he went to the library himself, where he was able to find books on Fortran and Simula and C. He needed to pick a language, and he needed to pick one fast. Each hour was an hour he'd fallen behind. He began spending every day in the computing lab. When it was time for him to teach, one of the secretaries called another secretary, who walked over and laid a note at the edge of his carrel. Back in Fine Hall, he stood before his classes, blinking. In his mind, tape spools jigged back and forth.

By now his rivals were months ahead. Years, even. Of this he was dreadfully aware. All the endless hours he'd been holed up alone, misguided by his intractable obsession.

Back in his office, the stacked boxes of drawings mocked him. He abandoned Fine Hall and returned to the computers, typing furiously into the glow, teaching himself about the new machine.

Somebody, he was certain, somewhere, was already pen-plotting the Abendroth.

"I ASSUME YOU saw this," said Hay, handing him a preprint.

"What?" said Andret. "No. I haven't. What is it?"

"It's been accepted at the *Annals*."

Andret scanned it, then raced through the pages. An unfamiliar name: Seth Kopter. "Commonalities of CW-Complexes and Hong Simplicial Complexes in Abendroth Precursors." It was due to be published in a few weeks.

"Why didn't you call me?"

"You know I prefer doing things in person."

Andret stepped to the window to read. Within a few seconds, he'd understood: Seth Kopter had elucidated a pivotal point. "Jesus," he said. "Of *course*." He flipped back to the front page. "Who is he?"

"He's out on the West Coast."

"Is that why I've never heard of him? Kopter?" He flipped to the end. "Stanford?"

"Palo Alto, Milo—good guess. But not Stanford." Hay shot his cuffs.

"What, Knudson?"

"Sit down."

"Goddamn you to hell."

"I'm not sure you want to hear this."

"Just tell me what you know."

"He's fourteen, Milo."

"What?"

"Fourteen years old. A senior at Gunn High School." Hay shook his head. "That's in Palo Alto, I believe."

When the lamp shattered, Hay looked wearily down at the floor. Fragments of blue and white ceramic were randomized across the rug.

"Who are you laughing at?" Andret shouted. He stepped over and pushed a stack of journals off the shelf, then kicked them across the floor.

"I'm not laughing, Milo."

"Yes, you goddamn *are*."

"My God," Hay said. "No, I'm not at all. You just broke my lamp."

"I need a computer, Knudson. Right now."

"Pardon?"

"I need my own computer. Today."

"Perhaps after you apologize."

"I apologize."

"Movingly put."

"I need a goddamn computer."

"Well, that's a bit of a tall order." Hay straightened his tie. "Nobody in this department has their own. Maybe in engineering, but not here. The one in engineering cost four million bucks, by the way."

"*You* have one."

"I'm the chair, Milo. And it's on loan."

"Well, I'm the Hyun Chair! I'm the Hyun fucking Chair! I'm the goddamn Hyun fucking goddamn Chair!"

Hay stood up. "Have you been drinking?"

"No."

"May I ask then what's wrong with the ones in engineering?"

"You don't understand anything. I need to work on this twenty-four hours a day from now on. From *now on,* Knudson. Twenty-four hours a day! Don't you get it? This son of a bitch from California just outflanked me. This fucking eighth grader!"

"Look, Milo." Hay rose and took him by the elbow. "Have you called Dr. Brink?"

"Let go of me."

"Have you called him?"

"Get your goddamn hands off me."

"You'll be fine, Milo. You incorporate this boy's work into your own. Christ, man, there's nobody on earth who can solve this problem faster than you. I'm fully confident of that. Milo, listen to me. And calm down." Hay took his elbow again and steered him toward the door. On the way there, he paused and said, "I really do suggest you get in touch with Dr. Brink, Milo. If you want, I could get in touch with him myself. He could give you a call in the morning."

Milo pulled back his arm. "Only a fucking moron would think I need a psychiatrist, Knudson. I don't need a goddamn psychiatrist. I need a goddamn computer!"

"What did you just say?"

"I said I need a goddamn computer. A first-rate one."

"Did you just call me a moron?"

"Look, I said I was sorry. Please just get me the fucking computer."

"You did? You said you were sorry?" Hay opened the door and guided him through. "Well, I must have missed it."

TREAD PICKED HIM up in his ruined car. Andret didn't like the arrangement, but Tread had insisted. When Andret pulled open the passenger door, a balled-up paper bag fell out onto the street. He picked it up and threw it back in with the others.

"You have the money?" Tread said.

Andret nodded. The inside of the car stank.

"May I see it?"

"What?"

"The money."

Andret showed it to him. "Where are we getting this thing from, Dewey?"

"From a little mouse I happen to know." Tread passed a flask across the seat, and Andret took a drink and passed it back. When they pulled away from the curb, the muffler dragged along the asphalt. Soon they turned north.

After a few miles, Andret said, "Okay, then how'd your little mouse get it?"

"My little mouse might have worked at a company. Or maybe one of his cousins did." He took another drink.

A few exits before Elizabeth, they turned off and drove down a rutted strip. Tread kept the flask to himself now. Here, only trucks were on the road. Alongside the pavement ran a long corridor of warehouses with shuttered windows. After a time, Tread finally slowed, then turned through a gap in the fence and pulled in behind a pile of filthy snow. The warehouse in front of them was no different from any of the others. Colorless steel. Steep metal roof. Icicles hanging theatrically from the eaves. When Andret got out, Tread said, "Where you going, Professor?"

"Aren't we going in?"

Tread held out his hands. "I'm afraid it's only me, pal."

It was the kind of thing you saw in the movies. In his pocket Andret ran his thumb over the wad of bills. He glanced around, then counted them out onto his friend's palm.

When Tread disappeared around the back of the building, Andret got back into the car, rubbing his hands together for warmth. A few driveways down, a truck was being backed into a loading bay and a man in dark coveralls was passing boxes onto a conveyor. In the other direction, there was nothing but empty road. Before him, every one of the building's windows was sealed with plywood.

On the way home, after they'd left the warehouse district, they turned up a side road into a neighborhood. On one of the smaller streets, they pulled over. Tread stayed in the driver's seat, sipping from the flask, while Andret went around to the trunk.

The printer wasn't what he cared about. It was a scratched-up old Centronics that they'd thrown in for nothing. He shoved it aside to get to the suitcase below it. With frigid fingers he clicked it open. In the center of the foam lining was a low-slung, futuristic-looking box made of gray plastic. The top cover was attached with mismatched screws. On the front, there was a rectangular hollow where the logo would eventually go. Andret figured he had maybe half a year, perhaps a little more. Then this thing would become available to the general public. Seth Kopter was probably only using a TRS-80 or a VIC-20. Maybe even a TI-99/4.

This was a prototype of the TI-120.

They drove the rest of the way home in silence. In front of Fine Hall, Tread kept the engine running, and Andret said halfheartedly, "You want to come in?"

"I look like I want to?"

At this hour, he might still bump into one of his colleagues in the elevator, so he took the stairs instead, running up as fast as he could with the printer and suitcase weighing down his arms. It was dark by now, and thankfully the hallway was empty. In his office, boxes covered the furniture, stacked three high. He threw the printer down on top of one. With the computer pressed against his side he elbowed clear the desk, the boxes breaking when they hit the floor. He kicked them away to make a path to the outlet.

Transire Suum Pectus

He didn't even want to take the time off. That was the irony. By the end of the week, everything in his life would be different; he knew this, but he couldn't even bring himself to give a damn. Three days that he wouldn't be able to work on the Abendroth conjecture— that's all it was to him now. The TI-120 was sitting idle in his office, and instead of learning to program it he was on a plane to Europe.

Warsaw, Poland. A cloudless morning. Industrial smoke at the horizon. From the airport, a black Trabant picked him up and drove him straight to the ceremony. Outside the lecture hall, scholars from every outpost of the mathematical world milled about in the high-ceilinged atrium. In deference to Hay, he made an effort to greet a few of them. But he'd arrived with almost no time to spare, and soon they were all in their chairs.

The hall went silent.

His name was the first to be announced. The applause rose, and he climbed the rostrum to stand next to the president of the International Mathematical Union. It was only then, as the dignified man leaned aside from the lectern, that he fully appreciated what had come to him. His vision blurred. For a moment he had to turn his head to the curtain. The citation was read carefully into the microphone: "To Milo Andret, of Princeton University, for his topological proof of Malosz's conjecture, for developing a broad theory of high-dimensional branching structures, and for establishing novel connections between topology, algebra, and harmonic analysis."

He straightened and proceeded to the judging table, where the elegant box was placed into his hands. Once more, the applause rose, then soon became an ovation.

At last.

He'd spent the entire flight over the Atlantic parsing the structural merits of Pascal versus Fortran versus C versus Simula, and up until a few moments ago he'd been imagining logical block sequences in his mind for an efficient entry point to his own algorithm. But now his thoughts unshackled. The applause moved over him like a wave; and then, like a wave, it lifted him. When he was set back down, he paused for a moment, then gathered himself and moved away to the side of the stage. Hands reached out to shake his.

Afterward, he went to only a single lecture, a sparsely attended talk on object-oriented programming, then found an abandoned room where he fell so deeply asleep he didn't wake till evening. Fortunately, the Trabant was still waiting outside to bring him back to the hotel. There he downed a couple of glasses of something called Krupnik—it had been placed on his nightstand—took a long shower, and emerged feeling better than he had in years. He had to give his own talk tomorrow, but that caused him no worry. He had another glass of Krupnik and headed out with the group for a night on the town.

The celebration started with a fine meal in an elegant, marble-floored establishment at the edge of Old Town, then proceeded to a nightclub. As the mathematicians rose to leave the restaurant, their beautiful young waitress leaned down to the table and handed him a wrapped gift. "For famous medal victory," she said.

He opened it. It was an expensive-looking bottle of vodka with a buxom mermaid carved into the glass. Someone hooted.

"From people of Poland," said the young woman gravely.

"Thank you," he answered, raising it in the air. "Thank you to all my colleagues and to every one of my distinguished hosts in your very fine city of Warsaw."

Later in the glittering night, a smaller crowd gathered around him in a pub along the Vistula. A worn, genteel spot with ancient windows that looked out upon a line of illuminated ferries angling through the dark. A perfect reformulation of his childhood. Inside the private salon behind the bar, he was at the center of the revelry and several times again found himself having to turn away his head.

On the long wood table before him lay the Fields.

It was examined by all in the room. No matter how prestigiously tenured, no matter how extraordinarily successful in mathematics they all were, every one of his colleagues was drawn to the deeply carved face of the medal. Its dull gold shine pulled their gazes like a flame. One by one, they leaned over the velvet-lined box, fingering the weighty disk, reading out his name where it was etched into the rim, turning it back over to the engraved figure of Archimedes, ringed by inscription. Everywhere around him, he could feel the density of admiration. This was the great elixir of his life. He'd missed it so badly.

He picked up the medal in his own hands. TRANSIRE SUUM PECTUS MUNDOQUE POTIRI: Rise Above Yourself and Grasp the World.

WHEN HE WOKE up back in Princeton his headache extended all the way out to the tips of his ears. On the flight home he'd read through all the manuals again and decided on the language he was going to use. Then he'd drunk himself to sleep.

He rose from bed now, shaved quickly, and dressed especially well. In the basement of the mathematics building he bought a can of orange soda and walked down the hall to Hay's workroom. Through its frosted-glass window he spied his chairman's rigid silhouette. The clatter of the pen plotter drifted out from under the door.

He made sure to wait a few moments after he'd knocked.

"Well, well, well—if it isn't the distinguished Fields Medalist," Hay said jovially.

"Good morning, Knudson." Behind Hay's head, there were no envelopes on the shelves.

"This was the news you wouldn't tell me, wasn't it?" Hay crossed the room and shook Andret's hand, then kept it in his own. "That's a pretty big secret to keep, my friend. Hearty congratulations to you, from everyone in this department."

"I know, Knudson, I know. Thank you."

Hay released him. "To what do I owe the pleasure, then, so soon after you're back?"

"I came in to apologize."

Hay clapped him on the shoulder, his eyes dropping to the can of soda. "I'm waiting for the punch line."

"There isn't one. I just wanted to say I'm sorry for what happened in our meeting the other day." He stepped over and set his briefcase alongside the desk. There were no envelopes there, either. "I just wanted to apologize to you in person. And to thank you for your decision about the Hyun Chair."

"This is the good Milo Andret?"

"As you wish."

"Well," said Hay. "I see that a little recognition has done you no harm at all. And to be perfectly honest, I didn't like that lamp much anyway. It was my predecessor's."

Andret cleared his throat. "I really am sorry, Knudson. And I really am grateful."

Hay reached down behind the desk. "As it happens," he said, "I have something for you right here. A little memento from all of us, in honor of your achievement." He opened a shopping bag and pulled out a wrapped box. "From the whole department, I mean. I think it makes sense to give it to you right now."

Andret opened it, and his heart fell: it was an antique, leather-bound copy of Euclid's *Elements*.

"The Heiberg edition," said Hay.

"I see that. Wow. Thank you very much."

"From all of us in Princeton mathematics—with our hearty congratulations."

Andret felt nothing. What he understood instead was that few of his colleagues would have attended a reception in his honor. This was why the gift had been given to him in Hay's office. "Well, good," he said. He tried to concentrate on why he'd come; but he felt himself collapsing. The weight of the Fields was already pressing down on him. He said, "I brought you something, too, Knudson." From his briefcase he pulled out the liter of vodka that the waitress had given him in Warsaw.

"Well, gosh," said Hay. "That's very kind of you." He peered closer. "And what an interesting bottle."

Andret smiled. "But enough of this," he said, stepping over to the clattering pen plotter. "What are you doing these days with the computer?"

There were no envelopes in the cabinet, either. Just the same books on Fortran and Pascal and Simula that were on the shelves of Andret's own office.

"I'm still learning to program," said Hay. "Just trying to keep ahead of the game." He went to the computer and proceeded to type in a logical statement that Andret pretended not to already know. Andret moved in dutifully behind him, scanning the room. There were no envelopes on any of the low shelves, either. Hay typed in another logical statement. He would input a line on the keyboard, then illustrate its application, opening the debugger to pause the program midsequence.

It was all painfully rudimentary.

After a few minutes, Andret tilted his hand forward and spilled the orange soda onto the floor. "Damn!" he said. "I'm so sorry, Knudson."

"Damn is right," said Hay.

The bathroom was at the other end of the floor, and Andret watched him hurry out the door and down the hall.

The envelope wasn't in any of the desk drawers, either; nor among the stack of folders next to the computer. As it turned out, it had been stored on the far side of the room, laid flat in a wire tray under some journals. The floppy disks were inside it, held together with a pair of paper clips. Footsteps approached along the hall, and Andret quickly snapped shut his briefcase, picked up Heiberg's Euclid, and pretended to be fascinated by the *pons asinorum*.

BACK IN HIS own office, he listened to the drive engage and then begin to read. The TI-120's cathode tube brightened—here he drew a breath—then flickered its green letters up the screen until finally the whirring quieted and in silent benediction the machine delivered its @ prompt. He exhaled. Even with C++ loaded onto the motherboard, the 120 would have enough memory to run a crushing series of calculations. He rubbed his hands together and pushed everything off the desk onto the floor.

This was it.

He knew he could manage the programming. There was no manual yet for this new language, but enclosed with the floppies was a photocopied sheaf explaining the syntax. And the logic itself was no more obtuse than any of the training exercises he'd completed for Pascal or Fortran. And *objects*—that was the whole reason he'd chosen C++: they would make his task immeasurably simpler. Kopter was obviously a programmer, too. Andret realized this now from the structure of the paper he'd read. But Kopter would have to struggle with one of the older languages: for a few moments, it almost seemed unfair.

Well, fuck you, Seth Kopter.

In the weeks that followed, he stayed at the machine day and night. Whenever he paused, he tried not to ask himself what a fourteen-year-old prodigy in Palo Alto might be doing at that very moment. On his shelf was a case of Maker's Mark and a water pitcher and a row of grocery bags filled with ramen. The flickering screen absolved him of the need for sleep. He saw Olga only a couple of times—she didn't mind that he raced out afterward—and Annabelle not at all. He went home every two or three days for a change of clothes and a shave, and otherwise merely took naps on the lowest row of boxes beside the door. They sagged now with the outline of his body.

THE FIRST TIME he tried to execute the program he discovered that it was filled with bugs. It had taken him a month to complete the structure, but when he ran it, it wouldn't even compile. The code was almost ten thousand lines long, and it took him another week just to whittle it down to something that the TI could read. When the machine finally took it, the first round of functions produced ludicrously inaccurate results.

He broke down the objects to make them more specific. This took time, too, but there was nothing else he could do. Every half hour or so, the TI would hang up in a memory leak. The quickest way to restore it was just to reach over and yank the plug from the wall. The program seemed to have its own spiteful resistance, and the printer paper, which he'd stolen from the engineering lab, tried relentlessly to roll itself back into a cylinder. His eyes were blurry. He ran a debugger for hours on end, pausing the storm of calculations that flickered upward on the screen, watching the compounding of his tactics and then the compounding of his errors that sent everything haywire, multiplying a thousandfold the misplacement of a single keystroke or the most trivial oversight in logic. This new engine of computation was brutal. It was a pitiless dungeon master, standing over him with a cudgel.

Now and then he thought of Brahe, looking out at the virgin sky from the windows of a Copenhagen attic.

ONE NIGHT, LATE, another knock at the door. He switched out the light and sat still. The clock ticked over to 2:35. The knock came again.

He found the C++ envelope and slipped it into a drawer.

"I saw the light go out in there, Milo."

He was confused.

"Is someone in there with you?"

"Annabelle," he said, rising. He switched on the lamp, and when he let her in he waved his arms over the disarray. "Sorry for all of this."

"A lovely welcome to Castle Dracula," she said. She stepped back to regard him. "And you must be Vlad the Impaler."

He needed to get back to programming.

"*Dracula* means *devil*," she said languidly, taking a seat on one of the sagging boxes. "In Romanian. Or some say the name came from the Greek, for *dragon*. You look horrible, by the way. You do look like the devil."

"Well, I feel like God himself. I feel ecstatic."

"Do you?"

"Listen, Annabelle, I might be onto something. This is one of the most powerful computers in the world. I need to get it to work."

"This one right here?" She stepped over to the desk.

"Please don't touch."

"*Insane* might be a better word." She fingered the belt on her coat, then pulled off her hat and ran her hand through her hair. "You do look insane, Milo. Have you gone insane since you last saw me?"

"Quite the opposite."

"I haven't seen you in weeks. Did you not realize that? I was getting a little lonely. I thought you might have spurned me."

"I didn't spurn you, Annabelle."

"Well, I *thought* you might have." She pushed out her lips. "Yev's out of town."

"I didn't know."

"I know you didn't. That's the point. You're one of the vainer men on the planet—do you realize that? And believe me, there's plenty of competition. Do you know you haven't called me since four Tuesdays ago? Actually, tomorrow it will be five. But why should you know that?"

"I'm onto something crucial here."

"Of course you are, and why should you know anything about *my* life? You're such an egomaniac, Milo. You *are* the impaler. You're *Milo the Egomaniacal Impaler.*"

"You've had a cocktail."

"I'm all alone in that fucking house."

"Annabelle, I've been working."

"Well, you're still a fucking monster, do you hear me? You don't have one single feeling in that misshapen head of yours."

"These are highly critical days, Annabelle. I need to get back to my work."

"You don't even know what a feeling *is,* do you? It's not the computer, it's *you*." Her voice was rising. "You can't love anyone. Do you understand that? You. Can't. Love. Anyone."

He sat down. It was going to be necessary to change strategy. "Well, it's not something I've thought about."

"Then think about it! Think about it right now!"

"There's no reason to shout. Shhh," he said. He rose and crossed to her, moving his finger to his lips. With one hand he picked up the bottle and with the other pulled her by the belt of her overcoat. The fabric was damp from the weather. He tilted the bourbon to her lips, then took another gulp himself. "Oh, I *do,*" he whispered. "I *do* have feelings."

Underneath the coat, she was wearing nothing but panties and a bra. And a scarf, which he unwound.

"Oh, my God," she said as his lips moved beneath her jaw. "I hate you, Milo. I hate you."

Where the collar of her coat had been closed, her skin went from cold to warm.

"But I want you," she murmured.

"I want you just as much."

She tilted back her neck.

A few minutes later, just after she'd climaxed, she reached for the scarf and began sniffling into it—muffled, underwater sounds that startled him with an unwelcome tenderness of feeling. He reached for her hand. But just as his fingers found hers, he realized that he'd reversed a pair of Boolean operators in the middle part of the program. By the time he'd typed in the correction at the desk, she was sobbing.

LATE ONE EVENING, he entered the code for another troublesome sequence, compiled the program again, and sat back to watch the calculation. He'd been working the same section for days, pushing his way through every detail but constantly finding himself stymied by oversight—he was accustomed to pausing the logic every few seconds to root out some flaw. But tonight, somehow, the execution was clean. Each time he added back another block, the little green automaton climbed up the left side of the screen and did what it had been assembled to do.

Before long, he'd ceased pausing the program altogether. He added the remainder of the blocks and simply let the whole thing run. For close to an hour, the green fire burned steadily, the drive and fan cycling irregularly—this was the sound of a successful implementation—until finally his attention returned with a start and he realized that the rhythm of the machine had changed again. The drive was whirring steadily now, without variation. This could signify only one thing: the logic board was repeating itself.

Another memory leak.

He was being tested by God.

Before he pulled the plug from the wall he took a short break to rest back in his chair. He might have dozed. When he came to, his glass was on its side and a puddle of bourbon was spreading. It hadn't reached the computer yet, but for a moment he thought about allowing it to. At this rate, Seth Kopter would demolish him.

Leaning forward in his chair, he touched his finger to the liquid. He made the lake first: Georgian Bay; then Saginaw Bay and the North Channel. Then the crescent where Cheboygan sloped in a half-moon to the water. With the tip of his pinkie he placed a drop where his old woods ran. For a moment, he nearly dozed again.

Then he wiped what he could off the edge of the blotter into the glass and leaned down to lick up what remained.

It was when he woke sometime later in the night, his head still on the desk, that he realized what had disturbed his sleep: the TI-120 had gone quiet. He looked up. The blaze on the screen had been extinguished to a single green ember, blinking calmly at the top. Something glowed steadily alongside it. He leaned forward.

A number.

He copied it out to twenty-one places and checked it the old way.

Annabelle answered the phone in a woozy voice. "Milo," she said. "Look at the clock on the wall. Tell me what time it is."

He took a breath. "It worked," he whispered.

Ant on a Rubber Rope

A DAY WAS a week now. A day was a month.

The Abendroth would be solved—of this fact there was no longer doubt.

In the morning he opened the door to his office. He closed it. The light grew. Faded. He opened it. Closed it. A week. Another week. Sleep was interruption. The energy of his mind was focused parabolically by the logic board, compressed to a scalding yellow dot like the pea-sized sun that had branded the whittled trinkets of his childhood. The TI-120 incinerated everything it touched. The numbers. The multivariable plots. The curve geometry. It burned and burned.

"MILO," HAY SAID. "A computer's nothing but a tool. Without proper direction, the tool would be useless. Completely useless."

They were in a back booth at Clip's again. This time, the outing had been Hay's idea. "But I've decided you were right about something else," he went on. He cleared his throat. "I'm going to buy machines for everyone in the department, Milo. Good ones." He sipped his drink. "Like the one in your office."

"What? When were you in my office?"

"I was walking by. Where'd you get that thing, anyway? I can't even tell what model it is."

"What were you doing in my office?"

"Dennis was in there, Milo. I happened to look in. I was up there to see one of your colleagues. That's a powerful-looking specimen you've got in there."

"Who the hell is Dennis?"

"The janitor, Milo. Dennis Alberts. He's been around Fine Hall longer than *you* have."

"Why was the door open?"

"I already told you, Dennis was in there."

"You came into my office when I wasn't there?"

"The door was open. I looked in to say hello."

"What janitor?"

"Are you kidding me, Milo? Let's not do this, please."

"What janitor?"

"Dennis Alberts, Milo. The Fine Hall janitor. I just told you."

"There's a janitor who goes into my office?"

"He's been here for twenty years, Milo. Do you think your wastebaskets empty *themselves*?"

"What was he doing in there?"

"Look, Milo."

"*What?*"

Hay took a drink, then placed his hand on Milo's arm. "I want to tell you something," he said. "Listen to me. You're a great mathematician, Milo. A truly great one. *This* computer, *that* computer— none of it has anything to do with what you are. You're a *world-class* mathematician—a theoretician of the highest order." He raised his glass. "And the world has now acknowledged it." He signaled to the waitress for another round. "That's all I wanted to say."

"Well, thank you, Knudson."

"You know who got you the Hyun Chair, right?"

"Yes, I'm well aware."

"It wasn't entirely easy."

"You already told me that. And I already said thank you."

"And because I believe in you, Milo, I want you to keep the floppies."

"What?"

Hay set down his glass. "It's fine, Milo. You can keep the C++ disks."

"I was planning to return them."

"I know you were. It's fine. I managed to get another set for myself anyway. Just keep the ones you have. I actually *want* you to have them."

"I was in a hurry, Knudson. I'm sorry."

"Well, to be fair, you could have just asked me to borrow them."

"And what if you'd said no?"

"Why would I do that?"

"I don't know, Knudson. *You* tell *me*."

"What, Milo? Okay, look—never mind. It's all fine. I know you'll do something much greater than I could with them. They're yours now. I have every confidence that they'll be well used."

More drinks arrived. Milo downed his.

Hay looked at the table. "I know what I'm not," he said.

Milo glanced across.

"I'm well aware of my own limitations," Hay continued.

"I don't understand."

"I'm not a great mathematician, Milo. I know that perfectly well."

Milo turned his head to the street. "You can never say that, Knudson."

"Yes, I can. I can say it with complete assurance. I'm no great mathematician. I've made my peace with it. But what I *am* good at is understanding *other* mathematicians. At taking *care* of them. At motivating them and bringing them along."

"I work hard, Knudson."

"That's not what I mean. I know you do."

"All right. Okay." Milo took a drink. Outside, an ambulance came into hearing. As it passed by, snaking through the traffic, its strobe detonated against the bottles on the back wall of the bar. He closed his eyes.

By MIDWINTER, HE'D prepared four papers. The four pillars of logic that would form the contributory proofs for his coup de grâce. Annabelle begged him to read the finished manuscripts for errors before she sent them off to the journals. But he could smell the final assault now and had already buried himself in the next round of derivations. So she hired an assistant professor to proofread what she typed up herself. She'd helped her own husband in the same way, years before. "And he never even thanked me," she said. "Do you know that?"

Andret looked up. "Well," he said. "Thank you."

As it happened, all four papers appeared in the same month. Two in a single issue of *Inventiones Mathematicae,* one in *Acta Mathematica,* and one in the *Annals.*

"NOT A BAD couple of weeks," said Hay. "Even for Milo Andret." They were in Hay's office this time, and he motioned for Milo to sit, then touched the line of reprints at the edge of his desk. "Without doubt the three best journals in the field. But that goes without saying, doesn't it? Drink?"

"Please."

"I can't imagine what this kid Kopter is feeling right now."

"I can do nothing *but* imagine it, Knudson. What's to stop him from still getting the jump on me?"

"No review would publish if he used your work without credit— that's what." He ran his hand along the reprints. "And you've got all the good ones covered."

"It's a new world."

"Not so new as you think." Hay raised his glass. "Truly, it's magnificent work you've done, my friend. It brings honor to this department. I called Manny Hyun last week, just to make sure he'd heard. Tell me, how close do you think you are *now*?"

"To what?"

"Why must you always test me, Milo?"

Andret's bourbon had been poured neat again. He downed the remainder. "I can see the whites of their eyes," he answered.

OLGA BECAME HIS only relief. She didn't talk, as Annabelle did, about his achievements. She didn't ask about his progress. She didn't congratulate him and she didn't goad him on. In her tiny bathroom one afternoon he spotted his issue of *Inventiones Mathematicae,* but it had been obscured beneath a scatter of last week's newspapers.

It was as though the exhaustion itself had charged him with hunger. Every few days, he came to see her. He found he wanted her two and three times a visit.

"My," she said one evening, after he'd outstayed his usual departure, "I think you must be eating steak this day."

"You're my steak."

"Is that so?"

She was atop him, her dark eyes burrowing into him like the lenses of a radiographic machine. He took her nipple between his lips.

"Answer me," she said.

"Answer you what?"

"Am I all you wish to eat?"

"Of course you are."

"Who is Annabelle then?"

"What?"

"Who is she?"

"I don't know."

In his ear: "You don't know?"

"Nobody. Where'd you get that name?"

"Where do I get it? That is not the question. The question is who is she."

She surprised him now by kissing him deeply. Then she was lifting his hips.

"Who is the mysterious Annabelle?"

"I don't know."

Again in his ear: "Do you think I care, Milo?"

"I don't know if you do."

"I do not."

"Then you don't."

"Yes, you are right." She quickened her pace now, her hands pressing down his shoulders. Her breath heaved as she pulled herself into his chest and then released, pulled herself in and released, shimmying up his body as though he were a tree she was determined to climb. When she drew forward he felt her hot breath on his face, and when she drew back he smelled her sweat, spiked with a smoky current of bourbon that weakened him like nerve gas. She was murmuring in Russian. At last she stiffened, closing her eyes.

Afterward, she lay next to him. He was looking out the window at the moon, but all he could feel was her gaze against the side of his skull.

"You are right that I do not care," she said. She lit a cigarette. "But I do think that *she* might."

ANOTHER KNOCK ON the door. Early morning this time. He'd been up all night working.

The knock came again.

"What is it!"

"It's me, Milo."

Knudson Hay.

"Milo, we need to speak."

"I'm busy. Not now."

"Then I guess you haven't seen this."

When Milo yanked open the door, it bounced off one of the boxes and smacked back against his shoulder. "Goddamn it, Knudson! I'm so fucking close! What now!"

Hay had an envelope in his hand. "I'm sorry, my friend," he said. "I still have every faith in you." Then he pointed back to the chair. "But you might want to be sitting down for this."

Andret kicked at the door. "What the hell is going on, Knudson?"

"It's Kopter," Hay said, holding out the envelope. "He appears to have found a proof."

THE MATRONLY OLD bartender at Clip's stopped in front of him. "Safe to say," she said, wiping at the counter, "that you're the only one in here reading a math article."

He'd asked her to leave his empties before him. The cut edges of the glasses were projecting stellate tessellations across the mahogany. He tilted one, and its rays shifted errorlessly along the matrix of prisms. Nature never broke its own laws. Every piece of code was encyclopedized within every atom of creation. And all of it was merely waiting. A pretty girl tapping her boot on the barstool while the cripple plans his heartfelt words. That was what he was—the cripple, deluded by a single kindly glance. A life devoted to an anachronistic dream of glory. A long-rotten version of the hunt. Even after the lamp at the cash register had warped in his eyes to a hazy oblong of yellow—this, too, was exactly explicable—he was unable to drive from his mind the fact that he'd taken a public beating at the hands of a fourteen-year-old boy.

Seth Kopter had used an entirely different method. He'd probably not even *known* about Andret's papers. And he'd made much better use of the computer.

"Keep my tab open, would you?" He slid off the stool toward the men's room.

"Of course, sweetheart."

He himself had probably been no more than a month away.

Reductio ad Impossibilem

IN CHICAGO, THE long winter's chain of filthy ice still crowded the lakefront. A crazed castle moat of gray-white flotsam stretching east a quarter mile from shore, heaving steadily in the wind. The waves lifted and settled the fractured sheet in slow rhythm, like a house-maid endlessly shaking out a tablecloth. He'd been waiting at O'Hare for his connection to Cheboygan but had taken a cab to the lake instead. What did it matter what he did now?

He walked from the pier to the waterline and set his foot on one of the slabs of ice. It was as long as a tennis court and rested half on the sand and half in the shallows, its surface pocked with sooty flecks from the traffic roaring behind him. When he stepped up onto the mass of it, it didn't even acknowledge his weight. And why should it? He moved out a few strides. Through his wing tips he could feel the knock of the current. When the wedges farther out on the lake struck one another, his feet vibrated. He walked forward until he reached the seam—a zigzag of black, bobbing with cigarette butts and sea-weed. The north wind was frigid, and with all the buildings to the rear of him the screeches from the deeper floes seemed to be trumpeting out from the shore.

When he looked up finally, there was a woman sitting on the pier. He pulled his coat tighter and leaped across the break onto the next floe, where he turned to wave. She made no response. But he could see her watching him. So he went farther, jumping the next break and then the next until he was a good part of the pier's length out from shore. The block he stood on now wasn't half as big as the first but still hunkered below him like a driveway. He tried to smile at her, but in the cold he wasn't sure if his lips had moved. She was too far away to see, anyway. He would have liked to begin a conversation. A conversation with a woman.

She turned away.

He was irrelevant.

The Abendroth was irrelevant.

Even the Malosz was irrelevant.

There was nothing, in fact, that was not irrelevant.

The truth of all of this could easily have brought him to his knees but instead produced a laugh—a short, low eruption that escaped his mouth and went to the ice like a wrench slipping from his frozen fingers. Out he went, deeper. Nothing he could ever do would elucidate even the most negligible force within a single atom. Let alone alter it. God was not the explanation of these things but merely a gripe with the puzzle of them.

The block that he was standing on now was pitched at greater depth but still touched the bottom, its prow parting the water like a boat anchored against the tide. At its front edge, the current made a hiss. But when he crossed to the next piece, his footing suddenly tilted: he was afloat now. His weight rocked, a gentle rhythm that he countered with his hips as he watched it occur in staggered delay over the whole field of jigsawed white. A molecule in the sea. An iota. That's all he was. He'd spent the good part of his life angling for a single glance at nature's scriptural code and yet was at every moment nothing more than an abject slave to its billions of unnamed postulates. That was the joke.

It was in his nature to get jokes late.

A long-remembered sensation came back then: the pleasure of his cold breath. The whole calm of winter. The traffic behind him was bellowing, but out here the sound was swallowed by the ice. This was a world that had existed alongside him all the time. He'd been the one to forsake it.

He turned to the pier and saw the woman still sitting there. She was watching him warily now, her expression a warning.

It's tragic how one can be saved. That's what he would think, many years later, when his only son asked him for advice. He waved at the woman, but again she made no response. Now, at least, he was in on the joke. When she rose and walked toward the street, he crossed back to shore himself, attempting to whistle but in fact making no sound at all that was discernible over the rush of cars.

THE NEXT DAY, a Greyhound took him the rest of the way to Cheboygan. Two stops and a change of buses. By the time he arrived, the sun was a good way down over the water. Across the street from the depot, the general store still displayed its tilting stack of sale wares— brightly colored garbage cans and the same repainted row of forest-green Adirondacks that had been advertising themselves on the day he'd boarded the bus for East Lansing, twenty years before. Hardly a detail had changed. Fertilizer bags. Shovels and trowels. A rope-tied pile of three-colored swim buoys. He stepped down and looked around. The cast of light off the lake. The sun's late-afternoon habit of seeming to shine up from the water rather than down from the sky. A tinge of iron on the breeze.

Mrs. Fredericks still drove the Brown's Cab.

At the door of his childhood house, he knocked.

Nothing. He realized he hadn't spoken to either of his parents since the Fields Medal. He knocked again.

Finally, the familiar dot-dash shuffle of his mother's slippers from the hallway near the kitchen.

"Lord," she said, scratching her head. "Look who's home."

. . .

WHEN HE ENTERED the back study, his father looked up from his reading chair, waved cheerfully, and returned to reading. From the door behind him, his mother said, "See?"

Back in the kitchen, Milo said, "That's how he's always been." He took his place at the table while she refilled her martini from a shaker.

"Are you kidding? I'm not even sure he knows you left."

"I left two decades ago, Mom."

"Well, go ask him if he remembers." She sniffed. "Top's come a little loose on the screws jar."

She set the shaker on the table and took a seat. Then she directed her gaze to the newspaper for a moment and pretended to be reading. Her tears were like the condensation on a glass of water. He looked away.

He poured a martini for himself. "My compliments on the recipe," he said.

"Thank you." She sipped. "While pouring the gin, dear, I thought briefly of the vermouth."

They sat there. The sun went behind the trees, dousing the kitchen in a last spray of northern light that made his eyes feel sharp.

After a time, he said, "Do *you* think I can ever love anyone?"

THAT NIGHT, HE went downtown by himself. Old Cheboygan. The boat slips empty for winter. Hardly a car on the streets. He parked along the channel and went into a deserted bar, where he took a place at the window and watched a Coast Guard vessel push slowly up the seaway. A low-transomed stalwart with rigging like a Christmas tree. Its crew hustled around the deck as it edged to a halt across the channel and slipped sideways into berth. From the tops of the gantry cranes, the sodium lamps snapped on. More men were onshore, moving around in the sudden brightness, shouting into walkie-talkies and steering the ramps.

He could have been part of some endeavor like that. His father had spent five years in the navy and then forty in the public schools. His mother had gone off every day to her work at the county seat. Now he'd spent his own life in solitary chase of something he would never reach.

In the dark entranceway of the bar he pulled out his wallet. The old card was still folded in behind his license. He dropped a fistful of change into the phone. She recognized his voice immediately. It heartened him.

"I'm watching a ship tie up in the dark right now," he said. "A huge one. It's all lit up. It's beautiful."

She failed to understand. "Yes?"

"Like a constellation. Like the one we saw in Sioux City."

Silence. Maybe he'd made a mistake.

"On the Missouri, Cle—don't you remember?"

"You've failed at something."

"What?"

"I can hear it, Milo. What happened? Was it the proof?"

"Yes." Then, "I was just a few weeks away."

"Oh—I'm sorry."

Another silence.

"I need you," he said.

"Of course you don't."

"You believed in me."

"Everyone did. Everyone still does."

"No. Only Borland and Hay. And *you*."

"Well, Hans Borland would tell you to get right back to work, wouldn't he?"

She was right.

"And what about that girl you brought to dinner? Where's she?"

He didn't answer.

"Well, I'm sorry to hear it. But I can't help you, Milo. I'd like to, but I can't. You have to go home and start again. I know you can do it. Life goes on."

Across the channel, a skid loader climbed down the ramp with a pallet in its stays. Then the lights snapped off again and the ship became a gray ghost against the night. The phone clicked, but he had no more change. Just before it disconnected, he said, "What makes you think I can do it?"

His mind was a paper bag that had been turned upside down and shaken.

The next day, he went out behind his parents' house for a walk. Along the edge of the coverts, he climbed a low hill and followed the line of giant birches that ran at the top of the crest. They were dropping long curls of bark now, like old theater lobbies giving up their wallpaper. When they finally fell—in a year or two, in ten—the aspens below would shoot up, consuming their old masters in a single season, as though with teeth.

Nonetheless, his old forest had hardly changed. Not a leaf was different because of the Abendroth.

He followed the gentle rise of the hill. Due east ten steps from the tenth trunk in the tenth row, but a few inches below the level of his chest now—it was he who had grown—he found the maple. *It* was the same, too. The star still there, a pale keloid in the dysplastic craze of bark. He rotated the notched bung and released the dovetail. At the bottom, the cavity was dry and the sack lay closed as though it had spent all this time at the rear of a sock drawer.

He hoisted it up and carefully pulled out the chain.

Years in the dark but no apparent harm. In long armfuls he laid it out along the ground, understanding for the first time what Mr. Farragut must have felt a quarter century before when it was set on his desk by a kid in first-semester shop. *He'd* been that kid. He'd sanded every inch in circumference, shellacked every link in isolation. Now the whole thing chimed like a woodwind as he spread it out on the frozen bed of peat. The sheer magnitude of the undertaking stunned him. Since then, he'd done nothing to approach it. Not even the

Malosz, whose solution, he sometimes thought darkly, had involved a piece of pure luck—luck that had come to him in these very same woods.

He gathered its length back into the sack, checking each link in his hands. Not a single one was flawed. His memory failed, but the intricacy of the design must have taken months. He might have thought years. This was something in his character, too. It had been there as a boy.

Now it had departed.

Why was it no longer possible to follow a thought toward anything but torment? Night suddenly closed over the trees, and he realized he'd forgotten a flashlight. An owl called out, and after a pause, its babies commenced their chatter. He pushed closed the burlap. Then he set out for home. In a gulley his foot slipped on a root and he sat heavily on the ground, the sack splaying out before him. A shout escaped. The owls quieted, and he lay back in the sudden hush. It was not unpleasant, actually, to rest there in the quiet and feel the winter earth below him, just beginning to thaw. He dug his hands into the leaves and smelled the vinegary ferment. He'd spent countless hours in these woods with no thought of anything but their welcome. He lay there quietly, waiting for the owls to resume, until he understood that tears were on his face.

It was necessary to find a way forward. But how? What would he do now?

A Scandinavian Weed

BACK IN HIS apartment in Princeton, he shook out his briefcase and rummaged through the drawers in his study, then went to the bedroom closet and turned out the pockets of his suits, pulling out matted scraps of paper until he came to what he was looking for.

The next afternoon, Dr. William Brink leaned back in a creaking wood rocker and let the knees of his pants show above the desktop. "And how may I be of help, Dr. Andret?"

"I need something."

"Yes? Something of which type?" The chair-front came down with a rattle. "Aid and comfort of a psychological nature?"

"No."

"Something more rapid?"

"I'm seeing things."

"Seeing things?"

"Things that aren't there, Doctor. Crazy, multiplicative geometries. I'm a mathematician, you know."

"Of course, I know that, Dr. Andret." Dr. Brink bowed his head courteously. "I know that very well. And by any chance are you hearing things, also?"

"No."

Brink gazed steadily across the desk at him. "And you wish to speak to me in detail about all of this? It's a bit unusual. It must be frightening."

"No, I don't. I don't want to talk about any of it. I just want something to take care of it."

"Ah. Something quick and efficient, then?"

"That's right."

He could tell that Dr. Brink understood.

"WHAT ARE YOU swallowing there?" Olga Petrinova said, raising her head from the pillow.

Andret looked down at the bottle. "I have no idea. All I know is that it works."

She turned lazily in the bed. After sex, she'd slipped back into the union suit, which despite its lacy bands gave her the appearance now of a Soviet factory worker rising for a night-shift. Andret was in the kitchen looking for something reasonable to wash down a pill with. On his first run through the cabinets, all he'd found was red wine. He didn't like her watching him.

"What?" he said.

"You should be careful with that."

"It's nothing to be careful about." He shook a couple of them onto his palm. "You should heat your apartment."

"Milo," she said, rising up onto her elbow. "You have been here for two nights now. You are eating tablets. What is going on? You are afraid of something, yes? Or some*one,* is it?"

"I'm not afraid of anything. It's damn cold in here." He slapped closed one cabinet and began rummaging in the next.

"You have never stayed before one whole night even. You do not tell me there is not something new here. Is this your mysterious Annabelle?"

"If you heated this place it might almost be comfortable."

"Why are you always such bastard? May I ask?"

"No, as a matter of fact. You may not ask."

What could he tell her? That though he was here with her for the moment, he was indeed longing for Annabelle—but that Yevgeny Detmeyer had just returned from England? That his actual taste in women ran severely to the bland? That with the Abendroth now in smithereens, he was careening?

Under the sink now, at last: some gin. He replaced his wine with it and downed the pills, shuddering as he looked closely at the prescription: it was Ativan.

When he turned again, Olga was beckoning. He took another drink.

Annabelle Detmeyer had typed his papers for him. She'd been alongside him when he'd come so close to the consummate work of his life. She'd believed in him. Cle had believed in him. He had a feeling that even Helena had once believed in him. Now he had Olga, waiting for him to perform on a sprung mattress in an apartment so cold his balls had disappeared inside him. He took another swallow of gin and walked back into the room. The world skidded past. Her rapacious mind, tactfully obscured. Her copy of *Inventiones Mathematicae,* poorly hidden in the bathroom. Olga was a mathematician, and everything that brought to mind mathematics brought to mind his failures, their vilely polluted flame burning blackly in his head.

THE NEXT AFTERNOON, when he phoned the Detmeyer house, Annabelle had to pretend on her end of the line that he was an appliance repairman. He pictured the Nobel laureate glancing testily at the phone: the deception thrilled him. When he called again in the early evening, Detmeyer himself answered. An ill-tempered voice and impatiently barked words. Andret, behind the shield of Ativan, considered a confrontation with the man but asked for an invented name instead. Let the bastard wonder. Then he hung up and called Olga. No answer. He headed out to Clip's for a refresher.

Nothing was right.

When darkness finally fell he walked back to his office, where the perfectly preserved wreck of his years of research rose up like a dead body to greet him. Failure. Failure. Failure. The damnable Abendroth and every one of its pitiable tangents. Boxes and boxes. A wasted decade. He swallowed another pill and washed it down with the last of the Maker's Mark. A mathematician had to strike early—it was generally over before the age of forty. Now he had no future unless he chose another target and started fresh, this time at the base of some other unfathomable mountain.

Hans Borland would tell you to get right back to work.

Well, what did Hans Borland know about any of it?

To make things worse, his mind, which since the defeat had been a sluggish forgery of itself, had once again been running too fast. He needed the Ativan to slow it. On the flight home from his parents' house, he'd had glimpses of his old troubles—warping lines on the plane's fuselage and fields of imbricated prisms shivering in the windows.

In the sloppy office now, he paced the perimeter, trying to bring some idea to bear. He would need to go back to the well. He moved thickly—an elephant fighting a dart—stumbling in slow sequence against the books and papers and piles of slumping boxes. The wall lamp blazed in his eyes so he threw his jacket over it. The computer, unplugged from the socket and already mottled with dust, was a relic of cheap plastic. He hit it with an open palm. The mount vibrated and dropped a screw. He kicked it aside. Round and round he went, circling the boxes of dead-end scholarship that littered the floor like gravestones. He recalled Hans Borland's desk. The cleared tableau. The neatly kept man himself.

There were other problems he'd considered before the Abendroth, but his mind couldn't even hold their fundamentals anymore, let alone evaluate the chances at a solution. The possibilities flew by him like bats in the dark. The first Kurtman. The Goldbach. A dozen others. He lurched against the wall, grasping at the shelves. He knew he would never find another idea. Not ever again. That's what the voice was whispering in his skull. The years of toil would never even begin. Never even *begin*. His brain was splintering to bits.

SOMETIME LATER, WHEN he woke on the floor, he felt decently refreshed. For a moment, his mind remained blank; but then the nightmarish tentacles reached up to drag him under again. A fourteen-year-old boy and a few weeks of work—maybe not even that. He rose and stumbled to the desk. Three more pills with the last drips of bourbon. The lamp had singed a hole in his suit jacket: that's what the smell was. He watched the threads blacken and curl, then balled up the ruined cloth and threw it toward the trash.

Then he dropped into his chair. As he hit the seat, the Ativan arrived in his brain like an ambulance swerving to the curb. He reached for the phone and pushed through the Rolodex until her name came back to him. He remembered that it sounded like a weed.

When she answered, he said in a composed voice, "You were right."

The sweet, rising calm flowing through him now.

"Who is this, please?"

"The Fields Medal. You were right about it."

He waited, rotating the bottle slowly on the desk.

"Is this the Princeton professor?" she said. "Is this Milo Andret?"

"Yes, it is. You already know, then—I won the Fields this year."

"Did you? No, actually, I hadn't heard."

Another blow.

The Ativan lapped right over it.

Soon they were chatting. She'd quit the *Times,* lived in Manhattan now, had married a banker at Goldman. Just like Cle—just like everybody else. A tinge of desolation flickered.

After a pause, she said, "Were you hoping to see me, Milo?"

"Why, yes, in fact. I was."

"Well, I'm not coming to New Jersey."

"I'll come to New York."

He heard her pouring a drink and longed for another. The ice shaken. Then a sip. "Three Pulitzers," she said. "Now—even more impressive—a Fields."

THAT NIGHT, A thought occurred to him: that despite Knudson Hay's long faith in him, that despite Cle's sturdy assurances on the phone, that despite a run of welcoming evenings in Olga Petrinova's bed, his grief at his defeat did not exist anywhere but in his own mind. It was not shared by Princeton University; it was not shared by the cosmos; it was not shared by his lovers. It was hardly even shared by his parents.

It was his alone.

Once or twice a month now, he skipped his lectures. Left a note instructing the secretaries to inform the class that he was ill, then spent the afternoon asleep on his couch. His students hardly seemed to care.

Elusive bits. Scattering intuitions. The instinctive way-signs eluding him. His ruinous failure outside the window day and night like an assassin.

Discovery

"I THOUGHT THERE were only *two* Pulitzers," he said the next afternoon, rising from the sheets. Thelma Nastrum's nightstand held a copy of *Architectural Digest* that contained a photograph shot from the very same nightstand. A foreshortened panorama of angles. The leaning pillows. The white credenza. The horizontal slabs of dark gray marble. He studied the picture, attempting to see whether it included a copy of the magazine itself. Several moments passed before he realized the impossibility of such a recursion. Another imbecilic mistake. A symptom. He was still no doubt good enough to make a killing in finance. Well, fuck you, Earl Biettermann: he would never ask for help.

"Oh, *that,*" Thelma drawled, stepping lazily from the dressing room. "That was—what, Milo?—five years ago? There's another one now."

"Another *Pulitzer?*"

"And a Fields, Milo. I choose carefully."

Thelma Nastrum. Perfect and brash. Her torso still ornamented by its lily-bloom cambers. The leaf-tip corners of her eyes. And aside from a remnant, professional inquisitiveness and the normal womanly attention, she was as uninterested in him as he was in her. He'd been spending day after day here. A seventy-five-minute commute on the NJT and the short, vitalizing cab ride in the cocksure Manhattan air. A husband who was gone past dark. Andret even wore the man's lush terry bathrobes that hung from their hoods on the wall of his dressing room, like a line of actors waiting to go onstage. An actor was what he felt like. A man pretending to a life. Thelma Nastrum wasn't his audience but another member of the cast. His audience was back in Princeton. His audience was in Warsaw. His audience was murmuring away inside the bellicose stone-façade tableau of Upper East Side striving that was thrusting itself into view through every steel-framed window in the apartment. The rest was immaterial.

"Tell me," she said one afternoon, "don't you still work?"

"I'm reconsidering."

"Reconsidering what?"

"My project. My career." He dragged on his cigarette. "My life."

"Please don't ash that in here."

"What are you supposed to do when your mind is gone?"

"Andret, please don't ash that. Throw it in the toilet or something."

"I haven't had a thought in weeks. A mathematical thought."

"They'll return."

"And what if they don't?"

"Well, what about your teaching?"

"Do I teach?"

"I thought you did. Look, Andret, that ash is getting quite long."

"I don't give a damn about teaching."

"Well, you've already won the Fields—what more do you still need to do in your life?"

He got up and paced the bedroom. As he walked he considered grinding out the butt into the dazzlingly white carpet. A nice touch-up to the photo in *Architectural Digest*. A hole of burnt brown to memorialize the desperation of his entire crashed-up life. Without mathematics, there was nothing in the world for him to hold on to.

In the end, though, he dropped it into the trash—he'd decided he wanted to be allowed to return—and sat down on the divan to light another. "I guess I don't know how to answer that," he said, pulling in the first, vivifying draw of smoke. "Let me think," he said, rubbing his eyes. "What is the answer to that question?"

"MILO—I DON'T THINK it's a good idea."

"I don't care. Then come over to *my* place."

"Just wait till tomorrow. Tomorrow he goes to Berlin. We have to wait twenty-four more hours. Can you wait one more day for me?"

"What time does he leave?"

"At dawn."

"I'll be over at nine, then."

"I have to prepare my lecture."

"Okay, ten."

"You can come at twelve-thirty. Just give me four hours. I'll make you a nice lunch."

"I teach at one."

"Oh, that's right. Then come on Thursday. We can spend the whole morning together."

"I can't wait that long."

"It's a day and a half, Milo. If I recall, you once left me without a word for five weeks."

"Why can't we do it tomorrow? I crave you, Annabelle. I need to see you. You're all I think about."

"That's very flattering."

"I'll come in the morning."

"I said I have to finish my lecture."

"Why does it take you so long?"

"It just does."

"I don't even write out my lectures."

"I know you don't, Milo."

"Can't you write it in the afternoon?"

"Milo, you know I don't do that."

"My place, then. Tonight."

"Goodness—what's gotten into you? You're acting like a teen-ager."

"I need to see you."

"Really, this is flattering. It really is."

"I can pick you up in a cab."

"Are you drunk?"

"Or you can meet me at a motel. Annabelle, please."

"Milo, you're certainly adamant, aren't you? But you'll just have to wait. You're very—I don't know. I can't wait to see you, either—but we'll both *have* to, we'll have to wait till Thursday."

"No."

"What?"

"I'm dying, Annabelle. *Dying.*"

There was a pause. Then she whispered, "You're incorrigible, aren't you?"

"Great. I'll be over at eleven."

"And my lecture? When am I supposed to prepare my lecture?"

"Perfect. Perfect. I'll bring treats."

BRIOCHE. BRIOCHE FROM the bakery on Witherspoon. He bought out the morning's supply, along with a pair of éclairs, some jelly pastries, and a strange species of fruit tart with dates stuck into the sides. He stacked them all into a paper bag and set the bag in the trunk. Then he went back inside for a cake. He really had no idea what she liked.

Behind the woods he parked the car and set off through the trees with his load. A man in the woods with a bag of pastries and a cake box. What if there was a bear? He was almost running. Across the street from the estate, a station wagon was idling in a driveway. 11:23. Damn, damn. He could barely keep himself in the shadows while a figure leaned against the driver's window and said a long goodbye.

He stamped his feet. When the car edged down into the road, he sprinted to the back steps.

His mind was a jar of marbles tilted onto a table.

At the door he kissed her, hungrily, hungrily, and pushed her back into the foyer. He threw his overcoat onto the chair and pulled her hands to the front of his shirt, then down into his pants. Now he guided her over the rug, around the kitchen counters, backward along the hallway to the stairs. Even in her embrace he sensed resistance, but this coiled him tighter. Upstairs in the bedroom he kicked the door closed and leaned her down against the mattress, licking her neck and kissing her breasts, pulling at the wrapped silk that hid them. She began to breathe heavily. Her breath tasted of bourbon. The smell of it began floating out of her skin.

"Oh my God," he whispered. "I missed you. I need you. You have no idea."

"My God—you're—you smell like the woods."

"I've been in the wild. I need you, Annabelle. I need you."

When he'd arrived she'd pretended resistance, but now he noticed the Maker's Mark and the two glasses on the bed table. And the brassy Spanish record that was still playing downstairs. And the silk top. Signs. Signs. She tugged off her skirt and then her slip and panties and kicked them onto the rug as he pushed her upward to the head of the mattress. She wasn't accustomed to speed but she seemed to like it. He climbed on top and reached for the bourbon. When she pulled him into her, he dropped the bottle clumsily onto the table. It wobbled and stilled. She gasped. He loved that. He was panting. He could feel his mind letting go of itself, drawing away and drawing away until at last it spun out of the top of his head and flew off into the air.

Afterward, he drifted for a moment.

When he woke he could still hear the muffled music from downstairs, which now sounded slightly comical through the carpet. A snare-drum military excitement behind a pair of wailing horns. She was rummaging in the closet. His glance fell on the curtain rod over the window, and its shiny knobs dimpled for an instant and tensed toward ovoids. He rose and ransacked his pants for the pills. They weren't there. His thoughts crowded. Then he was up and into the house. Down the stairs to the kitchen. He rifled the bag of pastries, then remembered the overcoat. Yes: he could feel them in the pocket. Three of the slippery things, down the hatch in a single swallow, and a breath of air at the kitchen window until at last he felt their arrival at the base of his brain. Ah, my lovelies. The yard looked normal: trees and birds. The sun between clouds. He raced back upstairs, the pastry bag in his hand. In the bedroom, another pull of bourbon. 12:35. He had another quarter hour before he had to leave for class. They could do it once more if he didn't rest. Hurry. She was already in bed. He shook open the bag and offered an éclair. She laughed and tore it from his fingers with her teeth. He laughed, too, and he heard with relief the calm in his voice.

He climbed onto the mattress and began kissing her neck. He whispered, "What did your husband do after the prize?"

"What?"

He lifted his lips. "What did Yevgeny do after he won the Nobel Prize?"

"I'd rather not talk about Yevgeny. Not at the moment. As you might imagine."

He touched his lips to her flesh. "Just tell me what he did."

"What do you mean, what did he do?"

"How did he go on?"

She pulled away. With her hand she lifted his head from the sheets. "My dear, it was the easiest thing imaginable. He always felt he deserved it. And he probably did. And then he won it. And now he's doing what he's always done, which is work. Work, work, work. Nothing's changed for him at all. I suppose he wonders if he'll win another." She ripped another bite of the éclair and pushed his head back down. "That's all I'll say about it."

"Really? Nothing's changed?"

"Milo, if you really—" Suddenly she sat straight. She pulled him up again, roughly, and looked at him with wild eyes, her words stacking themselves into a stammer. Then silence.

That was when the door opened. There he was, a bellman with their room-service order. Stocky legs. Polyester dress shirt too tight in the chest. Oily hair. Kyphotic slouch. Not exactly one's vision of a Nobel laureate: from the bed, Andret actually laughed. Annabelle screamed and pulled the blanket to her neck. Yevgeny Detmeyer cursed, then kicked over the floor lamp before starting across the room with his fists cocked at the shoulder.

THE FOLLOWING MONDAY, Andret met again with Knudson Hay. Their second tête-à-tête on what amounted to the same subject. Milo's face in the mirror that morning had been green-black, the cheekbones still blazingly tender, as though they'd been scalded.

"What are you going to do?" Milo said. "Fire us both?"

"No, Andret, I'm not. Professor Detmeyer is not under my jurisdiction." He cleared his throat. "But it *is* tempting to fire *you*."

"He's the one who started slugging."

"Milo, this is an embarrassment to the university. It ought to be an embarrassment to *you*. Yevgeny Detmeyer's a Nobel laureate. You were in his house. You were in his *bed*, if what I heard is correct."

"He was supposed to be on a flight to Europe."

Hay stared at him. "Are you really telling me this?"

"I'm a Fields laureate, Knudson."

"Look, Milo. What you ought to be doing is hoping that none of this makes the papers. And then you need to figure out how we can be sure nothing like it ever happens again."

"And I'd be a *Nobel* laureate if there was one—everybody knows it. Everybody fucking knows it. What's this meeting really about, Hay?"

"What this meeting's about is that we'd like to help you." His chairman rapped on the desk. "That's what it's about."

The door opened: a uniformed figure stood in the hallway.

"What the hell, Knudson? Is that a cop?"

"Campus security, Milo. We're going to give you one more chance."

"You're *what*?"

"Frankly, I'm not sure why."

Inventory

MILO ROSE FROM the mattress. In the ruthless winter light he stepped to the window to gaze out at the fields. Last night, his bunkmate, a fussy man named Drake who sold Yellow Pages advertising in Racine, Wisconsin, had neatly set his reading glasses on top of his Bible before climbing into bed on the other side of the room. Drake's wife had sent him, had packed his things and put him on the bus one morning after church. Milo stared out into the snow, listening to the man's untroubled breathing.

What was it like to have someone in the world who loved you?

Princeton had flown him here. Eaubridge, Wisconsin. The Walden Commons Addiction Center and Residential Treatment Facility. Arranged and paid for. The chaperone from campus security, a quiet and decent man—he'd graciously changed out of his uniform for the flight—had let him drink on the plane. Had even joined him for a scotch after takeoff. But when they arrived in Eaubridge, Milo had been started on Valium for withdrawal and packed off to his room, where they searched his bags. The huge black orderly found the flask in his sneaker and the bourbon in his mouthwash, unscrewing them both with his elephantine hands and pouring them down the sink with a flourish. He had a sidekick for a witness, a tattooed, wiry Irishman as pale as a corpse who leaned against the counter, observing the dealings like the detective in a hard-boiled procedural. Neither said a word as the booty was discovered, noted, and disposed of, the wiry one merely letting out a short yap of a laugh when his comrade shook the pair of rolled-up socks and the soft rattling of pills could be heard. Both were graduates of the program themselves. Green-and-white ball caps. Green-and-white polo shirts. Everything noted in triplicate on the green-and-white clipboards. The place seemed to be an employment agency, as well.

Welcome to boot camp.

Across the meadow, at the base of a distant slope, the bright morning's snow lapped itself in diminishing semi-ellipses along the staggered rise of a cattle fence.

IT WAS so strange to be sober. Every blade and hammer of the world suddenly unsheathed. The light in the fields. The trees tipped with ice. Inside, he heard sound harshly and could no longer discern the importance of detail. The voice of the staff counselor at the front of the room interrupted by the squeak of a shoe at a desk behind him, in turn intruded upon by the violent slamming of a door, somewhere down the corridor. His nerves were threads. His cheekbones still burned. When he held out his hands, they shook.

The Valium helped. It doused the heat. So did the cigarettes. He hungered for them.

Yevgeny Detmeyer. Andret's mind had been incinerated into a single foul charcoal of loathing. Noxious black smoke carrying his fury outward. The nasty blows. The humiliation in the presence of Annabelle. In the mornings, the Valium quelled such feelings, but by noon they were back, and then before dinner they peaked, his nerves pulling themselves into wires that shrieked in his ears.

There was a rumor around that Detmeyer had moved out of his own house. The news had made it out to the woods of Wisconsin— a scrawled postcard with DeWitt Tread's shivering signature crammed in beneath the address. Detmeyer had been seeing a woman in Washington, D.C., for years now—or so Tread wrote. A famous socialite. Milo gulped at the thought. The avaricious pig in a polyester thug's shirt sucking at the teat of the rich. The sloppy sneer. He wore that fucking prize like a coxcomb.

His counselor urged him to talk.

Andret wouldn't.

Why had Knudson Hay sent him all the way out to the Midwest? Was this another insult? Was it just so that he wouldn't hear such life-giving rumors of the repulsive prick's demise?

He was polite in his sessions. Made a point to dress well—better than anyone else at the place. The Borsalino fedora. The suits. At meals, he handed out cigarettes like a supply officer. Smoked silently and found others who preferred the same. At daily therapy, the questions came in slow succession. It was easy to smile. The thought of answering was off the table. He was slow to understand the new words. He'd heard such Creole before but had never spoken it. Meanwhile, at night, his tidy suitemate orated methodically from the far side of the room: a recumbent minister.

The 12 steps. At least the numbers were calming. *I am Powerless. I will Believe. I will Decide.* The primes: *I will Believe. I will Decide. I will Admit. I will Humbly Ask. I will Improve.* The Fibonaccis: *I am Powerless. I am Powerless. I will Believe. I will Decide. I will Admit. I will Become Willing.* The Pells: *I am Powerless. I will Believe. I will Admit. I will Practice.* The relations buzzing in his mind like a torn-open hive of bees while he sat mutely in his sessions, a beaten man on a hard plastic chair. Sometimes he pictured his mother, frowning over her martini.

The bright snow. The cigarettes. The quiet.

Whenever the Valium wore low, his mind raged on to Detmeyer.

THE MORNING OF his sixth day at the center, a Sunday, he woke before dawn.

He'd never heard quiet like this. Perhaps, in such a state, an opening to the Abendroth would come.

No. The past came tearing out from his dreams again.

He stepped to the window for a cigarette, his hand on his still-bruised cheek.

He'd been pummeled. That was the truth. Ulrich Abendroth. Seth Kopter. Earl Biettermann. Knudson Hay. Yevgeny Detmeyer. Pummeled before the assembled aristocracy of Princeton University and the whole nasty birthright elite of the entire Eastern Seaboard. Hans Borland and his cashmere suits. Cle Wells and her high-toned annunciations. Yevgeny Detmeyer and his cheap, schoolyard hammer punch. His stomach clenched. Yevgeny Detmeyer—a man as low on the ladder of strivers as Andret himself. Lower even! Ugly Russian peasant with a damnable work ethic as desperate as his own. Andret had launched the first blow, but Detmeyer had staggered him with a kick. Mongrel on mongrel. A storm of punches and finally a boot to the face. Andret's head snapping back and the floor rushing up to deliver the final wallop. Whipped like a dog.

Annabelle, wrapped in the blanket, had been screaming.

He couldn't exactly reproduce the event—had she tried to intercede?

His cigarette was down. He lit another.

They'd signed him up for a month. Group meetings. Counseling sessions. Exercise walks. Long smokes on the patio. Public confessions. He had the feeling of a gulag. Ruminations on his exploded career. And always beneath it, the nasty memory of the blows. In his dreams, the careening laughter of every despicable enemy he'd ever made. A churning vortex of noisy accusation. The Valium administered four times a day by the lumbering orderly who leaned in to watch him swallow. Green and white. Jolly and menacing. A clown in a nightmare. Made him open his mouth to show he hadn't stowed the pills in his cheeks.

On the sixth morning, after breakfast, his group was taken into town for coffee as a reward for their effort. By then most of them had been tapered to lower doses of the drugs. His dorm-mates congratulating themselves. By luck he saw a Greyhound bus boarding in a grocery lot across the street.

It took him as far as Milwaukee.

WELL PAST NIGHTFALL, the cab arrived back at his apartment. On the road home from the airport, he'd had the driver stop for flowers and bourbon. In the entry hall, his answering machine was already blinking: messages from Knudson Hay and the dean. Hay was concerned. Walden Commons was concerned. Every one of them was concerned.

"Well, fuck you all," he said, tapping out a cigarette from the pack and blissfully double measuring a shot.

When the glass was empty, he changed his clothes, downed a trio of pills, rewrapped the flowers in tissue, and went outside for a stroll. In the falling snow, the footing in his oxfords was slippery; he picked up an oak branch as a walking stick. The flowers in one hand, freckling themselves with dustings of white; the thick branch in the other, leveling his step. An endless, muffled silence, extending among the lawns and trees and dimly glowing colonials of the place that was as much his home now as anywhere—Princeton, New Jersey. He'd been here the good part of a decade. His mind, he realized, was his only friend.

At the Detmeyers', he stood at the door, unsure who would answer. He had a speech in his head. Annabelle, if given the choice, would choose *him*—of this he was more and more certain. Could it actually be that Yevgeny Detmeyer had already moved out? No cars were in the driveway. The Ativan was a waterfall of hope. In its radiant shower he stood unflinchingly. A single lamp glowing from the bedroom—her side of the bed. He pulled back the knocker. Four loud blows on the ornamented brass. A calm hand and a clear sound. The firm, unhurried tolling of destiny. Annabelle. He stepped behind one of the grandiose porch columns, out of view of the window, shook the flowers of their snow, and rapped the slate pavers with the walking stick. At that moment, a doe stepped from the trees into the glow of the streetlamp and looked up at him peacefully.

There was no such thing as a sign from heaven. But this was a sign from heaven.

Oh, Annabelle.

When it was Yevgeny Detmeyer who answered the door, he was thoroughly surprised. That was the problem with his thinking: it neglected the obvious, glued itself to the trivial and followed it to extinction. Yevgeny Detmeyer. Nobel laureate in economics. Street-trained pugilist. Self-promoting thug. The man leaned out from the doorway, looking around, then stepped out onto the porch. Andret forgot his speech. Words wouldn't serve anyway. He sprang instead from behind the column and broke the heavy piece of oak over his rival's thick and hideous back.

PART TWO

Restatement

I Confess

I'VE BEEN UNTRUTHFUL.

This man—Milo Andret: he was my father.

How else to tell the story? He told me most of it himself, and I've filled in where I've had to. I haven't left much out—only the few particulars that I truly can't bear to record. I hope I might be forgiven, for example, for omitting the bedroom scenes with Helena Pierce—although he recounted them in as much detail as all the others. Bit by bit, he told me the story of his life. This was all later on, when he was ill.

I'm still trying to understand him, really. To come to some reckoning—the great effort of my life, I suppose. As the Book says: *a searching and fearless moral inventory.* Of both of us. I'm the same age now that he was on the day he first arrived at Princeton.

D'où Venons Nous? Que Sommes Nous? Où Allons Nous?

Not long ago, when I was in my late twenties and already pretty much gutted by the outlandish blossom of my adopted trade, I came back home to take care of him. By then he'd been living by himself for most of a decade on the shore of a muddy lake in the middle of an underpopulated forest in a long-forgotten county of rural central Michigan. In his cottage the duck-print wallpaper was peeling from the plaster in long, twisted strips, like the birch trees of his child-hood. Now his health was failing.

What was remarkable, actually, was that it hadn't failed earlier. When I was a boy, his breakfast had consisted of two boiled eggs, two slices of bacon, and a glass of bourbon. I thought this was nor-mal. I thought it was normal that he didn't touch the eggs. In fact, I used to pour the bourbon for him while my mother cooked the bacon, and when he finished the bourbon and the bacon, I ate the eggs. My sister and I were raised in Tapington, Ohio, near the cam-pus of Fabricus College for Women, the small Baptist institution that had taken him in—sub rosa—after his two dismissals, first from Princeton and then from the College of Lake Ontario.

By the time I came back to help my father, my mother had already divorced him. Of course, theirs must long have been an abysmal marriage, or at least one predicated on a particularly despairing see-saw, at one end of which Dad had stacked every ounce of his logical brilliance, his highly purified arrogance, his Olympian drinking, his caustic derision, his near-autistic introversion, and his world-class self-involvement, and at the other end of which my mother had placed her two modest parcels of optimism and care.

And perhaps a third: her humor. Even amid the decline of their marriage, she maintained her mild, tardy habit of one-upping his banter in a softly offered voice, after a long pause, that was like a ten-nis player reaching a ball just before the second bounce.

I can still picture him in those days. Tall. Gaunt. Distracted from us but not yet distracted in general. Still focused on something out-side the room. He walked around with his hands behind his back, his feet swinging wide, his head tilted back, like an Old World European skating on a pond. Long before things had gone bad, he'd also be-come as direful a smoker as he'd been a drinker. My most prominent memory from childhood, in fact, is the smell of his cigarettes, a smell that was rooted in every corner of our house and in every piece of clothing that any of us ever wore. I didn't mind it, but my mother certainly did. She washed and washed. She tidied and tidied. And that was just the beginning. She encouraged and encouraged. Apologized and apologized. Tried and tried. How can I describe her? She was a creature who lived to serve others. If that is the criterion one uses for loveliness, then my mother was the paragon of loveliness.

And she was devoted to him. That in itself is another mystery.

As it turns out, she never did get her degree—but not long after my father mentioned art history to her, she indeed took it up, just as he'd suggested. She did it on her own, without even telling him, but she did it with unwavering dedication. That's the way she was.

YES, HELENA PIERCE is my mother.

She married Milo Andret in a courthouse, the day before the two of them left Princeton together for Buffalo, New York, to the locum tenens position that Knudson Hay, ever loyal, had found for my father. The College of Lake Ontario was a small-enough, experimental-enough, ambitious-enough liberal arts venture to have taken a gamble on a man whose office had been packed up by campus security. There was no honeymoon, of course, but Mom and Dad took the train north and rented an apartment not far from Niagara Falls. Unfortunately, the fresh start lasted only a few weeks itself before my father had insulted the director of his new department as well and been shipped out all over again. This time to Tapington, Ohio, where—*miraculum miraculorum*—an offer had come through from Fabricus College. In March of 1984, my parents bought an old Country Squire station wagon and headed south on Route 77. My mother has lived in Tapington most of the time since.

My father, I'm sure, would have preferred a two-seater—or at least a coupe—over a family car. But his new bride was practical. Either by nature or because she knew what was coming.

I was born at the end of that year, and a year later came my sister, Paulette.

.   .   .

BY THE TIME Paulie and I were old enough to go to school, my mother was already dragging us to art museums. I mean, dragging. There were plenty of perfectly fine ones around us in Ohio—in Columbus and Cincinnati and Dayton, to name just a few—but the one she insisted on going to at least twice a summer was the Art Institute of Chicago, which, like a well-contemplated punishment, lay at the end of a sweltering, five-hour drive. My sister and I endured the trip in the rattling old Country Squire, whose black vinyl interior by then smelled like a dog kennel set down in a decaying forest. My father, of course, didn't come along. In the rear seat, Paulie and I read our puzzle books and stared out the dusty windows; in the cargo bay, Bernoulli, our Bernese mountain dog (partly), whom everyone but Dad called Bernie, lounged on his side with a shredded nylon bone propped near his mouth; and in the front seat, stiff backed and smelling mildly of Dial soap, my mother drove with both hands on the wheel, now and then wiping the sweat from her neck with a folded handkerchief. The air conditioner had long ago stopped working.

By that point, in fact, the Andret family station wagon was well known around Tapington. A Fabricus colleague once asked Dad if he'd been wounded in the shoot-out—a reference to the strikingly linear formation of rust holes that perforated the left front quarter panel. Our next-door neighbor, who washed his car every Sunday, used to spray off our Country Squire out of helpfulness, or perhaps concern, and then lean down to inspect the interior through its sap-streaked windshield. Dregs of yellow foam bulged from the upholstery, and above the cargo bay the cloth lining of the roof had been taped back to the frame. One of the backseat doors could only be opened from the inside, and on humid days the electric windows worked only if we tapped the rocker buttons in rapid succession, like a ship's telegraph operator broadcasting an SOS. In the glove box, Dad kept a can of starter fluid.

My father, of course, would have bought a new car in a heartbeat.

My mother, of course, would never allow it.

The car's darkly carpeted floor resembled the mulch of a long-untended garden, composted from used-up drawing pads, dried-out felt markers, and waterlogged reproductions of the Old World masterpieces that my mother handed out before our trips. (For at least a year of my childhood, a mud-obscured figure of Jesus—from an April calendar page depicting Giotto's *Christ Reasoning with Peter*—looked up at me sideways from between my sneakers.) The musty odor of the seats was catalyzed by a yeasty damp that seemed to be entering through the footwells.

Yet before every trip to Chicago—or indeed before any trip of more than about an hour—my mother gave us another mini-lecture on another long-dead artist, then handed out another mini-sheaf of masterpieces, generally cut from the museum calendars of a bygone year. (Paulette had been named after Paul Erdős, by the way—one of the few contemporary mathematicians who was not despised by my father—but her middle name was Artemisia, after Artemisia Gentileschi, the virtuosa oilist of the Italian Baroque.) My mother herself had always enjoyed painting, but I also think she devoted herself to art history as ardently as she did—and tried to devote *us* to it as well—because it was as different from mathematics as a field could be.

Art history was also impractical. In fact, the impracticality of my mother's education, which had been entirely self-administered, might have been the true reason she remained married to my father for as long as she did. (Which makes me wonder if this is why my father had suggested the field in the first place: *Pluralitas non est ponenda sine necessitate*.) As a young woman, Mom had been accepted to the College of New Rochelle but by necessity had gone to work instead, at Princeton, where, as you've already read, she met my father. I don't imagine that she ever desired to be a secretary again. Dad at least could support us, if only in Tapington, if only in a peeling house, if only in a ruined station wagon, on his Fabricus College salary.

I should add that, from my mother's ministrations, I can probably guess what that salary was. After she paid the bills, which she did on

alternate Sundays while sipping tea at our kitchen table with a heavily erased figuring pad before her, she had him carry the checks to his
office for mailing. Fabricus College had stamps. It also had envelopes,
on which she would neatly black out the college's engraved insignia
(although she liked to leave the outline of the steeple and sometimes
the silhouetted pair of wood ducks) and write in our own return address: 1729 Karnum Road. When she finished with the current Sunday's checks, she would prepare the next Sunday's set of envelopes,
tear up the worked invoices, and then carefully hang her tea bag from
the kitchen faucet to dry. My mother used a tea bag twice.

Such unyielding frugality was not just her own instinct but the
conscious foundation, I think, of a lifelong effort to launch my sister
and me into the world. (Even now, she worries.) Whatever my father
brought home, she would multiply. That's what she did: she multi-
plied. Sunday was the day we ate meat, for example, and on Monday
and then again on Tuesday she served a soup of the bones. Times
three. With rice and carrots, of course. Times four. Or potatoes.
Times five. The carrots grew wild in the sunny unsectioned flat of
land behind our house, and the potatoes were the queerly shaped re-
jects that were delivered by truck to the parking lot of the Tapington
public library every Friday afternoon, in thirty-five-pound bags.
Agricultural topology, as my father used to say. My mother made it
abundantly clear in those days that money was to be saved, even if
my father had no inclination at all to save it. She sewed most of my
sister's clothes, and she procured my own rudimentary attire from
the ubiquitous church sales that served as the town's rotating charity
enterprise. (St. Andrew's Memorial Church was called by my father
"the Family Andret's Sartorial Hutch.")

About clothing the two of them fought without actually fighting,
which—in the beginning at least—was the method of warfare that
they generally adopted. My father still wore the Borsalino fedora, for
example, which he freshened in the mornings with a brush, along
with a rotating arsenal of tailored suits, also from his Princeton days,
that he regularly dropped off at the cleaner's. He accented the suits

with pale-colored shirts from a mail-order house in New York City. My mother countered by procuring her own wardrobe from St. Andrew's Memorial, then altering it on a tag-sale sewing machine that she'd restored herself. She was good that way. She could generally repair—since my father rarely bothered to (although he could be surprisingly adept at it)—whatever item in our house had clogged, broken, burned out, worn through, or generally declined. Drains. Curtains. Hair dryers. Carpets. Windows. And certainly whatever didn't fit, like clothing.

They also fought, without actually fighting, about our education.

Paulie and I were both talented, of course. In mathematics, that means. And because Dad didn't trust the public schools to teach his subject, he took it as his duty to lecture us on it himself. Naturally, my mother countered. From the stacks of the Fabricus College library she brought home tomes on every unrelated topic she could find, the farther from mathematics the better. Anthropology. Rhetoric. Law. Philosophy. Zoology. Literature. And, of course, art history. The studying we did at her behest from an early age seemed to be another counterweight to my father's outsize influence—that is to say, another ancillary sort of saving, not all that different from her husbanding of provisions. She would pack us up to our rooms to read her latest acquisition with the same unvarying forthrightness with which she doctored the Fabricus College envelopes or hung to dry her squeezed-out tea bags—as a counterpoint that illustrated frugality and discipline, if not actually reason.

As soon as we'd disappear to our work, she herself would sit down at the kitchen counter with either a tome on some obscure Florentine painter or a gruesomely illustrated textbook from one of the nursing courses she'd been enrolled in since the year my sister entered elementary school. This was my mother's own task of betterment. Her plan was to obtain a certificate in practical nursing, via the night program at Ohio State. Though she certainly labored withering hours just taking care of the three of us (not to mention Bernie), she was nonetheless determined to finish a degree. She took one course per year, a pace that put her on track to graduate at about the same time she might become a grandmother. But such a triviality wasn't going to stop her—not Helena Pierce Andret.

To my mother, I suppose, all of this—the books, the museums, the asymptotically far-off degree, all the carefully observed habits of discipline to which she unyieldingly bound herself—was as close as she could ever come to insurance. For her children, that is. Moral insurance. Emotional insurance. For what other reason, after all—other than what she already knew of her husband's life—would a frugal woman discourage a subject as economically viable as my father's and encourage one as economically improbable as her own? There was a multitude of things that Paulie and I could do in the world: that's what she was telling us with her exertions. Art history just happened to be one of them.

Of my father's own particularly stilted genius in the visual arts, I should add, I have few examples. Nearly all of his later drawings were highly ambitious renderings of the hyper-complex intersections of imagined shapes—rotating tesseracts overlapping at their vertices, 3D manifolds spun about planes in 6D space—and all but a handful of these pages have been lost. Nor do any of his portraits of famous mathematicians survive—not in my possession, anyway. In a silver frame on my kitchen wall hangs a single, elaborate depiction of the front of my childhood home, stupendously accurate in its detail up to the top-left corner of the paper, which remains untouched. And next to it is displayed a nearly photographic reproduction of the one misaligned sidewalk square that for as long as I can remember bulged between 1729 Karnum and the driveway to the north. This concrete square was portrayed by my father with mammoth foreshortening of the frost heave in the background and colossal magnification of the thick-capped property stake in the foreground—as though the whole scene were viewed by an ant. The stake lies on *our* side of the raised edge. That was the point of the exercise, which Dad had performed for legal reasons. Our neighbor—the one who liked to spray off our car—had tripped. My father had taken it upon himself to reproduce the facts of the tort, which, while lying on his belly, he did without shame or apology (he was capable of neither). There were no lawsuits in Tapington, of course, but he was very familiar with belligerence and on top of that had once lived in the East. Otherwise, in those days he drew nothing that I remember of the recognizable world, and he never mentioned his depictive talents. It was as if they didn't exist.

Still, my mother was constantly on the prowl for our abilities.

Anything but math.

The museums were the summertime front in what would eventually become their Fifteen Years' War. The June that I was eight and Paulie seven, my mother put Bernie in a kennel—my father disliked dogs nearly as much as dogs disliked my father—and drove my sister and me to our aunt's apartment in Hammond, Indiana. There we stayed for three full weeks without him, my mother delivering us by car every morning to a day camp on Michigan Avenue in Chicago, run by the staff of the Art Institute, then driving back to Hammond to spend the afternoon with her sister, talking about what surely was by then a disintegrating marriage. Along the lakefront in Chicago, two-dozen seven-, eight-, and nine-year-olds sat in front of Georges Seurat's *Un dimanche après-midi à l'Île de la Grande Jatte,* carefully executing their pointillist imitations, while one of them, using his brush handle as a surveyor's transit, concentrated on a minimally extrapolated estimate of the number of painted dots (ca. 1.2 million!) on the billboard-sized canvas.

That would be me: Hans Euler Andret.

Failed mathematician.

Volatility Smile

I'D BEEN NAMED for mathematicians, of course, and in the fall of my ninth year on earth my father finally grew serious about my education in mathematics. In Dad's mind, all the other academic disciplines—including the physical sciences, which were his own father's profession and his own mother's college major—were irrevocably tainted by their debt to substance. Biology, chemistry, engineering, geology—not to mention all those lesser endeavors that Mom brought home to us in her fraying GO WOOD DUCKS! tote bag—were polluted by their reliance on observation, on the vicissitudes of blood, force, and element. Blunderbusses, all of them. Mathematics, on the other hand, required no concession to the perturbing cant of the world. It was pure logic, streaked with pure imagination. Although I admit that this might be an oversimplification, I maintain that there was something distinctly religious about my father's devotion to the pure. Mathematics, though invisible, acted and existed everywhere at once, as did the Almighty.

Not even physics could boast such a birthright. My father was nettled all his life, in fact, by the idea that he'd left a university with the greatest mathematics program in the world to teach at a place where the mathematicians had to share a hallway with the physicists. The Fabricus College Department of Mathematics *and* Physics. Imagine!

I heard him say more than once that the two fields were like cricket and baseball: alike only to those who knew the rules of neither. This was the kind of pronouncement he liked to make at cocktail parties and departmental picnics, if he was dragged into any kind of conversation at all. There were not many people in Tapington, Ohio—not even at Fabricus—who could respond to such a statement with anything more than a nod. In a way, this might have been his problem all along: that human beings would never quite conform to his Occam's parsing.

The thing is, I had a good time with him. I'm not sure why, knowing what I now do. Maybe it was my mother's influence—her highly developed penchant for looking at the shinier side of the coin. Things were normal, actually—at least they felt normal to *me*—for most of my childhood.

I remember moments. One afternoon that October, we were sitting under the mulberry tree in our front yard, as we'd done nearly every weekday afternoon that fall, working our way through the foundations of my father's field. At that point, Dad still hadn't fully accepted his personal and professional failures—not that I knew of, anyway—and although he'd already been drummed out of Princeton, he was still young and in my mind still a formidable expert on the workings of the world. In the yard, the citrus smell of his cologne was mingling pleasantly with the mild vinegar of the crab apples that lay about on the grass. Paulette was with my mother indoors. On that day, I remember, my father had just led me through a derivation of the fundamental theorem of calculus (James Gregory's version—he found Isaac Barrow's less impressive, even if historically superior to both Newton's and Leibniz's). This might sound like an outrageous exercise for a boy my age, but I can tell you now that in no way is calculus beyond the grasp of any reasonably talented, if isolated, seventh grader (my sister and I had both skipped three years in school). I could offer other examples—the educational systems of various Eastern cultures, the experience of quite a few homeschooled children, or the statistically reliable presence, in any given year, of dozens of preadolescents among the freshman classes of our great universities—but all that I really need to say is that by that age I'd already mastered every precursor—algebra, geometry, and trigonometry—with no difficulty at all, sitting with my father on a rotted wooden bench beneath a gnarled old mulberry.

I should also add that, among a cohort of future mathematicians, my overall development might actually be considered *slow.* (There were other reasons for this.) By way of example, Paul Erdős, the great Hungarian savant, could multiply three-digit figures in his head not long after he could walk. In my own case, before I'd even stepped through the doors of a junior high school, my father had explored with me every antecedent of Newton's and Leibniz's work, along with all the variously powerful methods that existed for mathematical proof, from the deceptively modest *induction* to the graceful *contraposition* to the thrillingly brutal *reductio ad absurdum* (and even to the reviled *enumeration of cases,* at which computers now excel and about which my father, for his own peculiar reasons, couldn't speak without his lips puckering, as though around a lemon). I'd learned it all, without particular effort. And I'd thought it all no less normal than his daily breakfast of bacon and bourbon.

"Hans," he said to me one afternoon, "this idea, this discovery that shapes can be described with incrementally smaller shapes, that anything at all can be approximated in such a simple manner, is what first drew me to mathematics. And it has guided me in much of my thinking since."

His conversation normally didn't require response.

"Mathematics is an invented science," he went on. (This was a peculiarity of his, that he always insisted on the word *mathematics,* when just about every other mathematician I know says *math.* (Although it should also be noted that, like every other mathematician I've ever met, he insisted on using the full phrase "the Malosz *conjecture*" or "the Malosz *theorem*" every time he uttered the problem's name; he would have never, unlike his son, simply called it "the *Malosz.*")) "But strangely," he continued, "the inventions of mathematics, which are wholly constructions of the mind, are in turn able to yield other inventions. That is why they often seem more like *discoveries* than *creations*. In fact the distinction remains a debate." He looked over at me meaningfully, his still-soulful eyes shining vibrantly against the pallor of his cheeks. "I also believe that this is why so many mathematicians feel that they have been privy to the language of God."

"I've heard that," I offered.

He thought for a moment. "Although I should also say that I've thought of it in other ways, too. As the language of the mind, for example. Or even"—here he turned to me more thoughtfully—"as the language of *language*. The underlier of grammar. The skeleton of cognition. The rails on which the train of human advance steams up and down, one hill after the next."

At that moment, a mulberry twig fell onto the lawn before us.

"Squirrels," I said, looking up.

He retrieved the bit of wood and turned it over in his hand. Once he was going, it was difficult to stop him. "Mathematics is like carving a wooden doll," he said, "and then, one day, you watch as your wooden doll gives birth to another wooden doll."

These words have stayed with me all my life.

We sat there for a time. By that age, I was accustomed to his drifting. I saw the squirrel now, trampolining in the branches. Now and then it shook loose a few leaves, which fell around us. I've often wondered if they aim at people.

"In fact," he suddenly resumed, "this is exactly how you will know whether your wooden doll is alive. If it yields *another* wooden doll."

Not so many years after that, during the summer when his disease finally became apparent, I remember noticing the altered shape of his belly, which had begun to protrude beyond his belt. He'd taken us to the public pool. By that point, I'd entered a premature adolescence and was already considering Caltech or MIT for my future (or, if for some reason neither saw my potential, perhaps Harvard or Princeton). My father had always been a slender man, practically gaunt.

Now his belly resembled a smoothly linear Gaussian curve, slightly downsloped and radially distributed about the nidus of what I would later learn, when I came back from Manhattan to take care of him, was called the umbilical ligament. His gut hung over his swim shorts like a water balloon.

"My God," I said to him as he sat down near the diving board, "what's that?"

"Statistical noise," he answered instantly.

"Fuck you, Dad."

"Fuck you, Son."

He smiled. That year, we'd somehow taken to saying this to each other. I was the one who'd started it, but to my surprise he'd kept it up, perhaps because he sensed that the joke of it deflected the serious battle between us that was already on the horizon.

That afternoon, I well remember how he didn't look like the other middle-aged fathers who were gathered beneath the faded sun umbrellas, their polo shirts amiably protruding. There was nothing roly-poly about Dad's new belly. Nothing that made him look approachable or paternal. Despite his clever answer, he looked sick. Tall and dashingly thin all the years I knew him, he seemed suddenly to be shedding another, boundaryless person from inside himself—a larger, jiggling, water-inflated homunculus, dusky gray in hue, that had begun pushing itself out of his skin. A wooden doll emerging from another wooden doll.

I was swimming that day with a boy I knew from school, and at one point, as I was crouching to dive, he looked up at me from the water and said, "Your dad's eyes are yellow."

"Everybody's are that color," I said, "if you look." Then I dived.

I'M A TEACHER myself now—high-school geometry, trigonometry, and calculus—and in my job I come across plenty of kids in trouble. It's not hard to notice the distracted quiet in the loudmouthed jock, the missed homework from the valedictorian, the escalating tardiness from the sleepy cheerleader who wears the same ash-stained blouse to class all week. I've made a point to be on the lookout for these kids, for the ones who are smart enough and adept enough to make it into my classes—and smart enough and adept enough, thus, to be ignored by the school's counselors—but vulnerable enough, if that's the way you want to think of it, to veer.

Teaching is a noble profession that way. You're given the opportunity to intervene.

But just in case you think of me in any other way as noble, I should also say that before I became a teacher I first became rich. Moderately rich by the standards of my former field, perhaps, which was statistical arbitrage; but extravagantly rich by the standards of, say, a doctor or a lawyer (and obscenely rich by those of, say, a teacher). Certainly I was already an outlier's outlier, considering the scant number of years I'd been alive at the time I retired from Physico Partners Capital Management, at an age when plenty of other young men are still carrying coffee upstairs to their bosses. Physico was a hedge fund. PPCM, LLC. For close to a decade, I'd been the mild-mannered wunderkind on their high-frequency trading desk, up there on the top floor of 40 Wall Street (once the tallest building in the world, I should add). I'd started in the days when high-frequency trading was still something of a secret, at least from the public. At Physico, I was set up in my own password-locked execution room, where, in return for a rigorously excised take of four-and-a-half points against the net—which, *not* including my generally staggering bonus, already gave me a payday of a little more than a hundred times what my father earned in a year—I sat at a brilliantly lit desk twelve hours a day, chasing the spread on just about every species of financial instrument then known to man. I chased it on the on-the-run bond issue across all the international exchanges; I chased it on deliverable corn on the CME; I chased it on three-point arbitrage in the Singapore currency markets. Or, to be more accurate, I chased the *shadow* of that spread. Didn't matter what the underlier was, my specialty was the derivative, which fluttered around the thing itself like the wind around a truck, full of gusts and eddies. That's what I did: I figured out which gusts and eddies were predictable. When I found one, we fed on it. That's it. It was all just mathematics. As the great Fischer Black liked to say, the markets *need* noise. We weren't taking positions in L'eggs stockings or GE for the long hold; it didn't matter if we were trading on the open exchanges or in the dark pools; it didn't even matter if we were shorting the very same securities that we had our clients long on; we were just plucking the data points from a proprietary set of statistical curves and taking them to the bank. And it was *my* set of statistical curves.

In those days, I wrote just about every algo that Physico ever used. I had put Fischer Black, Eugene Fama, and Robert Merton into a blender and made one big patent-green smoothie on which all of us were hungrily slurping. (During my years there, by the way, our Sharpe ratio never budged from the stratosphere: we were inching our way toward the microsecond-scaled, end-to-end market data processing that, by the end of my era, was supporting every Tom-Dick-and-Harry trader with a Ph.D. in mathematics. But when I started out, the whole thing was *new,* and we all felt like *pioneers.*) By the time I retired, the only moral principle to which I still hewed was to never stay on a trade for longer than it took the electron to make the single expository round-trip that gave us the clue we needed. In everything we ever did, we stayed a few milliseconds ahead of the tape.

I'd started at seventeen. Five days a week, while other kids were struggling with their trigonometry homework, I was under my row of broad-spectrum fluorescent lamps, following the sun around the globe, from New York to London to Moscow to Tokyo to Los Angeles. In front of me was a nine-panel, semi-hexagonal, superbright CRT display that winked the ask and offer in various accelerated colors of warning, like the dashboard on a space vehicle preparing for reentry. The computer would do the math for any of the traders, of course—although, in deference to my father, I should say it would do the *computation*—but it certainly helped that I was the one who'd programmed it. It also helped that I, when you took into account the moment the other traders required to glance from one screen to the next, could do the math faster than the computer.

Yes—for a decade, I was Earl Biettermann.

When I eventually did quit Physico (before it met its unkind fate), the atmosphere I reentered was the normal one. On the day I stepped out of my charcoal suit for the very last time, I wasn't even thirty years old and I'd already made enough money to either retire or spend the rest of my life chasing a *truly great* fortune. But the thing was, I wanted it all to disappear. I wanted to start over at everything—and so did my wife—as far from that life as we could find.

Lasserville, New York, was where we ended up. George Westinghouse Senior High School, where both of us are now on the payroll.

Audra does remedial reading and writing, part-time, and I do math, full-time. For me it's five classes a day, homeroom, lunch, and two free periods, in which I usually tutor or grade homework. I also do boys' cross-country, Math Club, and Curriculum Committee. For Audra, it's two classes, three days a week, plus PTA liaison and tennis team in the spring.

Go, Wildcats!

We keep busy. She's on the town Greenery Committee and I'm an assistant leader for the Cub Scouts. She's a great cook, and I'm a decent one. She does the bills, and I clean the kitchen. (I like to.) We have a girl, Emmy, and a boy, Niels, both still in elementary school, both already adept at the Andret family skill. Emmy, especially.

We don't discourage it. But we do try to find other things for them to do.

NOT LONG AGO, I helped lead the Cub Scout pack on a hike near here. Niels is the scout. But I always take Emmy along, too, even though she's the only girl. The Brownies in our area don't do the kinds of things she enjoys, like taking long hikes through wallows of mud.

We went to a place called Middleton Caves, a chain of narrow caverns that descend into a single mammoth chamber fifty feet into the earth. There, the scouts can stand together behind a metal fence and stare openmouthed while I shine my cave light on paintings made by the Haudenosaunee Indians, a thousand years before any of us were born. An Art Institute of Chicago carved out of rock. The cave itself is difficult to find, and the entrance can only be reached on a winding three-mile hike from the parking lot. It's been raining pretty steadily here lately, and on the morning we left, the ground was making sucking noises where we stepped. Before we'd gone a hundred yards the mud had pulled a boot right off the foot of one of the younger kids; but Bill Granting, our scoutmaster, isn't the type to cancel an outing. I succeeded in getting the boot back onto the kid's foot, and then we set off again.

The trail that morning was crossed by brooks and standing puddles of muddy water that rippled with larvae. It was late spring, and the gnats and mosquitoes had already hatched. The foliage was a jungle. The terrain around Lasserville is hilly and the forest hardly varies, so it can be surprisingly difficult to track. There aren't many spots where a hiker can gain a vantage, and there's no great river to fix the directions. It's not dangerous land—if you walk long enough you'll eventually reach a parking lot—but even so, people do get lost. We walked for a good half hour, and then our scoutmaster made a wrong turn. The pack followed him. I intended to follow myself, from my position at the back of the line, even though I knew he'd made a mistake. Niels skipped happily along and disappeared around the bend; but when Emmy reached the place where the other kids had taken the wrong turn, she stopped and looked back at me. She'd recently turned nine. She and I had glanced at a map that morning, just briefly, but I knew what she was thinking. I pretended not to. I waved her on, and all the rest of us followed. Mr. Granting led us down the path that Emmy and I both knew would lead us in the wrong direction.

Nothing came of it, of course. We eventually found the caves. But the trip took an hour longer than it should have, and by the time we came out onto the pair of tightly pinioned boulders that mark the entrance to the first cavern, we'd done a five-mile hike instead of a three-mile hike, with seventeen boys between the ages of six and ten, most of them in new boots, and one girl, in a pair of red-and-white high-tops. Scoutmaster Granting believes that this is a coddled generation, so there were no snacks and only one stop for water.

You can imagine.

From there, we found our way down into the caves. In the dimness below the ground, we stood on a planked horizontal outcropping of shale lit by a single yellowish light on the wall. To get there, we'd crawled through a dozen narrower rooms, a couple of them no wider than my shoulders. I could hear the younger kids whimpering and a few of the older ones trying to soothe them, their voices chiming bravely in the gloom. I flipped on the lantern that I'd carried in, and the scouts lifted their eyes to the opposite wall, where the Haudenosaunee glyphs climb the rock in clusters and the faded, red-tinted bison narrow into running herds. I looked down at their faces. Dried tears on some of them (though not on Emmy's or Niels's); mosquito bites on them all, along with sweat and mud and the slash-shaped welts that are the telltale mark of the stinging nettles that grow around here in hellish profusion.

There was the usual amazement. Cub Scouts are appreciative by nature. I tilted the light from our narrow shale balcony toward the underground river that runs below it, a wide stream of nearly fluorescent liquid sludging past like frozen limeade poured from a can. The exclamations grew louder. Kids that age truly do love this kind of thing. But underneath the *cools* and *awesomes*, I still heard the not-quite-squelched hiccups of a few of the younger ones who'd been whimpering at the end of the hike. Blisters from the new boots, probably, and all the hot irritation of the mud. I knew with dread in my heart that to reach the vans we'd be walking home along the same route.

When we came out of the caves, Emmy turned around again and made a quizzical face at me. Both of us were blinking in the brightness of the trailhead. If we went to the right, we'd cut short the return by a couple of miles. But Mr. Granting led us to the left again, following our own slouching footprints back into the jungle.

After a few minutes, Emmy slowed, until finally she'd fallen back to the spot just ahead of me.

"Okay," I whispered from behind her. "Look at it this way. If we walk at this pace, how much longer will it take us?"

"Depends on average speed." She glanced sideways at me. "Like, *duh*."

"Well, you'll have to figure out that part, too," I said calmly. "Otherwise it's trivial. Now catch up to where you were."

We all made it home, of course. But when the boots came off in the vans, there were blisters and nettle scars and vicious red stripes everywhere. And back at headquarters, when the kids saw their parents already waiting in the lot, a few of the younger ones started crying all over again. The older ones were eerily silent, like soldiers liberated from the trenches.

But all in all, it turned out fine. I'd brought a change of clothes for Emmy and Niels, and on the drive home the three of us stopped for slushies. Later that evening, when we pulled up in front of the house, Niels bolted from the car, no doubt to tell his mother about our adventure. But Emmy stayed in the seat behind me.

I could hear her breathing as I went about with forced good cheer collecting our boots and clothes from the floor.

"Fifty-two minutes," she said from behind me. "Fifty-two minutes and maybe about forty seconds more."

"Good."

I whistled nonchalantly and finished packing up. But underneath all the pleasant sounds I was making, I could hear that she was still thinking. Emmy thinks the way my father used to—silently, for long periods, and in the midst of others.

Finally, I had no choice but to turn and look at her.

"You could have figured that out, too," she said.

ONE AUTUMN EVENING, not long after I'd noticed my father's belly at the pool, he leaned back at dinner and said to my mother, "Temptation sell everything, force 'em forward till the nigger strains."

"Pardon?" she answered. In those days, my mother was somewhat conservative politically, but my father had always been a wild liberal, a man who ranted at the car radio about all the various strains of bigots who lived around us in southern Ohio.

"All the curlings," he said (or something like that—he wasn't speaking clearly), "sky, bit-grass. Feed of it, for all know—to the nigger strains."

My mother's eyes went to his glass: about half full.

He stood up. His evening gait had always been distinct—getting up from dinner, he tended to walk like a man on a ship, his head lowered and his eyes pinned to the spot where he was heading—the liquor cabinet, usually, or the reading chair. Now we watched him totter to the kitchen door. "Front, back, front," he said, though I'm not sure any of us could understand him.

My mother rose halfway from her seat.

At the threshold of the room, he coughed once, harshly, without bringing his hand to his mouth. It took me a moment to connect this action with what I saw a moment later on the doorframe—a dark purple blotch the size of my fist, as though someone had smashed a pomegranate against the wood. I watched it slide slowly to the floor.

As it turned out, he'd caught hepatitis from some contaminated seafood, exacerbating what must have been, for some time by then, his hidden condition.

He recovered quickly—after only two nights in the hospital. But it gave our family the first glimpse of what would one day come home with him to stay.

.   .   .

A WEEK LATER he was back teaching his classes, churning out another generation of Fabricus baccalaureates to the nursing schools, secretarial corps, and real-estate agencies of the upper Midwest. And his belly, just like that, had receded—the integral had gone to zero. Yet I couldn't help remembering the blotch of dusky purple on the wall, which I'd cleaned up later that night, after he'd been admitted to the GI ward at Southern Ohio Lutheran. By then the color had faded to an unremarkable brown against the white linoleum floor, and the surface had hardened to a dry, stretchable crust, like the skin inside an old can of paint. But from underneath it when I scraped—also like the old can of paint—an eruption emerged of brilliant crimson. I allowed the blood to spread onto my fingers and then forced myself to examine it: my father was coming undone in my hands.

The Great War of the Calculus

AT THE AGE of eleven, I entered Tapington North High School. By that point, of course, I'd already been tutored for several years by my father in serious mathematics and encouraged by my mother in various aspects of English, civics, and the arts. But for my first year at Tapington North (there was no Tapington South, just fading hopes for one) I worked diligently all the same, not because I needed to study but because I knew of nothing else. There were no woods to explore behind our house.

What there was was Old Blair Creek, a narrow depression at the bottom of a low ravine that rose with runoff in April and was mud by the end of July. Our yard lay downstream from a Ford light-truck factory that had been shuttered a decade before, but a scattering of chemical and manufacturing plants still thrived in the county and accounted for a good part of my backyard entertainment. At certain times in the spring, I could sit on our porch and watch sluggish continents of brownish foam drift past the property. Sofa-sized icebergs of leaf-flecked suds would slide along, rotating in the eddies, until they either made it around the bend or were caught by the branches of the willows. It was a game of mine, betting on how far each one would reach. It's a complicated problem—wind, current, and angular velocity, to name a few—but even at that age I was convinced that the outcome wasn't exactly random.

I should add that I had no friends in the neighborhood and only a few friends at school. Midway through my freshman year, Tapington North's principal, Mr. Dowater, had called me into his office. By then, I'd already made my way through calculus and differential equations and had recently coregistered for a night course in Fourier analysis at OSU.

"So," Principal Dowater said. "Tell me your name."

"Hans Andret."

Obviously he knew my name. How could he not know the name of a boy like me in a school like North? And anyway, he'd called me Hans when he'd first beckoned me in from the secretary's office. He was just trying to see whether I could speak. But I *could* speak. Like my father, I could speak well.

"Hans Euler Andret," he said, reading from his roll book.

"The middle name rhymes with *toiler,* actually."

He laughed.

"It really does, Mr. Dowater. Most people think it rhymes with *ruler.* But it rhymes with *oiler.* As in Leonhard *Oy*-ler."

"You're named after a mathematician, then."

"After three of them, in fact."

"I see." He didn't waste any time thinking about it. "Tell me, Hans, how do you expect to take a night course at the university while you're enrolled during the day at North?"

His question wasn't logical. I answered anyway. "My mother drives me."

"Well, that's awfully nice of her."

"She's taking classes, too."

This seemed to catch his interest. "In what, may I ask?"

"Nursing."

"She wants to go into the healing professions, then?"

I couldn't decide on a response. It seemed to me that in reality she didn't want anything of the sort, that in fact she'd enrolled in nursing school only so that she could drive me to my course in Fourier analysis. But this didn't fully make sense to me, either, since her goal had always seemed to be to extend her children's education beyond mathematics. In fact, what I secretly suspected was that she was driving me to Columbus every Tuesday and Thursday evening because she hoped that while I was there I would sign up for a course in art history.

"I suppose she does," I said.

He nodded. "And tell me, Hans, how's it here for you?"

"It's good, Mr. Dowater."

"Excellent, then." He looked up wryly. "And the other inmates," he continued, "they treating you okay?"

"I don't really notice."

He picked up the Panthers calendar from his desk and flipped the page. "There's a math competition that our seniors go to every year," he said. "Has Mr. Kirpes told you about it?"

"I don't like competitions."

"I agree. I agree—but now, this is a statewide event. Even at your age, you'd probably have a good chance at taking the prize. For North, I mean. I think it would bring a few hours of glory to this old place. Glory to you, glory to our untiring Mr. Kirpes, and glory to the Panthers. It's only in Dayton, you know."

I didn't answer. Mr. Dowater had a reputation for deadpan humor, a humor that was strangely similar to the low-level, sarcastic sniper fire offered by the school's underbleacher population of stoners and class-cutters. It didn't really pay to engage it. After a moment, he set down the calendar and dropped the cheer from his voice.

"At the rate you're going, anyway," he said, "you'll be out of here in two more years."

"I know."

"And then what? We haven't sent a student to the Ivy League in quite a while. I imagine you'd be a strong candidate for either Harvard or Yale."

"I don't want to go to Harvard or Yale."

"I agree. Just don't tell me you want to be a Buckeye."

"Not in a million years, Mr. Dowater."

He eyed me approvingly.

"I want to be a Beaver," I said.

"A what?"

"Caltech. The Beavers. Beavers are the engineers of the animal world. Caltech is the best school in the country."

"I see."

"Or MIT," I said.

"Yes, another fine university. And what are *they*?"

"They're the Beavers."

Now he eyed me suspiciously. "I thought you just said that Caltech was the Beavers."

"I did, sir." I kept an inscrutable face. "But so's MIT. They're both the Beavers."

He blinked a few times, then absently lifted the handle of the paper cutter on his side desk. "Well, that's a little strange," he said.

"Indeed it is," I answered. "Indeed it is."

It was that spring, just as I was making the turn into the middle leg of my high-school career, that my eyes were finally opened.

One Saturday morning, the family set out in the car for the Macon Dalles, which was perhaps the only locale in Spartan County that could in any way be noted for its geologic grandeur. The Pitcote River, which for the vast part of its course meanders oleaginously through the rolling farmland plains of south-central Ohio, at one point strays into the quartzite underpinnings of the Allegheny foothills, which mark the geologic end point of the eastern United States; there, in the first rock bed it has ever encountered, it speeds itself into a panic. For a few hundred yards, it crashes through the landscape, churning past boulders and casting rainbows into the air. These are the dalles. At the end of them, the river makes another turn and widens again, slowing abruptly back into its old self—a fat, sandy-brown stripe that curls off into the unremarkable plains of the western part of the state. At this point in the landscape, there is a geologically striking run of steep and—for our part of the country, at least—dramatic cliffs that look out in both directions, west over the calm river and east over the raging one. The state park here was where my mother liked to walk.

At a certain turn in the trail, which looked down on a stretch of whitewater that foamed and leaped over refrigerator-sized boulders, she would set down our picnic blanket. The spot was only a short distance from the parking lot, but its topography was as wild and wooded as anything you might find in a state a thousand miles to the west. The roiling water, fifteen feet below the path, was thrilling. To me as a boy—although of course I understood the volumetric dynamics of why it had sped up—it was frightening as well: a frothing, cauldronic reminder of what our familiar river could become. My mother sometimes hushed us as we ate so that we could listen to its roar. You could discern the whole orchestra in it, from upright bass to triangle.

I suppose I could look now at her choice of lunch spot as emblematic of her desire to pretend that she was any place else other than southern Ohio, that she was sightseeing any place else other than along the last western afterthought of the Allegheny Mountains, that she was making her life any place else other than among the flat, soy- and corn-bearing farmland that is the eastern precursor to Indiana, and that she was married to a man who was anyone else besides a brooding assistant (yes) professor of mathematics, in a department composed of him and a pair of semi-retired colleagues, at what was essentially a secretarial college almost two hours' drive from the nearest art museum. Sometimes she sat quietly for the entire afternoon.

On this particular day, though, she and my father had been arguing. My mother had forgotten one of the picnic baskets, and on the drive to the dalles my father had been reduced to drinking from two six-packs of Leinenkugel that he'd picked up at a gas station outside the town limits (Tapington in those days was dry). In the front seat of the Country Squire, the two of them were exchanging words, biting them off under their breath while staring straight ahead, like a pair of spies on a park bench. The six-packs stood between them, taking up a good part of the upholstery, and my mother had moved all the way over against the door. My father always replaced his empties into the plastic rings—this was long before Tapingtonians recycled anything—as though he were assembling a new set of especially light beer cans that might be sold back at the next grocery. By now he was about two-thirds of the way through his day's supply. He'd stopped once already along the road to pee, and now he stopped again.

When he got out of the car to do his business, my mother stared straight ahead. But I turned to watch. There was always something wild and charismatically uncaring about my father's demeanor in these moments, some mysterious abandonment of his frowning and cogitative state that already meant a lot to me, even though at that age I understood almost nothing about him. Paulie had long ago stopped whispering *"Perv"* to me for observing him as he relieved himself. She, of course, kept her head in her novels.

I remember that it was cold that day, and windy, but that the sky had been cut from the crackling blue gem field of a late midwestern April. Outside the car, as other families sped past, my father stepped to the leeward side of the open door, then leaned back from the waist and at the same time forward from the ankles. His penis poked out from his zipper. For this part, Bernie always stood up at the rear window. My father paused for a moment, rocking slightly while a few indistinct words played on his lips. Then, just before his stream started, he tilted back his head, as though there were a code written in the sky that allowed the event to begin. This was the moment I waited for. The movement seemed to be a marker of his own private devotion; as though despite his unshakable atheism, as though despite his sour, entirely analytic approach to every affair of life, he nonetheless felt the need to acknowledge the heavens in regard to this particular function of the body. I don't know—perhaps I sensed that he simply enjoyed it in a deeper way than I did. It was possible, I already recognized, that the eye-narrowing depth of his physical delight in that moment was relative to the paucity of other delights in his life. But in any case, the prayerful uptilting of his cranium always seemed to democratize him for me, to make him, for a few moments at least, a regular man. Bernie let out a bark.

"Is he done?" asked my mother.

I opened my window. "Almost."

In fact, he was still in the midst. My father peed like a horse. His urine flowed in one great sweeping stream that started suddenly and stopped just as suddenly, a single, winking arc of shimmering clarity that endured for a prodigious interval and then disappeared in an instant, as though the outflow were a solid object—an arch of glittering ice or a thick band of silver—and not (as it actually approximated) a parabolic, dynamically averaged graph of the intersecting functions of gravity, air resistance, and initial velocity on a nonviscous fluid, produced and exhibited by a man who'd just consumed more than a gallon of midwestern beer. The flow was as clear as water. When it struck the edge of the gravel shoulder, the sound was like a bedsheet being ripped. Beneath this high reverberation, he let out a protracted, appreciative whistle that culminated in a tuneless gasp, his lips flapping at the close like a trumpeter's. In the viny topsoil, a gap appeared, a wisp of vapor rising from its center. Then a meandering river pushed its way forward, excavating a skier's course downhill. After the liquid had been absorbed, the foamy sluice continued to steam at the edges, as though it were not dilute human waste he had emitted but some caustic effluent. He shook himself. From my vantage he appeared entirely unashamed. Bernie bumped about in the cargo bay. My father moved up close to peer through the windshield, zipping his trousers and smiling through the glass at my mother. I realized that the yellow that should have been in his urine was unmistakable now in his eyes.

"Thank goodness," my mother said when the car door closed again. "I was getting a little bored in here."

In those days, this was her version of malice. My father had been on the attack since he'd discovered the second picnic basket had been left at home, and for most of the drive my mother had been parrying him, meeting his disjointed and rambling accusations with her own incremental admissions, coyly humorous questions, and occasional nods of agreement, like a boxer using the ropes. This was not an admission of defeat but a tactic. Time was on her side—we all knew this—and once my father had downed a few bona fide cocktails and gotten a bit of lunch into him, he would reliably retreat. My sister and I were witnessing nothing but the feel-out punches of the day's early rounds. We knew not to say anything ourselves, or he'd turn his spite against one of *us*.

But this morning, somehow, the beer wasn't calming him, nor the pretzels that my mother kept proffering across the seat. The twelve cans were already as light as a bag with a sandwich in it.

We were most of the way to the dalles when he turned and said, "I just would've thought that someone would have taken it up by now. And built something significant on it." He slowly pulled open the tab of the penultimate beer, allowing it to hiss. "That's all."

"That's because it's authoritative" was my mother's immediate answer.

Paulie was reading *The Hound of the Baskervilles* and *I Know Why the Caged Bird Sings* (to this day she maintains the habit of reading two books at once), and I was working my way through the Fabricus College library's pristine copy of Martin Gardner's puzzles from *Scientific American*. Bernie, leaning over my shoulder from the rear, was poking his head out the window into the passing air and cambering his snout up and down, a ritual that my father always referred to as *testing his principle*. (This was a reference, of course, to the Bernoulli principle of inviscid flow—although, actually, Bernie had not been named after *Daniel* Bernoulli, the physicist and mathematician who'd elucidated the principle, but *Jakob* Bernoulli, the pure mathematician, who'd sided with Leibniz against Newton in the Great War of the Calculus. (Naming a dog after an ally of Leibniz in the calculus wars, by the way, no doubt reflected my father's sense of irony as well as his quite durable sense of grievance.)) In any case, I can't say how I knew, but I understood immediately that my parents were discussing the Malosz theorem. My father's single crowning achievement had been the hidden stage work for most of the serious clashes I'd ever witnessed between the two of them. It was a historical fact as old and mysterious and yet as ever alive to our family as slavery might be to other families, or the bomb in Hiroshima, or the Holocaust. It put him into a mood. He'd published the paper twenty years before, but the proof had only a handful of times been used as the basis for another mathematician's work.

I set down my book of puzzles.

Glancing back at us, my mother opened her side window so that the sound of the wheels would cover her words.

I sat forward.

"Don't be nosy, Clever Hans." This was Paulie. She called me Clever Hans not because she thought I was quick-witted but because a German farm horse by that name had once become famous for being able to do arithmetic with its hooves.

"I'm not nosy, Smallette. I'm *interested*." (*Smallette* was the best I could do for *Paulette,* to my long-standing disappointment.) I leaned my temple against the back of my father's headrest, hoping he'd think I was sleepy.

"Nobody's come near it in years," I heard him say.

"That's because they're intimidated," Mom replied. "They're intimidated by its brilliance."

I remember marveling at my mother then, noting that despite the unrelenting weight of what must have already been a thoroughly one-sided marriage, she was immediately drawn to the encouraging word. For a few moments, I thought the impasse had ended.

But after driving silently for a time, my father turned to her and muttered, "Bullshit."

When there was no response, he said it louder. "Bullshit!"

Of course, I also knew exactly what he was talking about. My mother's imperturbable kindness was infuriating even to me— although, being young, I was confused by such a feeling.

"Okay," she said gently.

"You know," he said, "you are such a *fucking* Pollyanna."

"What I said was the truth, Milo. No mathematician can come near what you achieved in the field. Not for a long, long time, anyway. Some work just puts an end to debate."

He slowed the car. "Why, might I ask, are you such a goddamn fucking apologist?"

My mother turned to look at me in the backseat, then at the traffic behind us. "Sweetheart."

He slowed further. A van roared past. Bernie barked.

"Milo. This is a highway."

"I wrote a fucking brilliant proof, Helena. And no one's taken it up. Not one fucking single other mathematician. Not one in twenty fucking years."

"That's an exaggeration."

"Not that much of one. It's a goddamn insult."

"It's just another mark of its power, sweetheart. That's all. Nobody followed Newton, either. Now please speed up a little."

My father continued at the same rate, working the eleventh empty back into its plastic ring as first one car, then another, pulled out to pass us. I glanced out the rear window, where a line of traffic was building.

When the Leinie cans were back in their place, he withdrew his hand and drummed his fingers lazily against the wheel, like a farmer plodding along in a tractor. "By the way," he said, glancing up into the mirror. "That's completely absurd. Barrow preceded Newton, and Leibniz followed Newton. You don't know a goddamn thing about it. You don't know the first thing about a goddamn thing about what you're goddamn talking about."

All of this was said slowly.

"We can discuss it," said my mother, "anytime you'd like." Then: "Will you kindly respect the speed limit?"

"Okay," he said, shifting his foot to the accelerator. "Kids, your mother says we should respect the speed limit." The engine growled.

We roared forward, pulling close behind one of the cars that had just passed us. A moment later, our engine shaking, we passed it. Then the two ahead. He pulled in finally for a semitrailer coming in the other direction, then pulled back out to pass.

I looked over the headrest: the speedometer was on eighty.

"Okay," my mother said calmly. "What's next, Milo? What exactly are you planning to do next? Children, are your belts on?"

"What's next is nothing!" But rather than jerking the wheel or stomping even harder on the accelerator, as I somehow hoped he would do, he simply slid back into line and laid off the gas until we had slowed again to fifty-five; and then, just like that, we were driving peaceably. My mother offered him another pretzel, and he took it straight from her fingers into his mouth. When the salty tidbit appeared to soothe him further, she handed him a few more.

My mother in those days had become quite adept at calming him.

Many years later, of course, when I understood what was happening to my father, I learned about the cognitive changes that can accompany a condition like his; and I have to say, as I read those medical articles on the Internet in his dank and ruined house—a father myself at that point—I was forced to rethink many of the things I'd believed about him. Nobody likes to do that. Especially if you've nursed a grievance of mistreatment for a good portion of your life. But this is part of why I tell this story—to understand the truth about him, including the idea that he can't entirely be blamed for what he did to us, and for what he did to himself, and for what happened to him.

At any rate, it was later that afternoon, at the Macon Dalles, that the real event took place. There was a liquor store not far from the park entrance, and as usual it lifted him into a brighter mood. We managed to have a pleasant hike, winding our way through a grove of sycamores that cast a thousand permutations of green onto the spring grass that was just coming out of seed along the paths. At the river, we turned south. Below us, in the first run of boulders, the water began its concert. When we arrived at the spot where the path moved onto the stone ledge above the channel, my father bent down and lifted Paulie onto his shoulders. An uncertain smile crossed her face. As we moved along the narrow sill of rock, he began wobbling like a tipsy horse. Bernie ran up behind him, barking. An iron railing was built into the outcropping, and when he leaned over it my sister squealed. I wasn't sure whether it was a squeal of terror or a squeal of delight, but when he leaned back to safety again I saw that her smile had deepened. She pressed her knees against his flanks.

"Milo," said my mother.

He leaned over the railing again, and Paulie squealed anew, letting go of his shoulders this time and waving her hands in the air as though her roller-coaster car had paused at the peak of the hill.

"Milo. Please."

Bernie nudged Dad's leg, trying to move him back from the edge, but my father pretended to stumble toward the water.

My mother inhaled sharply.

"Mom, it's okay," said Paulie. She rolled her eyes.

"No, it's not okay, honey. It's not okay at all. Milo, please set her down."

"It's okay. I like it, Mom."

"Set her down, Milo." Then, louder: "Milo!"

He turned and looked at her, shaking his head. Then he complied. As soon as Paulie was on the ground, he bowed to all of us with an exaggerated flourish, like a rickshaw driver.

"Wow," said my sister, rolling her eyes again, "Mrs. Kill-the-Party."

"Thank you, Paulette."

"Miss Fall-off-the-Cliff-and-Break-Your-Neck," I said.

"Nobody's going to fall anywhere," said my father. "Are they, Bernou?" Then he said, "Here, boy," and patted Bernie on the head.

This was the end of the conversation. We walked on, and when we reached our picnic spot, my mother spread out the meal. Ham salad and coleslaw and sugar cookies, all of my father's favorites. We ate. But I could tell that the incident had upended his optimism. He sat so that we couldn't see his face, his head turned toward the churning water, and rather than let his wife fix his drinks for him in the glass tumbler that she'd lugged up the trail, he kept his liquor-store bag next to him and lifted it straight to his lips. The paper had formed itself to the neck of the bottle. As soon as he finished his sandwich, he took the bag with him and walked to the edge of the cliff.

The rest of us remained behind, sitting cross-legged on the checkered red blanket that was covered with our half-eaten sandwiches. I remember his silhouette that day, standing against the cellophane sky. There weren't many places in Ohio where a man could oversee vastness; but that was what he was doing, his somehow heroic frame contemplating the remaining westward reach of a continent that, over the last decade, he'd been slowly recrossing.

"Your father's feeling philosophical," said my mother. She'd risen to her knees and was putting away the utensils and sliding the uneaten coleslaw from his plate onto mine. His sandwich was being finished off by Bernie.

"He was fun today," said Paulette.

"Yes, he was," said my mother. "Your father does enjoy these outings."

Just then his silhouette bent forward at the waist, and over the rumble of the water we heard a staccato cough. His free hand went to his mouth, and the one with the bag in it went out to the side, to steady his balance. He remained bent forward for several moments before he stood again, still facing away from us. Then he brought the bag up to his lips.

My mother's hand touched mine. "Hans."

She rose and began moving toward him.

She was stepping gingerly, as though sneaking up on a bird, and as I followed her I did the same. At one point, her arm came back and found mine. He still hadn't turned, and when we neared him she slowed again, approaching watchfully. She said, "Milo?" First she tapped his shoulder, then she took hold of it.

He turned, and his eyes were red. I wondered how she'd known.

"The thing I will never do," he said, wiping his cheek with the bag, "is hurt them."

"Of course we know that," said my mother.

"I will never, ever, hurt my children."

"Of course not, my love."

Tears were on his cheeks.

I stepped up next to my mother. I should have turned away, should have given him the privacy he wanted, but I found, as always, that I couldn't. I couldn't ever turn away from him when he was like this, when the battle-dented armor behind which he spent his days had momentarily been lowered. For a moment I could see the man behind it.

"Never ever hurt them," he said.

"Of course not."

"Get away from here, Hans," he said through a sob.

"Fuck you, Dad."

He recoiled as though he'd been slapped.

"Hans!" said my mother.

"I was kidding. We always say that. It's a joke."

My sister came up behind. "Get away, Hans," she hissed. "You're making it worse."

My father turned on her. "You," he said, pointing. "You're one, too."

"One what?"

"One silly, fucking Pollyanna."

"What?" Paulie sat down on the ground.

"Jesus H. Christ," said my father. "All of you, get the hell away from me!"

"We're right here," said my mother. "It's all right, Milo."

"It's not all right," I said.

"Correct, Hans! You are *correct*." He turned to us, smiling weirdly now, then emitted another sharp sound, something between a laugh and a hiccup, and covered his mouth again with his hand.

"Why don't we all go finish our sandwiches," said my mother.

He pivoted once more to the water. For a few moments, we all just stayed there, frozen, my father looking off into the distance, my mother smiling determinedly at his back, while from behind us came the *hzz-hzz* of Paulette's sniffling and the *ph-hah, ph-hah* of Bernie's panting. Then my mother touched him on the shoulder again. That's when he wheeled. As though shooing a pernicious fly, he swung his hand and struck her backhand across the face.

She fell to the ground.

Paulie screamed. I grabbed Mom under the shoulders and stood her up, then led her away across the rock. At the blanket, I let go, and she slumped down into the ruins of the picnic. Bernie was baying. I turned angrily to my father, who'd resumed his posture on the cliff; then back to my mother, who lay crumpled on the ground like a dropped marionette, tears on her cheeks.

Paulette approached, sniffling.

"Shut up, Smallette. What's the matter with you? He *hurt* Mom."

"He hurt me just as badly. Did you hear what he said?"

Now my mother stirred. She rose, wiped her cheeks on her blouse, and looked around. Bernie was sprinting back and forth between the cliff edge and our blanket, as though doing line drills. "Please, you two," said my mother. "Please, I'm fine."

"Are you sure?" said Paulie. "We don't have to go back with him."

"Then how do you propose we get home, Smallette?"

"We'll leave him here."

"Please," my mother said again. "Please."

"Are you sure you're all right?" said Paulie. "You can tell us."

"I'm fine, honey. I'm sure he's terribly sorry." But these words seemed to affect her almost as deeply as the slap had. She slumped forward again, and the tears came freely. She was leaning on all fours now, trying to control herself, her gasps punctuating the rumble of the river. I saw my father turn toward the sound, then back to the water.

He stood there like that, his back to us, for a good long time while my mother's crying slowly diminished. Soon Paulette had stopped sniffling, too, and with a starched-blouse propriety she set about gathering up our picnic trash. She knelt rigidly and replaced everything in the wicker basket, her face a mask now of resolve. I think my sister had always imagined herself a war nurse; and here we were at last, at war.

I myself was passing the skirmish by rubbing my mother's shoulders, and she was raising her head now and then to thank me.

It might have been a quarter of an hour later that my father, at the edge of the cliff, finally turned to us again. He leaned forward and set both hands on his hips, then dropped the bag to the ground.

My mother rose to her knees.

He tilted up his head so we could see his face—he was smiling, rather sheepishly, it seemed. My mother smiled back.

Then he coughed again.

Afterward, there was a moment marked only by the tympanic rumble of the river and by the wobble of his slightly swaying torso against the sky. The next cough was shorter but strangely crisp, like the snap of a stick. His hand moved to his breast pocket. When it came away, I saw it—the smashed pomegranate again. He looked up, frightened. The globule had attached itself to his shirt, like the gaping, purplish wound from a bullet. I swallowed. I was still on my knees, still patting my mother's shoulder, and she was still looking up at me, still vaguely puzzled, as though I were a sympathy machine that she'd somehow forgotten how to switch off; but suddenly she shoved away my arm and sprang to her feet. The blanket was in her hand, and we were running. When she reached him, she pressed it to his face and lowered him to the ground. My father thrust away her attempts and cupped his hands over his own mouth. He was on his knees now, every few seconds spasming forward at the neck and emitting from his lips another crisp hack followed by a bright red stream of blood, a stuttering river that quickly became a spreading puddle below him, into which he leaned forward finally and collapsed.

Professor Gamble

LATER THAT MONTH, on the way home from the Southern Ohio Lutheran Medical Center, where Dad had been recovering, we stopped at the Greenway Shopping Center, and my parents went into the A&P together for groceries. Dad had been in the hospital for three weeks, and his gait was still wobbly. He was pale, and there were weirdly colored bruises all over his hands. As the doors of the A&P closed, I saw him bump into a shopping cart and almost fall over.

A few moments after that, as I watched from the backseat of the station wagon, I saw him emerge without my mother from a side exit and limp away down the alley. I couldn't tell where he was going, but several minutes later when he returned to the car, I could see the bulge under his jacket.

Perhaps he did intend to try. I give him credit for that.

During those first weeks at home, he slept late every morning, took a nap every afternoon, and retired early every night. For my daily mathematics sessions, I sat on my mother's side of the mattress. But he was clearly less interested in the material now, and we spent a good amount of time reviewing things I'd learned long ago. It wasn't even clear to me that he remembered what he'd already taught me. "Hans," he said one afternoon not long after his discharge from the hospital, "I don't think this stuff is all that important, actually."

"What? Why not?"

His eyes moved about nervously. "What we're doing right now. Integration by parts. It's heuristics, not mathematics. And it's plainly obvious. Why don't you just go outside and play?"

Through the window I could see the top branches of the mulberry, under which we normally sat for my lessons. In the shade of that tree was where he'd taught me this very material several years earlier. "Well, for one," I said, "I wouldn't know what to do."

"You wouldn't, would you?" He looked out the window himself for a moment but quickly shifted his gaze to the door. Then he shifted it back to me. I could see that something was agitating him. His eyes jumped around as though they couldn't decide how to look at anything. "Neither would I," he said. "Not anymore."

He raised his right arm from the sheets then and examined it. He'd been in the hospital for the good part of a month, and the arm itself looked like something that had fallen out of a rotting tree. My father at the time was not much older than fifty, but the flesh hung off the bone like a shirtsleeve. "Look at this," he said. "Look at the fingers."

He pointed them into the air. They were pale but otherwise appeared normal enough: chicken-bone knuckles, one of the digits bent slightly inward, as it always had been.

"What?" I said.

"You're not looking."

"The middle one's bent?"

"It's been that way since I was younger than you. Look closer."

I leaned in. "Your hand's shaking," I finally said.

"That's correct."

"Can't you stop it?"

"I probably could. But I find it riveting, don't you? I want to explore the theory."

"The theory?"

"The theory of human strangeness. Look at it, Hans."

I did. Extending all the way up his arm was a shivering tremor, as though somewhere near his shoulder a clock motor had been sewn into the flesh. With the other hand he reached behind the mattress, came up with a bottle, and took a gulp. "This stops it," he said. He held it up. "This is the cure."

"I see."

"But it's running low."

He let the arm drop and took another drink, then set the bottle back behind the headboard. For a time, we just sat there, staring out the windows. A few minutes later, when he raised the arm again, the tremor had stilled. "Hans," he said. "I need your help."

"Fuck you, Dad."

"Fuck you, Son."

We both laughed.

"What did you need me to do?"

"Never mind. Your mother wouldn't approve anyway."

I looked at him. Something in his face had changed during his stay in the hospital. Some aspect deeper than the purely physical. Whatever it was, it had occurred abruptly. He rubbed his brow, and when the arm came away, sweat showed on his hand. Since his return, the tilt of his outlook had somehow been reversed; he'd always been an introvert, yet his eyes had always looked unmistakably out at the world. Now they pointed inward. The pupils drifted this way and that.

"What did you need, Dad?"

"I said never mind."

"Come on, I can do it."

"It's all useless," he said. "Look at me. I've been *possessed*."

He held up the hand again. The trembling had resumed.

"Watch this," he said.

His wrist suddenly collapsed, then righted itself.

"Keep watching," he said.

Within a few moments, the wrist collapsed again, then instantly straightened. And before long, it was performing a strange, half-steady dance, plunging suddenly and then righting itself, like a chicken pecking at corn. After a time, he let it fall to the mattress, but even in the sheets it wouldn't quite stop. Finally, with a grunt, he rolled over and stilled it with his weight. Then he reached behind the pillows and brought out the bottle again.

MR. KIRPES DROVE us to Dayton. I sat in the front seat of the van with him, while, behind us, four seniors from advanced calculus lounged in their sandals. Mr. Kirpes bantered a little as he drove, mostly about the Bengals, who'd lost both games to the Browns that year. I knew nothing about sports, but you couldn't live in southwest Ohio without acquiring at least a conversational knowledge of the Reds and the Bengals. Otherwise, the trip was silent. The boy behind me was practicing clarinet by looking at sheet music and playing it with his fingers, blowing through his embouchure and tapping his feet in rhythm, even though he had no clarinet with him. The drive took an hour. I'd made it several times before on our way to the art museum.

We arrived early at the University of Dayton. Mr. Kirpes bought us milkshakes at a drive-through, then dropped us off at the auditorium on the edge of campus. In the hallway outside the exam room, a crowd of kids milled about. I didn't like being around other math whizzes. They were from all over the state, and they paced in the atrium or slouched on the floor by the entrance, flipping through flashcards and quizzing one another. I was at least five years younger than most of them, but I already knew that flashcards and quizzing would be of no help in what we were about to do. The kids who were *studying* for this kind of test had no chance.

When the bell rang and the auditorium doors finally opened, everyone pushed inside to get to the front-row desks. There must have been 150 people in there, every single one of them accustomed to being the smartest in the class. I made my way to the rear and took one of the last open chairs.

The test was ridiculously easy.

I'd figured it might be. There were a few questions on probability, a few on algebraic representation, and then a run of simple Euclidean figures. The first questions were truly elementary, and only after the middle section did they become even mildly involved. But whenever I looked up, I saw that plenty of the other kids were puzzled. The first part had been designed to encourage everyone, I realized, but this also had the effect of startling the weaker ones when the material picked up a notch. The last half-dozen problems at last grew tricky. By this point, several kids were looking off into the distance, only pretending to be thinking. One of them near me was in a jacket and tie, and he was putting on a show of loosening the tie so that he could see my answer sheet. On the second-to-last page, I figured out all four problems, then darkened all four answer boxes in one pass. Out of the corner of my eye, I saw him drop his head into his hands.

The thing was, I knew that there was a group of us in that room who were having a good time.

What I myself was enjoying most were the questions on number theory. In those days, I had particular affection for number theory because it seemed to have no practical application. Only a few cryptographers, a few pure mathematicians, and perhaps a few species of thirteen- and seventeen-year cicadas cared about things like prime numbers. And now I could add to this list the five or six other kids that I could sense around me in that auditorium radiating pleasure as we moved through the questions. There was a group of us, even in southern Ohio, who were in love with mathematics.

The last page contained a single problem:

Professor Gamble buys a lottery ticket, which requires that he pick six different integers from 1 through 46, inclusive. He chooses his numbers so that the sum of the base-ten logarithms of his six numbers is an integer. It so happens that the integers on the winning ticket have the same property—the sum of the base-ten logarithms is an integer. What is the probability that Professor Gamble holds the winning ticket?

(A) ⅕ (B) ¼ (C) ⅓ (D) ½ (E) 1

I thought about it. If the sum of the logs of the professor's numbers was an integer, then their product had to be an integer power of 10; since the prime factors of 10 were 2 and 5, then the six lottery numbers also had to have only 2 and 5 as prime factors. This left only 1, 2, 4, 5, 8, 10, 16, 20, 25, 32, and 40. Since the product of the smallest six of these numbers was greater than 10^3, and since there were only six factors of 5 on the list, the product of the winning numbers had to be either 10^4, 10^5, or 10^6. The rest was simple. There were only four possible combinations that would produce one of these exact products. Professor Gamble had a 1 in 4 chance of winning. The answer was B.

Forty-five minutes remained, and I'd finished. When I looked up, I could see that every other kid in the room was still working, even the ones who loved math. The boy next to me in the tie was five pages back. I set down my pencil and lifted my arm. In front of me I held it out straight. Slowly, as I tensed it there, it grew heavy. Eventually, it began to shake. By concentrating, I turned the shaking into a tremor. Around the room, a few heads came up. When enough people were looking, I willed the tremor to increase, and somehow it did. For a minute or two, my hand shook as though an electric current were flowing into it. Abruptly, I stopped it. I lowered my hand, picked up my pencil, and darkened the oval next to the letter B. Then I stood, sauntered to the front of the room, and turned in my test.

THE FOLLOWING AFTERNOON, I left school at lunchtime and walked by myself down to the Greenway Shopping Center, where I leaned against the telephone booth in front of Buckeye Spirits. Hardly a minute had passed before a rusted old Datsun pulled up at a slant and a coughing middle-aged woman struggled out from the driver's door with a cigarette in her mouth. She left the engine running and moved toward the entrance in the kind of forward-leaning gait that I recognized. It was 12:35 in the afternoon.

I pulled my baseball cap down over my eyes. "I'll pay for yours, ma'am," I said, "if you'll buy me mine."

. . .

THAT EVENING IN his room, Dad was skittish again. His eyes went from the curtains to the ceiling, from the ceiling to me, from me to the door. "How'd it go?" he said.

"How'd what go?"

His fingers worked the sheets. "The test, Hans. How was the state test? Mom told me you went to Dayton."

"Oh, yeah. Fine. Some of the kids had flashcards."

He smiled. "Flashcards?"

"Yeah."

We both laughed.

My gift for him was still back in the closet of my room, hidden in a grocery bag behind a pile of shoes. I'd decided to present it to him in the morning, when his mood would be better. He always became agitated after dusk, but every morning he emerged from bed fresh and strangely buoyant. Now as I stood before him, he grew quiet. After a time, a cloud crossed his features. He looked, for some reason, terribly sad.

"Dad?"

That's when his gaze abruptly dropped. His presence—whatever presence defines a human being—just disappeared. A moment later, the room stank of urine.

"Fuck you, Dad."

He didn't seem to hear me.

At the start, there was just a high-pitched grunt, then a single fierce jerk that flipped him over onto his side, as though someone had violently upended the bed. For a moment, he was still; then suddenly his arms were yanked behind him. It looked like a policeman was trying to force him into handcuffs but that Dad was resisting. His shoulders were pinned back, but he jutted his chest and then began ratcheting in a circle, driving forward his hips and wrenching himself around the mattress like a gearwheel. His teeth were clenched, and his legs caught in the sheets, then ripped through them. Now he was jerking all over. His head was at the bottom of the bed, and when it hit the footboards I reached over and cradled it in my hands. The skin was on fire. I tried to hold him steady, but his feet kicked everything off the table, then kept kicking the table until it fell over, then kicked at the air. The lamp smashed against the wall, and his shins were smeared with blood.

Then, just as suddenly, he was still. He curled up on his side, blinking.

I pushed a pillow under his head. "Dad?"

His color was returning, but still he made no sound. At last came a low gasp, then a short, ugly bark as he vomited. A moment later, I smelled the stench of his bowels.

It was only then that I shouted for my mother.

MOM HAD PILLS. Pills she'd kept on hand for some time, apparently. That evening, she gave him the first of them. She was a kind woman, my mother, forgiving to a fault; but she was also vexed for a good part of her life by a loyalty and a hampering self-consciousness that could seem like a prison. It was this self-consciousness, I think, that stopped her from calling the doctor. I'm fairly sure she understood what had happened, but instead of sending him for treatment, she treated him herself. With an old bottle of tranquilizers that she told me she'd found in his drawer. Before sleep that night, she gave him another.

I believe she was ashamed.

The medicine took him through until morning, and when I woke the next day I went in directly to see him. He was still alive. In fact, he appeared to have been restored almost to normal, sitting upright against the headboard reading his copy of *The Nation*. The agreeable smell of his cologne once again filled the room.

"Hans," he said without looking up, "your mother tells me you helped me out yesterday." He flipped a page. "Thank you."

"Are you feeling better?"

"I'm fine. A little slow, maybe." He rubbed his neck. "A little sore, too. But I've taken something for it."

I stood next to the bed. I could hear my mother downstairs, speaking in a low voice with Paulette.

When I pulled the bag from behind my back and placed it on the mattress, he set aside his reading. A tentative, quivering crease appeared on his face. He touched the brown paper, and the crease spread across his features until it ran all the way from his darkly scabbed lips to the haggard-looking corners of his eyes. "Oh, God," he whispered. "You figured it out, didn't you?"

"I did, Dad."

He pulled out the neck of one of the bottles and turned it to read the label. "Hennessy?" He set it back in and pulled out the next one. "All of these are *Cognac*?"

"The woman at the store must have misheard me."

A look of puzzlement, then of what I might call a thoughtfully considered determination, crossed his features. "That's fine, Hans," he whispered. "It'll do."

He shifted his features into a full-out smile then that twitched just faintly at the ends. I don't think my father had ever looked upon me—or has looked upon me since—with such thoroughly felt gratitude. "Oh, Hans," he said. "This is perfect. Thank you." He took my hand and squeezed it. "I knew I could count on you to understand."

WHEN I LOOK at my own children now, by the way, it would be Niels who would have understood. Niels who would have gotten me what I needed. This in itself is an intelligence, as poorly explained as any other.

What is brilliance, anyway? The great Indian autodidact Srinivasa Ramanujan derived many of the foundational theorems of mathematics while lounging on the steps of a dilapidated hut in Tamil Nadu. As a boy, he mastered Bernoulli numbers and Euler's natural logs. Then, when he finally found his way to university, he failed miserably at every single course that wasn't mathematics. What can one say about this? That brilliance is just an obsessive kind of love?

A man like Ramanujan looked only at what it pleased him to look at. As do most of us, I think. Einstein once said that God is subtle but not malicious, and I have to agree: success in mathematics is in good part a question of merely wanting badly enough to look. To look inside the mind, I should add—for that is where the field, like a pinhole camera, has thrown the universe, perhaps even backward and upside down. The actual sharpness of one's vision might even be secondary to the mere love of looking. Ramanujan's ardor, coupled with a faith in the absolute knowability of it all: those are the keys. Dawkins once said that he opposed religion mainly because it taught us to be satisfied with not understanding the world.

Faith and love—that's what it comes down to.

And what of life's other brilliances? I believe that my daughter is a good deal more talented in mathematics than my son, for example. It's Emmy's name that we might one day read in textbooks, the way we've already read my father's. The thing is, Emmy would never know what anyone secretly needed. Niels, on the other hand, would know it deeply, without ever having to be asked.

ON THE WAY home that week from OSU, where my mother and I had both taken midterms, she turned to me in the passenger seat and said, "Are you worried about your father?"

"Not really."

She kept her gaze on me. "Good," she said. "You just focus your mind on your studies." Then she looked back out at the road.

We were in the long stretch of empty land about three-quarters of the way back from Columbus. Whenever a car neared from the other direction, I could see her peering forward into the lights. My midterm had been on eigenfunctions, and hers had been on the circulatory system. "How'd you do on your test?" I said.

"Not bad. How about you?"

"Not bad, either."

She smiled and lifted the milkshake to me from the carton be-tween us on the dashboard. We always shared one on the way home, but tonight she hadn't taken any. It was my favorite: strawberry.

"What do you think's the matter with him?" I asked.

On the outskirts of Tapington, the traffic was thickening from a shift change at the appliance plant, and the cars turning in and out of the parking lot were lifting opals of light across her cheeks. "I really don't know," she said. "But I do know that you and your sister shouldn't be worrying about it."

"Hans," said my father. "Tell me how old you are."

I glanced at him. "Is this a real question?"

"Absolutely. It's not easy when you have more than one kid, not to mention a wife. The figures change at irregular intervals."

"Let's see—I've lived three hundred ninety-four million one hun-dred eighty-three thousand six hundred eighty-"—I glanced at my wrist for show—"eight seconds, Dad."

"That's what I thought."

We were in his room again. He'd returned to the world now in most of his previous capacities, but whenever he came back from teaching he still went upstairs for a nap. I had the feeling that it had become a permanent habit. Every day, a little before four o'clock, just about the time Paulie and I returned from school, he retired to bed. While he slept, the rest of us went about the house quietly, and after I'd finished my homework and read a few pages from one of the science fiction novels that I'd started to enjoy in those days, it would be time to go upstairs to say hello. I would tiptoe along the carpeted hallway, then stand at the door to his room. After a mo-ment, he would blink open his eyes, without turning his head, like a lizard.

Now, of course, I realize I was probably checking to make sure he was still alive.

"Did I wake you?" I would say.

"You're implying that I was asleep."

He seemed to move less now. In the bed, his arms lay across the blankets like pieces of wood. His hair was matted, his cheeks sallow, and his forehead devoid of all the old grimaces and narrowings that it used to display. He looked normal in every detail but somehow not yet himself. Like a statue of himself, carved by an artist who had technique but not soul.

"By the way," he said, "as I know you know, that was just arithmetic. That three hundred ninety-four million seconds. You're twelve years old. I'm well aware of that."

"Okay."

He sighed. "The true mathematics would be figuring out why every second seems like the last."

"Clever."

"Maybe, but not in any way true." He appeared to think for a moment. "Or perhaps when you get older, you'll see that it is indeed true. Just not mathematically so." He patted the sheets, and another whiff of cologne reached me. "Anyway, twelve is about the right age for what I'm about to say." He reached behind his shoulder and from under the pile of books on the headboard produced one of the bottles of Hennessy. "I've been tapering," he said. "You're about to witness the last drink your old man will ever take." He shook the bottle to show me that it was nearly empty.

"The last drink in your life?"

"That's right, in my life." He tilted the neck, gulped down the last bit, and held out the bottle. "By the way," he said, "it's not as bad as they say."

"I can get you something better next time."

"I could get something better *myself* next time, if I wanted to. That's the point. I *don't* want to. You're my witness." He reached out and shook my hand. "So help me God."

I didn't know what to say.

"I've done some difficult things in my life, Hans. This is just going to be one more." He sat up now, swung his feet stiffly over the side of the mattress, and began pulling on his socks. "People said I couldn't do some of those other things, either. But I proved them wrong."

"What things?"

"Well, some difficult problems, for one. I've solved a problem that was thought to be unsolvable."

"I know, Dad."

"And I learned that only a small part of it is talent. The rest is determination. Stick to your ramparts, my boy, no matter who else is trying to shout you off of them." He shifted around to look into my eyes. With his head turned, the arm on the far side began to quiver. "The will is everything," he said.

"Okay."

He held my gaze. "Look at me."

"What?"

"Do you agree?"

"With what?"

"That the will is everything."

"I guess so."

"Then say it."

"Say what?"

"Say, *The will is everything.*"

"I'm not going to say that."

"Why not?"

"I don't know. It's corny. I don't want to."

"Well, why don't you want to? Don't you believe it?"

"I didn't say I don't believe it. Maybe I do. Maybe I don't."

"Say it, then. Say, *The will is everything.*"

"I won't."

"Just say it, Hans. Say, 'I, Hans Euler Andret, will never give up.'"

"No."

"Come on now, Hans. 'The will is everything. I will never give up.'"

"No."

"Say it!"

"No!"

He thought for a moment. Then he smiled. "Good," he said.

Nunquam Cede

I knew I could count on you to understand.

Did my father recognize something in me that I hadn't known existed? Was he warning me about what was coming?

As it turned out, it was that very week that I, Hans Euler Andret— mathematics prodigy, namesake of mathematicians, aspiring Beaver, son of a woeful addict myself—began using.

Why? Believe me, I've thought about it—I've thought about it now for *years*—and I still don't have an answer. Why then? Why at all? I'd just watched my father nearly bleed to death on a cliff, then practically succumb in his bed to delirium tremens, then vow in my presence to never drink again. Of course I should have taken it all as a warning.

But I didn't.

I don't think it was a desire for my own destruction, nor a claim on my father's scant attention, nor a fear of unseating him (or an attempt at it), nor the will to differentiate myself from my sister, nor a stab, even, at shooting myself down from the dizzying trajectory at which I'd been flying—all theories that have been offered to me over the years, by my wife, my friends, my sponsor, and my shrinks. Instead, I think that it was nothing more than the long-delayed satisfaction of a physical craving that must have been inside me since birth. My clock had simply run down.

I wonder now if my father recognized this fact.

Tapington was a small town, with almost nothing to recommend it except a few churches, low real-estate prices, a women's college, and quiet. Still, I discovered a whole menu of choices: Pot. Speed. Meth. Coke. Crack. MDA. Whippets. Not to mention every manner of downer (in a county that didn't need any more downers: we already had a closed polymer plant, a closed aerospace plant, and a closed Ford plant). I didn't try coke or speed. I smoked a little pot with another kid from the math team; then I went straight to MDA.

The *Mellow Drug of America.*

That's what my friends called it, anyway; or, sometimes, for reasons I never understood, *Mr. Dowater Agrees.* (Ecstasy, by the way, MDA's more beguiling cousin, hadn't yet appeared in Tapington, or at least not yet at Tapington North—a fact that actually might have saved my life.) When the dealers saw who was waiting out back for them between the bleachers and the cafeteria dumpster, they made easy work of me. They roughed me up. From having skipped all those grades, I was already on everybody's list; and, of course, I was small for my cohort. When I came back, they roughed me up again, a little harder. But ever since my father's stay at Southern Ohio Lutheran—the first one, now more than a year before—there had been a disquiet inside me: part anger, part sorrow, part bewilderment. For some reason it was relieved, at least temporarily, by being pushed around; and then, later, by the drugs. I came back a third time.

Never give up.

Finally, on a warm Friday afternoon just a few minutes after the three o'clock bell, one of them sold me a couple of tabs: one green; one yellow. The silhouette of a butterfly stamped across the face of each. It was a new world. I didn't know anything about it. I didn't know, for example, if the different colors meant different drugs. Or different doses. Obviously, I didn't ask the kid who was selling it.

Instead, I pretended at both nonchalance and skepticism. I remember making a snide comment about the butterfly design—I was afraid he was selling me children's vitamins—but he just said, "See you next time."

As soon as I got home, I took the first one. In the seed-headed grass behind the dilapidated toolshed in our overgrown backyard, looking out over our foamy creek, I lay down alone, while not thirty feet away from me, in our chipmunk-ravaged garden, my mother and Paulie bent to their weeding. My father was upstairs napping. Several days before, he'd ruefully enjoyed the last afternoon drink he'd ever allow himself to indulge in. Now, it seemed, I was taking over for him. Our lives were perched on a fulcrum. I'd intended to try the green pill on Friday and the yellow pill on Saturday; but as it turned out, I tried the green pill on Friday and the yellow pill two hours later. Some people don't like drugs. Some people don't like giving up control.

Well, I wasn't one of those people.

The whole experience felt primordial to me, as though, until that moment, Hans Euler Andret had existed only inside of an egg—a rich, nutritionally fortified yolk insulated by a cushioning white—and now he was finally pecking his way out into the world. And I'm here to report that the world, as first seen by an organism emerging from a shell, appears astoundingly bright.

It also appears astoundingly meaningful, like a slideshow of your own life. My father, stepping tentatively onto the porch after his nap, lifting his frail hand against the sun. My mother, slapping the broom on the garage steps until a cloud of dust rises up around her. My sister, leaning down to count the wisps on a dandelion without picking it. It was all there in pictures. My extravagantly sad family.

Before long, I was buying seven hits a week.

At the outset, I got the money from my mother, leveraging her reliable kindness. Soon I began stealing from her purse. When she caught me at it (I should have known that she would know the total in her billfold), I turned to stealing from my new buddies (also MDA heads, it goes without saying), although stealing from thieves wasn't as easy. Before long, we were stealing from the lockers at school. Then from the coach's office, where the concessions lockbox was kept between games: I was the one who figured out the combination, of course.

Looking back, I see that this period was the only one in my life in which I had a good number of friends. (Nothing I pity myself for— I've never particularly wanted friends.) We MDA users were an emotional bunch, coaxing brotherhood from our methylated oxy-amphetamines. April and May of that year, my pals and I spent every free period under the bleachers at the far end of the football field, observing the behavior of the newly fertilized grass. Sometimes it grew into whispering green towers, or herds of grazing green cater-pillars, or stalks of swaying, green aluminum. My companions were dead-end kids, every single one of them, and they treated me like a dignitary who'd crash-landed in their midst. Their planet was a rav-aged one. They roamed it, looking for yellow and green. I followed, doing the same. Nothing was beyond my desire. I did their home-work for them; I laughed at their jokes and shared in their bitter asides about the teachers (whom I invariably still respected and in a few cases still loved). I wrote a college essay for the daughter of my honors English teacher. I wrote a term paper on Puritan ethics for the son of the town's Methodist minister. Everything in return for tabs, naturally.

All the while, I should add, I knew almost nothing of my father's history.

Most of Dad's early life—which would obviously bear on what I was doing—was only revealed to me later; and everything that was happening to him now, though it couldn't have been a more dire warning or a more minatory clue, seemed to be of no relevance.

On top of which, I couldn't have cared less.

In the afternoons, Dad and I had ceased studying mathematics al-together. The first time I told him I wasn't going to sit with him and review the day's requisite theorems, he merely shrugged and wandered off toward the kitchen. He was back at work now and seemed in no mood to waste any more time. Later that afternoon, I finished the homework for my class in Fourier analysis; but the next morning, I failed to mail it in to my professor at OSU. The same thing happened the following day. All five afternoons that week, in fact, I did my homework but then failed to mail it in, and all five afternoons I went instead with my newly made friends to a freshly built house at the south end of town. I don't blame my father for ignoring my descent—he had his own ruin to think about.

The house belonged to the parents of one of the dealers, actually. Suburban-style construction was new to Tapington, and the empty two-car garage and the refrigerator's built-in water dispenser were objects of amazement. That part of Tapington looked over the shut truck plant, whose burglar-proof windows had been attacked so many times over the years by crowbars and baseball bats that they were held together now only by the remains of their reinforcing wires, which glinted defiantly back at the town. A decade of winters had pierced the tar roof in a hundred places, and the brick walls of the assembly line were studded with holes where the pipes had been hacked away by salvagers. The entire building looked as though it had been the target of a sustained bombardment. That Friday afternoon, just before I swallowed my pill, I imagined my father looking out at the mulberry to see whether his son the prodigy had experienced a change of heart.

There was a shadow city living inside the Ford plant, stooped men who went out late in the afternoon as though leaving for the swing shift but returned an hour later to resume their vigils under the eaves. They slumped like rag dolls with brown paper bags in their hands. One of them, a skeletal figure with an amputated arm, looked a lot like Dad—the same startled brow, the same peculiarly fixed look of hope—and under the influence of the pills, I began, without warning, to feel sorry for him. For my father, I mean.

I understood suddenly that his misshapen intellect had narrowed the world to a deadened, claustrophobic slit; that it had given him a past far greater than his present or future; and that in such afflictions he was somehow already akin to this filthy one-sleeved man whose head nodded from side to side as he stared into the neck of a bottle, as though reading something in there. Through the chain-link fence at the perimeter, I watched him with concentration, the way a previous version of myself might have solved an inverse Fourier transform or a tricky contour integral. The MDA filled me with benevolence and a sort of microscopic, retrospective, emotional savantism. I might have even been feeling forgiveness—who knows? For hours on end, I could just stare.

I should add that I turned out to have a rather superhuman capacity for my chosen empathogenic amphetamine. Some of my friends were in pretty good condition themselves; they rolled two or three times a week. This took stamina.

Not knowing any better, I rolled every single day.

I suffered none of the comedown. None of the follow-on depression. None of the dried-out lethargy or achy misgiving that I've heard about a hundred times since. As soon as I began descending from one high, I began thinking about the next. Years later, in fact, when I chronicled my adolescent habits to a high-paid substance-abuse counselor during my intake interview at a place called Stillwater Farms, he looked up from his notepad and said, "Wow, you must have a very unusual brain chemistry."

The problem, though, was that it was not unusual *enough*. Two months later, on my second-semester final exam in Fourier analysis, I got my first grade lower than an A.

It was an F.

IN PEOPLE LIKE us, the craving is as strong as the craving for food or water, the yearning for touch or light or love. I was looking for something—a diversion, an occupation, an unwavering force—that would elevate me, that would lift me out of the melancholy dissection of my own interior geography that otherwise would have consumed me pitilessly, as it had my father. I wanted to fly above myself—if only for a few hours—and look down in tranquillity upon my life.

I'm an addict. I'm told I always will be.

Scrivener's Errors

THEN, JUST AS I was ejecting myself from the flame-spewing launch of my own blazing mathematical career, my father decided to re-dedicate himself to the dying embers of his old and desiccated one. For as long as I'd been alive, he'd been teaching his subject and going to his dismal faculty meetings at Fabricus, recycling his hoary tests and quizzes, and perfunctorily assigning the lowly semester grades that in time would keep his students out of veterinary schools and pharmacy schools and nursing schools across the Midwest; but in all the years that I'd been even marginally aware of his life—and though I'd always been cognizant of his early renown—I'd never known my father to engage in any of his own research.

I'd gone with him many times to his office at the college. It was on the top floor of the sciences building, at the end of a short corridor that housed a single physicist and the three members of his own department. His name, typeset in white on a rectangle of brown plas-tic, was screwed to the door. Inside, a small steel desk stood below a faded wall calendar that read, for the whole length of my childhood, GO WOOD DUCKS!—MARCH 1984. Next to the desk was a blackboard, but in none of my visits had I ever seen anything written on it. In fact, I'd encountered absolutely no evidence in that tiny room of anyone actually thinking about the field of mathematics. There wasn't even chalk in the chalk holder.

Somehow, the fact of this had never puzzled me.

Now, though, upstairs in our house, Dad established a work space. One afternoon not long after I'd witnessed his final drink, he pulled into the driveway with the rear door of the Country Squire propped open. He wedged out a wooden door and a pair of old metal filing cabinets, then lugged them up to the guest room, where he set the filing cabinets a few feet apart on the floor and laid the door between them. A desk. On it he placed a Tensor lamp, a coffee cup filled with pencils, a half-dozen pads of paper, and a bowl of caramels wrapped in cellophane. On the carpet below it he lined up three cardboard boxes, which closed with tight-fitting tops. On the first one he printed the word RIGHT; on the second WRONG; and on the last ??.

Then he sat down to work.

I'd never seen him do anything like this before. In all the time I'd known him, his job had been something he drove off to in the morning and returned from in the midafternoon, sucking on a cigarette and reaching for a drink (or for *another* drink, I realized later). But now, as soon as he got home, he went upstairs to his desk, where he sat until dinnertime. The door was usually closed, but now and then he left it open, and on those days I would stand in the hall and watch him. His back was to me, and his head was bent so low over the paper that I could see the vertebrae on his neck. Every few minutes he might straighten a little and make a mark with a pencil, or sometimes a small drawing, and every once in a while he would tear a sheet from the pad, glance at what he'd written on it, and, reaching below the desk, assign it to one of his three categories. Of course I was dreadfully curious about what he was putting into each of those boxes.

Yet, somehow, even then, I understood that I would never allow myself to open them.

Perhaps this was because, despite the turn my life had taken, I, too, was already a mathematician. Not that I would ever have claimed to be. Not even—strange as this may sound—that I had so much as thought of myself as one at any time during my short existence, despite my obvious precocity and my deep love for the subject. My life was still nothing more than the world that had presented itself to me. And what had presented itself in the recent months seemed no more significant to my future than what I had experienced for all the years before. (I realize now that I wasn't even sufficiently curious about my own psychological nature to know that I lacked psychological curiosity.) During that time, I was rolling pretty much every weekday afternoon, and on the weekends I was doing it four or five times.

To be fair, I might have been somewhat more aware of my father than most kids my age—if only because of his inturned but nonetheless imposing personality, or perhaps because I'd twice nearly witnessed his death—but I still had not yet reached cognizance of the very basic idea that he, Milo Andret, was a human being in his own right, that he was *separate from me.*

That he'd pursued his own ambitions, for example. That he still harbored them, even. That he'd endured his own failings, too. That he was living a life, which included my sister and my mother and me, that might not have been the one he would have chosen.

And being almost entirely unaware of him as a person, I was almost entirely unaware of myself as well. (My wife believes this to be a marker of the Andret family line.) Yet I somehow knew enough about him—because I somehow also knew enough about myself—to understand that his uncompleted thoughts were the lifeblood of his being. This was why I stayed away from those boxes. His thoughts were the ship on whose prow he stationed himself while the ice-strewn seas leaped and dived below. They were matters of calculatedly outrageous assumption, elephantine diligence, missilelike prophecy, and an unending, unruly wager regarding their eventual worth; they were going to be attacked with branching, incremental logic, and met after months of toil—if not after years of it—by either the maniacal astonishment of discovery or by the shame-tipped dart of folly. The fact of all of this was like genetic information inside me. I knew it even as a teenager. I knew it even as a teenager on a substituted, entactogenic amphetamine. I had probably known it as a child. And I knew equally well that the risk of the toil he now began performing every day upstairs in his new office, despite the apparent risklessness of his quotidian life, might at any time overwhelm him, even more so in his fragile state. I knew that these mortal risks were hidden away each evening, that they were held at bay till the following afternoon by the cardboard tops that he placed over his boxes.

I understood, even at the age I was then, and even in my newly altered condition, that the work was to be hallowed.

I would come upon this revelation again, just a few years later, when I was a graduate student myself in mathematics and making my own initial forays into a dissertation. (No, I never finished.) The dissertation I'd embarked upon involved Shores-Durban partial differential equations, which—at the time, at least—were still a relatively ignored branch of probability theory. They were ignored, I quickly discovered, because they were so goddamn baffling, even for a mathematician. And yet at sixteen years old, which was the age I was when I began my research, I set out to master them. Not only to master what was already known about them, but to develop their conclusions further than they'd ever been developed, by some of the most prominent mathematicians of the century. I was standing on the shoulders—really, I was attempting to *jump off* the shoulders— of Bachelier, Osborne, Black and Scholes, and the great Benoit Mandelbrot.

By then, I was living full-time in Columbus, in a moldy-smelling, subterranean two-bedroom apartment that I shared with a couple of OSU undergraduates majoring in sports communication and sports psychology. The place was as clean as you'd expect such a place to be. My bedroom doubled as the living room, which opened through a front door into the public hall of the building. Although everything else in my quarters, from my sleeping bag on the floor to my clothing tossed in either the clean pile or the dirty pile, reflected the adolescent disarray of my life, I nonetheless kept my desk elegantly bare—just the cup, the paper, and the bowl of wrapped caramels—in order to focus my thinking. And I kept the three boxes near at hand, in order to archive it. Of course, I kept them closed.

I can't say whether this arrangement was an imitation of my father or simply the exact piece inside my own brain of whatever was exactly inside his. Every night of my graduate-school career, I would gather up my notes and calculations, date them, and lay them neatly in either the RIGHT box, the WRONG box, or the ?? box, just as I'd watched Dad do. The tops fit snugly. Closing them was like putting my children to sleep for the night.

Before long, my roommates had begun referring to them as "the bank vaults."

Whenever my roommates returned to the apartment on a Friday or Saturday night, in fact—usually accompanied by a pair of girls who smelled of the sugary margarita mix that was dispensed in sixteen-ounce cups all across the campus—they had to pass behind my desk to get to their bedrooms. They'd find me at my seat, of course, headphones over my ears, working away on my Shores-Durbans (or on the undergraduate math homework that I corrected for my official university job and also completed—locum tenens—for Sigma Chi and the Phi Delts). With good-natured shrugs they'd say hello to me and introduce me to the girls they'd talked into coming home with them. I wasn't a complete dork: I knew what they were doing. I knew that I was an oddity, a conversation piece that subtly aided their cause. I watched them maneuver their prey toward the next set of doors, which were the all-important ones. While doing so, they invariably interrupted my mathematics, at which point they'd slap me on the shoulder and pretend to stumble toward the boxes or to accidentally knock off one of the tops as they walked past. My roommates were decent guys, but they were in their twenties already, and though I was a long way ahead of them in my studies, I was still, socially, their public ward. For my own part, I generally enjoyed the arrangement. In answer to their questions, I'd offer something without irony about my day's work, using a term like *group cohomology* or a name like *de la Vallée Poussin,* as though they'd understand the inferences. They'd nod. The two of them wanted the girls to see them as protective, kind to the lame, and, although it might not have been apparent an hour before at the margarita bowl, wickedly smart.

"Hans, my man," one of them might say, ruffling my hair or flipping through an equation-filled tract on my desk. "What'd you put into the bank vaults today?"

Their dates would smile—even when intoxicated, OSU girls could be counted upon to pet a dog or greet a child—and after the bedroom doors closed I would hear their gentle, muffled giggles, like kittens inside a box.

I DIDN'T KNOW what my father was working on. I assumed it was something new. His field—birthed in the eighteenth century by my namesake Leonhard Euler and his epochal curiosity about the Bridges of Königsberg—saw many advances in those years, from holomorphic dynamics to directed algebraic topology. My father liked to draw, and he liked to reason with pictures. From various clues, I believe he was working on the analogies between noncommutative algebras and knots.

One Sunday not long after he'd set up his desk, I wandered upstairs in the early afternoon and found the door open and Dad already sitting in his chair. When I saw him hunched there, I was seized with a particular hunger to know exactly what he was thinking. I'd already spent an hour with my friends at the Ford plant; but we'd been doing yop that week—the powder form instead of tablets—and the dose hadn't exactly been clear. In those days, I was in the throes of a particularly gargantuan run, and as I entered the upstairs study I found myself on a rope that had been winched to a quivering tension. If I moved to one end of it, I could see a number of colors in the room that hadn't yet been named. If I moved to the other, I could sense the tangled, adhesive lines of attachment that ran from me to every other human on the globe, Dad included. If I stayed at the midpoint, I could see into his heart. This small room with a desk and three boxes in it became the world. I'd probably taken more than I meant to, judging from the effects, and yet I was aware that my high still hadn't peaked. When it did, I wanted to be in the spot where I could see the things he'd hidden from me.

He sat leaning forward over a pad, his toes pointed down at the floor. His knees were pulled up, and one fist was bent under his chin, just like the sculpture of Rodin's *Thinker* that stood in front of the steps at the Cleveland Museum of Art. (This sculpture, by the way, had been bombed off its pedestal by the Weathermen long before I was born but put right back up by the museum staff without being repaired. As a child, every time I saw the shredded bronze wounds where the explosion had torn the feet from the legs, I thought instantly of my father, for no reason I could then explain.)

He jotted something, then lifted his pencil and continued thinking. I knew not to interrupt. Next to his chair was a tiny sheet of paper that had fallen to the rug. I was pulled toward it.

Without turning, he said, "Hello there, Hans."

His words pulled me back. Then the lengthening silence pulled me toward the paper again. He was pulling me in and pushing me back with the antipodal magnets of his thoughts.

"What are you thinking about?" he said.

"Not much."

He reached forward and made a few strokes on the pad. "Then why are you grinding your teeth like that?"

"Am I?"

Without answering, he returned to his calculations. I was forced to relinquish my desire to know him. My attention was stolen once again by the paper, which had begun now to emanate a pale blue light, as though a piece of the sky had fallen through the ceiling into the room. I swung my head until parallax was achieved. Now I was at the near end of the rope again, where the lines on the paper according to their slant and shading emanated the precise meanings of words. The drawing was of a rotating tesseract with thick strokes that showed the anger-riddled affection that my father sometimes expressed toward my mother. It was a cantellated tesseract, and it had been divided scrupulously by the paper itself, which had been folded into eighths and then unfolded before being drawn upon, each octant equally.

Something loud sounded outside. My concentration flickered. The sheet was no longer a piece of the sky. It was just a piece of paper, and I noticed that it had been freshly pulled from the pad. In fact, it hadn't been folded at all. The second-order folding of the figure had been achieved with my father's pencil. He was an extraordinary artist. This fact split me in two.

"Say 'I will never give up.'"

"What?"

"Say it, Hans."

"Not again."

"Remember—*the will is everything*. Remember, Hans—Andrets do not give up."

I stood there until he looked over at me. A whiff of his cologne had reached me now, and I was following its different components like the separate stripes on a waving flag, back to a distant field of lime trees in the sun.

"Are you all right?" he said gruffly.

"Yes."

"You're still grinding them."

"No. I stopped."

He continued to look at me. "Go ahead," he said, nodding. "Put it in the box."

"What?"

"Put it back in the box."

He pointed to my hand. The piece of paper was in it.

"Go ahead," he said. "Put it back in the box."

"Which one?"

But I already knew which one. The ?? box had taken on the same blue glow now that the paper had, undulating in gentle ripples as though the sky had been reflected on water. I stepped over, carefully loosened the lid, and placed my scrap on top of all the others.

"WHAT THE HELL is this?" Dad said the next evening before dinner, waving an envelope in the air. "Is this a mistake?"

Above the kitchen sink, where in the past his bottles of Maker's Mark had been stored, my mother had stacked her casserole dishes. She was reaching to lift one down. "Milo," she said.

"What."

"Leave him alone." She set the casserole on the counter. A moment later, she added, "Perhaps his father's the one who's failed."

"What the hell is this," he said again, waving the envelope in front of my face, then holding it open so that the letter dropped out into my hands. "I'm hoping it's a mistake."

"Oh, that," I said evenly. I unfolded it. "It's my grade report."

"From OSU," he said. "And?"

"And I got an F."

"Yes, you did, Hans. You got an *F*."

"Only one, Dad."

"Yes, that's true—only one." He cracked his knuckles. "But that's *all* Fs, isn't it? *Since you just took one class!*" Then he leaned forward until his face was in front of mine. "You're the math champion of the state of Ohio," he said slowly. "And you're proud that you got all Fs?"

"Math *co*-champion." (Another boy had tied with me.) "And I didn't say I was proud."

"Then what happened, may I ask?"

I know what he expected me to say. *Computational errors* had always been my available excuse, all through my academic career. Like so many mathematicians, my father assigned almost no value to figuring. He was giving me an out.

Instead, I said, "You can't make me into the thing you wanted to be yourself."

I looked up to see how he would react. I was on the downslope of the afternoon's yop and immediately felt the weight of my words. But I'd seen him furious plenty of times before, and nothing fazed me anymore. This was his chance to redeem himself.

Instead, he seemed to look right through me, as though he'd had a glimpse of one of his own solutions. His face went placid. "That's right," he said. "That's exactly what I was thinking myself."

THE NEXT WEEKEND, a few hours after I'd wandered home from the Ford plant, my father rounded up Paulie and me and put us into the station wagon. He drove us out Lincoln Road and along the banks of the Pitcote. This stretch of river was steadily coming back after decades of dumping from the polymer plant and the truck plant, and in one of its marshes now, to the derision of Tapington's laid-off workforce, a conservation area had been established. In the sandy shallows, a long cedar boardwalk had been laid through the willows. The boardwalk formed a sort of widening maze over the inlets, which were as still as ponds. In the distance, the rows of smokestacks on the outskirts of Tapington were no longer connected to the heavens by their kinked ropes of white. Dad parked in the gravel lot and said, "We're here."

It was evening. Bernie loved this place, but he'd been left at home. Paulette and I followed Dad into the thicket of plankways. The water was swathed in a rug of algae, and the vegetation rang with peeper frogs. On the drive over, Dad had been unusually quiet, and now he was quiet again, striding purposefully ahead of us. The philanthropist who'd paid for the preserve had been from New York City, and instead of building a factory for the unemployed population of Spartan County, he'd bought hundreds of acres of prime industrial riverfront and turned it into a nature preserve. On most days, you could walk for the entire afternoon and not see another human being.

We'd been out for maybe half an hour, looping and backtracking along the decks, when Dad suddenly stopped and said, "Hans, Paulie—you two stay here. I'll be right back. If I'm not back in twenty minutes, you can come get me." He nodded. "I'll be in the car."

"What?" said Paulette. "I don't want to be alone out here with him." She pointed at me, wrinkling her nose.

"Hans, take care of her."

Then he departed, nearly running. It seemed that Paulie and I were both shocked. From behind the wall of vegetation his footsteps thudded away like a line of rocks falling off into the water. Then they grew faint. Finally, the sound of the frogs rose again. Dusk was approaching, and their peeping was like an orchestra of piccolos waiting for a conductor.

"Great," said Paulette, sitting down to dangle her legs over the water.

"Snapping turtles," I said. "Watch your feet."

"Right. This is terrific. Stuck in a polluted jungle with a paranoid dopehead."

"What are you talking about?"

She didn't answer, but she lifted her legs up onto the planks anyway. Then she stood and moved beside me. "Well, Hans," she said. "If you haven't guessed it yet, Dad's pissed."

"At me?"

"Yes, at you."

"Why?"

"Are you kidding me? Look at you, you dopehead. You're Captain Fuck-Up."

"Because of the grade?" It had occurred to me, strangely, that my father, who never mentioned my trips to the truck plant, in fact knew all about them—while my sister, who accused me all the time of being a drug addict, had no idea.

She leaned down to pick at a sliver of board. We stayed like that for a time, standing alongside each other, waiting for the sunset. But the sky was cloudy and the air so humid that the sun never did set; it just gave up in exhaustion a few minutes later and disappeared. Before long, the bullfrogs began croaking. Soon they sounded like a bunkhouse full of alarm clocks, a new one going off every few seconds from a different direction. Finally, Paulie said, "He thinks he's wasted his time on you."

This meant something to her, I knew. We were both aware that *she* was mathematically talented, too, even if our father ignored it. I put my hand on her shoulder. "Those cattails look like priests," I said, pointing to the row of white rectangles that glowed around us in the dusk.

"Quit it, Hansie. That doesn't make me feel any better."

"Look, Paulie, I just want to know where he went. What the hell's he doing? He's been away a lot longer than twenty minutes."

"He wants to figure out whether you can find your way back, Hans."

"What?"

"To the car. In the dark. The way *he* can."

"Great."

"Well, can you?"

I looked around. There was no moon. To the east lay black sky; to the west, the distant glow from town. Around us, the faint light attached itself to the silver docks and the tall white cattails but slid off everything else. "It's night, Paulie. We were walking a long time. There's no way I can do it. Didn't he give you a flashlight?"

"*I* can," she said. "*I* know how to do it." She pointed in the direction of the parking lot.

I knew, too, of course. I'd always been able to do exactly what my father could. But instead I said, "Why don't you lead us, then?"

In the dark now, her eyes were shining. She lowered herself onto the boards again, and I heard the brush of her sandals against the water. "Because I'm the backup," she said. Then she added, "I'm tired of being the backup."

"Come on, Paulie. Go ahead."

"*You* have to do it."

I shook my head. "He's just trying to make me into a miniature version of himself, Paulie. And you know what? Fuck the great Milo Andret. I'm not turning out like him. No goddamn way."

Her smile glowed like a cattail.

Twenty minutes later, when we reached the car, she knocked on the front window, and Dad leaned across the seat and opened the back door for us. "Nicely done," he said, reaching over the headrest to shake my hand.

"He had to follow me," said my sister.

"Did you really? Is that right, Hans?"

"Yes, it is," I said.

"You know," my father said the next day. "I really don't care whether you end up in mathematics."

"You don't?"

"I didn't intend to end up here myself."

He'd caught me in my bedroom just after my day's outing. I'd noticed recently that if anything got in the way of the peak of my roll—my sister saying hello from the porch swing as I shuffled up the stairs, for example, or my mother asking me to set the table when I passed through the kitchen—I would whip around like a rabid dog. Even Bernie, who ran out to the fence whenever I came near the house, no longer did so with a stick in his mouth.

My father examined me. "Some kids might be curious about a statement like that—that their father doesn't care what they do."

"So?"

"So," he said back.

He walked over to the corner of my room and let his fingers graze the leaves of my ficus plant. A couple of inches under the soil I kept maybe a hundred hits, divided into three film canisters, each one taped inside its own plastic bag.

"Dinnertime," I said.

"Wait."

"What?"

"I know where you've been heading."

I sat down.

"What does that mean?"

"It means exactly what it sounds like. I know where you've been trying to go."

"Which is where?"

"Away from where you know you ought to be going."

I looked at him. "Oh," I said. "That."

"You can't fight who you are."

"That's an interesting thought. What's the proof?"

"It's an axiom."

"And which axiom would that be?"

"The first."

"Ah."

He looked at me closely. "You're a mathematician, Hans."

"You just said you don't care if I'm one or not."

"You're right," he said. "I *don't*." He grimaced. "But you *are* one. That's all I mean. You can't run from it. It's your destiny."

"Yawn."

His look changed now. "The thing is—" I could see that thoughts were crowding his brain.

"What?" I said. "What's the thing?"

"The thing is"—his hand moved near the ficus again—"what we do, it's—"

"Yes?"

"Mathematicians, Hans." There was something in his voice now. "We're the stooges, you know. The fix is in. We can't ever find what we're looking for." He shook his head and turned to the window. "We're destined to lose."

He was facing away from me, but I saw it anyway: he wiped his cheek.

I got up from the bed then and tapped him on the shoulder, and when he turned, I pulled him into a hug. It was the first time I'd touched him, probably, in years. He smelled of limes, the way he always did, but he was quivering minutely again, like a hummingbird. My grip grew tighter. I leaned my head until I could see my arms on the far side of his back and his narrow shoulder blades rising and falling. I can't say, truly, who was doing any of it.

Within a short time, though, he calmed. His hand reached up, and I could tell that he was wiping his eyes. He stood a little taller then, which caused me to loosen my hold. When I finally released him, guiding him around the ficus toward the door, he turned and looked back at me. "Thank you" was all he said.

OVER THE YEARS, many things happened between my father and me, but few of them could have been more important than that one afternoon in my bedroom, when I hugged him. Sometimes when I look back on my life, I wonder if I'm alive today only because of that moment. From a certain vantage, it all traces back, like a proof.

I still believe what he said: *We are destined to lose.*

In those days, I was in the throes of gravities—dark forces whose counterforces had not yet emerged to right me. And my father, of course, was still fighting a friendless battle in his own long and godless war. In the months that followed, he tried a few more times to convince me to study mathematics with him again. And a couple of times I acquiesced, taking my seat on the bench beneath the mulberry. He'd abandoned his methodical progression through the four branches of the discipline and begun lecturing me instead on unrelated topics, a tactic that I see in retrospect was meant to tempt me back into the fold. He was hoping that something far-flung might win my attention. He began dwelling not on the orderly foundations of logical thought but on the great, thrilling problems that in those days remained unsolved: charismatic enigmas to people like us. The Riemann hypothesis. The Poincaré conjecture. Kepler's obdurate question on the packing of spheres. He was hoping once again, I think, to share something with his son.

But I wouldn't let him.

Not then, anyway. Made newly wise by the drugs, I felt the distasteful cheapness of his longing. My F in Fourier analysis was followed six weeks later by a D in partial differential equations, and then by a D again in numerical methods. By the end of that semester, my nine hits of MDA per week had grown to twelve or thirteen—a staggering number even for a healthy adolescent male. Whenever I came home, which was invariably late at night, I went straight to the sink and drank three full glasses of water. Otherwise, I think, I might have dried to a smudge of cheap white powder.

We are destined to lose.

I don't know if I've ever felt such relief from a single piece of knowledge.

I SHOULD ADD, by the way, that my roommates at Ohio State turned out to be right. Those boxes did indeed become bank vaults. Shores-Durban partial differential equations, we now know (thanks in part to my unfinished dissertation), are applicable to microfluctuations in almost all types of massively multiplayer servo equilibria, including—as Marcus Diamond, vice president for technology recruitment at Physico Partners Capital Management, did not fail to notice during his recruitment trip to Columbus—the derivatives markets.

Conjecture

The Tristate Singularity

THEN ONE DAY in the summer of the year I turned fourteen, not long after I'd graduated from high school, everything I thought I knew about my family changed once again. One warm morning in June, my father rounded up my sister and me and herded us into the Country Squire, where my mother was already waiting. We didn't stop at the town limit; we didn't stop at the county line. We didn't turn east toward the Macon Dalles or west toward the rickety wooden waterslide whose fading picture above the words COOL DOWN! constituted Tapington's single billboard. It wasn't until we'd driven a full hour north that I noticed the two bulging, belt-strapped suitcases in the rear of the car. Bernie was resting his head on one of them.

It was a Saturday, and I was already three or four hours into my roll.

"Mom?" I finally said. "Where exactly are we going?"

"I don't know, honey."

Paulie looked up from her book. "How can *you* not even know?"

My mother showed us her profile and grinned shyly across the seat. "Because your father won't tell me."

"Then why are you smiling like that?" said Paulie.

"Because I do know that we're going on a little vacation."

"What?" said Paulie. "You didn't tell us that!" She tapped my father on the shoulder. "You can't just take us somewhere without telling us, or telling us *where*." She tapped him again, then again, like a woodpecker. "That's kidnapping."

"I won't tell *you*, either," he said, swiping at her hand.

"Tell us!"

"I won't."

"Why not?" I said.

"Because it's a mystery."

"Interesting, Dad," I offered. "That's a solipsism."

"It's not a solipsism, Clever Hans. Solipsism is a philosophy. It was just a self-documenting sentence." (At twelve, my sister was a disciple of Kurt Gödel.) She added, "People misuse the term."

"It's a solipsism, Smallette."

"It's got nothing to do with solipsism. Solipsism is the idea that the mind knows only its own constructs. It was a self-documenting sentence."

"Which is a type of solipsism."

"Enough," said my mother.

Silence. In that silence I was driving in a car with my family while watching myself drive in a car with my family. Sometimes I was watching myself watch myself. I knew that we were approaching a singularity, the point on the map that was shared equally by three different states—Indiana, Ohio, and Michigan—and yet belonged to none; but soon we bent a little to the east, and I understood that our chance had passed. Before long we crossed under a sign that read WELCOME TO MICHIGAN. It was a bright new sign but felt like a cheap greeting card. I turned and watched it disappear. Soon after that we came to turnoffs for Detroit and then Kalamazoo. Past these we went. Then we were moving through runs of narrow electric-blue rents in the landscape that I quickly understood to be slits connecting us to the other side of the earth. The sky on the other side was also the color of day. I began to doubt most of the things I knew. "Well," I said at last, to break the mortal silence.

"Lake country," said my father, turning to smile at my mother.

"Beautiful," she replied.

Oh, of course: lakes.

Paulette was staring at me.

"What?" I said.

"What?" she said back.

With that single utterance, my roll dropped away. Words could do that sometimes, could shift everything in an instant from a luminous ether to my family's dense, gravitational drab. I sat numbly. Miles of forest continued to speed upward across the windshield. Bernie moved behind me and metered his hot breath against my neck. My roll revived, shifting into its quiet phase. Thoughts stuck to the roof of my cranium, where if I leaned back I could observe them, clinging there like bats. Details halted in my eye. The smoke of my father's cigarette, cleverly snaking its way toward the narrowly opened window. The synchronized pendula of my mother's earrings. We were following a sinuous two-lane county highway, and I could feel the bends of the pavement as segments of a great, broadening circle, each one evolving into the ever-widening circumference. The bodies of water we passed announced themselves with a thinning of the conifers, then with a bend or two of wetland stream, dotted with lilies that looked like women's hats floating away on the current. I was aware of the women beneath them, stepping carefully across the slippery bottom.

On we drove. The black-green slashes of the pines. The blood-dot wildflowers on the road shoulders. Every now and then, through a gap in the trees, came another lake—a startling pane of aquamarine festooned with the day's high silver clouds. For lunch, we stopped at a beach, and just as we were finishing our sandwiches, the trees bent at their crests and began to rustle.

After lunch we swam, each of us in our own style. Dad plunged under, held his breath for a few seconds, and retreated howling to the bank. Mom stroked a metronomic line to where a boulder breached, then turned and stroked back. Paulie stood in the shallows, dipping her hands to wet herself like an old woman in a tub. I performed a serene breaststroke in the deep, while Bernie, my lifeguard, paddled beside me. If I looked down, I saw the same brightly glowing pebble every time I looked, winking at me from the depths.

After the swim, we dried ourselves in the breeze and climbed back into the car. It was late afternoon now, and my roll had dwindled. Silently we continued. Somewhere northwest of Jackson we exited the paved highway and entered a narrow two-track that began in gravel, then crossed uphill over a long meadow and sloped down again into trees. The chassis scraped over roots. Mosquitoes appeared—first outside the car, then in. My mother leaned over and slapped my father's neck. Bernie bumped at the windows.

An old wooden-plank bridge. A wide muddy creek sludging beneath it. My father stopped the car and climbed down the slope to the edge of the water. The land here was swampy. He took off his shoes and stepped into the reeds, then pushed his way through them until he was leaning heavily against one of the pilings. Finally, he climbed back up and walked the length of the span. When he returned, he said, "Solid." He started the engine.

"You're sure?" said my mother.

"Yes."

"One hundred percent?"

"No," he answered, steering us up onto the span.

"Nothing is one hundred percent, Mom," I explained. "Not even gravity."

This was one of the cornerstones of my recent thought: that physics was merely a dynamic averaging, and that all of us—our lives, our fates—were merely weighted, statistical trends in which outliers might indeed occur. In fact, they were obligated to.

The bridge held.

Under our wheels, though, its boards rattled raucously, and after a few moments—moments in which my mother's hand first went to her chest, then to my father's shoulder, then to the door handle—the ramp sloped us down again onto a peninsula of forest. It might as well have been a jungle. My father managed to open the windows into air that stank of mud and bark. Here and there as we pressed forward on the two-track, the curtain of vegetation had been trampled into low-ceilinged tunnels that gave intermittent views onto a featureless body of water. We swung toward its shore. But even from close, we could hardly see it. Just occasional fragments of a slack, humid brown, lazily misting.

When we exited the trees at last and encountered the house, my mother showed us her profile again. Then she showed us her face. She was puzzled.

My father shut the engine. A ramshackle wooden cabin simmered in a patch of gnat-strewn sunlight.

"Milo?"

"Yes."

"You're sure this is it?"

"Perfectly."

The front stairs were split, the roof was carpeted with blooms of green moss, and the dull-gray paint had been worn away in long, vertical strips, as though a bear had been sharpening its claws on the siding. Two cracked windowpanes glittered beside the door. A hum could be heard.

"What's that?" said my mother.

"The life of the forest," said Dad.

"Insects," said Paulette.

My mother sat up stiffly. "Well, has it at least been cleaned, honey? Did they know we were coming? Did you at least have them tidy it up for us?"

"It's a *lake* house," said my father. "We wouldn't want it tidied up."

BY THE TIME we'd pulled the suitcases from the car and lugged them through the weeds to the doorstep, my mother had already appeared on the stairs with a broom. She held her nose, walked to the edge of the brush, and emptied the dustpan onto the ground. I saw a dark body and a long, reddish tail. Then she returned to sweeping.

The main floor resembled the dining hall of a long-abandoned summer camp. A gouged wooden table. A still-greasy iron pot and a stack of rusting enameled plates. An old fireplace that puffed the smell of wet ash when my father kicked open the door to the porch. Dusty, framed paintings of ducks on the walls.

Upstairs was a pair of plain bedrooms packed tight under the eaves. My mother pressed one of the mattresses with her fingertip, and a puff of dust shot from the button. She picked up the broom again.

"How long are we staying?" she called down to the living room.

"Till the end of the week," came my father's jaunty reply.

I had enough in the lining of my jacket to last about three times that long.

Mom looked over at me.

"That's okay with me," I said.

"Good," she said. Then she added, "Perhaps I'll have it clean by then."

THAT EVENING, MY mother joined me at the dock, which stretched over the shallow end of a long, muddy cove. In one hand she held a glass of wine, which was unusual for her, and in the other the bottle itself, which was unheard of. She took a place beside me. I'd been pre-enjoying my next day's dose.

"Well," she said, "I believe your father has found the only mud-bottomed bog in the entire state of Michigan."

"It seems he did, Mom."

Around us, the fauna was bringing out its instruments for the evening. The crickets were marking out a metronomic beat, and a lone bullfrog, somewhere in the reeds, was blowing a contrapuntal bass run, over and over. A huge cloud of ungainly insects swirled above us, ricocheting off one another, then spinning down in frantic, coupling pairs to the water. Each pair would land on the surface and stir up a tiny, buzzing wake before a small, gulping splash would sound.

My mother looked up at the cloud of wings and feelers. "Mayflies," she said.

"They seem to be committing suicide in pairs."

"You're right." She leaned back and let out a sigh. "They're mating."

She took a drink, then laughed ruefully.

"I kind of like it here, Mom."

She made no answer.

"It's peaceful," I offered.

"Sometimes I do like a glass of wine," she said. "I really do." She turned to smile at me, and when I lay back against the dock boards to look up at the sky, she did the same. The crazy looping of the mayflies had thinned by now, and soon the last straggling bachelors and bachelorettes were spiraling down to the lake. Before long, even the fish had lost interest. Then, as though a shift whistle had blown, a smaller species of insect sprung into being. Thousands upon thousands of furtively darting specks appeared, gradually whirling themselves into a single roiling cloud that hummed above us like a high-voltage wire.

"Hans," she said, "would you mind if I asked you a question?"

"You already did."

I waited.

"Well?" I said.

"Oh," she said. "Oh." She pointed up. The moon had risen now, and against its halo we could see that some kind of rapacious bird had entered the fray. It winged crazily into the thicket of insects, diving and lunging, snapping this way and that, then disappeared out the other end into the black. Soon there was another one, adding its dark, vulturine missile to the circus.

"Are those seagulls?" she said.

"I don't think so, Mom."

"Swallows?"

"I think they're bats."

"Bats?" She sat up. "Yes, you're right. They're definitely bats." I heard the *lup-lup* of a pour, then the bottle being set down against the wood. Presently, she said, "Your father used to have a beautiful apartment, you know. Leaded windows and a stone fireplace. He was an endowed professor." She sipped.

"It's okay," I said.

"Bats."

"They're mammals, Mom."

"There were beautiful lanes all around Princeton, Hans. Country lanes where you could walk for an afternoon. There are plenty of lakes in New Jersey, too. And they've all been tastefully settled. You can get fried clams along the sea there. I hope you get to taste a fried clam on a beach someday, sweetheart. There are all kinds of worldly human beings in the East who do interesting things and travel to interesting places and work to elevate themselves."

She rubbed her hand in my hair.

"Sometimes I think about that," she said.

THE NEXT MORNING, I woke to the scrape of waves against the shore. From the rubberized mattress I sat up and looked out through the screens of the porch. On the other side of the pollen and spiderwebs, the water was as brown and still as a mudflat. That's when I realized what the sound was: my mother was on the steps already, working a broom.

Paulie sat up behind me. "Why are you cleaning a rented house?" she called.

My mother stopped. "Because that's what life is, honey."

My sister smirked. "I don't understand that," she whispered.

"Think about it, Smallette."

"I *have* thought about it."

"It's a simile," I said. "Life is cleaning a rented house."

"But it doesn't pertain. It's a logical phrase, but it's not logic. That's Mom for you. And for your information, Hans, it's a metaphor, not a simile."

"Please, Hans. Please, Paulette," said my mother. She was standing against the screens now. "Let's treat each other kindly. Can we do that? Can we do that for a week?"

"Sure," I said. "Till Saturday."

"God," said Paulie. "I would enjoy that. But it would be a world record for him."

"Enjoying *anything* would be a world record for you."

"Please, you two—can we?"

And somehow, for a few days, we did. A truce. After breakfast, Paulie and I walked together down to the shore. By the time the sun was over the trees, we'd grown tired of catching the grapefruit-sized bullfrogs. After a few hours, we just sat down in the waist-high grass and waited like Buddhas for them to hop into our hands. This idea had come to me on the upslope of my dose. I'd rarely been on the upslope in the presence of anyone but my friends, and now I found myself regarding Paulie with an unfamiliar esteem. (In fact, I'd taken a smaller amount than usual—a yellow instead of a green—but by that point in my career, I could conjure most of the drug's observatory powers without actually taking anything; nonetheless, it was exactly this sort of benevolence, exactly this sense of kinship with the world, that I craved. It suddenly seemed plausible to me that Paulie and I would be friends.)

"Wow," I said. "Look at this. Look at all of this."

"I am, Hansie."

Our palms were slick with excretions. Around us in the tall reeds, the narrow blue bars of the damselflies jerked up and down like elevators. Closer in, amid the jungle of stems, an infinity of insects climbed and burrowed and hopped and marched. When I lowered my head I could see that entire civilizations had developed on the bottoms of leaves. When I lifted it, I could see that other civilizations had developed on the tops. Winged ants and dusty grass-colored moths. Tiny, six-legged, triangular helmets of green. Life was perched on every incline and level, either stalking or hiding. Egg sacs submitted their designs to *The Encyclopedia of Tenacity* or *The Encyclopedia of*

Disguise. Evolution analyzed the data on dispersion versus adhesion. Spiderwebs attempted to prove what the tree limbs had merely conjectured. Alongside the cabin's crumbling chimney, an enormous woodpecker in a bright red hat hammered at the roof. Below it, Mom rapped the ceiling with a broom handle.

"God," I said. "Are you seeing all this?"

"I am," said Paulie. "I am."

We watched a pair of red ants pitilessly drag a thrashing inchworm across the sand. It was like the ending of a great novel.

"I used to think I was so important," she said.

"I know exactly what you mean."

Then she glanced up at the cabin. "Hans," she said, turning, "do you think he's all right?"

"Why do you ask?"

"Because he stopped drinking, for one. Then he took us on a vacation. He took *Mom* on a vacation. He looks—I don't know—he looks *better*."

"I AM BETTER," Dad said as he made his way ahead of me through the woods. It was evening, and he shone a small flashlight in front of him. Pulling back a branch, he said, "I'm *much* better." Then he added, "Don't worry, we're almost there."

He stopped to point the light. "Can you see it yet?"

"Is it the old outhouse?"

"No, it's another bungalow. It's small, but it's part of the estate. That's why I chose this place."

It was a tiny hut. There was a padlock on the door, but he had the key in his pocket. The inside turned out to be hardly bigger than a closet and contained nothing that the padlock might have protected. Just a small, splintered table and a wooden swivel chair tilted up against it, as though someone had been holding a spot at a library. A dusty, diamond-shaped window looked out into the trees. There was only enough room for the two of us to stand close against the walls, one on each side of the table. Paulie and Mom were back at the cabin.

He flipped on the light. "I'm going to do my work out here," he said, as though I'd asked him a question. "I'm ready to do something again."

THAT EVENING, I was watching the sun from the dock. It was an orange tennis ball lowering itself back into the can.

"You were standing in this exact same place last night," said Dad from behind me.

"Oh, hi there."

"What do you busy yourself with out here?"

"I listen to the universe."

An owl hooted.

"Tell me," he said. "Is it laughing?"

"The owl? Or the universe?"

"The universe."

"No. It's weeping."

"That's correct, Hans." From off to the side, I heard the strike of a match. "Mind a little company?"

"It's a free country."

The dock creaked. Over the far shore now, the sun was half a grapefruit turned down on a saucer. As soon as it dipped below the horizon, the mosquitoes arrived. Their whines circled us, the rise and fall of the pitch marking out a narrowing orbit.

"Listen to that," Dad said, grinding the cigarette into the boards. "Christian Doppler was the first to describe it. Such a basic idea." He lit another. "But so clever to get his name attached."

For a while then, we were both silent, except for his long inhalations and our periodic slaps. The wind had calmed, and the cigarette smoke settled down around us. Presently, he said, "This is going to be our life here, you know. It might be good for all of us. And not just this one week. I think we're going to stay a while."

"A while? How long is a while?"

"I don't know. A couple more weeks, maybe. A month. But I do know this: I'm going to do something again. Right there in that shed." The boards creaked, and in the twilight his glowing cherry was pointing. "I've always worked best in the woods, Hans. I should have realized it a long time ago."

He walked to the other end of the dock, where his body showed itself against the brightness of the house. He raised his hands to his face, as though hiding his eyes; then lowered them and looked up at the sky. After a few moments, he said, "I can feel it, Hans. I have one thing left."

IN THE COOL mornings, Paulette and I explored the remnants of the trails that wandered through the woods. They usually went to water or high ground, but sometimes they ended in unexpected places—splits of sunlight or views. One path cut its way through a thicket of blackberries to a promontory of rock that faced, I realized the moment I stepped out onto it, directly east. Someone had come here to watch the sunrise.

One morning I woke early and walked out to watch it myself. I arrived before light, and as the sky took on its first paleness I swallowed my dose and sat down on a rock.

I'm not sure I can describe a Michigan sunrise on oxyamphetamines.

Mathematics still hasn't exactly succeeded in explaining time. Newton, who observed the world, deduced that time proceeded as a constant. Einstein, who refused to observe the world, deduced that it proceeded as a variable. Others have contributed. Minkowski added his four-dimensional manifold; Poincaré his transformation, named for Lorentz. (No matter that some of these men called themselves physicists: what they were doing was mathematics.) The previous theory of time and space had revolved around a concept called the luminiferous ether, which is now spoken of, by men like my father, with a quaint smile. Yet I myself resist. Luminiferous ether is the closest I can come to describing what I saw while sitting on that slab of limestone, over a brightening Michigan lake, my neurons excited by a twice-methylated amphetamine, as the sun rose in a ball of rainbow flame from the far side of the earth.

Neither is there a satisfactory mathematical explanation, I should add, for why time shouldn't be able to run backward.

Several hours later, alone in the woods and weary, I rose, acutely aware of my own meaninglessness among the buzzing ricochet of particle motion that was the cosmos. In the growing warmth, I stumbled back through the thicket. Trees dropped the last of their dew on my head, and nettles stabbed at my pants. Nearing the house, I came upon Dad's shed. I was turning down toward the water when the door opened. "Hans," he said. "Come in here."

He'd already set himself up. On the desk lay the stacked pads, the cup of pencils, and the candies. Above him in the rafters stood the three boxes. He motioned me in. "You're up early," he said.

"Carpe diem."

He laughed, glancing quickly in my direction. He sipped his coffee and set it down. Next to where he set it on the blotter was a drawing of a tree, viewed from below. "Here we are," he said. "In nature."

"I think you're right."

He looked at me again, more carefully. "Are you okay?"

"More than that."

"You're doing that thing with your jaw again."

"No, I'm not."

"Look out the window, then. What do you see?"

"The luminiferous ether."

"The what?" He pointed through the glass. "I want you to look at the trees, Hans. That one right there, in the sun over by the clearing—the cherry. It's a black cherry, from what I've read. Tell me about its leaves."

"They're lovely."

"Mathematically."

I leaned closer. "Two ellipses, intersecting."

"Or?"

"Two crossing hyperbolae."

"Of?"

"Contrary orientation."

"The formulae?"

"That's trivial."

"Tell me anyway."

"$TF_1 + TF_2 = K$." I licked my lips. "I'm not a kid anymore, Dad."

"Indeed. And the hyperbolae?"

I considered my options. "The centers of a set of circles externally tangent to a pair of their brethren."

"Very clever, Hans. I see that you're still capable of thought." He moved closer to the window. "Well, think about this then. Think about the men who discovered those relations. Think of the men who extracted those truths. From the universe, I mean. Two thousand years ago. Ptolemy. Euclid. Nicotoles. It was the undoing of kings. Now ninth graders write it on their flashcards." He looked back at me, smiling at the word. "But at the time, these men were tearing down the foundations of their cultures. They gave their lives in pursuit."

He stopped. His hand went idly to the rafters above him and brushed against the WRONG box. "You and I," he said in a softer voice. "We're the same."

I made no answer.

"Your mother, though—she's not like us. I wish it weren't so. But I can see that you have what I have."

"Which is what?"

"The curse."

"Ah," I said. An earwig poked out of a crack in the desktop. "That's neither provable nor disprovable."

"Have you read about Euclid's doubt? Have you read about his struggle?"

"No."

"How about Apollonius of Perga? Have you read of the grief that became *The Conics*?"

"Ditto to that one, too."

"That's because it was never recorded, Hans. None of it ever was. But I can assure you—I can *guarantee* you—that it was there, for every one of them. For every one of *us*."

"I don't think either of us has any curse."

But my words glittered cheaply in the air. My father smiled at them sadly.

"History is merciless, Hans. That's the truth you and I both know. The struggle doesn't matter. The struggle vanishes. What remains is the work, and the work either stands or falls."

IT WAS ONLY as she was cheerfully cleaning up from breakfast the next morning that my mother said across the table, "Who did we rent this from anyway, honey?"

Dad looked up. "Nobody."

She lifted her coffee mug and sipped, puckering her lips at the taste. "I don't understand," she said. "Someone didn't just *give* it to us."

"Nope."

"Milo, did we just stay in somebody's house without their permission?"

My father leaned forward, drew butter onto his knife, and ran it across his toast.

"Milo," she said. "Are we in somebody else's house?"

"No," he said. "We're not."

"Well, that's good."

"It happens to be ours, Helena."

She set down her mug and smoothed the front of her blouse. "What did you say?"

"We bought it."

"Please, honey."

"It wasn't much more than a new car."

"Milo, *please*."

"And we have plenty of time to pay it off."

Flatland

THUS BEGAN THE last summer I ever spent with my family.

The next morning, I found my mother sitting in a chair before the screened window on the porch, staring out into the morass of vines that reached from the boggy lake to the sides of the house and in a few places came in through the screens. A glass of cheap wine stood on the floor beside her. Over the morning it slowly lowered. In the air above her head, a sign was visible to my sister and me, and probably to my father also. It read:

DO NOT SPEAK TO ME

Paulie and I fixed our own lunches. I ate Special K from a chipped coffee mug and then a few slices of bologna while my sister cooked a strange-looking vegetable that my mother had brought up from Tapington. Since our arrival, a pair of rooty orbs had been sitting on the counter like diseased organs from a surgery. Paulie cut one up and threw it into the skillet.

"What is that thing?" I said.

"Celery root."

She searched the cabinets until she found a bottle that still contained a little bit of oil.

"I thought the celery *was* the root."

"Are you kidding me?"

"No."

"It's the stalk, Hans." She sprinkled in a palmful of pepper. "Did you really not know that?"

"Knowledge isn't the same as intelligence."

"You draw fine distinctions, sir."

I sat down behind her at the rickety table. At school that spring, she'd been running with the oddball crowd. "Are you a vegetarian now, Paulie?"

"Some of the time, yes."

When she'd finished, she sat down at the table with me and ate straight from the skillet, staring out the window the way my mother had been staring all morning. I watched her until she was nearly finished. Then I said, "Are you happy here?"

"What?"

"Are you happy here like this, with our whole family together?"

"I don't think about it."

"Ah." This was a revelation: my sister didn't think about it. My dose was still spreading, and I saw all the complicated lines of entanglement again, radiating out from her in a silken web. The thickest strand went straight to my mother, who had moved her chair outside now into the warming sun. My mother didn't think about happiness, either. Not her own, and not ours. She thought about our *well-being;* she thought about our *health;* she thought about our *futures.* But her concern did not include anything so poorly cageable as happiness. From me, on the other hand, the thickest strand shot straight through the window, climbed the brush, and arrowed through the narrow door of the shed to where my father sat gloomily over his papers. Happiness was something my father would never in his life have considered; in fact, it was something he regularly scoffed at; but I saw then, with bruising clarity, that it was the single prize he'd always chased. His devotion to the solvable. It was the momentary lee of his torment.

It was the same way for me.

THE NEXT DAY, right after breakfast, Mom held up three strips of wallpaper against the mantel. Felt City, the town at the end of the road, had a general store, but the general store didn't offer much in the way of decorating samples. "Which one do you like?" she said to us.

"The fish," answered my father.

"Which fish, dear? There are two different kinds." She smiled like an elementary-school teacher and held up the wallpaper again. "See?"

She was being cheerful. This was the punishment she inflicted when she was especially hurt.

"The trout," he said.

"Are these the trout?" She flicked one.

"Yes."

"I like the other ones," I said. "What are those? Bass?"

"Pike," answered my father.

"That's a guess," said Paulie.

"Or muskie," he said. "And one of them is a walleye, possibly."

He was trying to be as cheerful as she was.

"If you two disagree," said my mother, "that leaves Paulie and me. What do *you* say, sweetheart?"

"The ducks," said my sister. "Without a doubt."

"Well, I'm not having fish on the walls of my house," said my mother. "Two to one, Paulie wins."

Mom did the work herself. The old mortar had a rough surface, but she used a lot of paste. When she was finished, clusters of bumps still showed through, but the wood ducks and mergansers and especially the mallards stood out elegantly. Their webbed feet splayed beneath the lightly drawn waterline, and their proud heads pointed hopefully toward the actual lake. When Mom was done, she mopped the whole cabin, then brought in wildflowers and set them in cups.

"PAULIE," I SAID. "I don't think he's doing as well as you thought."

"Why not?" It was a warm morning, and we were standing in the upstairs bedroom together, looking down through the window. Below us, Dad had just crossed the clearing, heading toward the shed.

"He's preoccupied," I said. "He isn't working."

"How do you know?"

"I was in his office. He isn't working on *mathematics,* anyway. He's drawing *trees.*"

She was silent. On the windowsill was an old fishbowl that she'd found in one of the closets. She'd filled it with lake water and a few rocks and put in a pair of crayfish. She tapped the glass, and one of them did a little threatening push-up, backing up quickly and waving its claws. She tapped again. Then she said, "You were in the shed with him?"

"Yes."

She picked up a stick and touched one of its pincers until the creature scooted into a corner. Then she just stood there, the sun through the window catching the edges of her hair. In a certain light, she was actually kind of pretty.

"I just happened to be walking by, Paulie."

"I walk by all the time."

"Well, he was in some kind of sociable mood. He was going on about how math is a curse." I laughed. "He told me that I have it, too."

She looked away. I could see the little shivers in her jaw. "Well," she finally said. "Good for the two of you."

A Marrow Lover's Feast

THAT WEEKEND, DAD and I returned to Tapington. Mom had made a list of things she needed. From the dock, she and Paulie lifted their iced-tea glasses and Bernie lifted his matted head as Dad and I edged out the driveway in the Country Squire. On the dashboard, the top page of Mom's pad fluttered in the air vent, shivering the thickly penned words THANK YOU! and DON'T FORGET! into my vision.

Dad drove fast, the windows down. At a gas station south of Felt City, he left me in the car while he used the restroom. In the hot asphalt fumes of the lot, I ducked down in the seat and took my dose. Then I picked up Mom's list. It was several pages long. The first page read:

> *Kleenex (full one, by fridge)*
> *Sun hats (Paulie's—cellar door?)*
> *SPAGHETTI POT (biggest don't forget LID)*
> *Drainer (spaghetti)*
> *Lid for pot*
> *Foot cream (white)*
> *Bernie nail clippers*
> *Nice cotton dish towel, yellow one*
> *Leather leash by door maybe on rack*

Hans shorts (khaki, second drawer, back)
Paulie sandals (skinny brown)
Pruning knife (garage, and clippers?)
Striped swim suit (haven't worn in years—call)

When Dad returned, I set the pad back on the dash. He buckled his seatbelt and said, "Me, for example."

"Me what?"

He pulled out a sweaty can of ginger ale from the cooler and held it up to the light. "I was young when I learned the importance of will," he said. He snapped it open. "I was young when I learned to appreciate difficulty. What it takes to do something that nobody thinks you can do." He took a long swallow, then turned and looked at me appraisingly.

I looked back like the hardened criminal I was. "Wow," I said. "Extremely interesting, Dad."

Sometime later, on the Ohio side of the border, we left the highway and started down a country lane. At the end of the blacktop, looking out over an astonishingly rectangular pond, stood a restaurant with a hand-painted sign over the door.

s'MAMA's

Folding chairs leaned against garbage cans. The lot was filled with every manner of vehicle, from rusted tractors to a cream-colored Cadillac with its leather convertible top folded down behind the seat. Black people worked at the counters, and white people sat at the tables. It was a barbecue joint. I'd passed this way on every one of my trips to Chicago with my mother, yet I'd never had any idea such a place existed.

Dad went to the counter. Something about the swaying car ride, the murmuring crowd, and now the salty smell of the meat—I could see it flaming inside the wall ovens—caused my roll to open like a sinkhole.

s'MAMA's

The so-nearly-achieved symmetry of the name began devouring me.

I sat down at a table. I was a crayfish in a tank, and people were studying me through the glass. I waved my claws.

"What?" said Dad. He was standing at the table with a pile of Styrofoam boxes in his arms, looking queerly at my face. "I didn't hear you."

I turned and gazed out at the pond. In biology that semester, we'd seen a film of gazelles at a water hole. At every moment that the herd was drinking, there was always one gazelle who kept an eye on the horizon. At the tables now, the human beings were doing the same thing. At each table at least one person—in our case, me—was watching for lions.

Eating.

People were happy when they were eating.

"Suit yourself," he said, smacking down the boxes and pushing in beside me. Ribs and corn. When he'd picked clean his first order, he slid a second one over in front of him. For many minutes we didn't speak. Now and then I rechecked the horizon. I'd managed to wrestle myself to the surface of my mind.

People were happy when they were eating.

That's why it made them vulnerable.

In the pond, fish were jumping peaceably, just often enough to signal that they were watching me. They were trying to calm me. Thank you, fish. I turned and made an effort to appreciate my father. He tore at his meal. He gnawed the gristle, then nibbled at the joints. He sucked on his fingers. When he was done with the meat, he dispatched two pieces of corn, sliding and turning the cobs like a machine designed to remove the kernels. Then he pulled a plastic fork from the bag and poked it around the hollows of the bones, looking for marrow. Finally, he picked up a thoroughly eaten rib and sucked at it again. "God," he said. *"Ribs."*

"Yup."

"Your mother doesn't ever make ribs."

Something had changed him.

"Sometimes she does," I offered.

"Nope. Never." He wiped his fingers on a sharp-smelling tow-elette and leaned back in the chair with his hands behind his head. "Now that was food," he said, gazing out over the table.

I realized why he was different: *she wasn't here.*

I was the gazelle watching the horizon. I was responsible for bringing us back to safety. After a certain amount of time, I said, "I know that, Dad."

"You know what?"

"I know what food is."

He narrowed his eyes, picking up the corn-fork again and poking it around. "You're a funny one."

"How is that?"

"I know you know what food is."

"Okay."

"That's not why I said it."

"Okay." I looked across at him. "I wish Mom could have tried this."

"Why?"

"I don't know. She'd like it."

"No, she wouldn't. Neither would your sister." He looked doubt-fully at me. "You haven't touched yours. You mind?"

My roll was a huge black bird inside me now that suddenly cawed and spread its wings. I gulped.

He reached. "You mind?"

"Please."

When he'd finished what was in my box, we returned to the car, and for the rest of the ride home he stared out the windshield while I stared out the side window, scouring the horizon.

I, too, was different when my mother wasn't around.

Not far outside of Tapington, he turned to me and said, in what sounded like an amused voice, "Do you know who Knudson Hay is?"

"No."

"He was my boss at Princeton. There's a conference at the U of M, and he's coming out for it."

"So?"

"Well, he's going to drive up afterwards and stop by the cabin."

"Well, that's nice, I guess."

He looked back at the road.

"I'm wondering," he said, "if I should tell your mother."

AT DUSK, WHEN we reached Tapington, my roll was still jackrabbiting around inside me. My father opened the front door of the house and led me in. Here we were, just the two of us, in a hallway as cool and still as a mausoleum.

I suddenly understood that the family who had lived here was dead.

The winter coats in the tiny closet were their mummies. A tall father, gruff and oblivious, dandruff pasted to his shoulders. A short mother, diligent and cheerful, her red rainboots pressed together. Two teenagers, poorly fit to the world. Folded Kleenex in the girl's pockets. Powdery traces in the boy's.

A broken umbrella on the floor by the door. Wobbly chairs in the kitchen. More clues. An orderly existence had begun to fail. As we stepped through the echoing halls, bits became clearer. The buoyant mother's efforts had in the end proved insufficient. Onward we went, through the cramped rooms. The smell of dust on drapes. The sourness of mold from the cellar door. Side by side above the mantel in the living room hung two old oil paintings, one of a barn and one of a stormy sea. The other walls were covered with faded prints of famous art—Fra Angelico, Caravaggio, Monet, Mondrian, Escher, Picasso—the history of Western civilization in counterclockwise order, pausing for the chimney.

These poor people.

My father had disappeared upstairs. When I arrived in the bedroom he was tearing through the closet, heaping clothes into a pile. Then he gave up and strode all the way down to the basement. Furniture shifted. Boxes thudded against the concrete. When he returned, he was dragging behind him the unattached sections of a wooden ladder. He joined them together, leaned the frame up against the trapdoor in the ceiling, and ascended into the attic.

More scraping. He appeared at the opening with a box in his hands. "Where does time go?" he asked.

"Depends on velocity."

"Ah," he said, climbing down. "I've raised a theoretician."

"What's in the box?"

"Something I made." He set it on the rug, broke the tape, and began lifting out parts. "When I was in school."

"What *is* it?"

"It's called a quatrant."

As he joined it together, it became obvious that not all the pieces would fit. He joined several at the rim and a few along the struts, but the dovetails and the sliding joints had all shrunk or cracked, and he couldn't close the radius.

"When I made this," he said, "I was in the midst of the most hopeful period of my life, but I was tormented by a problem. I thought that if I devoted myself to it, no matter how difficult it turned out to be, then my devotion would reveal the truth."

"And now?"

"I think that the problem was the only thing that allowed me to exist."

WE LEFT THE next morning before dawn, the Country Squire piled high with our take. Tied-off garbage bags and rolled-up sheets, all of them filled with the things from Mom's list. Her summer coat hung from a hook over the back door, and three pairs of her shoes were wrapped in dish towels inside the spaghetti pot, which sat atop its own lid next to a taped-up box of cooking utensils. Beside it all lay the quatrant, its parts rolled into a blanket. I could barely see out the rear window.

Dad was in an expansive mood. As he drove, he talked. He told me about how he'd first gotten the idea for a quatrant from a book he'd found as a graduate student. For years, a man named Tycho Brahe had used a quatrant to record every single incremental change in the position of the heavens above his attic in Denmark. He sipped at his soda. "And do you know what came of it?"

"No," I said.

He looked over. "Nothing, Hans. Nothing at all."

The sun was just beginning to rise. His thin smile became a parenthesis of thought. After a moment, he said, "Actually, that's not true. What came of it were the Rudolphine tables."

I turned and watched a pickup truck drag a cloud of dust through a field.

"The Rudolphine tables were his life's work. They were his signature accomplishment. A record of every celestial body in the sky." He glanced over again. "Listen to me, please."

"I am."

"They surpassed the Alphonsine tables in every way. They were a thousand times more accurate." He reached his hand back and touched the rolled blanket. "The Rudolphine tables were a masterpiece. They ended the Ptolemaic system and brought about the heliocentric one. They were the beginning of modern astronomy."

For a few moments I considered his words. "Then why have I never heard of him?"

"Because he only collected the data, Hans. He never actually published it. Do you know who finally did?"

"Tell me."

He turned and looked at me significantly. "Kepler. Kepler published Brahe's data."

We were in the rolling farmland now at the northern edge of the till plain. I'd not yet taken my dose. The hour was still early and the road stretched before us toward the brightening horizon. My father was driving twenty miles an hour over the speed limit.

"Kepler started as Brahe's student, but then he became his rival. And in the end, he killed his old master." He shook his head. "By disproving the Tychonic theory."

"Okay."

"Just like that, one man was dead and another was ascendant. Brahe knew that the planets circled the sun, but he was stuck on the idea that the sun circled the earth."

"He was close, I guess. It was a reasonable idea for the time."

He looked over. "He got it wrong, Hans."

"Obviously. But he was on the right track."

I could feel his gaze.

"Nobody cares if you're close, Hans. Brahe was blinded. That's why he missed it."

I looked out the window.

"Listen to me."

"I am."

"It wasn't even that he hadn't thought of the possibility. He *had* thought of it. But he insisted that the earth *couldn't* be in orbit around the sun, because"—here he paused to smile—"because if it had been, the stars would have exhibited a parallax."

"And they didn't?"

Now his look was disdainful. "Yes, of course they did. How else could it be?" He opened his window and spat.

"Well—"

"Brahe just flat out ignored it. If the earth was the thing that was moving, he knew that a parallax had to be there. He knew it would be maximized at six months' orbit. His own student was humiliating him. They were both looking straight at a parallax, and they both took the observations, and yet one of them failed to see it. It was obviously there."

"Maybe it was too small for his instruments."

"Well, it wasn't. It was just ignored. Brahe somehow convinced himself that it wasn't there." He cleared his throat. "Hope overcoming reason."

"It's not so bad to be hopeful."

"You've been talking to your mother." He leaned across the seat. "Tycho Brahe clung to a lousy idea, Hans. That's all it was. People like us—you must know this by now—we can't do that. We know damn well when we're right. We know a long time before anyone else even suspects it." He cleared his throat. "Or when we're wrong. That's how we live. That's how we die."

After that, we drove in silence. Just north of the state border, we stopped for gas, and when he walked inside to use the restroom, I took out one of the film canisters that I'd pulled from my ficus pot earlier that morning. I swallowed my dose. I had enough now to last me through the summer.

We were in a country filling station—one pump, a service bay, and a buzzing Coke machine. The sky was already white with humidity. As I waited, I turned and fingered his row of books on the floor behind me. On one end was Jordan's *Cours d'Analyse,* which I'd read that winter, and behind it a copy of Hardy's "A Mathematician's Apology," whose title still drew me, despite the fact that as a boy I'd given up on it after a few pages. Next to the books was the quatrant, and when I lifted the blanket around it I saw again how old and dried out it was.

But then I saw something else that he'd wrapped inside with it: a box. It was newer and made of varnished wood. I pulled it out and set it on my lap, and for a few moments, as I waited for the day's roll to introduce itself, I looked down at it. Then I opened it.

It was, as I somehow already knew, his Fields Medal.

I knew this even though I'd never before seen it in my life. I knew it even though, until that moment, I'd never even realized it was an actual *object*. But from the velvet lining now I tilted out a golden disk the size of a dollar coin. I lifted it to the window and saw the writing that was engraved in tiny, precise letters around the rim. His name glowed in the morning light.

By the time he came back from the restroom, I was leaning over the rear seat again, pretending to be looking through his books. The box was back inside the blanket, but as the car steered onto the highway he glanced over at me, then held my gaze. I considered what I'd say if he asked me about it. In my hands I still felt the cool ghost of its shape and in my ears I could still hear the waves of applause, stretching off into a dark auditorium.

But he turned back without a word.

It was only later that evening, as we were lugging the bags into the cabin and my dose was finally letting go of me, that I wondered why he'd bothered to bring something like that up there at all.

THAT WEEK, MY mother set to work clearing the land. She started close to the house, using the clippers and pruning saw that Dad and I had brought up from Tapington and a crowbar that she'd found under the porch. She used the crowbar for the roots, wedging it underneath them and levering until a great snake of a shape began to reveal itself in the mulch.

" 'Out, damn'd spot,' " she said to me one morning, holding out her palms. On her gloves, rust from the crowbar had mixed with juice from the vines until the leather looked like it had been soaked in blood. " 'Out, I say!' "

" 'Hark,' " I answered gravely, " 'she speaks.' "

We'd read *Macbeth* that year in English class. Though it wasn't anything I cared about, I still had a memory for it. This pleased her. She rose and kissed my cheek. Then she wriggled the tool from the soil and plunged it in a few inches up the line. She'd been working since dawn on a patch of undergrowth no bigger than a Ping-Pong table. Though the sun was hardly over the trees, she was already covered in sweat. She wiped her brow and said, "How's your father doing?"

"Why do you ask?"

"Because I thought you might be the one to know." She leaned forward on the bar and bounced.

"He's working on something," I said. "He wants to do something big again."

"Yes, I know." Then, "He's been saying that since we moved to Ohio."

"Oh." I dug listlessly at a root, then sat back to rest. "That was a big deal for you, wasn't it?"

"Wasn't what?"

"Moving from Princeton."

"Why yes, Hans—yes, it was." From the corner of my eye, I saw her watching me. "I don't mind saying so."

I turned and regarded her in full now. Her face was wet, of course. Dripping. The sign above her head this time read:

ASK ME

I set down the spade. "Are you upset that this is where you are, Mom? I mean, that you moved to Ohio? And that you're up *here* now?"

"Not at all." She laughed, but at the same time the sweat seemed to thicken on her cheeks. Finally, she said, "Anyway, there's no point."

I turned away. I was incapable, especially in those days, of understanding her. Though she talked with us openly, and though she sometimes appeared to tell us her private thoughts, these private thoughts always seemed to be in the service of other even-more-private thoughts; as though beneath all the laid-together pieces she'd forgotten what she'd first set out to conceal. The kindnesses, the confidences, even the tears—they were all just layers. My father, on the other hand—who rarely spoke to us with anything that might be termed *kindness*—had never in my experience been anything short of forthcoming. He wore his own pain, and the malice it yielded, as nothing more than a fact.

She said, "Your dad's wrong, you know."

"About what?"

"About math being a curse."

"He told you that?"

"No, Paulie did." She nodded toward the cabin. "Neither of you has any curse, Hans. Do you hear me? That's just your father being— I don't know—dramatic. You have to ignore half of what he says."

"I already do."

She turned and looked at me—proudly, I think. For a time then we just sat there.

"I'm just not sure it's the right half," I said.

This brought out a laugh. Then she rose and wedged the crowbar under another root. "Now," she said, lowering her weight onto the end, "tell me what he's working on."

BUT OF COURSE I didn't know. I never did. Dad's work—though it was our family's livelihood and though it would later become the work of both his children—was still performed in a far universe. That universe now included his desk at home and his tiny, moss-rimmed shed in the woods, but it was still a universe none of the rest of us was allowed to enter.

In the mornings, he vanished.

In the evenings, he reappeared.

One such evening, not long after our drive back from Tapington, I was sitting on the porch with my sister when we heard the slap of the shed door. A moment later, Dad was at the clearing. Instead of coming across to the cabin, though, he turned and headed down to the water, where, at the shore, he dropped to the ground and did a dozen push-ups. I'd never even seen him do a single one. I wouldn't have thought he was even capable of it. But he was. He did them easily. He was skinny again, and when he stood, his arms glistened.

When he stripped to his swimming trunks and stepped into the water, I felt what I might have felt watching a polar bear emerge from a cave at the zoo, tread thickly across the patio, and slip into the pool.

"God," I said to Paulie. "Is that really who I think it is?"

She looked at me, rather closely. "Who else did you have in mind?"

Dad waded in. The wind had died, as it usually did in the evenings, and the inlet was perfectly calm. When the water reached his chest, he stopped walking and stood with his arms crossed, breathing heavily.

"What's he doing?" I said.

"He's hyperventilating. He has this idea that he can make it all the way across." She looked at me closely again.

"Underwater?"

"Yes, Hans. Underwater. He's been doing it since we got here. Where have you been? It's sixty-five yards. I measured."

At that moment, he slid under. A foot kicked at the surface and then he disappeared. For a few seconds, I could see his pale legs beneath the brown.

"That's a long way to go without breathing, Paulie."

"Not for him it isn't."

Judging from the timing, he might have been halfway to the other side of the cove when the sound of a boat engine came into range. A moment later, the craft itself swept into the mouth of the inlet and pulled up short. It was followed by a skier—a girl about Paulie's age—who came racing around the edge of the trees. They were still a hundred feet from where Dad was swimming. The girl lifted her ski rope and tossed it, then slid magically across the surface until she was alongside the boat, where she made a tiny S with the ski and sank to her knees. There was laughter, which carried brilliantly, as though the entire family were sitting on the porch with us. The man at the wheel reached from the side of the boat and took hold of her hand.

When she was over the transom, he wrapped her in a towel and hugged her across the shoulders.

At this point my father surfaced. He stood, rubbed his eyes, and looked out at them.

From out deep came another round of laughter. A boy stepped up onto the side of the boat this time and cannonballed into the water. The woman in the front seat leaned out and skipped the ski to him. Then the boat nosed around, gurgling. A moment later it roared off, the boy popping up behind, shaking out his hair as he rose from the water. Just before they disappeared, he cut the ski in a long arc that threw a fan of diamonds all the way onto the beach.

"Wow," said Paulie. "Did you just see that?"

"I did, Paulie."

"Is that—" She stopped. "Is that—"

"What other families are like?"

"Yeah."

"I think it is, Paulie."

Dad had apparently seen it, too, or at least the final part of it. He stood shielding his eyes. Then he turned, and I could see him taking his breaths again. After a moment, he bent his knees and slipped under. Without coming up for air, he made it all the way back to the sand. When he emerged, he dried himself with a towel, then walked up through the front door of the cabin, not even bothering to say hello as he passed.

BELOW ME IN the warm night, a creature the size of a softball bat was nosing the pilings. I'd been studying it from the dock. Whenever I pointed my flashlight, it would still its fins and look up at me; if I moved the beam to a different patch, all would be tranquil for a few seconds; then the minnows would part, and a moment later its pale body would glide stealthily back into the brightness, like a dirigible appearing out of the night.

When I heard Mom's footsteps, I said, "I believe it appreciates the attention."

"Of course it does." She leaned down and poured something out into the lake.

"Oh, man—what was that?"

"Paulie's crayfish." With a clank, she set the bowl down on the wood. "She'll just have to find new ones." Her steps paused. "Oh, my Lord—what *is* that thing?"

"Some kind of suckerfish, I believe. Possibly a mutant. I've been watching it for a while."

"Lord," she said. "Bats. Mosquito swarms. Now suckerfish. What do you think we're going to find next?"

I lifted the flashlight into the midsection of the pine tree alongside the house. Two pairs of glowing eyes stared back at us from the branches.

"Ah," she said. "I guess we'll need a garbage can with a lid."

"Why are you still awake, Mom?"

"The heat. And the smell of those crayfish." She nodded toward the cabin, where I could see the fan now, turning in the open window of their bedroom. "And listen."

"What is it?"

"The sound of your father, in the wild."

Amid the rhythmic trilling of the insects, I hadn't noticed it until then. His snoring sounded like a hog snuffling at the edge of the woods.

"The heat and the stink," she said, "*and* that sound. That's what's keeping me awake. That sound has kept me awake most nights of my adult life, actually." She leaned over the dock now and peered down into the water. "It looks kind of like a daikon, doesn't it?"

"Yeah. A huge, sorrowful daikon."

She leaned farther out. "With a pinstripe down its back, floating alone in the dark."

Although I might not have been able to say so at the time, that was one of the things I liked about my mother: that she was as interested as I was in the world. Together, we watched the creature's gray-rimmed side fins open and close.

"Paulie likes daikon," she said.

"I know, Mom. She likes it sautéed with ginger. And you like it plain."

She regarded me. After a time, her hand brushed my shoulder. Presently, in a clearer voice, she said, "What I meant to tell you when we were talking the other day is that *nobody* ever chooses the right thing. I mean, *exactly* the right thing."

"I'm trying to figure out what you mean by that."

"I mean you can only choose what you choose. After that, it's up to you to make it right." She sighed. "Of course I'm happy I live in Tapington. And what I said the other day about Princeton—that stuff doesn't matter. I was just feeling sorry for myself, for a *moment*. I enjoy my life a lot. I consider myself an exceptionally lucky person. I consider all of us to be exceptionally lucky people."

She moved closer.

"Things are better now," I said. "Aren't they? Since he quit."

"Yes, they are, Hans."

Below us, a second creature slid out now from the dark, as big as the first and of the same depleted white. It began moving parallel to its comrade.

"Oh, good," she said. "At least it's not alone anymore."

"And I guess it's not a mutant."

In the dimness we watched. Gradually their toil brought the two of them to opposite sides of the same post, where in chiral symmetry they undulated, facing each other across the hairy wood. Their tails beat long sweeps that kept their lips tightly pressed to the algae. It was as though a single pale suckerfish had come out in the night to look at itself in the mirror.

"What about you, Mom?"

"What about me?"

"Do you ever think *you're* alone?"

"It's the human condition, Hans." Then, after a moment, "But it's different when you have children."

"I suppose it must be." I flicked the light on and off. "I'm going away to college, though. And Paulie goes the year after."

"Of course you are. But neither of you is leaving for a while yet." She clicked her tongue. "And I'll be fine when you do. I'll be more than fine."

For a few minutes then, amid the thrum of the crickets and the occasional hoot from the owl, we continued to scrutinize our two giants. Then she said, "Your father is a great mathematician, Hans. But he's certainly done some things that haven't helped his career."

"I know that already."

"You do?"

"Well, it's not too hard to figure out." I threw a pebble into the water and watched the creatures eye its descent. When it hit the bottom, they both nosed down and sniffed at it. "Mom," I said. "What actually happened to him at Princeton?"

"Your father? Well, he did a few ill-advised things. It's a long story."

"That's okay. You don't have to tell me."

"He wasn't getting along with people, for one. And then he allowed some unwise things to take place. But he's still the same mathematician that he always was. *I* know it, and I think that *they* know it, too."

"Shhh," I said. "Listen."

"What?"

"He stopped."

"Did he?" She cocked her head. "Oh, yes, I think you're right."

Out beyond the cattails now, the bathroom light flickered on.

"I saw his Fields the other day," I said.

"Did you really, honey? When you were at home together?"

"No. He brought it up here."

She glanced over. Then she touched my arm again and looked out at the water.

"Mom?"

"Yes?"

"His old boss is coming up to see him."

"What?"

"Dad's old boss from Princeton. He's coming up here."

She took hold of my shoulder and turned me toward her. "What do you mean? Are you talking about Knudson Hay?"

"You look shocked."

"Well, I sort of *am*."

"He has a conference in Ann Arbor, and then he's coming up to see us. Dad told me on the drive back. I wasn't sure if you already knew."

"Well, no, actually, I *didn't*. But thanks for the tip." She turned again and looked up at the house, where in the tiny bathroom window now my father's silhouette appeared. Then the light went out. She said, "I just wonder when he was planning to tell me."

A Nonconforming Interval

AND SO BEGAN one of the rare periods in my family's life in which I can fairly say that together all of us might have been called—for a time, at least—*happy*. It was my mother's influence, I think—as such things always seemed to be. After I told her that Knudson Hay was coming, something changed in her.

For this particular stretch of our existence, for those few high weeks of midsummer, she once again became capable of the persuasive, outspreading delight that I recalled so clearly from my younger days. She spent her mornings on her outdoor projects, singing lightly as she worked. The sound of her voice, even from a distance, was like another drug to me. My sister, who'd always been a barometer of my mother's moods, came out and sang beside her.

As for me, when happiness arrived it felt like lethargy—like a distant, narcotic stillness that laid itself over my unease. The disquiet that had for so long existed within me—a disquiet that I'd hardly noticed, strangely, until it began to wane—became more apparent with each day it diminished. One morning, I woke before dawn and hiked to the head of the marsh, where I found a family of beavers swimming in the pools. One of their tails slapped the water like a rifle shot, and in an instant the whole group vanished into the depths. But soon they were abiding me. Before long, I was their regular visitor. I would rise each morning, take my dose, and hike to their lair, where I would sit on the shore and watch them work their dam. That dam was a marvel: a crisscrossed wad of tightly tied brush anchored by barkless trunks that had been sharpened at their felled ends like pencils. The first time I'd seen it, I'd thought it was the ruins of an old railroad bridge; but one morning I witnessed a forty-foot birch being toppled and added to the girding. It slapped the water like one of their tails. I sat there as a clan of swimming rodents floated it expertly into place.

Ordinarily I would have wanted to tell somebody. But the drug now was a friend in itself. Not only did it tell me things, but I could tell *it* things.

The feeling I had then—the feeling that I told the drug I had then—with the sun just beginning to halo the trees, with the glinting, silver wakes of a family of beavers fanning out in the stillness, was unmistakable: I was happy.

On my way home that day, my roll finally fading, I passed through the woods behind the shed. There, through the tiny window, I stopped for a moment and watched the back of my father's head. It dipped. It rose. It dipped. I felt another charge of joy. Like the beavers, he was working.

THAT EVENING WHEN he finished in his shed, he sauntered down to the beach in his bathing suit. He kicked off his flip-flops, waded into the water, and stood hyperventilating in the shallows at the end of the dock. A few feet away, the rest of us lay on the boards in the last of the afternoon heat. It was during this period that Dad, even when I wasn't rolling, was becoming a creature of particular interest to me—a pale-skinned, nervous, highly familiar being and at the same time something entirely strange. I suppose it was typical for a boy my age to begin taking notice of his father. He was part of me and not part of me. Part of all of us and not part of all of us. What could I actually learn of his life beyond my paltry and distorted view of it? A tic shook the stringy muscle of his shoulder. He splashed lake water on his face and rubbed his hands through his hair. Then he bent at the knees and ducked under.

The muddy brown inlet closed over him, and all we saw then was his bulging wake plowing forward, as though a great, determined sea creature had somehow found its way into our cove. I glanced out at the spot, a few feet farther than the one from which he'd emerged the week before, where his shaking head would soon pop back up into the air.

The surface grew still. A pair of minks peeked out from the boulders. Partway up the beach, Bernie sat up and barked.

Suddenly Paulie said, "Why can't he just be like everyone else?"

Mom looked over at her.

My sister shielded her eyes with her hand, shook her head, and dropped herself back to the dock. "Why does he always have to be *working* on something?"

My mother turned to the deep then, where the prow of his wake had appeared again, pushing steadily along the surface. "Because it's the only thing he knows how to do," she said.

IF YOUR FATHER was never like other fathers, if he never tossed the ball with you, if he never talked with you about your day at school while you walked the dog together in the evenings, if he never brought you to a hockey game or played tag with you in front of the house when he arrived home from work, if he was always late when he picked you up, if he swore when he tripped on curbs and stumbled when he got out of cars, if he spent his days in battle with the underpinnings of the universe and his evenings with the bottle, then you might understand what it felt like, at that susceptible age, to live for a few months with the buoyant, outgoing man who seemed to emerge in the woods that summer from the dark husk of another man's ruin.

I had no idea whether his work was going well. It might have been. At times I could sense what felt like hopefulness.

One afternoon, I heard an unfamiliar noise coming from the bushes, and when I walked up to the road I found him standing at the end of our drive alongside a towering heap of soda bottles. They were piled all the way to the limbs of the cedars, as though a dump truck had just dropped them off. He was busily dividing them into garbage bags. I watched him from the cover of the trees. Half liters were going into one bag, liters into another, two liters and jugs into a third. As soon as one bag was filled, he would pull out a replacement. There must have been a thousand empty bottles in front of him.

Without looking up, he said, "I'm assuming you know about the economy here in Michigan."

I stepped out. "As a matter of fact, I don't."

"Bad," he said. "B-a-d. I'd say Detroit's already a goner." He pulled out a roll of duct tape and sealed off a bag with it. "A Faygo plant went under out on Sixty-nine."

"What's a Faygo plant?"

"A *bottling* plant, Hans. Faygo's a soda—local company. I got their clean stock. At least, it was *supposed* to be clean." He tossed one of the bags into the driveway, where it bounced down the slope like a beach ball. "Ten bucks," he said. "This whole pile cost me ten bucks, and we're going to make something you'll remember for the rest of your life."

The man in front of me still looked like my father.

"Yes, Hans," he said. "They won't soon forget."

"Who might that be, Dad?"

"You. The neighbors. Everybody. The whole goddamn world. Even your mother." He pointed up and down the cove, then pulled a pair of bottles from the pile and wound them together with tape. "This is our mahogany."

"Okay."

He squeezed the taped bottles together until a popping sound erupted and the structure suddenly deformed. "Polyethylene terephthalate," he said. "Radially corrugated. Remarkably resistant to compression."

"I see."

"Hundreds of them, Hans. All we have to do is lash them together. The corrugation is the brilliance. It's what makes the structure achievable. You can figure the displacement yourself."

"Of?"

"Of what else, Hans? The *hull*."

"AND HOW MANY bottles would bring neutral buoyancy?" he asked that night at dinner.

"What size are the bottles?" said Paulette.

"Two liter."

The questions in our family always went to my sister first. If she made an error, I would get my turn.

"Who's in the boat?" she said.

"I am," answered Dad.

"In fresh water?"

"Good question, Paulie. Yes, fresh water."

"How much does a bottle weigh?"

"Fifty-two grams exactly."

"Empty?"

"Of course."

"With the cap?"

"Yes."

"Well," said my sister, "how much do *you* weigh, then?"

Dad shook his head. "Estimation is a mathematical skill."

"Of course it is," I added. "Otherwise it's just arithmetic."

"Brilliant, Clever Hans."

"Excellent point, Smallette."

"And what about the ullage?" she said.

We both looked at her.

"And what about the *what*?" said Dad.

"The ullage. The part of the bottle that's empty, under the cap."

"Forget the ullage."

"Yeah, Smallette, forget the ullage."

"Okay," she said. She walked to the end of the table and stood in front of his chair. His body had long ago returned to normal. His belly was flat, his skin was tan, and his hair had been carefully combed. His eyes darted around intelligently, the way they had when I was younger. He looked, I remember noticing, exactly like my father.

"One sixty?" she said cautiously.

"*What,* Smallette!" I nodded sagely. "*I weigh *one sixty*. Try one eighty. How about one seventy-five, at the very least?"

"One fifty-eight," he answered.

"I told you! 36 bottles for neutral buoyancy in fresh water. And another for the weight of the plastic. That's 37."

"35.83, Smallette. Plus .93 for the extra. That's 36.76."

"Try putting the cap on 76 hundredths of a bottle, Clever One."

"This is math, Smallette, not boatbuilding."

"No, it's not," said Dad. "It's boatbuilding."

He turned to my sister.

"Thirty-five in salt water," she said triumphantly. "Plus another for the bottles. Thirty-six."

"And for two-thirds freeboard, Paulie?" he asked.

"What's freeboard?"

"The part above the waterline," I snapped. "A hundred and eleven in fresh! A hundred and eight in salt!"

"That was trivial, Hans!"

"We don't need to buy any boat, kids!" Dad stood up, pulling my mother into a quick hug. "That's the beauty of it," he said, releasing her and pointing out the window. "Sailors!" he boomed. "To the task!"

IF YOU WERE standing on the shore of our cove the next morning as the sun burned the last mist from the shallows, you would have seen three skinny figures hunched in a line along the bank, fastening together something long and low and shiny from a pile of strangely shaped objects that was heaped beside them. A big, hairy dog was ambling in their midst. It's possible that all four beings would have appeared content, possibly even joyful. At the very least, the three who were working were doing so with singular concentration.

This, I now understand, is what a mathematician would call happiness.

Paulette and I were assembling one end while Dad assembled the other. From our wrists hung thick rolls of duct tape. We unspooled it meticulously, trying to prevent the lengths from adhering to themselves. (This aspect was particularly gratifying: I'd taken my usual dose, of course, and in my hands the eager ribbons bent toward their sticky sides with what I understood to be the molecular equivalent of affection.) Paulette held everything in place as I taped. Then we switched, and I held the pieces for her. My father preferred to work alone—as he always did—by clamping the bottles between his knees. Bernie panted faithfully, shuffling back and forth among us. A few of the containers had bits of soda in them still and we spilled these onto the bank, where a line of ants was filing in from the woods, their feelers trembling. Bernie sniffed at them.

They, too, were concentrating.

Up on the porch sat my mother, happily reading. She was another ant, I understood then, trembling with her own intention. My sister was pausing now and then to glance up at her.

Before the sun reached its peak, the main hull had grown to length. We stood back to admire it. When I whistled—my father whistling in return—my mother looked up, then set down her book and clapped. The main deck was twelve feet long by then—exactly the length of my sister and me head to toe, with one of my high-top sneakers laid between us—and six feet wide. A dozen courses in length, a dozen and a half in width, and two in height. Four hundred thirty-two hollow, truncated biconics of DuPont polyethylene terephthalate, corrugated at their bottoms, lashed with duct tape to exclude a volume exceeding the water-equivalent mass of any combination of Andret family who might wish to brave an expedition. The whole thing rested like a gray iceberg on the sand.

We broke for lunch.

AFTER WE FINISHED eating, Paulie and I walked down to the shore again by ourselves. I began taping a course for a side rail, but Paulie just sat down on the sand. "Go ahead and relax," I said.

"I am."

I looked out at the lake. A mass of bottom weeds had been torn loose by the wind the night before, and now the waves were edging them toward us. "No, really," I said. "No problem. I'll do the rest myself."

"I heard you, Hans."

"Good. Because I was just wondering." I pulled out a length of tape. "Because if you really did hear me, then maybe you want to help."

She watched me with a disdainful smile. Then she said, morosely, "You'd do anything, you know?"

"Excuse me?"

"You think you're a rebel, but you're the worst kind of conformist. You'd do absolutely anything he thinks of." She nodded toward his shed, where through the window we could see the top of his head.

"You're full of it, Smallette."

"If he asked you to stab yourself in the chest, you'd say, 'Should I put the knife back in the drawer when I'm done?' "

"What's the matter with you?"

"Don't you see how futile it is?"

"What do you mean, futile? We just built a boat together."

"Half of one. What about the sides?"

"I'm working on them by myself."

"That's not what I mean."

"Well, then what *do* you mean? We could finish it today if you helped."

"I'm talking about *him,* Hans. He doesn't give a damn. Don't you see that? He only cares about one thing." She pointed toward the shed.

"He helped us all morning, Paulie."

She laughed. "Well," she said, "let's see if he helps us tomorrow."

EVEN AT THE age I was that summer, I was precocious enough that I could have discussed with my father whatever mathematical endeavor he'd embarked upon. But I never even asked him about it.

That kind of curiosity—a curiosity about the man beyond the effects he had on my own life—wouldn't arrive for years.

Paulette was right: he never did help us again with the boat. The next morning, while my mother made breakfast for the two of us, we heard the porch door slap shut and a moment later watched him make his way out to the shed.

My mother glanced over at Paulie. "I'm sorry," she said, slipping more eggs onto her plate. "But if it makes you feel any better, what he's working on right now could be of major significance."

My sister didn't even look up.

It took Paulie and me the whole day to build the transom. Then another day for the bow and the side rails and then an entire weekend to lash all the parts together. We matched up the deck and the rails, then wedged the necks of the deck bottles through the diamond-shaped gaps in the sides. The whole thing had been my father's idea, and it had been the prospect of working with him that had driven both of us to the task. But we finished alone.

Paulie was right: I did want to please him.

But something else was happening, too: every day now, I found myself ingesting a smaller dose. By the end of that week, I wasn't sure whether I was even rolling anymore or whether the magnitude of the task Paulie and I were doing had simply produced in me a state of meditation that was no different from the drug's.

Late on a Sunday afternoon, we made the final assembly on a patch of beach near the waterline. When we'd taped together the straps between the gunwale and the transom, Paulie stood back and rested her hands on her hips. "Look," she said quietly.

I slung my arm over her shoulder. "A boat," I said.

It had required more than 750 bottles and a dozen rolls of tape. The pitch of the deck was steadied by a keel of oversize jugs.

"We did it, Hans."

"I guess we did, Paulie."

"*We,*" she said. "You and I."

That evening, when Dad emerged from the shed, he watched us lift it into the shallows. We carried it across the muddy bank and set it gingerly down on the surface, where of course it floated. High on its beam. Dad went back to the house and returned with his camera, then snapped pictures of the two of us as we held our arms together across the bow. He walked up to the cabin again and came down with the garden hose. I took it from his hands and filled the jugs in the keel. As the last one reached its brim, the whole craft sighed and settled into its draft.

Now my mother came down from the porch. She walked up the dock like the Princess of Wales and lifted her skirt elegantly over the transom. "Splendid," she said. "Splendid, splendid, splendid."

On the deck, she kicked off her sandals and shook her hips. The craft, which was the size of our Country Squire but which—with the keel jugs empty, anyway—weighed no more than Bernie, stood firm. Bernie, as though to acknowledge the equivalence, lowered himself off the dock and pushed on it with his paws. The rails hardly dipped. Even the minnows came out of the shadows to look.

"What are we calling it?" said Paulie.

"How about the *Victory*?" said my mother in her British accent. She glanced slyly around.

"The victory over what?" said Dad.

"Over nothing," said Paulie.

"The *Victory* was Nelson's command ship," said Mom. "It was fleet command at Trafalgar."

"And this is our Trafalgar," said my father.

My mother laughed. "Our what?"

He laughed, too. He didn't laugh that often, but when he did it was almost a bellow. The sound filled the cove. My mother watched him.

"Do you perhaps mean our *Waterloo*?"

"Oh," he said. Then, "Perhaps I do."

Paulette said, "We can build a *Royal Sovereign,* too."

"Good, Paulie," said my mother.

"The *Royal Sovereign* was Nelson's second-in-command," said Paulie.

"I know that, Smallette."

"No, you don't, Hans."

Mom turned to the deep. "I pronounce you, then"—here she gestured grandly over the bow—"the HMS *Victory.* Congratulations to the entire family of Andrets, boatbuilders and scholars."

"Thanks, Mom."

"Thanks, Mom."

My father stood with his camera on the dock, shaking his head distantly, laughing more softly now and smiling queerly down at all of us, like a man I'd never seen before.

THE NEXT AFTERNOON, Paulie and I started on the *Royal Sovereign.* Paulie was the one who insisted. She wanted to refight the great Battle of Trafalgar.

I carried down the bags of bottles to the beach. She'd just come out from a swim and was pulling off her wet bikini top by extracting it from her sweatshirt. (As a younger boy, I'd been fascinated by this trick, which I'd first seen at the public pool in Tapington. But by elementary school, I knew enough topology to trivialize it: in the topological world, size was utterly irrelevant, and things stretched or shrank at will. If you imagined my sister in her bikini top, wearing a sweatshirt that grew continuously (or if you imagined my sister shrinking continuously) until the sweatshirt was miles away from even touching her, it was obvious that she could change whatever wet clothes she wanted, without removing the dry clothes that covered them.) She pulled the dripping top out of the armhole of her sweatshirt, as though it were a ferret that had crawled up her sleeve, and hung it on a branch.

"The great Battle of Trafalgar?" I said. "They were both Nelson's ships."

"Correct."

"That means they're both on the same side, Paulie. How can we reenact a battle with one side's navy? Answer that one."

"It would be a metaphor."

I looked at her.

"For our family, Hans."

By the time Dad came out of the cabin and walked past us to his shed, we were at work. By the end of the next afternoon, all the sections were complete; and by the end of the one after that, we were running the strapping around the deck. "You know," Paulie said as we set the last jug into the keel. "We just have to stick together now."

"Who does?"

"You and I, Hans."

I loved my sister—I'd realized it again that week, working at her side in the shade of the cedars while the adrenalized generosity of even my diminished dose misted through me. I loved her, even if we would always be in battle. "That's a little dramatic," I said. "Don't you think?"

"It's intended to be."

"He's busy, Paulie. He can't play around with a couple of kids."

"He's not *that* busy. And we're a couple of *his* kids. He gets this little fantasy going, then he leaves it to us to finish." She measured out a length of tape and in an even voice said, "He's unreliable. That's what it is."

"So?"

"So, I never know if he's going to come out here with some idea like this or just sulk around like an asshole inside that shed."

I whistled.

"Shut up. It's the truth."

"Maybe."

"There's no better word."

"Which word, Paulie? *Asshole*? Or *shed*?"

"Unreliable."

"Oh, come on." I touched her elbow. "Things could be worse."

She looked at me as though I'd slapped her. "Not really. There aren't many things that *could* be worse. Not for a girl, anyway. There's not much worse than having an asshole for a father."

I held a length of tape against the gunwale, and she pushed it sullenly into place. I drew out another, and we attached this one across the bow. But when I handed the roll to her for the other side, she wouldn't take it. Her eyes were damp.

"You don't understand, Hans. It's like *quicksand*. I keep trying to push myself up, but the ground keeps sinking. That's him. He's the quicksand I grew up on."

When I entered, Dad was at his desk, using a screwdriver to scrape the rust off of something. Mom had sent me out to the shed with a sandwich.

"What's that?" I said.

"Humanity," he answered. He set down the screwdriver. "Humanity trying to defeat its limitations. Otherwise known as a dynamo. This one powers a lantern."

"Okay."

"But it's just another example of man against God." He blew rust from the desk blotter. "Which, if anyone asks, happens to be the purpose of life. Look at this." He held up what looked like a flashlight crossed with a pistol, set onto a stool from a dollhouse. When he squeezed the handle, a metal gear turned, and after a few pulls a bulb on the end began to flicker.

"God appears to be winning."

He laughed. "For the moment perhaps. It's still pretty rusty." He bent forward and began digging at the teeth again.

"Can I ask you a question, Dad?"

"You already did."

"Fuck you."

"Fuck you, back. What's the question?"

"Are you happy?"

"Nope. Nobody is."

He hadn't even stopped to think about it.

"What about when you're working?"

"Working?"

"On mathematics."

He set down the dynamo and looked straight ahead, so that I saw his face in profile. In the corner of the shed I could see that there were a few other rusty gadgets, too, along with some old tools. "Do I look like I'm working?"

"No."

"Do I look happy?"

"I guess not."

I glanced up then and noticed that there were also more boxes on the rafters. All of them, at least all the ones that I could see, said WRONG.

"It's not about happy, Hans. It's about not giving up."

He turned back to the dynamo then, and I set down the plate with the sandwich on it.

"Happy isn't even a real idea," he said. "It's just like love. A reasonably skeptical person doesn't even know what it means."

AT SUNSET, PAULIE and I unveiled the second boat. I waited in the shallows while she walked up to the cabin to retrieve our parents, who took their places on the beach. At the side of the dock, the *Victory* and the *Royal Sovereign* were tied toe rail to toe rail. Stable of keel, shallow of draft, moored abreast of each other in the lowering sun. In the perfect calm, they looked as though they'd been set out for display on a glass table. Next to them, the minnows made their perfect shadows of the hulls, now in silver, now in black.

Mom held her hand over her mouth. Dad stood beside her with an appraising look.

The Reluctant Cartesian

As we walked up from the water a few mornings later, my father glanced back at the dock, where the boats were still moored. They looked like a pair of naval statues glinting in the sun. "Impressive," he said. "Quite impressive."

"Thanks, Dad."

He turned and peered into the distance, toward the curve where the road left the highway and crossed into the meadow. He knocked me on the shoulder. "Our Trafalgar," he said amiably.

"Our Trafalgar," I answered, just as amiably.

Today was the day Knudson Hay was arriving.

When we entered the cabin, I saw that Mom had already changed into her yellow dress and her cocoa-colored stockings. She was sweeping the floor, but the way her wide belt held her upright made her look as though she were holding her breath as she worked. When she was finished, she walked through the rooms turning on table lamps. Bernie had already been brushed.

When Knudson Hay's car appeared, a silver glare between the trees, we all went to the windows. A few minutes later, when it nosed out of the woods and began crawling down the narrow driveway, my mother smiled at my father like an actress. "Go," she said, pushing him toward the porch. At the threshold, she rose up on her toes and kissed his cheek.

Dad nodded, then opened the door and stepped outside. I heard his strangely jovial call. "Well, you don't say, Chairman Hay! Up here in the north woods! An honor, Professor, an honor! Up here with us in the great north woods!"

"I REALLY DON'T care," said my mother.

"Neither do we," said Paulie.

It was early evening, and Paulie and I were sitting across from my mother in a booth at the back of the Green & White, a truck stop on the state route north of Felt City. My father and Knudson Hay were twenty minutes farther up the road, at the Belle View Supper Club, the only establishment within an hour's drive of the cabin that served a steak.

"Life's just fine in Tapington," said my mother. In her cinched dress, she still seemed to be holding her breath. "I have to admit, though, it would be nice to be able to go shopping every once in a while."

"Like at Lord and Taylor," said Paulie.

My mother smiled. "Yes—well, that's true, isn't it? There's one on Fifth Avenue near Grand Central. I once bought a purse there."

Paulie sucked thoughtfully on her Coke. "How far would we be from New York?" she asked.

"Well, from Princeton Junction it's seventy-five minutes on the train. And then you're right in the middle of Manhattan, on Thirty-fourth Street." She sipped her tea. "It's quite thrilling, actually."

"So, what exactly is he here for?" Paulie said.

"I'm not sure, sweetie."

"Yes, you are," I said.

My mother wouldn't smile. "Well, for one, they haven't seen each other in fifteen years."

"Why don't you just say it?" I turned to Paulie. "They're talking about Dad getting his old job back."

"We know that, Hans."

"Then why'd you ask?"

"Because I wanted to hear what Mom had to say about it."

"It's important to remember," said my mother, "that life is fine where we are. We don't *need* anything more than what we already have." She looked meaningfully across the table. "Tell me that both of you understand that."

THAT NIGHT, WHEN the phone rang, I rose from bed and leaned through the doorway. "Was that him?" I said.

"It was, honey." Mom was at the table with a glass of wine. The clock radio on the counter flipped to 1:12. Behind me on the porch, Paulie snored softly.

"Is he okay?"

"Go back to sleep, sweetie. They're going to be a while. They're still talking, I guess." She squinted across the room at me.

"Are *you* okay?" I said.

"Oh, Hans."

I moved into the kitchen and sat down across from her.

"This all makes me a little nervous," she said.

"You want to go back there, don't you?"

"Oh, I don't think I really know."

"You'd have things to do."

"I have plenty of things to do in Tapington."

"You'd have friends."

She sipped her wine. "I like the people in Ohio."

"But they're not really your friends."

"Well—perhaps not. But they're fine enough people." Then she added, "And I have your father, and I have the two of you. I don't need any more than that. We don't know what's going to happen, anyway. He's probably just out here saying hello to Dad."

"Dad's not your friend."

She laughed. "You're wrong about that, Hans."

"You wish you had *real* friends."

"He *is* my real friend."

Out on the lake, a boat engine started up—a flashlight fisherman, out for catfish. We watched the red bow light slide east in the darkness, then shift to green as it turned north.

"You make a decision," I said, still looking out the window. "Then you turn it into the right one."

"That's right," she answered.

SOMETIME LATER, WHEN I woke again, the moon was low in the screens. I tiptoed into the living room, where Mom was slouched in a chair. In the dark, I could see Dad's overcoat in a heap on the floor. On the couch behind her, then, I saw him, sprawled across the cushions.

Later still, when the slam of a car door woke me for good, the lake was in full light. The silver car was in the driveway, and my father was standing alongside it. Knudson Hay looked up from the steering wheel. Dad was in his usual pose, his hands against his sides, his gaze to the ground. They shook hands through the window. Hay gave a short salute and turned to back out. My father watched him move up the drive.

By the time he was inside, I was dressed.

"Good morning, everybody," said my mother, ducking to peek out at the road. She sat down on the couch. "Come in, honey," she said to Dad. "Why don't you sit down and tell us what happened?"

My father didn't move from the door. "It was a long evening. We talked about a lot of things."

Paulie walked in from the porch, rubbing her eyes.

"Well," said Mom, "did he?"

"Did he what?"

"*Ask you,* sweetheart. Did he ask you to come back?"

Dad looked out the window. Then he said, "What do you want to hear, Helena? Yes, he *did*. You were right."

"Oh, honey." She turned to smile at Paulie and me. "That's wonderful."

Now Dad went to the window and leaned down to see all the way to the water. "I just need a little more time to think about it," he said.

"Of course you do. There's no hurry."

He shielded his eyes and gazed out at the cove. "Look at those boats, kids. You built a couple of marvelously seaworthy craft out there. They're quite something, aren't they?"

"Well, thanks, Dad," said Paulie.

My parents were not affectionate people—certainly not my father—but my mother rose from the couch then and crossed to him, smoothing the front of her blouse. At the window she reached her arms around his neck and rested her head for a moment on his chest.

"Who'd like to have a sea battle in one of those things?" said Dad.

"I would," I said.

"I think we *all* would," said Mom. "Wouldn't we, Paulie?"

"Good," said Dad. "Because that's just what we need right now— a good old sea battle. A good old Battle of Trafalgar. How about it, everyone?"

The Real Are Almost All Irrational

AT DINNER THE next day, my mother made pork chops and apple-sauce and scalloped potatoes, my father's favorites. She left every-thing heating in the pans until we heard the shed door slap shut. When we saw him making his way down from the woods, we all sat at the table. He was finishing off a cigarette, and his cheeks were sun-burned from our day on the lake. Something about him seemed quite different. Mom clicked her tongue and whispered, "Don't say a word till he's had a chance to eat something. He'll bring it up when he's ready."

He came in and sat down. He took a sip of water, then turned his head and glanced back up at the shed.

"You look stricken," said Paulie.

"Shh," said my mother.

"Well, no. I'm not stricken at all."

My mother dished out his applesauce and went back to the stove for the potatoes. "Well, how did your work go out there today?"

"It went fine, Helena."

"Tell us," said Paulie.

"Sweetheart," said my mother.

"What do you want to know?"

"Paulie—shhh, *please*."

"Are we going to move or not?"

"Paulie!"

"No, I'm happy to talk about it." He leaned over and crushed his cigarette into the ashtray on the windowsill. "What do you want to know?"

"Well, okay then," said Mom. She looked at Paulie. "In that case, I, for one, would like to know how he asked."

"In the normal way, dear." He took a bite of pork chop and slowly chewed it. "There's a position open, in topology."

"Oh, Milo!" My mother set the applesauce at the center of the table and slid back into her seat. "That's perfect."

He cut off another bite of pork. "It's not perfect."

"Why not?"

"Because it's *algebraic* topology, Helena."

"Well, close enough."

"Close enough? To what?"

"To what you do."

"It's not close in the least to what I do."

"Well, that's okay."

"It's a bunch of equation hashers."

"You'll just have to make it your own, then."

"I'll just have to do *what*?" He dropped his fork and turned to the window. Then he said, "And it's probationary, on top of that."

"Well, what does that mean?"

"It means it's an"—he could hardly say it—"it's an *assistant* professorship."

There was a silence. My mother reached for the water pitcher and refilled our glasses. "Oh dear," she said. Then, after a moment, "Well, I think that must be procedural."

"*Procedural?*"

"I just don't see Knudson doing anything like that himself. Remember, you're a Fields Medalist."

"You're damn right I remember that."

"It's some kind of university work-around. I'm sure it's a technicality."

"The technicality, Helena, is that they'd have my balls in a nutcracker."

I laughed. Dad glanced over.

"No, they wouldn't," said Mom.

"I never expected to have to go begging."

"You didn't, Milo. *They* begged. Knudson came all the way out here to ask you."

"So what? If it were an endowed chair, I might consider it. But it's not. It's an *assistant* professorship. An assistant. Fucking. Professorship." He pushed back his chair and got up. Then he moved into the kitchen and bent to drink from the faucet. Over his shoulder, he called out, "But at least the *pig's* out on his ass."

"What is that, Milo?"

"Yevgeny Detmeyer's on his way out—to Chicago, I think. At least I got *that* much." Through the door I saw him spit. "Good riddance to the bastard."

"Oh, honey, I wonder if that's why it happened so suddenly."

"*Suddenly?* I left fifteen years ago, Helena."

Paulie said, "Are we moving or aren't we? Mom, what happened?"

"Your father and I will have to discuss it."

"Oh, no we won't."

"Of course we will. We can talk about it after dinner. But right now we want to hear *your* thoughts about it, kids." She turned. "Tell us what *you* think of the news."

"It's not news, Helena." He strode back to the table and pulled out his chair. "I like it fine right here. *That's* the news. One crappy last-minute offer from a washed-up tyrant doesn't change one goddamn thing. I'm fine right where I am."

"I am, too, but—"

"It's too late, Helena."

"Of course it's not."

"It is."

"Milo. Please."

"Helena, I already said no to them." Then he sat down, took another bite of pork, and said, "So, kids, what do you think of *that* news?"

Thomson's Lamp

I FOLLOWED THE sound up the bed of the creek. It wasn't coming from the beaver marsh. As I moved upstream, it grew louder. A dull, steady cracking, like the unhurried blow of a hammer. The sun had just risen, and I was a half hour into my dose. I'd taken a strong one.

At the peak of a rise, I climbed into a pine tree. When I reached a certain height, I saw him. He was a short way ahead in the clearing, swinging a branch against a tree. After one of the blows, the branch flew from his grip, and he picked it up again, stumbling. He swung it against the next tree, falling over when it hit. Again it flew into the brush. Again he rose, stumbling, and set off after it.

THAT NIGHT AT dinner, the sign above my mother's head read:

I HAVE BEEN WOUNDED

I looked over at Bernie, who was crowded into the corner on his mat. He wouldn't meet my eye. I turned to Paulie, who took no notice. Mom had made hamburgers. My sister was eating hers the way she always did, as though she'd never tasted one before. After each bite, she opened the bun and looked inside.

"So, Paulie," I said. "How was *your* day?"

She looked up curiously. "What?"

"How was your day?"

"What do you mean?"

"I mean, how was your day?"

She glanced at my mother. "Did something happen to him?"

My father was examining me, too, tearing off bites of his burger and eyeing me across the table like a cop deciding whether to pull his handcuffs.

That's when my mother made a sound—a single high-pitched gulp that might not have been so startling if it had been included among wails or sobs, or even among a string of odd laughs. But it wasn't. It stood there alone, a solitary, warbling gasp like the call of a loon. She took a sip of water and kept the glass at her lips.

"What on earth was that?" said my father.

"Just be quiet, Dad," said Paulie.

He tore off another bite of burger. "Was it Princeton?"

"Come on, Dad."

"Is that what you're crying about? About Princeton University? Well, I'll tell you"—he looked around the table—"I'll say it again. Fuck. Princeton. University."

My mother set down her glass. "Do you really feel that way?"

"I feel *exactly* that way."

"Why, Milo?"

"Because it's the truth. It's all a waste."

"What is, Milo? What exactly is a waste?"

He dropped the burger onto his plate. Like a stage direction, an arrow of ketchup appeared on the tablecloth, pointing at me. He looked down at it. "My son, for one. He's wasted his entire life."

Bernie barked. At the sound, my roll breathed in. "Ah," I said. "Interesting."

"You," he said, thrusting his chin at me. "You're going to throw everything away."

There was a silence. I watched his words drift down like snow in a paperweight.

"Well," I said mildly. "I'm not sure what any of that means."

My father's face reddened. "I know all about you, you lazy little fuck. Do you hear me?"

"What?" said my mother.

"What exactly do you know, Dad?"

"I know that you're never going to make anything out of yourself, for one. That, I know for goddamn *sure*."

"What?" said my mother. "How can you say that to your son, Milo?"

"Because it's the truth, Helena. Because someone around here has to tell him the goddamn truth for once in his life. He's a fucking waste of talent. Do you all hear me? Waste of brains. Waste of life. Waste of everything I've ever given him, right down a hole."

"What on earth, Milo?"

"Every fucking thing I ever gave him. Which is all he goddamn has."

Mom rose. "What in God's name have *you* ever given him besides your—oh, you're some kind of creature."

"It's okay, Mom," I said.

"No, it's not," said Paulie.

My mother said, "My Lord, why I ever—what on earth have you been doing out there in that shed, Milo?"

"Why you ever *what*, Helena?"

Paulie said, "Married you."

"Oh, is that it?" Dad rose now. "Is that what you were going to say, Helena?"

My mother didn't answer.

Inside me, a crack opened.

"Well, you're right," he said. "You should never have married me. You should have stuck with someone at your own level."

"Please," I said. "Both of you—why don't we all stop? Let's just sit back down and eat these burgers."

"You two stay out of it," said Mom. She was pulling on the cord of the floor lamp now so that the light was going on and off. "You mean, I should have stuck to someone on a *civilized* level? Instead of some egomaniac—"

"Hold on, everybody," I said.

"No. Go on, Helena. Please, absolutely—go on. Some egomaniac, who *what*? Whose work has never amounted *to one fucking thing*. Is that what you were going to say?"

"Children," said my mother. "Outside now, please—both of you." She turned to him. "How dare you?"

Paulie said, "We're staying right here, Mom."

"You little cunt," said my father.

"Oh, my God," said my sister.

"Oh, that's great," said Mom. "*Another* brilliant one, Milo. Milo Andret, *Ph.D.* After fifteen years, *that's* what you come up with?"

"You were never smart enough, were you? You wanted everyone at Princeton University to think you were halfway uncommon. Then everybody at Fabricus College *for Women*. Now everybody in the stinking fucking woods of central fucking Michigan. Sweet little good-hearted Helena Pierce. But you're not. You're—"

Paulie said, "She married you because she felt sorry for you."

Right, I thought: *of course.*

"Sorry for me? Well, you can shove that one, Helena. With a god-damn sharp stick."

Paulie blanched.

"Yes, Milo," said my mother. "Sorry for you. Didn't you know? Don't you know that we all *still* feel sorry for you? That's why we're all still here. Why don't you go find another one of those five-dollar little friends of yours and just get the hell out of our house."

"You're the little five-dollar whore around—"

Paulie's boot hit the wall near his head.

When I stood, my father wheeled. "And *you*," he said. "You should never have been born."

"I feel sorry for *you*, Mom," said my sister.

"Well, I feel sorry for her, too! Mother to a deadbeat like him." He jabbed his finger at me. "Pissed away every goddamn talent I ever gave him."

"Milo, get out of this house."

"*You* get out. All three of you, get out! All three of you fucking ingrates!"

"Tell me, Dad," said Paulie. "Did *I* piss away my talent?"

"What?" he said, without even turning. "No, you didn't, Paulie. You never had it to begin with."

When my mother swung the floor lamp, the cord yanked it from her hand, so that instead of smashing the wall, it leaped backward and wobbled against the baseboard. My father leaned over, picked it up, and threw it through the window. The pane thought for a moment; then was gone. Shatters covered the carpet. He stepped over and began stomping them. Paulie screamed.

My father reached through the empty window frame and lifted something in from the porch. When he turned, I saw my mother's crowbar in his hands. Paulie launched herself against him, shouting, "I hate you! I hate you!" Dad lurched toward the wall, smacking the floor with it as he tried to shake her from his back. "I hate you! I hate you!"

"Milo," said my mother evenly. "Put that thing down."

"Fuck all of you."

"Put it down."

"Get her goddamn off me, then!"

"Hans," said my mother.

"Paulie," I said. "Perhaps—"

My mother grabbed for him.

When he swung it, I don't believe he intended it to come anywhere near her, but by the time it cleared his shoulder, she was standing right next to him. I saw the dark flash and thought, *This is how—*

But she ducked, and it passed over her head. He shouted "Jesus, Helena!" and a spray of dust shot out from the wall.

"Oh my God," said my mother. She straightened, trembling, and Paulie dropped from his back. "I hate you," Paulie said. "I truly, truly hate you."

The hook of the bar was still wedged into the plaster, and with a grunting lurch he twisted it free. But then he brought it to his shoulder and rammed it in again. The boards splintered, and a bright triangle of lake appeared. The next blow shook the house and opened a gap to the corner. He smashed again. The planks tore away like cardboard. I could see most of the dock now and our two boats tied together in the sun. Then the whole run of land to the water. Bernie was barking wildly. My father kept smashing. A quivering tangle of vines popped into the room. "Jesus fucking Christ," he shouted. Paulie screamed, "Idiot!" He shouted, "Fuck you all!" Paulie screamed, "You crazy idiot!" He tore at the vines, then hooked the blade over the slats and pulled. When they ripped clean, he crashed backward onto the carpet, glass scattering all around him and the crowbar skittering away.

As I bent to pick it up, I heard my mother say, calmly, "Enough."

When I turned around again, she'd dropped to the floor and was wrapping him in her arms.

"No!" Paulie shouted. "You can't do that!"

"Quiet, Smallette."

"You make me sick! You make me sick! He's crazy, Mom!"

"Quiet now, Paulie," I said. "Just, let's be quiet."

Then suddenly my sister calmed. She cocked her head and brought her hand to her mouth. On the floor, my mother had blanketed him with her body, the way she might have blanketed a child, leaning down over his chest and cupping his face in her hands. Under his harsh breathing, I realized that she was whispering to him. Paulie stood above them, ashen, and even Bernie had flattened himself against the rug, so that after a moment I was able to make out her words. Her lips were pressed close to his ear. "I love you," she was saying. "I love you, Milo. It's all right. Everything's going to be all right."

Disciplina in Civitatem

THAT WEEK, I waited for the apocalypse, for the universe to finally acknowledge the rent that had been torn in the fabric of Andret family life. But first one day, a partly cloudy one and mild, then the next, sunny and humid, floated peaceably by. My mother cleaned up the mess. We ate breakfast. We ate lunch. We ate dinner. We spoke, though somewhat cautiously, when we passed one another on the paths. In the daytime, Mom went back to working on the clearing. Dad went off to his shed.

Today was Saturday, finally, and my father was washing the hallway rug in the lake. It seemed to me that this was his first acknowledgment, in any form, of what had happened. Mom and I were sitting together on the porch, watching him. From the end of the dock, he dipped it into the water, then lifted it, spread it onto the boards, and squeezed a bottle of soap over it.

I couldn't imagine him ever apologizing: but this was close.

"Those things," my mother said suddenly. "Those things I said. I want you to know that you had nothing to do with any of them. What I said about why I'm still here with your dad, for example. You must know how upset I was."

"I do know, Mom."

"I wish I'd never uttered a word of any of it. I wish none of us had."

"I know *that*, too."

"Of course you do. We were all crazy up there for a few minutes." She set down her mug. "Except for you, I suppose. You kept your head better than the rest of us. Thank you for that."

"You're welcome. I guess."

We turned to watch him again. He was leaning over the fabric, kneading the soap into foam, his fingers picking out what must have been the last bits of plaster in the weave.

"I think he's a little better now," she said. "I think he might be back to normal."

I lifted my head and looked over the cove.

"What's the matter?"

"*Normal* people don't swing crowbars at their wives," I said.

"He wasn't swinging at me."

"Then who was he swinging at?"

She looked down at him, then up at the woods. "He was swinging at *that*," she said. She pointed. "At whatever's going on in that shed up there."

"Well, normal men don't rip holes in their houses either, just because a proof isn't going perfectly." I pointed the other way, behind us at the cabin, where a man from the hardware store had nailed up a sheet of plywood the day before. "Or because they decide a job offer is some kind of insult."

"Ordinary men don't do what he does."

"Please."

"He goes in there every morning with no idea of what he's going to find, Hans. He never knows if any of it will pay off. For him or for us." She shook her head. "For you and Paulie, I'm talking about."

Out on the dock, he pulled the rug back up onto the boards, rolled it, and began pressing out the water.

"That's why he swung a crowbar at you?"

"He was mortified about that."

"*Mortified?* And how about the stuff he said to Paulie?"

"You're right—that was inexcusable." She turned her head and looked with a pained face out at the water. "But he wasn't in a normal state. He really wasn't." Then she added, "One day, you'll understand."

"What, when I'm a mathematician?"

"When you have a family."

He rose then and lugged the sopping mass up the dock. When he reached the stairs, he unrolled it and hefted it over the railing. He looked up at the porch then, miming the weight. Then he actually waved.

Mom waved back.

"He's acting like nothing happened," I said.

"No, he's not. He's acting like something dreadfully wrong happened. *I'm* the one who's acting like *nothing* happened."

Dad smiled a little, came down the steps, and started making his way through the woods toward the shed. We watched him. After a time, she said, "You know, Hans, human beings will always be tested."

"Is that why you're pretending it didn't happen?"

She looked out at the water again, then back at me. From far in the trees, we heard the shed door slap shut. "No," she said.

"Then why are you doing it?"

"Because I don't see that I have any choice," she said.

IN HIS SHED, the box that held his Fields Medal was sitting at the corner of his desk. He'd called me out there to speak with him.

"You know," he said suddenly, "you can't make time run backwards."

"Does it look like I'm trying to?"

He actually laughed.

Then he reached into the drawer. "Now we're going to stop bull-shitting each other," he said. "Things are about to change around here."

He pulled out his hand. In it were a half dozen of my pills.

"Oh," I said. "Well."

He balled his fist and shook it. "They're a drug, aren't they?"

"I have no idea."

He looked at me with disgust.

"You've never seen them before, right?"

"As a matter of fact, I haven't."

He opened the drawer and threw them back in. Then he stood and stepped toward me, leaning close. He gazed into my pupils. I could see the tiny scabs at the corners of his lips and the web of capillaries on his nose. But there was no recognition at all in the sorrowful irises that stood just a few inches from mine. Not any that I could see, any-way, even with my dose at its peak.

"You're high on them right now," he said. "Aren't you?"

"I don't even know what they are."

His laugh was a bark. He shifted back on his heels and for a few moments just stood there. Then he sat again and began rocking in the chair, its wheels squeaking. "Well, that's funny," he said. "Because I found them in your closet."

"That *is* funny."

"Let's see"—he glanced at the calendar—"about three weeks ago now."

"Well, I don't know what to say."

"How about nothing?"

"That sounds good."

He stared at me for a long time. Finally, he pointed up at the raf-ters. "Take a look," he said.

I followed his finger.

"Take a look, Hans." He leaned sideways and pushed a crate against the wall. "Go ahead. Take a glance at the work I've been doing."

He tapped on the crate.

When I stepped up onto it, I was staring into his rows of boxes lined up along the rafters. The ones in front of me were all labeled WRONG or ??. Behind them, I could see a corner of one that said RIGHT.

"What do you want me to look at?"

"Just take one of them down."

I suppose I should have known merely from being his son, not to mention from the way he'd been acting lately, or even from the sound the cardboard made as my arms bumped against it on the ledge; but my thoughts were no longer tying themselves together. I reached and pulled a box to the edge, then guided it down. Only when it was on the rug did I understand that I'd picked the one that said RIGHT.

Despite everything, I was still as hopeful as my mother.

"Go ahead," he said.

"What?"

"Open it."

I did.

Inside were bottles. Empty ones.

For a moment, even then, I failed to understand.

He brushed his hand toward the rafters. "Every fucking one of them," he said.

He'd wadded paper between them, but I could still see the red wax melted on the necks. I pulled one out. Not a drop left inside.

"Birds of a feather," he said.

"You didn't quit."

"What does it look like?"

"Like you didn't."

"Well, I *did,* actually. But I couldn't make it stick."

I sat down on the floor.

"You can be through with me," he said.

"I don't want to be. Don't say that."

"If you are, I'd understand. I'm washed up."

"No, you're not."

"Yes, I am. I'm good as dead—as a mathematician, anyway. Haven't done a thing in a decade. Not one fucking thing in my entire life, probably." He pointed at the box, shaking his head. "Never give up."

"You didn't."

"Yes, I did. A long time ago." Something appeared in his eyes. But then he waved his hand, and it seemed to go away. He pulled open the drawer again and glanced in at the pills. "What are they, Hans?"

"They're MDA, Dad."

"Jesus."

"The Mellow Drug of America."

He dropped back into the chair then, swept a hand through the drawer, and held his fist out over the trash can. Then he seemed to think better of it. When he turned and opened his palm to me, I saw a clot of yellows and greens and light blues: 80s, 120s, and 160s. His sweat was already sticking them together.

I reached to take them.

"Goddamn it," he said. "I guess it's over for both of us."

I BELIEVE NOW that he never did tell my mother.

At first I wondered if my own silence was expected in return—quid pro quo. But later in my life, when I had my other troubles, I realized that it was probably more elemental: he really *had* given up. Not only on his work and on me, but on all the relationships he'd ever had—on every one of the distressing amalgams of mystery and pain that had puzzled him since childhood. In the mathematical world—indeed in the *entire* world—he had not a single friend; at home, my sister already treated him like a stranger; and by that point, no doubt, my mother was halfway gone.

Later that summer, I realized why he'd brought the Fields Medal with him up to the lake. In September, two days before school started, my mother and sister and I drove back to Ohio in the Country Squire, with Bernie sitting like a king on the empty side of the front seat. My father stayed behind to close the cabin. He was going to take the

Greyhound home to Tapington in time for his own classes, which began the following week.

But by the time the semester opened, he still hadn't appeared. One evening not long after that—and not long before I went off to college myself—my mother answered a phone call from the dean of faculty. After a few moments, she went upstairs to the bedroom extension.

As it turned out, she never did finish her nursing degree. By the time I moved to Columbus, she was working again, full-time, as a secretary in the offices of the Fabricus College administration.

That was how their marriage ended—quietly. My father just never came back.

Molly and Sally

I DIDN'T THINK he would be the type to write letters—especially under the circumstances—but he did: they appeared every week or so in my new PO box at OSU.

I knew he was writing to Paulie, too, back home in Tapington, but Paulie wouldn't even open the envelopes.

Or so she told me. She said she threw them out as soon as they arrived.

As for me, I read them over and over.

He was a surprisingly elegant writer. The sentences were scrupulous—short, lucid descriptions of the changing seasons and the animals he saw as the woods progressed through the cooler days of autumn into the true cold. He came across porcupines and weasels. He befriended the same family of beavers that I'd befriended myself, and in the winter, after I'd mailed back the first of my responses, he began reporting on their doings. They obviously understood the predictability of fulcrums and levers, he told me, and had evidently mastered the majority of man's own mathematical innovations up through the Renaissance. *As soon as it's warm enough, I plan to teach them the remainder, at least the geometry and trigonometry. Although I worry that like my students they have an eye only for the necessary.*

In his seclusion, I suppose, it was natural that he began to pay attention to the theater of nature, the way he had as a boy. Am I wrong to think that all of us—if left alone—would return to the same comforts?

Sometimes he was philosophical. In one letter, he wrote, *Certain categories of thinkers cross canyons. Before the same canyons, a mathematician—a scientist—takes only the smallest, most measured steps.*

There were drawings, too, on the backs of the letters or folded inside them. Truly remarkable renderings of the tiny lake as the fall came over it. Then the winter. Then the spring.

On the back of one envelope, in a loop of tiny cursive that twined around the postage, he'd written, *I come into the presence of still water.*

In Columbus, when I first read about the effects of MDA, I realized how lucky I'd been. Around the country, kids were dying—regularly enough to notice, if you were paying attention. In every college town and big city by then, an army of basement chemists had added the methyl group and turned MDA into MDMA, which first was called window but before long became known as ecstasy. Kids began passing out at raves. They began dancing and hooking up and jabbering in the glow of their own body heat, forgetting to drink at all, communing with the theological verities and releasing into the ether their instinctive commonality until the rising potassium in their blood stopped their hearts.

Somehow, I'd avoided such a fate. And by the time I arrived at Ohio State, at the age of most eighth graders, I'd somehow made up my mind to quit. I'd had an earlier start than my father, and I suppose this allowed me an earlier exit.

But still, I couldn't help thinking about what he'd said: *I guess it's over for both of us.*

Well, was it?

My first week in Columbus, I joined NA. Going cold turkey was easier than I would have imagined, although later, when I mentioned this to my sponsor, he stayed to talk to me after the meeting. He was a man my father's age, a night watchman who, like my father, reminded me of one of the Ford-plant occupants back home. "Folks like us," he said, pointing at himself first, then dropping his voice. "Easy stand. Easy fall."

In fairness, the jury remains out.

With my father removed from the picture, my soup of anger, sorrow, and bewilderment had finally found a place to cool. That first semester, I dabbled in art history and political science. The art history, at least, was interesting—and of course I'd had a head start. Sometimes I imagined my mother standing behind me in the classroom, smiling her insistent smile, and my father standing behind *her,* turning his head to snicker.

By the end of the fall, though, I'd declared mathematics.

Applied mathematics, anyway—which to my father might as well have been Himalayan transcendentalist studies. Because of my high-school curriculum, I went straight to the upper-level courses. My first day in Mathematics 5702, Curves and Surfaces in Euclidean Three Space, the professor took attendance and stepped to the blackboard, then turned to me and said, "Well, Hans, how *is* the great man?"

Summation

Salads

IT WAS FIVE years later—by which time, at barely nineteen years old, I was already the owner of a four-story brownstone in the West Village and a hundred-acre estate near Litchfield—that the envelope arrived in my office. The word PERSONAL, in heavy pencil, slanting down both sides. No return address.

Inside was a mathematics journal: *The Northern European Review of Enumerative Combinatorics,* volume 13, number 2. September 1999.

The fall I'd left for college.

Otherwise, nothing: not even a business card. Just an old rubber band around a poorly glued binding. On the cover, a single title had been circled in the same heavy pencil: a paper by Benedek Fodor, a mathematician I'd revered in graduate school. But the paper had nothing to do with Shores-Durban equilibria—in fact, when I glanced at it, I saw that it had nothing to do with my work at all—so I didn't read it. And I'd never even heard of the journal.

I was busy in those days.

If I'd already known of Earl Biettermann, of course, I would have read the article with great care; but Dad hadn't yet told me any of those stories. In fact, if it weren't for the esteem in which Fodor was held by just about everyone in my field, I would probably have just thrown away the whole thing.

But something must have stopped me: it might have been the rubber band. I'm no topologist, but I still have my feelings about stretchable curves. This one, drawn tight where it doubled around the binding, was beginning to crumble. Along one edge, as all such shortened annuli must minimally be, it had been twisted exactly twice. Whoever had sent it had taken care to minimize the twists and to migrate them to a single segment.

That was interesting.

But all kinds of my quant colleagues were in the habit of sending me all kinds of interesting quant things, and I usually had no time to even glance at them. I remember pulling the stretchy little noose off the binding and playing with it a little in my fingers. I might have even thought for a second about giving the article another look, but it was at that moment that my Southern Hemisphere terminals began chiming—the three rising low-pitched bongs that signal the opening of the São Paulo exchange—so I dropped the journal on a shelf, brushed off my desk, and sat back down to work.

BY THE END of that year, the rubble from the Trade Center had been cleared and most of our competitors had high-tailed it for either Connecticut or New Jersey, where they were running their tired old algorithms out of glass-and-brick low-rises with lawns around the parking lots. But not Physico. Over at 40 Wall Street, where I'd been employed since the morning they'd airlifted me out of graduate school, we'd kept our noses tight against the grindstone. For people like us, those were the halcyon days. The private equity markets on the West Coast had already made and lost their billions. The Dow had recovered. Bin Laden was on the run. The weak hands had folded, and now, apparently, we were all moving on.

The quants in particular were surfing a wave. At Physico, I was developing a strategy to capitalize on a certain species of put/call mismatch that existed fleetingly across a whole host of currency platforms worldwide. Didn't matter if those markets were headed up or down, of course. That was the point.

In those days—at the beginning of those days, anyway—I was about the only one doing it.

Two years before, on a Physico jet, I'd landed at Teterboro Airport, carrying a taped-up box of mathematics books and two fraying duffel bags, one of which contained the first third of my dissertation on Shores-Durban equations. By the end of the day, I was sitting in my own private office on the top floor of the Trump Building. From my window I could look west, back toward Columbus, and watch the weather roll in. There were no other traders on my floor, mostly because any red-blooded trader would have served me up on a skewer if he'd discovered how old I was, not to mention what I was about to do to his livelihood. The strategy I was developing was fundamentally conservative—every bet I made was soundly hedged—but it stood to put more than a few Wall Street types back in school.

It was not so conservative, I should add, that my employer wasn't making a potful of money on me pretty much right out of the gate. I happened to be the first one down the well with my particular drill. We bought and sold the prediction of just about anything, as fast as the hardware could do it. One of my early gambits was the spread between the futures that were traded in Chicago and the securities they predicted in New York City. I used the fastest computers in the world over a network of fiber optics that gave Physico Partners, over the 790 miles between my west-facing window and the LaSalle Street exchange, a microsecond execution advantage against just about any other house, large or small, on the whole Eastern Seaboard. As we quants liked to say ourselves: money in the bank.

From my first morning in a suit, I was placing well long of a hundred thousand orders in an hour. On my job interview, as a sixteen-year-old doctoral candidate in a scarlet-and-gray windbreaker and Birkenstocks, I'd been flattered into showing a group of men in Ferragamo loafers how Shores-Durban equations could forecast the swell and shrink of just about every type of large-market inefficiency that existed anywhere—inefficiencies that until that point had been dismissed as noise. I could tell that nobody in the room, not even the other stat-arb quants, understood exactly what I was talking about. Nonetheless, Physico took less than an hour to offer me a signing bonus that well exceeded the salary my father had earned over his entire career. I waited a few days to accept; but when I did, a limousine was dispatched to the front door of the OSU mathematics department.

Take that, Seth Kopter.

Two years into it, though, my system still wasn't perfect. I was still programming every night after the close, still triangulating my executions until they asymptotically approached the optimums for my newly hatched breed of computational microstructure trades, which, to put it boastfully (but accurately), swarmed like piranha around the clumsy, staggering hooves of our rivals. And I have to say, I was liking it. At any hour of the day or night, I was capable of laserlike concentration, knifelike thought, and hoglike greed. Occasionally, well into morning, my mind might crystallize into something more pure: I would glance at the stapled-together dissertation notes on my shelf and imagine Isaac Newton during the plague years, leaning over a table in Woolsthorpe-by-Colsterworth, deriving his fluxional calculus. But that didn't stop me. My Sharpe ratio was scoffing at the bulge bracket from the top of a very tall building. I could locate a micro-inefficiency anywhere in the world—Chicago, Hong Kong, you name it—and without even bothering with the indignity of leverage could turn a remarkably reliable profit in the nanosecond it took a cesium 133 atom to oscillate a bare handful of times between energy states. It was all fun and games.

In fact, I probably would have done it for nothing.

What really drove me was the thing I knew instinctively, every single day that I was swept up in that silent elevator to the seventieth floor of the Trump Building: that an even-more-accurate algorithm lay out there somewhere. I knew it in the way my father had once known, staring at the flats of San Francisco Bay, that he stood at the edge of absolutely the correct abyss. I would place my million trades a day, then sit at my glass-topped desk well into morning, doing and redoing every move in my mind.

Ah, recidivism. It's the fly in the ointment.

The only obvious problem with my life—that is, the only one I was worried about at the time—was that to a numerically inclined mind like my own, the economics of normal existence were becoming untenable. How could I go for a half-hour walk in Battery Park when it meant $25,000 in income? Was a coffee at Starbucks worth the price of a Mercedes?

I'd been raised on mathematics. Now I was starting to doubt a few of its dictates.

At some ungodly hour of the night, I would at last allow myself to quit. The empty elevator whisked me back down to the lobby, where Lorenzo, my Astoria-Italian driver, would be idling at the Pine Street entrance in his Town Car, waiting to take me home to the brownstone, which was on Perry Street near the river.

In the living room of that brownstone was a Mpingo coffee table that had cost as much as Lorenzo's Lincoln. I'd bought it with about an hour's salary.

THE FIRST DINNER my father and I had together in New York was at Le Pinceau. A warm, ginkgo-scented fall evening not that long after I'd started at Physico. I'd only seen him once during the whole time I was at OSU, a single weekend in the middle of my second year when I took the bus up to Michigan to talk with him about my thoughts on the Shores-Durbans. We ate every meal at the Green & White, and he gave me a couple of good ideas about the mathematics, which I have to admit might have been helpful if I'd ever gotten around to writing a dissertation.

Now, here he was in New York, looking rather well. Dapper, even. Pale linen suit and the old Borsalino. His belly was flat, and his

face was aglow with the burnished sunburn that he'd started to ex-
hibit despite the fact that he was living full-time in a woods. He
moved solidly across the dining-room floor to the seat across from
me. He'd flown in from Detroit, first class. Courtesy of me, of course.
I'd walked down the block from the office.

"I'll pay for my own dinner" was the first thing he said.

"No need. Really."

He looked around, smirking. "Not many mathematics professors
in here, I see."

"Not many Fields winners, anyway."

This softened him. Undoing his coat, he glanced at the menu.
"They serve decent scotch. I think I'll try the Laphroaig first. What
about you?"

"Nothing for me, Dad."

He raised his eyebrows, then smiled from one corner of his mouth.

By the time our appetizers arrived, he'd tried the GlenDronach,
too; and by the time the endive salad was rolled to the table and
dressed with ground peppercorns and a twenty-five-year-old Mo-
dena balsamic, he'd offered opinions on the St. Magdalene and the
Glenfarcias, each of which he'd dispatched in a single appreciative
slit-eyed swallow that looked a little bit like a snake putting the
final touches on a mouse. For the main course, he ordered a bison
steak and a mound of shoestring potatoes, then sat back for another
GlenDronach.

At a table a few feet from us that night was a young woman dining
alone. Not a derivatives trader. Not even in the financial business, I
could see from her wardrobe, whose warp and brownish palette
brought to mind sheep rather than tiger. I'd noticed her while waiting for Dad. She was pretty. She was sitting behind me, though, and
a little off to the side, so that I'd been reduced to angling my water
glass against the dining-room mirrors to get an occasional view of
her features. When my father ordered the first GlenDronach, I noticed in my reflector that she glanced up with hardly more than an
eyebrow. Still. She was older than I was—who wasn't?—but none-

theless a little young to be dining alone in a place like this, even in New York City: somewhere in her mid- to late twenties was my guess. I straightened my tie, which was a dark Hermès picked out by one of my secretaries, then nodded gravely over Dad's shoulder, signaling for the waiter. I was spending a lot of time in those days trying to look older.

"I didn't think she'd do it," my father grumbled, starting right in as we waited for our food. Of course, he was talking about Mom. That year, she'd finally contacted a divorce lawyer.

"She has her own future to think of, Dad."

"She used to think of mine, as well."

"Yeah—and then you left her."

He sniffed. "Well, fuck you, Son."

"Well, fuck you, Dad."

In my reflector, the girl raised her eyebrows again. I smiled into my water glass to make it clear that Dad and I were joking.

"Well, her future should be fine, either way," he said. "I'm sure the judge is going to take care of her in style."

"And she deserves it."

"Oh, so you're one of *those*."

"One of *whats*?"

"One of the apologists." He boomed the words, gesturing for another scotch. "Just like the two of them."

I didn't get a break from this kind of banter until after dessert, which he didn't touch. But at last he rose from the table to use the men's room. By then, I was pretty much beaten. I looked into my water glass and found the girl watching me. I smiled.

When the waiter arrived with another GlenDronach and set it at Dad's spot, I reached across and downed it.

A moment later, I heard, "That was a fast one."

I checked the glass: she was standing right behind me. "Oh," I said. "He won't even remember. I was actually doing him a favor."

"I was just on my way to the ladies' room."

I pointed. "It's over there."

"Thank you, yes."

Her voice was surprisingly southern and surprisingly lovely—though also surprisingly firm, like a magnolia trunk. (I could tell even then.) Her blouse was buttoned all the way to the neck, where a turn of white silk had been folded. And now I noticed that her nose contained a single, breathtaking bend, about halfway down. She pointed to the empty glass. "I hope you didn't actually need that."

"Well, I did."

"Just to speak to me?"

"You weren't here at the time."

"Technically not." She looked at me rather sharply. "That's your father, isn't it?" She nodded toward the far side of the room, where I saw now that he'd taken a seat at the bar. Another shot was being poured for him.

"Well, yes," I said. "It appears to be."

"Then if I were you," she said, turning to make her way, "I'd be a little more careful."

"You seem to be far from an apologist, by the way," she said.

"You were eavesdropping."

"You were spying."

"That's true," I said. "Could you tell?"

"Either that or you found the water in your glass extremely interesting."

"In fact, I *did*." I smiled. "The randomness of molecular behavior is overestimated. Brownian motion. It bears on my field."

She smiled back, not as though she understood the thought but as though she understood why I might have had it. "And besides," she said. "I wasn't eavesdropping. Your father's voice carries."

"He's a professor."

"Of math?"

"That's right." I felt a twinge. "Of *mathematics*. Or at least, he *was*. How'd you know?"

"The same way I knew you weren't an apologist."

We were on our first date. Every evening of that week, I'd left the Trump Building early and dined alone at Le Pinceau. I'd become transfixed. Transfixed and suddenly lonely—a strange turn for a man who'd never thought much about companionship. How did you find a person you'd spoken to only once in a city the size of New York? Actually, it was the type of mathematical problem for which my training had perfectly prepared me. An intersection of probabilities, each one small. After my sixth night at the same table—my sixth pepper steak, my sixth gratinéed potato, my sixth dully bubbling glass of mineral water—I was reaching for the door handle at the exit to head back up to Physico for my sixth round of late-night brainstorming, when the door opened ahead of my hand. *"Quod erat demonstrandum,"* I said, under my breath.

"You look as though you were expecting me."

Within moments, she'd agreed to dinner. (Sometimes, like my father, I could talk.) The waiter said nothing as he brought me my second pepper steak of the evening.

Texas. Small town. Alone in New York now, employed in book publishing. These were the facts, which she related to me while sitting straight, like a dancer, across the white-linened table. She kept her head tilted just slightly up, and I couldn't keep my eyes off that tiny bend* in her nose.

"Women's prison," she said.

"What's that?"

"Book publishing."

I pointed out the window, where, from up the block, 40 Wall Street was casting its stony stare at the sidewalk. "Then I suppose I'm in men's prison."

"Here's to the inmates."

When we set down our glasses of mineral water, I said, "I'm just

---

* For those who care for an approximation of the tilt and bend:

for $y = 0 \dots 180$, $x = 170e^{-.00016(y-23)^2} - 9.4e^{-.0025(y-47)^2}$.

wondering—how does a girl in book publishing manage to eat at Le Pinceau?"

"Carefully," she answered. "And occasionally. And using a little secret."

"Which is what?"

But she only smiled. She took another look around and asked if I minded going for a walk.

Minded?

I called Lorenzo (discreet nod of approval as he shut the door behind her) and had him bring us up to Central Park, where, sitting on a rough stone archway alongside the apple-scented horse trails, eating an oversalted pretzel from a cart, she told me about: (1) the collapse of her engagement (older man, a professor at her college); (2) her Hill Country childhood (rattlesnakes, imaginary friends); (3) her current dreams (children, a literary salon); (4) her family (brother, older, drying out for the third time).

She asked me about: (1) my own childhood (not much that I wished to recount); (2) my parents (the mulberry tree, the Art Institute, the cabin in the woods); (3) my sister (MIT, now Caltech, on faculty); (4) my work (the Shores-Durbans); and (5) my dreams (I'd never actually come up with any).

Like my father, I didn't want to talk about my life. Like my father, I fell in love with the first girl who asked me about it.

UNLIKE MY FATHER, however, I married her.

Non-Brownian Gray

DAD SHOWED UP in New York City one more time, a couple of months before the wedding. Audra thought I should have dinner with him alone, but she offered to join us for dessert. Le Pinceau again—his choice. The same five whiskeys with the same appetizers and the same main course. Then another couple of Laphroaigs as we waited for her to arrive. I'd seen him in his cups before, on plenty of occasions, but now he seemed to be pushing himself up one last, terrible hill.

By the time she joined us, the dessert plates were on the table. At that point Dad had finished off an Irish coffee, too. Not five minutes later, as he was telling her about his early years at Princeton, he knocked a newly arrived GlenDronach onto the floor, lunging for it and nearly going over himself. The waiter was there in a moment, but he didn't bring another.

"Doesn't matter," Dad said gruffly. "They've been watering them all night anyway."

I could see him fighting somebody. His head was circling. His chin had dropped, and he was looking out at the two of us over the tops of his glasses. Audra asked him about the Fields then, which warmed him for a moment. He was bred to charm any woman he met, and I understood that my fiancée was no exception. But when he finished telling the story of his trip to Warsaw, the head dropped again.

I leaned to Audra's ear and whispered, "I'm sorry about this."

"Don't be. It's not your fault." She opened her hand on the table, and I took it.

"You're lovely," Dad said suddenly, reaching for her other hand. She let him take it.

"You remind me of someone I used to know," he said. "Look at her, Hans. Isn't she a vision?"

"She is, Dad."

"Whom do I remind you of, Mr. Andret?"

He looked right at her, his eyes fixed on her face. This didn't rattle her in the least.

"Dad?"

He snapped his glance away. "It doesn't matter."

Then he descended into the true dark. He'd been picking at the cookies at the center of the table, but now he pushed them away and let his head fall all the way to his chest. He mumbled something. Then he snored. He woke cursing.

"Dad?"

"*What?*"

"Audra and I have to go now. I'll get you a cab."

"Good riddance, then."

But he got up with us and pushed back his chair. As we crossed the room, I had to take his arm to steady him. The last thing he said, after we'd made it past the bar but before we reached the door, was "Fuck you, Hans."

"Fuck you, Dad," I answered, patting him carefully on the back.

But he hadn't said it like in the old days. This time I could barely make out the words.

At the door, he stopped and made an attempt to gather himself. He tugged at his jacket, pulled his arm out of mine, and leaned heavily against the door to open it. Just after I went through, he said, "You two go wherever. I'm just going to sit at the bar for a moment and finish up some thinking I've been doing."

. . .

THE WEDDING WAS at the Winston Club in Sagaponack. Next to the grass tennis courts was a slate patio that turned out to be a landing pad. On the morning of the ceremony, four helicopters set down on it: Physico people, naturally, in their charcoal suits with slightly brighter ties. A couple of them might have been called my friends, but the rest had come mostly because they were beholden to me—to an underaged, corrupted mathematician who couldn't help observe that the distribution of monochromatic attire around the bar was further evidence of the Shores-Durban nonrandomness of profit-motivated entities. Together, we'd been trimming the world of its shaggy billions.

Almost all the rest were Audra's people, including the priest. Her people could be described as genteel, astute, and Texan. Country folk who read plenty of books and discussed them as though I'd read them, too, but who also knew how to mend a cattle fence. She and I had known each other not quite a year, a fact that seemed to worry half of them and please the other half.

Mom came by herself, and Paulie with a young man who might or might not have been a boyfriend—I could see my mother trying to arrive at a hopeful conclusion. By then, my sister had grown into a rather formal young woman. She was an associate professor now at Caltech in Pasadena. Homological algebra. She hugged me and kissed Audra on both cheeks, but I could see that she was no longer the girl who would catch a frog in her bare hands.

Well, I guess I wasn't the boy who would do that anymore, either.

As the ceremony approached, I calmed myself with some Shores-Durban extrapolations, and just before I went into the anteroom I indulged one last therapeutic pull from the gangster-style hip flask that had been offered to me by one of my charcoal-suited pals. Then I walked back out to the tent. A few minutes later, Audra stepped up the well-mowed aisle on the arm of her father and took her place across from me on the platform. The priest leaned forward and caught my eye, as if to say, *Are you all right in there?* The next thing I noticed was Audra lowering her chin, also to catch my eye, edging it lower until I smiled. She winked.

My mind cleared.

There are several possible explanations for why our marriage has lasted. Audra is forgiving, for one. In the end, I'm as impulsive as my own father; but like him, also, I'm obliquely hoping to be led.

Also like my father, I've always known when the solution is at hand.

DAD, AS YOU might have guessed, didn't make it to the wedding. I called him a week before, but all he said was "Yeah, I thought I answered that already."

Analysis Situs

A LITTLE MORE than half a decade later, on a warm afternoon in September, Lorenzo drove me out to LaGuardia to pick up Mom. I'd offered to come get her myself in Ohio, in one of the Physico jets, but she'd assumed I was joking. I'm not sure why. The winter before, when I'd flown out in one of those same jets to help her prepare the house, she'd watched from the front seat of a sporty new Ford Focus as the pilot taxied me right up to the parking lot fence. (It had been hard enough to get her into that car in the first place, I should add: the salesman from the dealership had to promise her he wouldn't try to sell the Country Squire to some other, unsuspecting soul— although my own guess is that by that point the old thing could barely have been sold for parts.)

In front of Terminal B now at LaGuardia, Lorenzo pulled the baggage cart behind us, loaded down with her strapped valises. With exaggerated Neapolitan grace he set them into the trunk of the Lincoln. As he did, she stepped off to the side to raise her eyebrows. "Very elegant," she whispered, once we were inside and moving. "You're living like a Medici, I see."

"Which one would that be?"

"Lorenzo, of course."

I laughed. "That's my driver's name, too, you know." I tapped on the glass. "Lorenzo, this is Mom."

From the front seat, the big Italian head tipped modestly to one side.

"Well, Lorenzo was the great one in that family," said my mother, leaning forward to tap the glass herself. "Most of the rest of the Medici were just—" She stopped.

"What, Mom? Bankers?"

"You know that's not what I mean. Several of them were popes, too, and one of them was the queen of France."

"That would be Caterina, madam," came Lorenzo's voice from the front. As we merged onto the Grand Central Parkway, he slid the partition the rest of the way shut.

Mom smiled. For a while she watched the traffic.

"Well, you've always wanted to come back east, anyway," I said.

"I have?"

"Yes, Mom. You have."

She sat back. Then, in an unhurried voice, she told me a few details about the move. What she'd kept, what she'd sold, what she'd given away. Then about the house, which she'd eventually managed to unload for a profit. I asked whether she had any second thoughts about coming to live in New York.

She didn't answer, just held up her purse. It wasn't a purse, actually, but an old Fabricus bookbag stretched until the zipper wouldn't close. Inside, I could see a stack of presents. "I'm looking forward to spending more time with my grandchildren," she said.

When the car idled at the tolls, she gazed out the window. It was a startlingly clear afternoon under a range of billowing cumulus; in the distance, Lower Manhattan shone in a precipice of light. She couldn't have picked a more inviting day to begin her new existence.

"By the way," she said. "When did I ever tell you I wanted to come back to the East?"

"You told me in Michigan."

"Well, frankly, I don't remember." She laughed. "Or maybe I just don't think about it anymore."

From the side window, I could see the Chase Manhattan tower shielding the Physico building from the north. It was a Saturday, and I needed to go back into work to run a few simulations.

She set her hand on my shoulder. "What are you thinking about?"

"You once told me how beautiful New Jersey was. You told me you hoped I'd get to eat fried clams on the beach."

She looked at me.

"Right before Dad turned down the job," I said.

"Oh, that." Her face darkened. Then she composed herself. She laughed again, turning back to the window. "Well," she said. "I don't think about *that* anymore, either."

WHEN WE'D FINALLY made it down to the Village, I pointed to the bulging bag of presents in her hand. "Have you been reading up on shock and awe, Mom?"

She blushed. "I just want to make sure they're happy that their grandmother is here." After a moment, she added, "Or I can parcel them out, if you think that's better."

"Of course they're happy you're here, Mom. Even without presents."

"Oh, sweetheart. You must not understand children yet."

At the house, Emmy and Niels were back from school. The two of them hadn't seen their grandmother in a while, and of course they were a bit bashful when I opened the door to the kitchen. Mom burst in the way she always does when she's nervous, letting out an overenthusiastic squeal. She clutched the misshapen bag to her side so that she bumped against the trim of the narrow door and caromed into the room like a pinball clanging off the bell. The kids looked up tentatively. But in a moment she was around the back of the counter and hugging them both, kissing them on their clean little heads while

Niels reached up to hug her and Emmy tried to get in one last bite of Cheerios. Meanwhile, Anna-Maria, the Ecuadorian nanny who'd started with us the month before, made her way out from behind the range island, smiling ecstatically, as though it were her own mother arriving without warning from a thousand miles away, and kissing her own two children on the head.

Mom was right. Within a minute, they were tearing through the things she'd brought. She slipped behind Niels the way she'd slipped behind Lorenzo at the airport. I turned away.

They were books, of course. Mostly art books.

That night, on the sofa, the three of them sat together reading them. Lorenzo had already driven Anna-Maria home. In those days, our kids liked to squabble with each other over just about anything, from whose milk had been filled closer to the top to which one of them had seen the quadruple peanut in the bag; but now they sat adoringly, one on each side of their grandmother. Like two disciples on the Giotto calendar page that used to look up at me from the floor of the Country Squire. Niels was on the right, where, just like in the painting, Mom was rubbing his foot; Emmy was on the left. Both of them had on their obligatory halos. Niels was Peter, of course (not that I know the first thing about such matters); but Emmy, it occurred to me, was Judas. Not because she would ever have betrayed anybody but because I could see that she was afflicted with certain thoughts that neither her brother nor any of the rest of us would ever have.

Mom calmed her. It was obvious. Emmy's brow was unwrinkled. Emmy's an Andret, through and through, but at that moment the Pierce quarter of her seemed to be exerting the same effect on her that in my own calmer moments it still exerts on me—the buffer against the storm of Andret genome that has tormented me for as long as I can remember.

One of the things I'd learned by that point, in fact, and for which I was already deeply grateful, was that Audra calmed me in the same way that my mother used to calm my father. On the day Mom arrived in New York, Audra and I already owned a house in the country but hadn't yet bought the one we live in now, all the way upstate and out of the way. Lorenzo's Town Car still sped me wherever I wanted to go. The stewards of legendary fortunes still called me every day. And yet the moment I took the seat next to Mom on the ride back from LaGuardia and closed the window to the horn-blaring cacophony of Terminal B, I felt myself enveloped in a nearly forgotten embrace. Really, it was a weighty thing. As we merged onto the Grand Central Parkway, the thick auto glass hushed everything, like a blizzard. There in front of me was the comforting bald shine of Lorenzo's Mediterranean occiput, rising cheerily from the headrest, and there around me was the childhood scent of my mother's soap. A peace fell over me like one I'd not known in years. I'd actually felt the urge to weep. But I'd turned to the window instead, where the landscape, looking strangely war torn, slid soundlessly past. My mother must have realized what I was feeling. Her familiar voice, in a cadence of reply—though I hadn't asked a question—had said simply, "It's good to be here, honey."

ON MONDAY, WE gave her a tour of her new apartment. It was two blocks from our house. Mom had stayed the weekend in our guest room, where Niels and Emmy had made an encampment on her floor. Her first night in New York, I'd tucked the two of them in on a pair of sofa cushions arranged around my mother's bedposts. On Monday morning when I checked in before work, I found three lumps in the bed. They were tight up against her like piglets. I could hear them all breathing: Niels as though climbing a hill, Emmy as though working the middle section of a test, and Mom as though reading the end of a Jane Austen novel. On the pillow, she opened one eye, smiled, and closed it again.

But the next evening, when we walked her through the new apartment, she said, "This won't do."

"What won't, Mom?"

We weren't two minutes into the tour. I was showing her the

kitchen, which had been remodeled by an Upper East Side firm, while Audra showed the balcony to the kids. Mom pointed below the marble counter at the two stainless-steel dishwashers. "I wash my dishes by hand, honey," she said. "Always have."

"Well, now you have a machine to do it."

We tried unsuccessfully to unlatch the handle of one of them, until I realized it was a sliding-drawer model. When at last we succeeded in getting it open, the electronics lofted up a pleasing arpeggio with the strangely recognizable cadence of "Well, Hello There, You!"

"Hmm," she said, peering over her reading glasses. "You know, you get things cleaner by hand."

"Well, now you don't have to."

"I *want* to."

"Ah."

"And I want the kids to, also. That's how you raise them. Not with dishwashers that pull out of the wall, and not with"—she hesitated—"a string of nannies." She used her hip to nudge the dishwasher closed, and it beeped a down-cadenced version of the same spry melody. With her glasses off she looked at me queerly, as though a strange but no-longer-threatening animal stood before her. "Of course you already know all this," she said.

AFTER TWO DAYS in the apartment, she invited us for dinner. Niels and Emmy had gone over ahead of time for their first Grandma outing, which we were surprised to discover had included the preparation of the meal. When I entered with Audra, Niels lost no time in informing us that they'd gone out to buy yesterday's bread at Pret A Manger, reviving its crust in the oven, along with last week's tomatoes from D'Agostino, which Mom had let Niels sauté in a pan and then Emmy cook into a frittata. At the center of the table it sat on a metal stand like a wedding cake. Mom pointed around the corner at Emmy, who, like someone else's child, was already scrubbing the pan in the sink. Audra's jaw actually dropped.

Mom moved behind Niels again, but again I wouldn't let her catch my eye.

AND THAT WAS how we lived, for a good long while anyway. Audra, who's always worked particularly hard, left for the publisher's every morning at seven. Forty-five minutes later, I walked the kids to school, then made my way back to the apartment, where Lorenzo would be waiting out front with the day's customaries: a triple espresso, a chocolate croissant from Flakey's, and the usual grooming kit unzipped to a set of German nail clippers and a Japanese razor. (On the far side of the pivoting desk there was also a pack of flossers, a tin of breath mints, a bottle of mouthwash, a shaving mirror, and four newspapers, all of them arranged on the tray like the tools of a particularly well-informed but hedonistic dentist.) In the afternoon, Anna-Maria delivered the kids to my mother's. At 8:30 or 9:00 in the evening, Lorenzo dropped me back at the house.

Mom changed everything. It wasn't that luxury didn't agree with her; it was just that she hated wasting anything at all—envelopes, tea, money of any denomination, time, or intellect. Squandering what the world had allowed us was to her the great sin of our epoch (a point with which I've come to agree). Within weeks, she knew most of the used-goods stores in Lower Manhattan. And the kids went along on her shopping trips as though exploring a newly charted land. Niels readied himself with a map. Emmy (who needs no map) brought along a reporter's notebook. One afternoon I opened it to a page that contained a matrix of milk, ice cream, and butter prices at all the markets in the neighborhood. She'd figured everything by the ounce.

Naturally, Mom also availed them of the art museums. I knew the more prominent ones myself—the Met, MoMA, the Guggenheim—from the money-related events I'd attended in their inner rooms. But Mom went further. She succeeded in doing for the kids what she'd once hoped to do for Paulie and me, on all those drives to Chicago. And the kids didn't even seem to mind.

Over the first months, they became familiar with just about every landmark, major or minor, on the New York art scene, from the Whitney to the Neue to the Folk Art. They went to the Chelsea and the Rubin and a whole slew of private galleries whose buzzered doors she scoffed at but still entered. The Frick didn't allow children, but she talked them in anyway. On weekends they went by subway to the Museum of African Art in Harlem and the Socrates Sculpture Park in Queens, where they picnicked from a wicker basket she'd bought from a street cart. I could well imagine all these expeditions: the kids, watching the paintings, being watched by Mom; Mom waiting saintlike for any sign of interest.

Emmy no doubt heartened her. Emmy will absorb whatever is presented—music, art, mathematics—and store it in the permanent collection. Niels will flit around like a bee. But when the bee settles on a flower, it settles.

I could imagine Mom charting their futures.

"They're interesting," she said to me one day. "They're not like you were at that age. Or Paulie, for that matter."

"Well, they've got plenty of Audra in them, too."

"Yes, yes, you're right." She nodded, as though the thought were new to her. "I can see that."

"Niels is like you," I offered. "More well rounded."

She eyed me.

"I mean that as a compliment."

"Thank you." She smiled, but after a moment, the smile thinned. "Emmy is the one—the one I worry about." She touched her head. "She could—"

"Yes, yes, I know."

"But she won't," said my mother. "We just won't let her."

OUR COUNTRY PLACE in Litchfield is an eighteenth-century colonial with a hundred acres of oak and maple out back. Out front is a brook whose course has been nudged with a backhoe so that it makes two gurgling passes beneath a pair of Japanese footbridges beside the driveway. At the loop of the bank, the old carriage house has been converted into an office—yes, the pads, the pencils, and the caramels, though not the boxes.

That's where I was when the phone rang one Saturday a couple of years ago. "Who's this?" I said, hearing a woman say my name on the line. Her voice prodded something in my memory.

"Cleopatra Biettermann," came the reply.

"Do I know you?"

"My husband and I are old friends of your father's. Cle Wells was my name then." She paused, taking a dramatic breath. "Your dad's not doing well, you know."

"How do you mean?"

"He told me that the two of you had some kind of falling-out. That's why I called."

"How's he not doing well?"

"When I spoke to him recently, he didn't sound very good."

I was still trying to place her voice. "Well," I said. "He can sound that way."

"I know he can." She paused. "Hans, your father is an extraordinary man. He's unlike anyone either of us has ever known."

"Well, on that point, we agree."

"Oh—" she said, inhaling sharply.

"What?"

"Nothing." Then she added, "For just a second there, you reminded me of him."

We were both silent. Then I said, "So, how exactly is he not doing well?"

"I think you need to go see him," she said.

7
Proof

Drunkard's Walk

ON THE PHYSICO jet, the waiter served a dry-aged New York strip with raspberry reduction and a plate of miniature asparagus spears under dill. In Detroit, I settled into a stick-shift Audi. I could have landed at an airport closer to the house, but I was looking forward to the drive. The GPS said 112 minutes.

I made it in ninety.

The thing is, I nearly missed the turnoff. That's how different it all was. The gravel road that in my childhood had curved down into a cedar-strewn swampland and over a shaky wooden bridge had been paved and straightened. Asphalt so black it looked as though it had been laid that morning. White lines down the sides like the stripes on a Ping-Pong table. At the intersection sat a new hotel—a Lakeland Suites with its bright green shamrock, slowly turning. Next door, a slickly rounded Speedway station, its line of pumps turned gold by the evening light. I had the thought that if I continued down that shining slice of pavement, I'd find a business park at the end.

And I almost did.

It was a housing development. Gray and beige saltboxes with steep green roofs, the dark living-room windows reflecting a dozen shimmering balls of flame as the sun moved down below the trees. Closer to the bridge stood a longer, lower construction with the same steep roof. A parking lot wrapped around three landscaped sides. I thought it might be a gym; then maybe a bowling alley; then a school. Then I read the sign: A SINNING MAN NEVER PRAYS—AND A PRAYING MAN NEVER SINS.

My father was passing a mega-church now every time he went into town.

Just before the creek, I made the sharp turn onto the rutted two-track. This part was paved now as well—the same darkly glinting asphalt and shining white borders. All of it burnished to amber by the evening. The old trestle bridge had been replaced by a steel one, with a fenced-in foot lane. On the far side, peeking from the trees every hundred feet or so, were driveways that ended in carved mailboxes—smallmouth bass and startled owls and friendly bears with their jaws open for the postman. People had taken to naming their cabins: TEES FOR TWO, A LONG DRIVE, ANGER'S AWAY! I could see the screened-in porches through the boughs and the lamps burning in the living rooms. Suddenly a row of streetlights blinked on.

Streetlights!

I'd last seen my father on the night at Le Pinceau with Audra—the night we had the falling-out that Cle Biettermann mentioned—and I'd last been up here to the cabin several years before that, when I was still a student at OSU. This entire transformation had taken place without me knowing. The lake was still the same humid brown, but it was dotted now with tiny white lozenges suspended in the darkness—speedboats on their shore hoists, glimmering in the long dusk.

A couple of hours after our dinner together in New York, when Audra and I had left him to his nightcap, Dad had thrown a tumbler against the wall behind the bar at Le Pinceau. Then a bottle. Then he'd stood and made his way down the row of $10,000 mahogany-framed mirrors, smashing them with a stool. When he collapsed, an ambulance had been called.

I know these details because I paid for them.

But in the few times since then that we'd spoken—the week be-

fore the wedding for one, and a couple of other, rather strained conversations after that—he'd avoided the topic completely. What I
knew was that he'd been sitting at the bar with a woman—a woman
who'd been kind enough to call me from Dad's phone when the para-
medics arrived to take him to New York–Presbyterian. As I pulled
the Audi along the darkening lane now, looking for the old gap in the
trees, I suddenly realized why Cle Biettermann's voice had sounded
familiar: she was the one who'd called me. She was the one he'd been
sitting with at the bar.

AFTER THAT, DAD and I stopped speaking almost altogether. In fact,
the next time I remember talking to him was one Sunday morning at
least a year after the wedding when he called me out of the blue. He'd
somehow latched on to the idea again that I was an apologist and that
along with Paulie and his soon-to-be-ex-wife, I was trying to ruin
him.

The phone had rung while Audra and I were asleep. "Now he
wants the whole house" was the first thing he said. No greeting.

"Who does?"

"The assassin."

That's what he called Mom's lawyer.

"Well, *you've* got the cabin. *She's* got to live somewhere, too, Dad.
Jesus, what time is it out there?"

"The same as it is out *there*. It's him, Hans. This is the assassin's
work. Your mother would never do anything like this."

"She might."

"What?"

"I said, she *might*."

"Don't tell me you're on *their* side again."

"I'm on nobody's side."

I thought I might have heard him take a swallow. I glanced at the
clock. "It's five-thirty, Dad. You know that, right?"

"Well, that's what time I get up these days."

I wasn't sure what to say to that. He didn't seem to know, either, so I waited.

"Are you keeping busy?" I said finally into the gap. "Are you working?"

"As a matter of fact, I am."

"Okay, good. On what?"

"On something. When I'm alone like this up here, I can think. I'm back on track."

"On track for what?"

His breathing changed. I could hear him deliberating. Finally, he said, "Who wants to know?"

"What?"

"Who asked?"

"*I* did. I want to know how you're doing. You just called me, Dad. You woke me up."

A silence.

"Things get out," he said.

"What kinds of things?"

"On the Internet. Things get taken."

"You think someone's trying to steal your work?"

"Computers have cameras now."

"Cameras? You think someone's taking screen shots of what you're doing?"

"Your mother. The assassin. All of them. People record everything. I'm talking about the Internet."

"I don't understand, Dad. You think people are watching you? You think someone's trying to steal your work off the Internet?"

"Kopter did."

Another silence. I was listening for the knock of the glass. Finally, I heard it.

Just before he hung up, he said, "Don't ever ask me to discuss my work again, Hans. Do you hear me? Don't ever ask that again."

.   .   .

ONLY THE LAST fifty yards resembled anything I remembered. Just before our turn, everything reverted, the pavement broken now by potholes and gashes and all the old spindly shrubs growing right through the blacktop. No streetlamps here, the Audi pushing slowly into the country dark. I opened the windows and smelled mud and iron. At the driveway, a fallen birch had been dragged just far enough to allow a car to pass. Rocks pinged the undercarriage. The parking area, which my mother had once cleared, and where I'd once watched my father bid farewell to Knudson Hay—and, later that summer, to all of us—had been taken over by wild. Curtains of vines around a narrow tunnel. At the end of it: the clearing. On the far side of that stood the cabin. Every light was off.

I'd called a couple of days before to remind Dad I was coming, but the connection had been bad. I'd given him the date and time, and right before we'd hung up he'd said in his thin voice, "All right, see you then," as though I'd been phoning from the corner about stopping over with some takeout.

I tried his number again now from the car. From the cabin I could hear the ringing.

When I hung up, I flipped on the high beams. Along the near wall, the siding was hanging with moss and was still patched with the same grayed-out sheet of plywood that had been there on the day my mother and sister and I had left. I pulled in behind a junky-looking car, my lights catching the holes in the rear where the FO of the logo dangled. It was an old Taurus. The trunk was spotted with Bondo, and the windows were whitened with ghosts of mud, as though the clouds had been dropping pellets of dust all summer instead of rain. On the trunk, someone had written WASH ME.

At least he was going into town, then.

A hundred feet down the bank, the lake was rippling. At the end of the beach, the lights caught a pair of metal legs protruding from the thicket: the old dock sections, thrown down on their sides. He hadn't put them back in the water after winter.

I wondered which winter that might have been.

Closer in, an angled bush stuck out halfway across the clearing. I peered into the dimness until suddenly I recognized it: the hull of the *Victory,* pinned down by vines. Behind it, the same blunted shape of the *Royal Sovereign.*

I shut off the engine and stepped out into the chirping night. "Dad?" I called.

Around the near side of the house, my eyes found a track through the undergrowth. Behind the screens on the porch, the old pair of wicker chairs stood next to the table. On the table, a glass.

I called out again, this time toward the upstairs.

At the rear, hidden in the gloom, I stumbled on a row of teepeed beans and a narrow patch of what looked like lettuce. At the far end, clusters of tiny tomatoes were silhouetted in their planters.

He was keeping up a garden, then. Also a good sign.

The porch stairs had been repaired with planks—a pretty competent job of it, actually: firm under my step, and the handrail steady. Through the dusty windows I could see nothing. I knocked on the door. "Dad?"

When I pushed it open, the only sound was the lap of water through the screens. I flipped the switch, but nothing came on. I flipped the next one. Was he not paying the electric bill? I took a few steps in and searched until I found the old lamp in the corner of the dining room. The same place it used to be. In the blackness I felt for the pull cord. To my surprise, it worked.

I looked around. The place was being neatly kept, at least. Another good sign.

Alpha

My FIRST SATURDAY at Stillwater Farms, Audra and I took a long walk together in the fields behind the center. Stillwater, which rented its excess acreage to the local farmers, seemed to be about the only business in that corner of rural New Hampshire that was turning a profit—although I doubt it depended on the crops. As a numbers guy, in fact, I'd admired the fiduciary spirit of the place from the moment I'd first laid eyes on its costs sheet. The local agriculture seemed to be part of the treatment philosophy as well, providing a serene but eminently practical view for the patients. I must say that I found it eminently and serenely therapeutic myself. Especially on those cool north-latitude afternoons when I was allowed to take an hour's walk with my wife.

In the distance, one of the farmers was driving a dark green tractor through the rows, a churn of dust following. I could see clods flying up behind the tilling blades, like mice jumping up from the fields. I was six days into my stay, and I realized I still felt like one of those mice.

Audra was here for the weekend. She'd been at a group meeting with me in the morning, then at a therapy session with me in the afternoon, and she'd be at another group meeting that evening with the other spouses, followed by the nightly speaker. Tomorrow she was flying back to New York. "Oh, Hans," she said, taking my hands and looking steadily into my eyes. "Thank God we did this."

Since my arrival, the nurses had been looking into my eyes just as steadily, with their pen lights.

"I'm glad, too," I said.

"I feel like we were snatched from an abyss."

"Maybe we were. I hope that's right." My gaze went to the farmer in his tractor. I noted that even this far into my stay, my initial thought persisted: that rather than being snatched from an abyss, I was being thrown into one.

I also knew, however—as I was learning to say that week—that this was the drugs talking.

AT STILLWATER, WE were encouraged to share. My suitemate, a garrulous man from a West Coast division of Wells Fargo, had no difficulty with the assignment. He was in the same business as mine, but on the retail end, peddling risk to attorneys and dentists. I bought and sold the shadow of the prediction of risk, for some of the richest men in the world, at a million times per second.

But these are details.

Stillwater was a far cry from Walden Commons, where my father had once been funneled into his own obligatory furlough. On the web, Audra had found the place in a single afternoon, along with several dozen reviews of its food, accommodations, gym equipment, and rate of recidivism. At the airport in Newport, a staff member picked me up in a Volvo, Vivaldi sparkling on the audio. A concierge nodded as he checked me in. An aide accompanied me to my room. Instead of searching my bags, he introduced me to my suitemate— the man from Wells Fargo—as well as to the trays of mints and macadamias in the pantry, the jars of juices in the mini-fridge, and the service intercom, which was available around the clock. Also, he pointed out where the ice maker could be found.

I was left alone to unpack.

Stillwater, in fact, made quite a show of not caring about the obvious. About what we'd brought with us, for example. About whether we would complete the treatment. The perimeter gates were kept unlocked, and the doors to the meeting rooms were always propped open. The Volvos were constantly available out front, their radios tuned to the classical station. In the coat closet of our Perry Street brownstone the week before, I'd divided a baggie of mid-Andes Bolivian between a stripped-out thumb drive and the battery compartment of my key-chain flashlight. When I landed in Newport, the flashlight was in my pants pocket and the thumb drive in my laptop. At Stillwater, nobody even checked.

We had to *want* to change.

My first evening in-house, I closed the door to my room, lowered myself into the leather chair, pulled out the thumb drive, and ruminated on its meaning. I was only half convinced that I needed anything to change. At that moment, actually, I'd say a good deal less than half. Even through the cap I could taste the bitter.

The picture in my mind was of Audra, backed up stiffly against the curtains. "Please don't," she was saying.

WELL, READER: *I didn't.*

That night was my first clean one in—how long? Half a decade? No, longer—it's hard to even remember.

MDA, it turns out, had been the quaint days. I wasn't a philosopher anymore. My thoughts didn't have anything to do with Sartre or Camus (or even Gödel or Frege). They generally had to do with mathematics. Mathematics in the modern world. That is to say: with money.

It pretty much becomes your life, I'm here to report.

So, why was I suddenly willing to change? It could have been my own cleaned-up version of the old Andret willpower. It could have been Audra's magnolia-trunk voice, still ringing in my ears. It could have been the beta blockers that Stillwater had prescribed at intake. It could have been the kids. But whatever it was, it held, just long enough that I'm here recounting all of this now. Stillwater assigned us to a course of lectures and meetings and to an exercise class before every dinner, and that night and the next day I went through all of it, clean and quiet and sober.

The therapeutic idea, I guess, was not to allow *too* many minutes—at least at first—for our own thoughts.

Well, what would those thoughts have been? That it was all pointless? That I was bound to fail, to follow the same, sad path that my father had? That it was, indeed, *over for me?*

Audra insists this is nonsense.

The Thursday before, I'd come home late from work. With the time differences to the Asian markets, Thursday nights were my ramp-up into the weekend. I remember needing my bother to go away. I remember needing to get back up on the elephant. Earlier in the day, in just a couple of hours, I'd cleared a medium-sized fortune for the firm—maybe twenty million—short and long on a pile of interest-only tranches that were bouncing like ball bearings on a flash currency raid out of Hong Kong. It was my third-best showing of the year.

At the brownstone, I'd found Audra in the kitchen. When I walked in, she was sitting at the table with Emmy, who was eating a bowl of cereal with bananas before bed. Niels must have already been upstairs.

Until then, I'd kept it out of the house. Even on the weekends, I'd kept it out of the house.

As soon as I entered that room, though, I knew that tonight was going to be different. The world had dulled. Dulled and darkened—over months, I'm talking about—but suddenly it was about to wink out. Maybe it was because of the day. I was still irritated by a certain slant in the run, a slant in which the Shores-Durbans had missed a decent-sized slice of the pie. To the tune of maybe two and a half million. I was sure they could have gobbled it, but they hadn't. *They fucking hadn't gobbled it.*

I was going to discover why.

If I could only get the world to shed its dark. I kissed my wife and daughter. As soon as possible, I stepped back out to the living room.

"Wait a minute," said Audra, a moment later, entering from the kitchen.

I was leaning down over the Mpingo coffee table.

"What are you doing?" she said, backing up against the curtains.

I lowered my head hungrily. With one eye I glanced up. "What do you mean, what am I doing?"

"Wait. Wait. Wait. What is this, Hans? Are you kidding me?"

I sprang up and shot through the kitchen door for the refrigerator, which dispensed the glacial ice water that I craved. I was alive now inside a flickering shell of light. At the table, Emmy looked up from her cereal bowl and said, "Hey, Daddy-o."

"Hey, love." I kissed her on the forehead.

Back in the living room, I mouthed to Audra, "North of twenty sticks today, babe."

She was still standing wide eyed against the curtains. She whispered, "What? Please, Hans—what is this?"

"North of twenty today, Aud!" It might have come out as a shout. "Not bad. Come on, honey. Sit down with me and celebrate!"

On the way home, I should also mention, Lorenzo had dropped me for a quick stop at one of the boutique hotels downtown. I'd done a couple of nice bumps there, too, with another quant I knew, on the dazzling glass towel shelf in the dazzling marble bathroom of a dazzlingly opulent bar. In those days, though, a bump lasted about as long as a breath.

"Hans," said Audra. "I have no idea what you're doing right now. In front of me like this, in your own house, and with your own daughter *right there*." She pointed through the wall. "What is this? Is this a joke?"

"The door's closed, Aud. She can't see anything."

I should also add: it wasn't as though my wife had never seen it before, herself. She'd even *done* it with me, once, early in my career—

some diluted Mexican street puff at a party during my first year in New York, on the medium-fancy roof deck of a midlevel, Midtown customer whose account already meant just a little less than nothing to me. I hadn't exactly pretended to be new to it all.

"Stop looking so shocked," I said. "How do you think I've been making all this bank?" I powered down the last of the water and shook the ice cubes onto my tongue. When I bit down I couldn't tell whether it was the cubes that were breaking or my teeth. "How do you think I've been making our shiny little nut, sweetheart? You think I just do all this *on my own?*"

She retreated into the kitchen. I heard her cellphone open. I heard it close. "What?" she said again, reappearing in the doorway, running her hands through her hair. Her mouth made the shape of a scream, but what emerged was a short, breathy wheeze. I was hunched at the table, licking up the dust.

"How do you think I've been keeping us inside our little pyramid of fancy?" I said. With quivering fingers I pointed at the blazing French Empire chandelier above the fireplace. The room was alive now with light. I ran those fingers across my gums and sucked.

Her next scream was real.

A Topologist's Apology

As I walked back through the cabin, I tried the rest of the lights. The dining nook. The staircase. The porch. They were all burned out except for the one behind me in the living room. In the narrow hallway, I took my phone from my pocket and held it in front of me, the dull-yellow walls and worn floors easing forward out of the dark. Finally, at the pantry door, the old fluorescent lamps flickered on.

The kitchen was clean, too. A couple of washed plates in the rack. A sponge standing in the sink. Water still dripping from the tap. I shut it off. "Dad?" Alongside the refrigerator I found the old broom on its peg. With its splintered handle I rapped the floor, the way Mom used to do when it was time for breakfast. "Dad?" I called out, rapping it again. Behind the cabinet doors were a few supplies. Vegetable oil. A jar of pickles. A loaf of wheat bread. In the refrigerator, a pack of hot dogs and a quart of milk.

I pulled out my phone again and dialed. From the living room came the startlingly loud ring. When I found the extension, the light on the answering machine was blinking. I knew what it would say, but I held the glow to it anyway: messages full.

I stepped to the bottom of the stairs. "Dad?"

Through the side window my glance fell again on his car. I saw now that it had a flat tire—left rear, all the way to the rim. He wasn't driving, then. Someone must be doing his errands for him.

A woman.

If I waited here, would he walk in with her? Standing at the window, I understood that this was exactly what he'd done. In five minutes, in an hour, he'd be coming in the door with some rumpled young thing on his arm. That's what I had to prepare for.

Or I could just drive back up the road to the hotel.

But then what? He wasn't even checking messages. When we'd spoken, I'd told him exactly when I'd be arriving. He wouldn't have forgotten: dates were numbers.

In the shallow closet at the rear of the pantry, I found the old sheets from my childhood bed. Stiff but still clean enough.

Upstairs in my old bedroom, the table lamp still worked. The same ancient shades with their bent-twig pulls still hung over the windows. The same oval rug still covered the floor. Paulie's framed drawing of a sunrise, still propped next to the mirror. I pulled the sheets over the mattress.

What kind of woman would choose a life like this? The tidy kitchen, the tended garden. But you still couldn't get around the fact of what it all was.

When I pushed open the door to my parents' room, I was wary. I guess I expected to see the first real evidence of whoever she was. I flipped on the light, and what I actually noticed was that it didn't look at all like the rest of the place—the blankets on the bed had been pulled into a heap, and the floor was scattered with cigarette butts. She wasn't taking care of him: that's what crossed my mind. It was only then that my eyes traveled across the room and saw that in the chair by the window sat an enormous, wild-haired man, staring out into the dark.

"I'm sorry," said a high voice. The head didn't turn. In the glass I saw the face.

"Oh, God—" I said.

The voice was a young girl's. It was my daughter Emmy's.

"It's you, Hans," he said feebly. "It's you, isn't it?"

"Oh, God, Dad. It *is*."

I'd seen him ill before, but this was different. He looked like two men—a fat one sitting on a thin one. His flesh had been stretched to bursting, and the weight of it had pulled him forward over his knees, where his huge arms hung like two more legs. They almost touched the floor. He was panting, and through his swollen eyelids he looked out from a pair of tiny crescents. At the corner of one, I could see a bloody wedge. That's where my gaze finally settled, on that rheumy red triangle at the side of his eye, which still seemed somehow like a view inside him.

"What's happened, Dad?"

"Entropy."

"It's okay."

"No, it's not. It's not okay at all. I'm sick." He lowered his head. Then, in his strange new voice, he added, "I'm sorry, Hans. I truly am."

IN THE KITCHEN I heated a hot dog in the skillet and brought it upstairs on a piece of bread. The hot dog and the bread were the only things I found that weren't inside a bottle.

"Entropy always wins," he said.

"I guess it does."

"What are you doing here? Did she call you?"

"She did, Dad. If you mean Cle."

"It's none of her business."

"Well, it's *my* business now. How come you didn't tell me?"

"What was there to say? I have something wrong with me. Dr. Gandapur can tell you the rest tomorrow."

"Does Mom know?"

He turned slowly to the wall. Then he looked down at a newspaper that was trampled on the floor. After a moment, he said, "Wait a minute—today's not Tuesday, is it?"

"It's Sunday."

"Well, the doctor comes tomorrow anyway. Every Monday and Wednesday." He smiled weakly, then returned his gaze to the window. "Turn off the light."

"What?"

"Just turn it off. Then come over here."

In the dark, the smell was stronger: bourbon and sweat and a sweet rankness like an open can of corn.

"Look at this," he said. "You can see the road." When I reached him, he managed to lift an arm to point. "I can see all the way to the end. Saw you drive up. Saw you poking around down there." He was panting. "It's all changed, hasn't it?"

Through the glass we watched a car advance along the cove. Halfway around, it turned in at a driveway, then stopped at a house. The garage door slid up. A flat of light elongated itself onto the surface of the lake, then retracted.

After a time, he looked up. "Well," he said, "thanks for coming, anyway."

The Prisoner's Dilemma

"AND IT SURPRISED you?" said Matthew. "It surprised you that your wife was so upset?"

"I have to say that it did."

"My God," said Audra.

Matthew was my therapist. I didn't know his last name. Stillwater didn't use last names. He was a bristling, muscly guy in his fifties—retired military, maybe—with an unexpectedly kind face. A powerful combination. And he did things his own way—a fact that I've since come to appreciate greatly. The first thing he ever said to me was "Welcome to Vermont, Hans, from one addict to another." Coke, booze, and gambling—those had been his own particular musketeers. This kind of matchmaking was one of the reasons the place was so expensive.

"And Audra," he said, turning, "tell me. You mean to say that you didn't know your husband had been using for—for what is it now, Hans?"

"I don't know. A couple of years."

He glanced.

"Two or three, or so," I offered.

He glanced again.

"No, I didn't," said Audra. "I didn't know."

"I'm sorry, honey. I just needed something to calm me."

"You needed cocaine to *calm* you?"

"Yes."

Matthew smiled. Familiarly, it seemed. "And why do you suppose"—he turned to me—"why do you suppose you picked that way to do it, Hans? Why in front of your wife, and with your daughter right there in the next room? Most addicts I know would have gone out of their way to *hide* it. Most addicts would have made it their number one *priority* to hide it."

"I wasn't doing it in front of my wife. And I wasn't thinking about my daughter. I was just doing it. In my own house. On my own time. They happened to be around."

"We were in our kitchen."

"Okay. In the kitchen."

Audra glanced at Matthew. Matthew cocked his head.

Audra said, "*Please,* Hans."

"Really," I said. "There really wasn't any other reason. The balloon was coming down. I just needed to get it back up in the air."

THAT WINTER, WHEN I'd stopped off in Tapington to help Mom ready the place for the realtor, she'd picked me up at the Springfield Airport. (Her new car was five months old by then, and it had a total of 235 miles on the odometer, *including* the 35 she'd driven to pick me up.) When we arrived at the house, I found that she'd been in the middle of packing up Dad's things. At that point, he'd been gone for close to ten years. He'd left nearly everything, and it looked as though most of it—if not all of it—was still there. She was sorting things into boxes. "You're not taking any of this with you," I said, "right?"

"Right, honey. I'm giving it away."

"Well, good, Mom."

I don't think she'd ever really hoped for his return; but maybe she'd thought it was important to keep his memory there for Paulie and me.

Or perhaps it was just that she'd always felt insignificant without him. That's possible, too. My father might have been right about that.

In the house, the living-room shelves were still crowded with his mathematics books. A boxful of tumblers was still taking up a corner of the pantry. I even found his winter coat still hanging on the metal bar in the hall closet. When I lifted it, it gave off the faintest odor of cigarettes.

The house looked entirely the same.

"I only kept it this way for you and Paulie," she said. "Just in case one of you decided to come back. But of course, neither one of you did. I can't say I blame you."

"I liked growing up here, Mom."

"Well, that makes me happy."

Slowly, we worked our way through the rooms. On the window-sill of the upstairs bath, the faded spine of my old *Scientific American* puzzle collection stood among the books. When I slid out the hard-back next to it—*Women Artists of the Romantic Era*—a gold pendant dropped out. "What's this?" I said. "It looks like some kind of saint."

"Oh, that? Yes—I think it must be Saint Francis."

"Is it yours?"

She reddened. "Yes, it's definitely Saint Francis, for what it's worth. Of Assisi. I guess I didn't feel right getting rid of it."

"What's on his head?"

"A sparrow." She took it from my hand. "Saint Francis spoke to the birds, you know." She shrugged. "I'm sure your father would have said he was crazy."

"Yes, he would have."

She shook her head. "You know, Dad once stole something from my apartment. Can you believe it? Just after we met."

"What was it?"

"A crucifix. He pulled it right off my wall."

"Ha."

"I took it to mean he was sensitive."

I laughed.

"Anyway, that's why I kept Saint Francis in the art book, because I knew he'd never look here." She folded its chain and nestled it behind the cover again. "I know what you're thinking," she said.

"What?"

"That I don't need to hide it anymore."

"I'm not thinking that, Mom. But you're right, you don't."

She lifted the window shade and glanced out at the stream behind the house. At that time of year, it was nothing more than a curled ribbon of ice. Some kind of dull-gray winter bird was hopping on it. "Just so you know," she said, "I don't believe in any of it. But that doesn't mean it doesn't console me."

"How's it been out here, Mom?"

She let the shade drop. "Cold. But not so bad."

"I mean, how's it been living out here by yourself?"

"Oh, that's such old news." She pulled a dried washcloth off the shower rod and dropped it into the laundry chute. "After a year or two, I didn't even miss anybody."

"Really?"

"Well, certainly not your father. And the two of you—maybe not as much as you might think. Mostly that's true. Mostly it's been okay." She stepped into the hall and moved toward the bedrooms. "Living without the two of you has been a little hard sometimes."

"Well, you'll have *me* now, Mom. And your grandchildren."

"And Audra. And Paulie. Paulie will fly out to see us."

We stepped into my old bedroom now. The books on the desk there, the smell of the sheets, the hammock springs inside the mattress—it was all an artfully preserved diorama. The only thing changed was the ficus, which had grown at least a foot and a half. It looked like a teenager I hadn't seen in a couple of years.

Next to it by the window, Mom lifted herself up onto the ledge and sat bumping her heels against the wainscoting. She actually did appear to be happy. There was something about her that was still girlish. Was *more* girlish, even, than before. She was sixty-one. "The ficus looks good," she said. "Doesn't it?"

"You dust the leaves, don't you?"

"Yes, I do." She rubbed her thumb across one of the tips. "Otherwise they don't breathe."

"Amazing."

"I'm just a housewife." She shrugged. "And not even a very good one, at that. I couldn't even do *that* very well. Your dad was right. Maybe I would have been better off with another kind of person."

Out the window, a pair of squirrels began shaking the mulberry. I peered out at them. They were hunched in the seam of a bough, chattering, and now and then one of them would race up and down the trunk. When I was a boy, my father had given me my first lesson in differential calculus under that very bough. "I hope you don't really believe that," I said.

"Believe what?"

"That you didn't do it well. That you didn't belong with someone like him."

"Well, part of me does."

"Dad was ill, Mom. He was—I don't know—"

"I don't want to talk about it." She turned, crossing her arms. "Your father's astonishing," she said. "That's what you need to remember." She hopped from the ledge and began folding towels from the laundry basket. I rose and turned the ficus on its saucer. The soil was dark with moisture, the surface dotted with tiny beads of white.

"You keep fertilizer on it, too," I said. "Don't you?"

"And I rotate it. For the light."

I looked at her.

"I don't have that much to do, honey."

"Did you ever find anything in here, Mom?"

She raised an eyebrow. "What would I find in there?"

"Here. In the ficus pot." The loam came up in moist clumps in my fingers.

"Hans, what on earth are you doing?"

"Did Dad ever tell you?"

"Tell me *what*?"

"About *me*?"

"I don't know," she said. She went back to folding the towels, but in a moment she looked up again. "What would he have told me about *you*, sweetheart?"

"It's a long story," I said.

"AND DID *YOU* tell her?" said Matthew.

"No, actually. I didn't."

"What?" said Audra.

"Not then. But I did. Eventually."

"Eventually?" said Matthew.

"The other day."

"You just told her *now*?" said Audra.

"Well, yes." I attempted a smile. "I skipped a couple of steps."

"And what did she say?" said Matthew.

"She was really surprised. Shocked, I guess."

"You didn't expect anything different, did you, honey?"

"I'd always thought—I don't know—I'd always thought that she *did* know. Once Dad did, anyway. Even though—" I shook my head.

"Even though, *what*?" This was Matthew.

"Even though I knew that Dad wouldn't tell her himself."

"And he didn't?"

"I guess not."

"Honey, if she'd known, of course she would have said something. *Your* mother? She would have worried her hair out."

"I didn't think about it like that."

"So you somehow convinced yourself that she knew," said Matthew. "Just because your father did—even though you were well aware that he'd probably never tell her."

"And you convinced yourself that if *she* didn't care—" This was Audra now.

I shrugged. "Yeah, then why should *I*?"

"It's strangely logical," she said.

Matthew smiled. Then he let a silence fall. The silence went on. With one hand he crumpled a sheet of paper and threw it across the room into the trash can.

"Nice shot."

"But that's not all," he said. He crossed his arms and looked over at me.

"Not all of what?"

"You're not telling all of it."

"Yes, I am."

"Why did you not tell your mother?"

"Because I figured she already knew. Either Dad would have told her or she would have figured it out."

"Yes, you've said that much." He crossed his arms and stared again. Then he glanced out the window. He crumpled another sheet of paper and without looking threw it into the trash can. "Well?"

"I'm a mathematician, Doctor."

"Indeed you are. Although I'm no doctor."

"Mathematicians require proof."

"And there's no proof?"

"No."

"But tell me, don't mathematicians play their hunches?"

"Yes, of course they do. But they don't publish them."

"Why don't you just give us your hunch then?" said Matthew. "Off the record. Why did you tell your father but never your mother."

He crossed his arms once more and stared at me in his placid way. So did Audra, in her own placid way. She actually crossed her arms, too, as though the two of them had trained together.

I finally said, "Because I didn't want to betray her."

Theodicy

I HEARD THE click of the cabin's front door and a few moments later the sound of things being set down on the table, then of the kitchen cabinets opening and closing. Finally, shuffling on the stairs. When the bedroom door opened, a tall, finely dressed man stood holding a medical case. He looked startled, then pleased.

"Your son, I presume?" He set down the case and offered me a hand. He was Indian or maybe Pakistani, the skin on his face still youthful but the eyes genially wrinkled. He might have been Dad's age. "Daneesh Gandapur," he said, bowing.

"Danny," said my father. "Or Dr. G. That's what I call him. Everyone else around here calls him Gandhi."

"Well, they couldn't be more wrong about that."

"A pleasure, Dr. Gandapur. Hans Andret."

"Sir, the pleasure is mine."

Dad pulled out a cigarette. "Hans is here for a couple of days."

"Ah, yes. Very good, then. See, Milo, it is nice to have a little company, is it not?"

"I told you, I don't need company. Don't need anything from anyone."

The doctor set down his belongings. "Not even your own son?" He glanced over at me.

"All I want is to be alone."

Dr. Gandapur shook his head.

"Dad said you're taking good care of him," I offered.

"As well as can be achieved under the circumstances." He glanced at the cigarette in Dad's mouth. Then he bowed again slightly, first to Dad, then to me. "And it is permissible for me to continue while the young man is present?"

"I suspect the boy's seen worse, Danny."

"I suspect he has."

The doctor arranged his supplies on the edge of the bed like a vendor arranging his wares. Dad watched, still puffing on his cigarette. But his eyes gleamed now as though he were about to receive a fix of the most astonishing drug in the world.

"I'm going to request that you put that out now, Milo."

"Whatever you say, Danny." He dropped the butt onto the floor, where his shoe moved over it like a slug over a leaf.

"And you have emptied your bladder?"

"Of course I have."

Two chairs came over next to the bed now, and the doctor helped Dad shift into one of them. My father lifted his shirt. Wrapped around his huge midsection was something like a truss—a shiny plastic girdle tightened with thick laces at the center. When the doctor untied it, a quivering mass of belly burst out, like a sandbag falling off a wall. It yanked Dad forward. He steadied himself, unbuckled his pants, and pushed the waistband down over his knees. When he inched his legs apart, the sandbag toppled the rest of the way out until it spread across the second chair. It was a jiggling, gargantuan version of the belly I'd first seen at the Tapington swimming pool, a dozen years before. He was straining from the weight.

From the edge of the bed, Dr. Gandapur reached across and scrubbed the skin. Then with one palm he slapped the flesh, which trembled like Jell-O. With the other, he made a swift movement, and when the Jell-O stilled, I realized with a start that a needle was poking out from the center of it. There was another flurry of motion, and now a coil of tubing curled from the needle. The doctor attached the other end of it to a jar. I turned away. When I turned back, fluid had appeared. A narrow straw-colored column that emerged from inside his body and pushed hesitantly around the loops, like a timid snake exploring the room. At the far end, drops began to trickle. At first, just a few; then more and more, until after a time, it sounded like he was peeing into a cup. When the first bottle was full, Dr. Gandapur switched to the second. Then the third. All the while, Dad's face was brightening.

When at last the needle was withdrawn, the man who rose from the chair looked something like my father again. The truss lay behind him on the floor. His belly slid easily back into his pants. "Lord, oh Lord," he said, coming forward, "I can breathe again."

He crossed the room and shook my hand, then the doctor's; then, from a bottle on the dresser, he poured us all a round of bourbon.

"BY CHANCE YOU took note of what I did for him?" said the doctor. He set his case on the kitchen counter and poured his drink down the drain. I took a sip of mine, then did the same. We'd left Dad dozing upstairs. "That was called a paracentesis," he said. "About a paracentesis there is little beyond the obvious. You place the trocar and allow the fluid to seek its own level." He smiled, busying his hands with his tool bag. "And yet it means everything for his comfort."

"Thank you, Doctor. I see that it did."

"I'm just pleased that I can do something to ease his burden. You know, I count your father as a friend now."

"That's generous of you."

He glanced. "And despite his condition, he is still the man who proved the Malosz theorem." He seemed to bow slightly at the words. "Of course, either of these two things would have been more than enough to bring me by."

"You know the Malosz theorem, then?"

"Of course I do. Your father would not have told you, but I once hoped to be a mathematician myself." He looked up at me. "Although it did not take me long to abandon the project."

"That would make two of us."

He reddened. "Except in my case, Mr. Andret, it was because it was beyond my capabilities." He opened the bag again. "Your father has of course spoken of you."

"What was your field?"

"Well, I suppose you could say I was a geometer." He continued busying himself with his instruments. "The only problem was that the Lord failed to inform me early enough that I was no good at it." Into his pocket went the stethoscope. "Treating a man like your father, however, remains one of the privileges of my profession. One does not encounter many Fields Medalists in these particular woods."

He moved to the counter then and picked up one of the bottles of liquid. "What we have here," he said, holding it to the light, "is the by-product of his cirrhosis. The fluid presses against his lungs until his existence, if I may be blunt, becomes rather uncomfortable." He tightened the lid and set the bottle into a box. "It feels like trying to breathe inside a packed suitcase. This is when I drain him. Whenever it is done, he can look forward to a period of relief."

"Really? How long a period?"

"This varies. A week or two. A month, perhaps."

"And then?"

"Sometimes the relief persists. He is a formidable person, your father. But this is a grave illness, and like all men who suffer from it, he waxes and wanes. I have seen him look entirely well for weeks."

"But, Doctor, may I ask—it *always* comes back?"

"So far—yes."

"How long can he go on like this?"

He set the other bottles gently into the box, gathered the last of his belongings, and moved toward the door. I opened it for him. "That is a good question," he said, stepping gingerly out onto the stairs, as though they might not hold him. "I wish I could say. His is a grave condition, but he is also a resilient man—like many with his particular history. The medical texts may not assign him the best of odds, but in my own career, I have yet to see a man who obeys the medical texts."

"He didn't look so resilient when I arrived."

"Well, that might be because you are accustomed to the flower in bloom. Did you not see how much better he looked today when we'd finished?"

I followed him across the drive. When he climbed back into the old Mercedes that was sitting beneath the trees, I leaned down to the window. "Tell me, then," I said, "in his condition, should he really be doing what he's doing?"

"Which is what, I might ask."

I gestured toward the upstairs window, where we could see him now with a cigarette in his mouth and a glass in his hand.

"Ah, Mr. Andret," he said, shifting the rattling coupe into reverse, "he still has his pleasures, hasn't he? If I were you, I would be happy that he can at least rise from bed to enjoy them."

"Paulie," I said. "He's in bad shape."

"Surprise, surprise."

"Worse than we thought."

There was a pause. "He's been in that kind of shape all our lives, Hans. Probably all his own, too."

"Well, this is different."

Silence. I was talking from the garden behind the cabin.

"Why?" she finally said.

"Why what?"

"Why's it different?"

"You've never seen him like this. He's got cirrhosis. He's enormous. He's swollen all over and he sounds like a girl. His voice sounds like Emmy's."

"But he's better now since the doctor came, isn't he?"

"The doctor said he's in *grave* shape, Paulie. That's the word he used—*grave*. I think you should come."

"He's been in grave shape before."

"How do you know?"

"I've talked to that doctor myself."

Upstairs in the cabin, I could see Dad sitting in the window again, looking down at me.

"What about Mom?" I said. "Do you think Mom would want to be here?"

"You're kidding, right?"

"No, I'm not. I think if she knew—"

"No, Hans. Mom does not want to be there. She's got her own life now. It's taken her a long time to get it."

"Well, then what about *you*?"

"What *about* me? I survived."

"I know that. I understand. Listen, Paulie—can I tell you what I saw in the bushes yesterday? The HMS *Victory*."

I could hear her calm breathing.

"And the *Royal Sovereign,* Paulie. They're both still here. I'd bet they'd still float."

Another silence.

"They're still here, Paulie. Don't you remember? In the bushes by the well pump. They looked like a couple of arks. You remember all that, don't you? Freeboard? The potato cannons? The Battle of Trafalgar?"

"No."

"Come on, Paulie. You're kidding. You have to remember."

"I mean no, I'm not coming out. Yes, I remember. Of course I remember. I remember a lot of other things, too."

"Are you serious? You really won't?"

"Hans," she said. "You still don't understand. This is the same old quicksand."

. . .

"You and Paulie, Dad," I said. "You're still not getting along, are you?"

"Your sister takes everything to heart." He lit another cigarette. "Just like your mother."

"Look, Dad—"

"Don't bother." He brushed his hand at me. He was leaning against the windowsill, and now he turned to the view. "I've heard it all already, Hans. In fact, I paid your mother's assassin for the privilege of hearing it."

"Mom's had to look out for herself."

"She had a job, Hans."

"Well, you could have one, too."

He laughed, miserably. "Look at me. Do I look like someone you'd hire?" He slapped his belly, which was entirely different from what it had been when I'd arrived but still echoed under his hand. "I wouldn't hire me to drop a rock down a hole." He lowered himself into the chair. Outside the window, a pickup had crossed the bridge and was making its way along the water. It turned in at a lot. "They found gas up here," he said. "That's what all the excitement's about."

"It's certainly different."

"Well, you have the speculators to thank for that. If you leave a door unlocked, they'll drill a well in your kitchen. Built a service center up the road, too. That's what all the houses are. This place might actually be worth something."

"Dad," I said. "Have you and Paulie spoken?"

"No, not in years. Look at that. You can see all the way to the bridge now. Look at all the garages. They built ten last year." He rose, straining to push himself from the chair. Once on his feet, though, he was steady again. He crossed to the window. Where the pickup had parked, a man on a roof was tilting up a pulley. We watched his partner unload a pallet of shingles from the truck, hooking them into a basket. The basket rose on cables, and presently the *ktchka-ktchka-ktchka* of a nail gun came ricocheting across the cove.

"Dad," I said, "I haven't really done anything with the mathematics you taught me."

He looked back at me. "I liked those dinners in New York well enough."

"Still, the mathematics—most of it was wasted."

He laughed. "Well," he said. "If that's the case, then that makes two of us."

ON MY PHONE, I went to RECENTS. She answered on the first ring. "Oh, Hans," she said. "I'm glad it's you. I've been worried about your father."

"He's okay, Mrs. Biettermann. He seems a lot better now."

"Good." There was a pause. Then, out of nowhere, she laughed. "Say my name again."

"What?"

"My *full* name."

"Cle Biettermann."

"Cle *Wells*." After a moment, she said, "My, my."

"I wanted to thank you for letting me know about him. I came up to the cabin and found him in pretty dire shape—you were right. I'm still in Michigan."

"But he's doing better now?"

"The doctor drained some fluid yesterday, and it seemed to help quite a bit."

"That little Indian fellow in the beat-up Mercedes?"

"Dr. Gandapur, yes."

There was another pause.

"Mrs. Wells?"

"Yes?"

"Well, nothing."

． ． ．

ON THE LAST day of my visit, I was awakened by the sound of scraping. The sun was just coming up, and when I looked out through the screens, it took me a moment to realize what was happening. Dr. Gandapur stood in the clearing. With the sole of his wing tip, he was working a shovel into the earth.

He was digging Dad's grave.

"Ah," he said when I arrived beside him. "I hope I haven't awakened you."

"Oh, no. I was just surprised to see you here this early. I was awake anyway."

I looked down: he was planting something.

"Ah, of course." I fingered the tomato stems next to the hole he was making. "I'd been wondering how he kept up a garden."

The shovel went in again. He set aside a measure of soil, then reached into his pocket and brought out a handful of bulbs. "Man does not live by bread alone," he said. "I would like to get in a few saffron crocus, to surprise him in the fall."

"And the rest of it? You've done this whole thing?"

"No, no—not all of it. Your father does a part of it himself. It lures him out of the house. You're seeing him at a difficult interval, as I think you know. These episodes come and go. He is a bull, though. He looks much better than when you arrived, don't you think so?"

"And the groceries in the kitchen—that's you, too, isn't it?"

"They are quite minimal."

"They're not, actually. Thank you."

He set a bulb into one of the holes.

"And the house?" I said. "Are you the one who's keeping everything in order?"

"He won't let me touch the upstairs."

"I can see that."

I considered taking out my wallet.

Somehow, he knew, and he raised his hand. "Ah, but you see," he said, "my own children are grown. My son is in Washington and my daughter is in Palo Alto. They are good children, but they have their own lives now." He dropped his eyes. "And my wife is no longer with us. So it is really for myself that I do it. We Jesuits—we have always embraced the concept."

"Which concept would that be, Doctor?"

"That serving others is in fact service to oneself." He turned and from his other pocket offered me a trowel. "Here," he said. "I would not refuse your help, though. I was hoping to get two rows parallel."

I took the tool from his hand. Tendrils of false grape were winding in from the periphery, and around them the soil was loose; but the roots still knotted together in every direction. It seemed something of a miracle that the beans and tomatoes had grown at all. "Does he mind," I said, "that you're doing all of this for him?"

"He doesn't seem to mind at all, actually."

"Even though he says he wants to be alone?"

"I doubt the veracity of that claim. I don't believe that anybody truly wants to be alone. Especially not someone of our age."

We went back to digging.

"I'm sorry," I said.

"Please don't be."

For a time, then, we worked in silence. He walked ahead, watering the rows from a bucket. Presently, he said, "We discuss maths, you know. I'm somewhat rusty, of course, but I still comprehend a reasonable part of it. I'm not too humble to say so. It is very exciting for me. I think he might in a small way even appreciate my company. He has told me about his new work."

"I'm sure he does appreciate your company, very much." I pushed the trowel along to make a trough for the bulbs. "So what did he tell you about his new work?"

"I cannot say." He looked sideways at me. "He believes there are those who would steal it, as you know."

"Yes, I do know."

"Well, what can you do?" He glanced up at the windows. "I can tell you that it's geometry. Low dimension. About any more than that, I have been sworn to secrecy."

"I understand."

He touched me lightly on the shoulder. "But truly, Hans," he said, dropping his voice. "Do you really think he is capable of doing new work? In *his* condition? Frankly, it would be hard for me to imagine."

"Of course."

"It happens." He turned again to the garden. "To the brain, I mean. It's the drink, naturally. And the hepatic function. But there is clearly something else occurring, too. Certainly in other men I've seen it. There is something in certain abilities that is never far from— far from—" He looked out at the lake. "I cannot really know."

"No, please go on."

"Far from terror, perhaps. It is not such a rare phenomenon, you see. I used to encounter it around the maths division when I was at university, and I have seen it here, even, in my little country practice. It seems to be quite primal. At its crudest, it is a bona fide paranoia. Plenty in the field are gone before the age of twenty. I've seen *that,* too. Perhaps it is a harbinger. I believe it to be physiological." He looked down. "I sometimes imagine it as God's revenge."

"Against mathematicians?"

"One must bear in mind that they might be considered spies." He was smiling now.

"By the Deity, you mean?"

"Indeed. Your dad's cantankerous nature, by the way—you know that this is his liver, too, don't you? And of course the drink plays a part in it—but it is also the man himself. The emotions are ablaze in him." He set down the bucket. "For people like you and me—well, we are shielded by all our damping circuitry. We maintain a cushion against the world, if you will. A comfort against the ravage. But I believe it is not so for him."

He regarded me. "Think of what life must be like for a mind like your father's. I mean, human existence is bounded by tragedy, is it not? And shot through with it, as well. I was born in Lahore, so I know this in a particular way. But your father, too—he knows it just as particularly, in his own way. I have learned to keep such thoughts somewhat at bay. And so have you. But for him, there is no ignoring it. There is no joy in God's creation. No pleasure in sunlight or water. No pleasure in a good meal. There is no pleasure in the company of friends. There is nothing. Nothing that might assuage the maw. He stands directly in its whirlwind. I've come to believe that this is the consequence of a brain like his. That this is the price for solving a puzzle as great as the one he solved."

BEFORE I LEFT for the airport, I cleaned Dad's room. Empty bottles. Sticky glasses. All the crushed-out cigarettes. On the floor by the door lay a mass of newspapers and magazines, heaped together. The spines were bent, the sections scattered in pieces, as though for months he'd simply been throwing everything from the bed. Atop the dirty blanket he lay snoring. I set about quietly moving everything back onto the shelves.

That's when I came across it.

It was resting on its side, in a gap between books, the rings of a glass darkening its cover. *The Northern European Review of Enumerative Combinatorics,* volume 13, number 2. September 1999. On the cover, the title of Benedek Fodor's paper had been circled in heavy pencil, just as it had been on my own.

The Expected Teaches Nothing

IT WAS A warm afternoon. Chickadees hopping in the tamaracks outside the window of Matthew's office. "What you said the other day, Hans," he said, "that you didn't want to *betray* your mother—what did you mean exactly?"

"I didn't want to betray her optimism."

"By telling her the truth?"

"Optimism is an attempt to circumvent the truth."

"Wow," said Audra.

I glanced at her. "That's how I see it, anyway."

"Couldn't it just be an attempt to influence it?" she said.

Now I turned to look at her.

Matthew said, "And you would have been threatening her optimistic interpretation."

"If I told her about myself, then I'd have to tell her about *him,* too."

"But didn't she already know about him?"

"Of course. But she did and she didn't. She was still good at believing it was going to get better."

"Indeed," said Audra.

"Believe me," said Matthew. "It's common."

"Maybe it's common," said my wife, "because it's common for women to believe that they have no choice."

Now we both turned to her. She folded her arms.

"True indeed," said Matthew. "But then what? What would have happened if you *had* told her? If you'd told her the truth?"

"About me?"

"About you, about your dad."

"You mean, that he was just sitting out there with a bottle?"

"I mean the full truth, as it would have affected all of you."

"That he was out there drinking, and"—here my voice actually cracked—"that he wasn't really *working* on anything?"

He waited a moment. "That's difficult for you to say, isn't it?"

"He was a mathematician, you know. The work—for him, it was everything."

"Tell me, Hans. People in your field—they make their mark early, isn't that right?"

"In my former field, you're talking about."

"I mean in math."

I think I might have cringed. "I'm not sure," I said. "That's what's often said. I don't know if it's accurate."

"But it's said?"

"By many people, yes. Abel made his mark early. So did Eisenstein. So did Galois. Hardy, definitely. Gauss wrote the *Disquisitiones* when he was in his teens. But Euler worked all his life."

"And you—you're awfully young, too—you're awfully young to be doing what you're doing."

"It comes at a cost."

"What's the cost?"

I pointed at the walls, then at Matthew, then at the wood-shake inn building, with its 120 rooms, that stood across the grass like the king of England's hunting lodge. "My father taught me most of what I know."

"In every respect."

"Yes."

"And if you'd exposed him?"

"It would have all changed."

He smiled. "What would have?"

"Well," I said, turning to the window. "My mother would have realized—realized what I guess she finally did realize."

"Which is what?" said Audra.

"That she'd tied herself to a great mind, who was finished now. Who was about to pull all of us over a cliff."

"So, WHY THEN?" said Matthew. It was the next day, our late-afternoon session. "Why all of this so suddenly? Why'd you come home one day and do a couple of bumps in front of your wife and daughter?"

Audra winced.

"You'd had plenty of practice at hiding it," he said. "Surely you're a better delinquent than that."

"I don't know."

"Take a stab." He glanced out the window. Out in the field, the tractor was stirring up a cloud again.

"I really don't."

He rose and stood at the glass. The tractor edged along a row, made the corner, and began working the next one. "Genius is a true degenerative psychosis," he said, "belonging to the group of moral insanity."

"Pardon?" said Audra.

"Cesare Lombroso. A criminologist. He died a hundred years ago, but now the neurobiologists are starting to agree with him. Fewer dopamine receptors or something like that. Psychosis and inventiveness seem to run along a kind of continuum."

I said, "I'd been thinking about my father."

He sat back down. "Tell us."

"He'd started talking to me about his life. When I was visiting him at his cabin. He was pretty ill then already."

"I'm sorry."

"When I was a kid, he'd never said a word to me about anything from his past. Like a lot of fathers, I guess. Then I went out to see him, in the woods where he's living now. And he told me things I never knew. Like that he was in a place like this himself once."

"And you never knew about it?"

"No, I didn't. His department at Princeton made him go. They sent a security guard on the plane with him to make sure he got there." I laughed. "Dad brought along a bottle, of course."

"I'd expect no less."

"They took it away."

"Not unusual, either. When was this?"

"Right before he lost his job and my parents moved to Ohio. Probably a year before I was born."

"And did the treatment work?"

"He went AWOL."

He glanced over. "You're free to leave, too, you know."

"I know that."

"Tell us what happened afterwards," said Audra.

"You know what happened."

"Tell Matthew." She turned to him. "His dad destroyed his career. Then he abandoned his family. Then he almost ruined *our* family."

"He didn't almost ruin *our* family."

"He didn't? Look at you."

"What about me?" I reached out my hand.

She ignored it.

"You don't agree with your wife?" said Matthew. "You don't agree that he almost ruined your family?"

"I don't think my father has anything to do with it anymore."

At these words, Audra actually laughed. "Sometimes, you're so thick," she said.

"Thank you."

"Audra, why don't you tell us what's on your mind then?"

"What's on my mind is obvious. Hans was *hoping* to be caught. Weren't you? Obviously, you *wanted* me to stop you."

"Why would I want that?"

"Because you couldn't just let it go on. You *needed* it to stop."

"Well, I don't—"

"Shhh," she said. "Just be quiet. Just think about it for a minute. You must have known it for a long time—that unless something changed—" Here she closed her eyes.

Matthew handed her the box of Kleenex. After a time, he said, "Well, Hans?"

"I guess she means that unless something changed, I'd eventually be in the same shape as my dad."

"And?" said Audra.

"And I guess I don't want to think about what that would have meant for our kids."

"That's one of the reasons we've never let them meet him," Audra said. It was her last session with me before she went back to New York in the morning.

"Your children have never met their grandfather?"

"It's not that we forbid it," I said. "It's just that it doesn't ever seem to happen. *He* certainly never expresses any interest."

"I don't know if Hans told you this," said Audra, "but he didn't come to our wedding."

"Was he invited?"

"Of course he was," she said. "But he must have been afraid to come."

"Afraid?" said Matthew.

"Of seeing my mother, she means."

"Do you agree with that, Hans? Do you think he was afraid of seeing her?"

"Well—yes, I think he was. And he was probably afraid to see Paulie and me, too."

"I can understand that." This was Audra again. "I can see why he wouldn't want to show up if all of you were going to be there. It was probably too painful. He was probably so ashamed of what he'd done."

"My wife is being generous."

"You see it differently?"

"I just see it as the way he is. He's a frightened person."

"Frightened of what?"

"Hard to say. Of people, maybe. Of human beings as unpredictable functions. I don't know how else to put it. I don't think he was actually ashamed. I don't think he operates that way. It's much more elemental, in my opinion. I think he was bewildered, and being bewildered scares him. He wouldn't know what to say to the woman who was about to marry his son. He wouldn't know what to say to her family. And he probably wouldn't know what to say now to our kids. That's why he drinks. That's why he stays away."

"And you prefer it that way?"

"I didn't say I do."

"But you *do,*" said Audra. "You're afraid of his influence."

"Well, aren't *you?*"

Matthew let Audra think about that one.

"I don't know," she finally said. "Of course I am. But it's already there, don't you think? I mean, honey—*look* at our two children." She laughed. "They certainly don't get it from *me.*"

"THERE'S ANOTHER THING," I said. Audra had gone home now, and Matthew and I were in our afternoon session alone. It was my last week at Stillwater, and I'd realized that I was probably going to make it. "When I was at my dad's cabin," I said, "I found something interesting—the same mathematics journal that someone had once sent to me at my office in New York."

"I don't understand."

"A few years back, someone sent me a copy of a mathematics journal. And I guess they sent one to Dad, too. The same article had been circled in both of them. But it didn't have anything to do with either of our fields. It was combinatorics. I was surprised to find it on his shelf."

"Combinatorics?"

"Pascal's triangle. The Rubik's Cube. How objects are ordered. I don't know much combinatorics, and I don't think Dad does, either. It was by a man named Benedek Fodor. There was one sentence in it. It wasn't even in the article, actually, it was just a footnote."

"Which said?"

"It said 'It has not escaped my attention that such a finding is at odds with one of the foundational proofs of twentieth-century topology.'"

Matthew sat back in his chair. "You know it from memory, I see."

"A sentence like that—well, for a mathematician, anyway—it's the strike of the sword. Fodor was referring to my father's proof."

"Of the Malosz theorem?"

"Yes."

"Then, you mean—there's a *problem* with it?"

"Well, that hasn't been shown. But there might be. There *might* be a problem with it. It can take a long time for a question like that to actually be sorted out. It can take decades. That's how it goes with these things. The Kepler conjecture was solved years ago, but still nobody's completely sure if it's right. Some people are still trying to verify it, and other people are still trying to find a flaw. And the Malosz conjecture might be even more difficult than that one. But yes," I said, "when a mathematician like Benedek Fodor says something like that, it casts doubt on what Dad did."

"Did your father ever tell you about this problem—this *potential* problem?"

"No. Of course he didn't."

"But wouldn't he have known about it?"

"Possibly. Not certainly. A proof like his takes years of work. Not many people in the world can even *read* a paper like the Malosz theorem, let alone track it. Fodor's article was in an obscure journal. It was published in Europe. It was a single sentence. It was another mathematician's thinking, in another field, in a footnote. All it did was raise a doubt. Dad might not have even heard about it."

"But the journal was on his shelf."

"Along with a hundred others."

"Still," he said, "it's a doubt that concerns you."

"I don't know whether it concerns me or not. It would take me as long to figure that out as it would any other mathematician. Longer, probably."

Matthew closed his eyes—he appeared to be thinking. "So your theory is that the same person might have sent the journal to both of you? Why do you think someone would do something like that?"

"I would have to assume as an attack."

"Against you or your father?"

"Against both of us, I guess."

"Well, that's upsetting."

"Of course it is. I don't like to think that I have enemies out there the way *he* does."

"Your dad has enemies?"

I laughed. "Dad has nothing *but* enemies. He makes them pretty much everywhere he goes. Pretty much everyone he ever works with. Pretty much every place he ever works. It's easier to count the people who *aren't* his enemies."

"May I ask you something?"

"Yes."

"Is that why you try so hard not to make them yourself?"

"Possibly."

He nodded, then sat back in his chair. For a time, we sat there together silently. Then he said, "Do you feel any better now?"

"Why would I feel better?"

"Because you told me about this. I would have thought there'd be other things much more difficult for you to talk about, but you talked about all of them without too much effort—at least effort that I noticed. This one—a doubt about a proof your father wrote before you were even born—this one took all your will. I can see it. Your wife's already left, and it's the very end of your time here."

"More difficult than a doubt about the validity of his work? For a man like my father? Nothing could be more difficult."

"I meant for a man like *you*."

I laughed. "I don't know why it's so hard. It shouldn't be."

He smiled. "You do feel a little better now, though, don't you?"

"As a matter of fact, I do."

"Confession is most of what we do," he said. "Isn't that funny? We have this state-of-the-art clinic. We have this highly trained staff. But in the end, confession might be just about the only cure we offer."

ONE SPRING MORNING, after I'd been back in New York for a few months, my phone rang at work: Dr. Gandapur had found Dad asleep on a bench down by the water with a bottle next to him. This was March, and the lake was still capped by an uncracked plate of ice. Dad was dressed in black wing tips, dark socks, and a pair of boxers. Nothing else. The wing tips were his old teaching shoes from Princeton. He'd shined them up.

"Well, the good news is that he's an extremely hardy creature," said Dr. Gandapur. "In fact, such an insult would have killed anything less. I think he was out there for at least a couple of hours."

"But he's all right now?"

"He seems to be, actually." Over the crackling line, he chuckled. "He's drinking a very cold bourbon right now."

"Well, good. That's a relief."

There was a pause.

"But I am indeed afraid," he said. "Well, to put it this way, is what you are doing out there—I mean, your current work in New York City—how difficult might it be to put it aside for a bit?"

Easy Does It

For a while, as Mom got used to Manhattan, she was at the Perry Street house every day. In the morning, she'd eat breakfast with the kids, then walk them to school. While they were gone, she'd bustle about. By 3:30, when they clomped back in through the front door, she'd already have made plans for the afternoon. First they'd put away their things, and after they'd had a snack and cleaned up the kitchen, they'd head out. They liked to walk uptown as a trio. Small galleries and secondhand shops in the old neighborhoods. Tea in the Russian pastry shops. Exercise in the public parks. Really, it was as though the two kids we knew had stepped out the door one day and been replaced by the resourceful offspring of pioneers.

As for me: well, it hadn't been that long since Stillwater, but I was managing to stay clean.

Every morning, Lorenzo drove me to Physico, where the Shores-Durbans and I still spent the day cutting tiny pieces out of the biggest, juiciest financial steaks in the world. I'd lost some of my drive, I suppose. But I didn't miss it—not yet, anyway. When the Town Car dropped me back at the house in the evening, I'd walk to the gym with Audra. Mom was with the kids then, too, strolling on the High Line or reading aloud to them on the living-room rug. *The Wind in the Willows* or *Art Through the Ages*. She supervised their generally

sparse practice sessions on the piano. With Emmy, she was also drawing a little, although Emmy seemed to have inherited none of that
particular aspect of my father's talent. For his part, Niels was turning
into an engineer rather than a mathematician. Even at his age I could
see it. Mom saw it, too, as clearly as I did, and the relief she took in it
was evident. From the public library she brought home books on
dams and engines and airplanes. Audra might not have noticed the
difference between engineering and mathematics, but to Mom and
me it could not have been more obvious. Cricket and baseball.

One afternoon I watched Niels build a rubber-band rifle from a
broomstick. I registered the sight with relief, the way my father must
have registered the sight of his own son, at almost the same age, sitting under the mulberry tree rescaling Euclid's proof on the infini-
tude of primes.

"Look at it," Mom said to me one night after the kids were asleep.
She held up Niels's weapon, which looked rather capable. He'd filed
down the end of the broomstick and cut notches in the tip, then duct-
taped a row of clothespins as triggers. Mom and I were on the terrace.
It had been a warm day, and she'd poured herself a glass of wine. She
set it down and sighted along the barrel of the gun at the lightly
dressed walkers who were making the midevening transition from
the restaurants to the bars. "Niels is so excited," she said.

"They live in such a different world now. Everything's old hat for
them. But this—*this* is new."

"It's the kind of thing that boys did during *my* childhood." She
sighed. "Now they've all seen everything."

A group of young women drifted by beneath us, their phones
glowing in the dark. All my life I've loved sitting with my mother,
watching the world move insignificantly along.

"I know that when *you* were that age," she said, "you played in the
backyard."

"It's what I had."

"And what a blessing that was, thank you. Your childhood was
an open canvas." She set down the gun and took a sip of wine. "Can-

vas and paint—and a few math lessons—that's what we gave you."
Then she added, less firmly, "And not even that much, really. This
generation—sometimes I wonder."

"People have been saying that for a thousand years."

She frowned. There was a pair of newspapers at her feet, and she
worked off their rubber bands and hooked one of them into a trigger.
When she fired, the rubber band whizzed up over our heads and shivered through the halo of the streetlamp. It paused at the apex, then
wobbled lamely down to the street and brushed the shoulder of a
man walking past. He touched his sleeve and looked up.

Mom ducked.

I waved.

"Wow," I said when she sat up again. "You seem—I don't know."

"What? Tipsy?"

"No. Happy."

"I *am* happy. I've been quite happy." She looked out at the busy
sidewalk. Then she added, "Not just here, though, Hans. For years
now."

For several moments, we were silent. I believe we were thinking
the same thing.

"Mom," I finally said. "He's sick. Things have gotten worse."

"I know, sweetheart."

"How did you know?"

"Paulie told me."

"It has to be—I don't know, upsetting."

"Of course it is. It's terribly upsetting."

She pulled out the other rubber band and hooked it into the
clothespin. But then she set the whole thing down on the floor. "I'm
not going out there," she said. "I just want you to know that."

"Nobody expects you to."

"I'm done helping."

"I know, Mom."

We were silent. Presently, she said, "It's serious, though, this time,
isn't it?"

"I'm afraid it is, Mom."

"Shoot."

"But he's strong, you know. He's very strong. You know that, don't you?"

"Well, no. He's not."

Then, as though to change the subject, she leaned over the railing. At the corner, a tow truck had pulled to the curb, and the driver was positioning clamps around the wheels of a car. He climbed back into the cab, and the car began rocking. Then suddenly it levitated, swinging in its noose. "They don't give you much of a chance around here, do they?" Mom said.

I nodded. I suspected she was remembering her old life in Tapington; I myself was remembering my own. In the truck's revolving strobe, the spreading ginkgo at the corner looked a little bit like our old mulberry.

She said, "I just can't care anymore."

"I know you can't."

"He had his chance. He had lots of them." She looked away. "Okay, honey. I've said it now."

From up the avenue then, the sound of a street sweeper arrived. Mom's glass began rattling; soon the whole table was shaking. A moment later, the vehicle appeared: a hunched, roaring beetle, nosing up a pair of brightly shining eyes from the alley.

"*You* go help him," she said.

"I will. I'm going back out there. For as long as he needs."

She looked out at the street again. "And what about your job?"

"And what about it?"

She took my hand. "Oh, God, Hans. I truly am sorry. I'll help *you*. I'll help Audra. I'll do everything for Niels and Emmy. But—"

"I'll take care of him, Mom. Don't worry."

She squeezed my hand. "This is just the way things have to go," she said. "Your father simply can't take anything more from me."

The Truth at Last

By the time I left for Michigan again, later in the month, it already felt like summer in New York. At LaGuardia, the limos were dripping puddles onto the concrete. Ninety minutes later, when the door opened in Grand Rapids, a maritime chill came hurtling through the cabin like water through a breached hull.

In another rented Audi I took the shoreline route. South of Holland, I pulled over onto the shoulder of the Blue Star Highway and watched the lake piling in behind the dunes. Here, winter was still in the air. The huge swells were slashed with white, and above the bluffs, the hawks were stopped dead in the air. I got back into the car. When the road bent east again, the shadows of the clouds darkened the countryside like another set of lakes, this one moving inland with me through the fields. Midstate, spring arrived. I opened the windows and breathed the familiar air.

At the cabin, Dad was in the garden.

Covered in sweat. Digging steadily. Planting something: more bulbs. A heap of them thrown down beside the tomato plants. Leaning forward from a rusted gardener's chair, the radio blaring a piano sonata into the woods. What I saw immediately was that he looked healthy. From the rear—except for the crazy white hair that hung past his shoulders—he looked no different from the man I used to know.

"Ouch!" he barked, when I tapped him on the shoulder.

"Did that hurt?"

"No, but you scared the Jesus out of me."

He kicked away the bucket at his feet and stood, sweat dripping from his chin. His shirt was soaked. His face was streaked with earth and his pants clung to his thighs. "Dad," I said, "you don't even look sick anymore. You're out here working yourself into a lather."

"That's because I'm *not* sick. Doctors are full of it." He raised and lowered the trowel in his hand like a dumbbell. "I'm on the upslope. Diet and exercise. Study and moderation."

He was still thin. When he spoke, the tendons moved in his neck.

"THIS IS BECAUSE I drained him again," said Dr. Gandapur. He'd joined us for dinner, then stepped out onto the deck with me after the meal. Earlier in the evening, Dad had grilled steaks on the patio, then retreated to the couch. Now he was asleep on it.

"He is slim and determined," said the doctor, "so no doubt he will look healthy to you. However, I will tell you"—he opened his fingers—"that he will fool us both. I took off four liters of fluid, you know, which is rather a lot. But it will return, Hans. This is something we will not be able to solve in the long run."

"I see."

"But yes," he said, patting me on the shoulder. "You are absolutely right. He looks remarkably healthy, does he not? He has been doing exceptionally well. This is what we should be grateful for."

"DON'T WORRY," DAD said, pushing away his plate. "I'll pay."

I'd taken him for lunch in Felt City, but the toothpicks were still in his sandwich. The diner was in the back corner of the general store, and as I ate I watched him eye a couple of customers who were shopping for hardware. Suddenly he said, "When you were a young man, you were using that drug."

"I'm clean now."

"Well, good." He nodded. "That's good."

"I don't think I've told you yet, but I was in treatment recently."

He looked at me. "Don't tell me you actually believe in that stuff."

"It's possible that I do."

"It's *possible*?" He raised an eyebrow. "Well, at least the doubt will serve you."

The waitress moved past our table then, and he pointed to his coffee. "I could use a refill about now."

She swept on without answering.

He called after her, "Just dip me one out of the lake."

He peeled back the tops on a handful of creamers and emptied them into his cup. When she passed again, he raised his finger, but she walked right by.

He leaned toward me. "Rolled in the hay with her once. Now she likes to make me wait."

"I don't think I want to know."

"Of course you don't. But it wasn't bad." He poured another creamer. "At this point, I thought you might be interested in the truth."

"Well, in this case, I'm not."

It occurred to me that the illness might be doing something to his brain.

"I was still with your mother."

"I said I don't want to know."

He smiled. "Look at her, will you? I love the small-time ones."

"Dad, really. I'll leave."

When she bent over the pie cooler now, he turned all the way around. But then he turned back and mumbled, "All right, you win." He rubbed his arm, stretching. "You know," he said. "I never cared about money."

"I don't care much about it, either."

At that one, he slapped the table.

"By the time I was your age," he said, "I already had you and your sister. That's the only reason I thought about earning a living at all. But you know, the money didn't mean a thing to me." He sipped his coffee, making a sour face. "For that matter, I wouldn't have said that you kids were a big part of my life, either."

"I'm aware of that. We both are."

"That's just how it was in those days. I was working. That's what we did." With a pinkie, he traced the pattern in the table. "I did my good work early," he said.

I finished my sandwich and sat back in the booth. The truth was, when he was my age, he hadn't even met my mother yet.

The waitress was laying out her dinner settings now, moving through the rows of tables. Dad was smiling at her, but she still wouldn't look at him. He snapped his fingers, but she didn't even turn.

"She'd had a bit to drink," he said.

"I'll bet."

He spit his coffee then, smiling as though I'd finally said something funny. But after a moment he winced, and the smile dropped. He rubbed his shoulder. "Goddamn," he said. "Whatever this is, it still hurts."

THE NEXT AFTERNOON, the phone rang: it was Cle Wells.

She wanted to come up.

I covered the receiver with my hand. Dad was on the couch, blinking from a nap. "When?" he mouthed. "When?"

"Next week, I guess." I held out the phone. "Come over and talk to her."

"No. Tell her it's fine. Just tell her to call in advance. Tell her to call when she's an hour away!" He swung his feet around and stood.

"He says he wants you to call before you get here."

"An *hour* before!" Dad whispered.

"When you're an hour away."

"He hasn't changed much," she said. "Has he?"

"I don't know. When's the last time you saw him?"

She paused. "It was a while ago."

"Well, then he might have."

"What's she saying now?" said Dad.

"Nothing."

"Is she coming alone?"

"Christ. Tell him to pick up the phone himself." She raised her voice. "Milo!"

I held out the extension.

"Just ask her, Hans."

"He'd like to know if you're coming by yourself, Mrs. Wells."

"Good Lord." She took a long breath. Then she said, "How's he doing?"

"He looks pretty good to me."

"Tell him Monday then. Early afternoon."

"Did she say *we*?"

"Dad, why don't you just ask her yourself?"

"Remind her to call when she's an hour away!"

"I just did, Dad."

"Hans, I'm looking forward very much to meeting you."

"Thank you, Mrs. Wells."

"Please," she said. "Call me Cle."

THE NEXT MORNING, we walked together to get his hair cut. There was a lady at the end of the cove who ran a salon out of an RV. Dad's stride was steady. He made it all the way out to the turn where the new two-story houses and then the big church came into view with the salon resting on blocks behind the parking lot. He climbed the steps and plunked himself down onto a stool.

She was country-waitress pretty. Reddish curls that bounced when she leaned down to tie the bib over him. But he just sat there silently before her. The scissors *snick-snick-snick*ing behind him. The clippings so white they disappeared into the linoleum.

On the way back, his stride wasn't as steady. Sweat darkened the front of his shirt. But the haircut flattered him. He kept touching it. As we walked he told me the story of coming to Princeton, of meeting my mother in the mathematics office. "I told her I was an assistant professor," he said, stepping slowly up the drive, "so she told me she was an assistant secretary."

"She sounds charming, Dad."

"She was." At the cabin steps, he paused. "But I didn't love her."

I took his arm and started us both up toward the door.

"I asked her to marry me, Hans. But I never had the feeling. I loved someone else. It was all a mistake."

"Mom deserves more than you gave her."

"I'm not talking about that. I'm only telling you the facts as I know them." He took his arm out of mine and laid it on the railing. "It was a programming error, Hans. Once it was made, it just kept compounding itself."

THE NEXT MORNING, he woke up and said, "Let's clean the place."

So we did. It was hard to fathom all the things that could go wrong with a house like that, sitting out there in a damp woods with only Dr. Gandapur to help my father with it. But we managed to set a lot of it right. It was the anti-universe of Physico. I clipped roots and unwrapped vines. I drove trunkfuls of trash into town and pulled mouse nests out of cabinets. I cleaned every screen. Dad would help a little, breaking for rests while I kept going. Every noon, we ate lunch in Felt City, and when we got back he'd take his afternoon nap. I'd work outside while he slept. When he woke, in the hour or two before dinner, he'd talk.

Something in him had loosened. He started telling me everything.

. . .

WHEN THE PHONE rang on Monday afternoon, he rose from the day-bed, pulled on a pair of pressed pants from the closet, and went into the bathroom to shave. "How do I look?" he called out.

"Handsome as ever."

He went to the window and sat down, looking out into the trees. For some time, he just sat there. Then, finally, he rose and went out-side. In his nice clothes, in his new haircut, stepping purposefully across the clearing, he looked like a respectable man.

At the kitchen window I stood watching. He sat down next to the plantings. The same spot where he'd been sitting when I pulled into the driveway myself, a week before. The same rusted chair. His feet in the same thin patch of strawberries. He laid a trowel at his feet and picked up a hoe. Behind him, the garden hose trailed back to the cabin. He set himself up carefully and looked out at the lake.

When the car finally appeared, turning briskly at the far end of the inlet and driving fast along the stretch, he reached back for the hose, opened his hand, and splashed water all over himself.

"PROFESSOR," SHE CALLED, emerging from the driver's seat. It was a French car—a Citroën. "Professor Andret!"

A striking woman—shrewd featured, slender in the way of the wealthy, her chin angled up and her white hair pulled back in a bun. The trunk lid popped up, and at the same time the rear door swung halfway out, then shut. Then pushed out again. Somebody was strug-gling with it.

She strode briskly around behind the trunk, and when she ap-peared again she was pushing a wheelchair. The passenger door fi-nally opened, and a pair of feet flopped out onto the ground. She bent over and snapped down the chair's stirrups, then stepped back. With both arms, a dark-suited man leaned out, grabbed the rails, and jerked himself into the seat.

"Professor," she called again. More cheerily this time. She gave the chair a push and bumped it ahead of her across the furrows. Her head was already cocked toward the rear of the house, where Dad was leaning forward in the lawn chair. "Milo!" she called brightly. "Milo, we're here!"

"Oh, Hans," said Audra. "That's so sad."

"I don't know. I'm not sure it's sad. Romance isn't everyone's expectation. It could mean any number of things."

"What could? That he never loved your mother?" I heard her set the phone down on the counter. It was five o'clock: almost dinnertime. When she picked it up again, she said, "He must have been afraid she'd never love *him*."

In the background, I heard the metronome click on and Niels begin a scale on the piano.

"He's been talking," I said. "He's told me things that I doubt he's ever told anyone."

"What kinds of things?"

"You wouldn't want to hear. Old flames he's gone to bed with. Ones he's been in love with. Plenty of it I didn't want to hear myself."

"Is he drinking?"

"Of course he's drinking."

"I'm sorry."

"It's doing things to his brain now."

The blender whirred. When it stopped, she said, "Well, then maybe you don't have to believe everything. Maybe you shouldn't be taking everything to heart. Just listen for a while. That's why you're there. You don't have to decide whether any of it's true."

The blender whirred again. Then came the sound of a spoon banging a bowl. The *tk-tk-tk* of the stove burners.

"It *is*, Aud."

"What is?"

"What he's saying. I can tell—it's all true."

Brompton's Mixture

EITHER DAD DIDN'T know or he hadn't remembered: Earl Bietter-mann had been in an accident. Cle unfolded a ramp for him at the door, and as soon as she was done, she asked Dad to show her the lake. While the two of them walked down to the water, Earl pushed himself into the house. He wheeled through the rooms, lifting curtains, jerking window knobs, bumping irately through the narrow doorways. At the bottom of the stairway, he leaned forward and peered up toward the second floor.

On the shore, Dad and Cle stood looking out at the cove. She made an elegant figure—loose-sleeved sweater, leather handbag, pale flats. An Upper East Side matron weekending in the Hamptons. Behind her, Dad leaned against a tree, pointing out the view.

"I don't want to be here," Earl said, moving past me. He stopped before the bookshelves. "In case you didn't know."

"I'm sorry you have to be, then."

"It's a bad idea. I'm not a man for bad ideas." He edged himself along the flimsy wall, the rubber wheels squeaking. "It's why I'm good at what I do." When he arrived at the window, he shook his head. "Look at them. They're fools."

"That very well might be true."

"Your father's always been a fool around her. And she can be a worse one around *him*."

Across the clearing, Dad was gesturing at something in the woods. The land must have seemed awfully shabby to her—pitiful, even—but she stood beside him and seemed to admire it. She nodded as he spoke, one heel crossed behind the other. Biettermann jiggled the brake on his chair. "I need to get to the hotel," he said. He moved before the wall mirror, but he wasn't looking at his own figure. I could see exactly where his gaze was pointed.

Even with the accident he was still a handsome man. Steep chin, bladed nose—the skin so deeply tanned that in the light off the lake it looked bronzed. It was a face I'd seen a thousand times on Wall Street—the cavalry lieutenant drawn from noble line—but the features were disturbed by the eyes. They looked unreal.

He glanced up. "I can't stand pity."

"I don't pity you."

"I get around fine. I get plenty done." He jiggled the handrails. "It's a misplaced emotion. Animals don't pity, they just get what they can." He felt around in his pocket. "Mind if I smoke?"

"You'd be about the first to ask."

He smiled for a moment. "I'm not asking. I'm just wondering if it bothers you."

As soon as he pulled out the cigarette case, I knew what it was: the same thick piece of silver he'd shown to my mother and father after Hans Borland's funeral, thirty years before. He'd probably been showing it ever since. He set it on the handrail, and on the front plate I recognized the row of screaming figures.

Earl was watching me. "Argentium silver," he said, tilting it to the light. "From the Ponte Vecchio. Cost about as much as my car." He flicked it open. "Italians might be even better thieves than the Americans."

When he held it up, I saw the coiling snakes and the terrified, screaming mouths of the damned. The cigarettes inside looked like pieces of art, too, custom rolled with a red thread dividing each.

"We're giving them a run, anyway," I said.

He allowed himself a clipped laugh. Then he snapped the thing shut and slid it back into his pocket. He looked up appraisingly. "You and I did what your old man never could."

"Which is?"

"Made something of ourselves. He had the same gifts, but he never did anything with them."

"You call the Fields nothing?"

He looked at me flatly. "Yes, in fact, I do." Now he backed up to take in the view again, drumming his fingers on the chair. Out on the dock, I could see that Dad was leaning forward now and rubbing his arms. He was getting tired. Biettermann turned away. "*You* provide for your children," he said.

"And so did my dad. All you and I did was sell out."

"The only ones who didn't sell out were the ones who couldn't."

"He didn't *want* to."

"That, I doubt." He rolled to the wall and began pulling books from the shelves, glancing disdainfully at their titles. "Everybody wants to."

"Not him."

"Well, look at what it got him. Ending his days in a place like this."

I turned away.

"What?" he said. "Look around. You wouldn't live here yourself."

"So what?"

"So, *you're* the one who said it—he won the Fields."

"And?"

"And?" he said, rolling closer. "That's the question, isn't it? The problem he never solved. And? And—*what*?"

"Everybody has a different answer to that one," said Dad from the doorway. He was standing at the top of the ramp.

Biettermann spun. "Bullshit," he said. "I could have told you a long time ago. I saw it all from the beginning."

"Told us what?" said Cle.

"How it would end." He pointed at my father. "I could have told you both how it would end up for him."

Dad stepped into the room. "Then why didn't you?"

"Why didn't I?" He perused us with his strange eyes. After a moment, he smiled. "Because I didn't want to spoil the surprise."

THAT EVENING, CLE and Dad stood together again at the waterline. Dad was talking, his hands moving before him in the air. Cle leaned toward him, her heel crossed behind her again, the white knot of her hair unraveling. After dinner, I'd driven Earl back to the hotel, and now in the kitchen I was cleaning the dishes. When I switched on the light, Cle turned and gazed up at the house. After a moment, she waved. I switched it off.

They moved back now along the shore. With a woman on his arm, my father looked ten years younger. No, *twenty*. Even in the moonlight I could see the pleasure he took in it. His elbow high. His shoulders straight. At the porch bench, they sat down; then she pulled a pad from her bag and handed it to him. She leaned back, gazing out at the water. He picked up the pad, opened the cover, and leaned down over it.

When we lived in Tapington, after he'd come back from the hospital, he used to disappear upstairs to his office and lean down over a pad of paper the same way, like a man in prayer. He could stay like that for hours. We used to start dinner without him, the table strangely calm. But we always knew we were waiting for him to break that calm. To break the unbearable hopefulness of that silence. I remember thinking sometimes that he'd gone away somewhere— I remember *wishing* that he had. But whenever he returned, I was also relieved, hearing his heavy step on the stairs.

A few moments later, when he turned on the bench and looked up at Cle, I realized he was drawing her.

THE NEXT MORNING, Biettermann said, "I hear the apple doesn't fall far from the tree."

"How's that?"

Behind us, Dad was asleep on the couch. After breakfast, he'd started a story about the history of the land up here—the Indians, the loggers, the gas drillers—but at some point he'd lost the thread. He'd tried again with something about the invention of the logging wheel, then trailed off. Now he was snoring.

"Rumor is, you don't drive alone," said Biettermann.

"Where'd you hear something like that?"

"You and I are in the same line of work."

"I'm fine," I said.

He looked up at me, appraisingly again. After a time, he said, "Does he ever talk about her?"

"You mean your wife? No, as a matter of fact, I've never heard him do that." I turned to the window. "And if he does, it's because his mind wanders. He's not well."

"Obviously not." He shook out a cigarette and tapped it on the chair. "But neither am I. That's life, isn't it? We make the best of it." He flicked closed the case. "Smoke?"

"No thanks." When he snapped the lighter, tilting his chin, I saw what it was about his eyes: the pupils were pinpoints.

"Are you in pain?" I asked.

"Lord" was all he said.

ALL THAT MORNING, while Dad slept, Earl conducted business on the phone from the side room, his voice ringing through the walls. He was working on some kind of private equity deal with a venture cap-italist on the West Coast who seemed to be having second thoughts.

For hours it ran on, Earl alternately ranting and flattering and cajoling. Hanging up and calling back. Speaking testily with his assistant in New York and obsequiously with the guy on the coast. The chair squeaking against the baseboards and bumping against the desk. Cle had gone into town for something. In the kitchen I turned up the radio.

Near noon, he finally quit. A few minutes later, when he rolled out into the living room, there was a dumbbell on his lap. He deposited it at the center of the rug and said, "But I don't let it stop me."

"All right."

"The pain." He unfolded a gym towel and spread it on his legs. "I'm sorry if I lost my cool yesterday. You had a problem. You tried to solve it."

"That's one way of looking at it."

"You want my guess?"

"Do I *want* it?"

"Blow." He tucked the towel around his legs. "Am I right?"

I said nothing.

"Typical." He pushed his hands into a pair of half gloves. "I mean, typical for a guy like you." He pinched and pulled the fabric over his palms. "It's the same old story. I've seen it a hundred times. You all make the same mistake."

He closed his eyes then and sat there, taking himself through a series of breaths that gradually slowed until he was hardly moving. Finally the chair rolled forward. At the center of the rug he scooped up the dumbbell, pressed it over his head, and set it back down. Fifty times he repeated this. Then he rolled backward, pivoted in the chair, and did the same thing again with the other arm. At last he sat still at the center of the room, sweat rolling off his temples.

"The real nature of your desire," he said. "That's what you're missing. It's the hole that can never be filled."

He dried his face with the towel. Then he closed his eyes until his breathing calmed, almost to nothing again. When he opened them, he jerked himself forward and repeated the whole routine.

. . .

THAT AFTERNOON, AFTER I'd driven Earl back to the hotel, a truck appeared in the drive. The back doors swung open, and two men started unloading furniture: a table, a set of chairs, a rug, a sofa. The rug was a Persian and the sofa was dark leather. They brought everything inside, then came in with a box of framed prints—black-and-white daguerreotypes of small-town Main Streets from the last century. Cle followed the men around, directing where everything should go.

As soon as they were done, Dad sat down on the new couch. He'd made no objection to any of it. Out had gone the chipped linoleum table and the ramshackle chairs. The cracked wooden bench beneath the window. When the old, thready couch was tilted through the door, he followed it with his eyes; but he said nothing. As the truck pulled away, Cle unpacked a box of candles in pewter cups and set them along the window ledges.

That night at dinner, she lit them. She'd picked up her husband by then, and he'd taken his place at the far end of the table. He didn't even seem to notice that anything had changed. His eyes were dull, staring out the window. While Cle served the meal, he turned his chin away and gazed into one of the candles. His lips were pale. My father, at the other end, ate steadily, clinking his fork, talking with the elegant woman beside him. Every now and then, he would turn his attention to Biettermann, but Biettermann didn't even look back.

With dessert, the conversation between Cle and my father at last quieted. Then came the evening silence. Out the window, the last light of day flared, the shorebirds *cheep-cheep*ing in the scrub.

Dad had eaten most of a steak, a salad, and a plate of pears. Now he leaned back in one of the new chairs, the sun angling up through the windows onto his cheeks. A line of violet flamed the row of prints on the wall. He lifted his head and gazed at them, his eyes lowering then to our faces. On Biettermann's they rested the longest.

.   .   .

THE NEXT EVENING, Cle walked up from the dock to ask if I would mind picking up her husband for dinner. She'd been sitting on the bench with Dad, watching a row of thunderstorms over the far hills, and now she walked back down again and sat beside him.

As I drove toward town to get Earl, charged air rolled through the car. The sky above was clear, but from the west, the thunder was steadily rumbling, like furniture being moved in the distant part of a house. I took the long route, pulling into the Speedway station at the crossroads and taking my time with a cup of coffee.

When I finally walked up the ramp at the Lakeland Suites, I heard banging from inside the room. The curtains were drawn. I stamped my feet a couple of times, then knocked. The banging stopped. Then it came again—one, two, three times, shaking the floor. When the door opened, Earl was standing in front of me.

"Oh—"

"What?" he said. "Where's my wife?"

The wheelchair was pushed against the bed.

"I'm sorry. I thought—"

"You wouldn't be the first." He screwed up his face, threw one arm out against the doorframe, and made a stiff-legged lunge, pushing off the wall with his fist so that he landed on the mattress. He pulled the wheelchair close and lifted himself into it.

On the drive to the cabin he told me the story: rainy night, fancy motorcycle—a handmade Ecosse racer that he'd been trying out for a friend. Full-face helmet and Kevlar suit. And just a couple of blocks from home. A teenager running a light.

"Are you ever going to be able to walk again?" I said.

"Not many have."

"I'm sorry. I didn't know."

"Didn't know what?"

"That you could stand up like that."

"And what? Lurch?"

"Walk."

"I can't walk."

"All right." By now, I was guiding the car over the ruts at the dark end of the cove. Night had fallen and the rain still hadn't hit, but across the lake, lightning was flaring the horizon. At the mailbox, I tapped the horn a couple of times before I turned in to the drive. I was distracted, and maybe for that reason, I said, "Well, it could have been worse."

He spared me by not answering. We pulled up to the cabin, and I'd already shut off the engine by the time I noticed what the headlights were shining on: Dad and Cle, still sitting together down by the dock. They hadn't even come up yet to start dinner. I couldn't find the light switch, so I tried opening the door. But the lights stayed on. Next to me I could hear Earl's steady breathing. He just sat there, looking implacably down at the two of them, until finally, with a click, they disappeared back into the night.

THE NEXT MORNING, when we sat down to breakfast, I looked out the window and saw that the ramp had been removed. "Where's Earl?"

"Back in New York," answered Cle. "He has a busy week."

Dad looked up from his plate and smiled.

The Sum of Infinitesimals

So THAT WAS how we lived, at the beginning of that summer. Just Cle and Dad and I, out in the woods in that tumbledown cabin, now nicely furnished. I called New York and extended my leave. What could Physico say? They'd have a pretty hard time replacing me.

The cherry orchards across the lake turned from white to green. In the mornings and evenings, I built a fire in the small hearth whose walls were black with soot; then soon, I was building one only in the mornings. Puffs of warm air arrived from the south like trumpet blasts ahead of an army. Geese crossed overhead. At the bench along the dock, Dad and Cle sat watching them.

Right before lunch each day, Dad and I would go down to the water together. Cle would use the time to drive into town for groceries. This was my hour with him. We'd sit on the dock or walk on the paths. I have to say, the days took on a malleability that I'd almost forgotten. The geese. The mergansers. The minks, scrabbling in the crags on sunny mornings. For a time, I called the office every day; but after a while, I just stopped.

Our dinners were quiet—the two of them sitting beside each other the way they did on the dock, but with me at the head of the table now, passing the food. Dad was eating, which pleased Dr. Gandapur. He could finish a whole steak. And though in the afternoons he still grew tired, his nap always seemed to revive him, and in the evenings he grew alert. There was the long, ruddy light. The sharpness of the cedars against the water. He would rise on the new sofa and look from Cle's face to mine.

ONE MORNING, I watched Dad dress himself. I could see that he was feeling good. Pressed slacks from the closet. A sweater from the drawer. The polished wing tips. Standing at the mirror, he combed his hair carefully and splashed cologne onto his collar.

When he noticed me watching he said, "Will you smell this?" He stepped forward. "What's happened to it?"

"I don't know, Dad."

"I'm only asking you what the cologne smells like." He pulled the collar toward me.

"It smells like lime, Dad. Same as it always has."

"What?" He sniffed the cloth. "It stinks. Don't you smell that? It's gone putrid."

"What? No, I don't. It smells the same."

He stepped away. In front of the mirror he busied himself with his cuffs, then leaned forward to examine the stubble on his neck. I could see that he was actually trying to smell his collar again. After a time, he said, "Isn't it amazing?"

"What?"

"I don't know," he said. "I just don't know what's happening to me."

HE BEGAN GROOMING himself like that every day now—like a dandy. The shined shoes. The combed hair. Sometimes he'd put on his old black Princeton jacket with its oiled leather sleeves. It had always been small for him, but now it fit. Cle pinned the cuffs so that they wouldn't hang over his hands. He wore it during the string of cool mornings that arrived midway through the month. The zipper halfway closed, the collar turned up against his neck. She would take his arm: together they would make their way down to the water.

He seemed to be entering the first turns of a maze.

It was hard to know why some days were better than others. In the mornings, he'd walk with her, his step a pace or two ahead. A glance over his shoulder, as though if she stumbled on the path he might still help her. Their spot was the bench at the tip of the dock. A couple of the boards halfway out had cracked, and he'd step past them, then reach back for her hand. His daily gentility. She would take his thin arm and step over. Then they would continue out to the end.

There's a moment I remember so clearly from that time. One of my father's spells of energy. A clear morning. A coat of dew. He and Cle making their way along the dampened boards. At the gap, she takes his elbow. Then the rest of the way out to the spalted bench, arm in arm. His bony fingers. Her pale knees. Her face turned to his.

I was washing the breakfast dishes. My mother's old chore.

Then: a small movement. A quick, upward tilt of her chin.

And suddenly they're kissing. Her hand comes up and touches his neck.

EMMY PICKED UP the phone saying, "Daddy!" She was packing her own lunch for school. She told me about a pyramid she'd built the night before from matchboxes. The number of boxes on each level was determined by a Lucas sequence. Did I know what a Lucas sequence was? I did. She recited the function anyway. She informed me that the Lucas numbers were only one example of a Lucas sequence. I told her I was proud of her. Of course, I was also touched with dread.

I asked her how everybody was getting along. She said, "I don't know, just a minute." She got off the line. Now Niels came on. He asked me how I was doing. He asked about his grandfather. He asked about the lady who was with us. He told me that Emmy was misbehaving a little bit, but only at bedtime, and that he missed me, although not so badly that he wanted me to come home. If I needed to stay with Grandpa, that was fine. He said he would understand. He would *understand*. He said he imagined I loved my own father the way he and Emmy loved me. I told him that this was really kind of him to consider. I told him that I loved him very much, too. He said that Mom was good and New York was fine. He'd already made himself a peanut-butter-and-banana sandwich for school. If Mom asked him to, he would make one for Emmy. She had a book report due that day. "Social studies," he said, lowering his voice. "Not a good subject for her." I told him she'd already made her own lunch. Then he said goodbye and went downstairs to load his backpack.

Audra came on. She asked me how I was. I told her. I asked her how she was. She told me about a fundraiser at the kids' school and about a contractor down the block who'd been sandblasting a brownstone that belonged to a sheikh. She told me about a weekend playdate she'd arranged for Emmy with a new girl from the neighborhood.

When she finished, I said, "So, how's Mom doing?"

"Oh, she's good. She's really good. She seems to have a lot of energy. She's gone out to visit Paulie."

"Oh, I didn't know they were doing that."

"It was your sister's idea. I guess she figured she'd get to spend some time with her while you weren't here." Then she added, "Actually, I think it's good for both of them."

As she talked, Dad appeared through the window and turned down the path toward the lake. A moment later, Cle came down behind him. When she arrived at the turn in the path, he reached back for her arm.

"So, how's Mom doing?" I asked.

There was a pause.

"Are you all right?" asked Audra.

"Yes, I'm fine. I'm fine. I'm okay."

"Because you just asked me that," she said.

The Witch of Agnesi

DAD'S HAND SHOOK, but he pulled the knife along the grain, canting his wrist so that the shaving curled away into his palm. I sat down beside him. "What are you making?"

"A whistle," he said. He held it out. "It's for your son. Here, blow."

It made two tones, one high and one low.

"Two frequencies," he said. "I learned that when I was Niels's age. I used to whittle things like this in the woods. Spent all my days out there by myself. Does he like that kind of thing?"

"Niels loves the woods."

Dad didn't look up. From his pocket he pulled a narrower blade and began slotting the end. He wedged out a chip and squared the opening. "I meant being alone," he said.

"No. Not really. He's the social one."

"Does he know where he is?"

I looked out at the water. "He can't do any of that, Dad. But Emmy can. I'm afraid she has all of it."

"You're right to be afraid, then." With the flat of the knife, he smoothed the barrel, keeping the blade parallel to the wood. "Well, he should enjoy this anyway," he said and blew another note.

A wind came up suddenly, bending the trees. Then, just as quickly, it calmed.

"What about Emmy, Dad?"

"What about her?"

"Do you think you could make a whistle for *her, too*?"

"PART OF IT," he said, "is a revelation. Look at the color of this." He pulled up the bottom of his shirt, where the skin was bronze, like tanning cream. "My liver's off. The proteins are gone. That's what Gandhi tells me." He tapped the lip of swelling that had appeared again. "Osmotic pressure. Simple mathematics, coming back around to take a swing at me."

"Well, it's better than it was."

"The things you take for granted. One part goes and everything else follows. You cross the line, you don't get another chance. When I shave, it bleeds for an hour. And look at my hands." He held one up. "It's all a perfect strangeness."

"Does that hurt?"

"No. But they're red as beets, aren't they? It's my joints that hurt. And sometimes I itch in places you wouldn't want to know. The itching's the worst. Most of the other stuff wouldn't really even bother me. Not that much, anyway." He looked at me sourly. "It's like watching a zombie movie, but you're starring in it."

When he scratched his shoulder, I saw the nail marks under his collar. He rose and undid the rest of his shirt buttons. "Did I ever show you these?"

"What am I looking at?"

"I'm turning into the thing I loved," he said. He parted the fabric of his shirt then, and two rubbery breasts swung out. When he dipped his shoulders, they bounced. "Not bad, am I?"

"I've seen better."

That made him laugh. When he caught his breath, he leaned against the chair and undid his belt, then let his pants slide down. From his shorts he lifted out one of his testicles. It was hairless and small. "And feel *this*."

"I think I'll pass, Dad."

He pulled out the other one. "They're just about gone, Hans."

He shuddered, letting himself down into the chair again. "Even my old friends have run for the hills."

THE PAIN IN his joints had begun to wake him from sleep, and one evening, Dr. Gandapur stopped by and tried him on a little morphine. Dad swallowed the pill and lay down on the couch. A few minutes later, he sat up and vomited.

Cle heated a cup of soup, and they tried again. This time Dad kept it down; but after Dr. Gandapur left, he stayed on the couch for the rest of the night, half sitting and half lying against the leather, licking his lips and staring wide eyed at whoever was checking on him, as though trying to figure out whether it was Cle or I who was plotting the attack.

The next morning, when the doctor drove back out to see him, Dad said, "Don't ever ask me to do that again."

"I understand," said Dr. Gandapur.

"No," said Dad, blinking across at him. "You *don't* understand. I need to be able to *think*."

"Even at night?"

"Yes, even at night."

Later, at the door of the Mercedes, I said to the doctor, "I'm sorry about that."

"Oh, there's nothing to apologize for. It was I who overstepped. He'll do fine on what he's on, perhaps with a little more at bedtime. A mind like his—the drug must perturb it."

"Frankly, I wouldn't think he'd give a damn about perturbing *anything* these days."

He laughed. "But you see, he still *does*." He settled himself in the seat. "We never rightly understand the existence of another, do we? Of course, he prefers the medicine that he already knows." He bowed his head, and his pale fingers came to rest on the mirror. "And that is what we will keep him on, for as long as it is possible."

CLE HAD ROASTED a chicken. I'd made a salad, from carrots and lettuce and the pink, box-cornered balls of wax that were sold by the Felt City General Store as tomatoes. The afternoon had been warm, but now the lake was dark and a wind was stirring the trees.

We were a good way through the meal when I realized that Dad had stopped eating. Cle had come in from the kitchen and was standing behind him, pouring wine with one hand and rubbing his shoulder with the other. Dad set down his fork on the table and looked up. Then he looked back at his plate. Beside him, Cle's eyes slowly rose. After a moment, I turned around.

Peering through the porch windows were Paulie and my mother.

A Unifying Conjecture

THE COMBINATORICS MEETING had been held at a plush hotel in the West End of London, which was a fifteen-minute walk from my plusher one in Mayfair. A chilly October day, not long after my first trip out to see Dad. The Thames that morning was alive with barges and seabirds. Out front of the hotel, the souvlaki vendors were hawking hot plates, the oily blue sheen of handprints streaking the lobby doors. It wasn't difficult to spot the mathematicians as they milled among the carts, comparing prices.

The meeting itself was more lavish than I had expected. A chandeliered ballroom with nineteenth-century oil paintings on the walls. On the side tables, carefully fanned advertisements for jet-shares. In the alcoves, the murmur of fountains. I wondered why mathematicians chose these kinds of places if they really wanted to stay in their math departments.

On the Internet I'd been able to find only a meager history of Benedek Fodor. His Wikipedia page was a grainy picture and one sentence about his interests, which were wildly divergent—matroid theory, tensor theory, Riemannian geometry. There was nothing at all about his life. I'd picked up bits on my own: he was an autodidact, the son of a cheese maker from a village in the Mátra. At nineteen, the Abel Prize; at twenty-nine, the Fields. There were only a handful of articles about either one, though, and all of them had been written from the same information. He'd not even bothered to appear at the ceremony for the Fields. No wife and no children. Still shared a house with his parents. In every article, I read the same quotes, from a local precinct official and a tavern owner and a policeman, apparently the only residents of his prefecture who would speak to a reporter. They were all aware that Benedek Fodor had accomplished something significant, but none of them knew what it was.

I'd left my Wall Street clothes back at the hotel.

When I found him, he was standing outside the door of the auditorium, poking his narrow head into a dismal-looking presentation on Dirichlet series. Inside were half-a-dozen mathematicians in a room that could have held a hundred. "Dr. Fodor?" I said, extending my hand. "May I introduce myself? My name is Hans Andret."

He kept his arms at his side. "Say his name?"

"Hans Andret."

"*His* name."

"Do you mean *Milo* Andret?"

"Ah," he said. Carefully, he raised his hand. The rough palm. The dirty shirt cuff. "Perhaps," he said, in a precisely edged accent. "Perhaps I know who you are."

I offered to take him to lunch. He glanced down at the carpet, then nodded. We stepped away from whatever new thing was being revealed about Dirichlet series and walked down the block to a noodle shop off the square, a place I'd noted on the way in. Not for the food but because it looked quiet enough.

He ordered two bowls of soup. When the first arrived, he ate it to the bottom, then lifted the bowl to his lips and sucked down the last bit of broth. All this before we'd spoken anything beyond pleasantries.

"You understand?" he finally said, setting down the dish. "You understand what is it?"

"Understand what what is?"

"The problem."

The waiter brought him his second soup, and he started in.

"Yes, I do."

He grimaced.

"So here you come."

"Yes."

"You are the first." He plucked a wedge of meat from the spoon and set it on the tablecloth. "You first to come ask about it."

"I suppose I'm happy to hear that."

"You are topologist like him?"

"No, I'm not. I work in a very different field."

He set another piece of meat on the tablecloth. "A dirty field?"

"A what?"

"A dirty field?"

"It's not mathematics. Is that what you mean, Dr. Fodor?"

"*Brother* Fodor." Into the new bowl he lunged. The waiter skirted past and refilled our water glasses. "Like my countryman, Erdős—every man's brother."

"Okay. Good."

"Financials?" he said over the steaming spoon.

"Is that what I do? Yes, it is."

For a moment he appeared jubilant. Then angry. Then puzzled. He poured his water into his soup bowl, twisting off the glass like a sommelier. "Clearly you are three times more intelligent than your father."

"Clearly not." I signaled to the waiter for more water, then for tea. "Look," I said. "I read your proof. I read it thoroughly. It's very good."

"Is logic."

"Yes, of course. It's logic. I understand how it pertains. I understand what it means." I composed my features. "About the Malosz theorem, Dr. Fodor. Brother Fodor." I cleared my throat. "It could disprove what my father proved. What he won the Fields for."

He smiled gaily. "The Fields is a plate of shit."

"Perhaps so."

"Yes," he said into the bowl. "Perhaps so. I love this. Perhaps so!"

I tried to smile.

He said, "I did for the curse."

Another piece of meat onto the tablecloth.

"The curse of knowledge." Steam drifted from his mouth like exhaust from a dryer. He was still smiling. "I did for the curse of humanity."

I looked closely at him. The oily lips, the damp glasses, the starved eyes. "Ah, yes," I said. "Of course. All for the *cause* of knowledge. The *cause* of humanity."

"Yes, excuse!" He laughed. "*Átok. Curse* is *átok.* I meant *cause.*"

His own mistake seemed to win him over.

"Would you like another soup?"

"Yes, please!"

The waiter was quick with the third one. Fodor poured another glass of water into it, then attacked. By now a half circle of meat dampened the linens. When he'd finished, he said, "Of course I do not wish to hurt anyone reputation." He set his spoon upright into the glass and folded his hands. "He is great man, your father. And he is the father, so you have come for defending."

"Yes, perhaps. Though perhaps we don't think of it exactly the same way. I'm obliged to defend him, but in other ways I don't feel that I am. I'm obliged more to the truth. That's what it is. I believe my father would agree with that statement."

He looked curiously at me.

"I meant no offense, Dr. Fodor."

"Tell me, he is well?"

"No, he's not well. Actually, he's rather ill."

"I do not mean to cause harm. Particularly."

"I can see that you don't."

"You are his friendly son."

"Perhaps."

"Why perhaps?"

"Yes, I am."

"Do you understand however?"

"Do I understand what? The proof?"

"Yes."

I sipped my tea. "Yours or his?"

"His. Mine is not proof. Mine is question. The maths are of your father."

"Yes, I do understand. A reasonable part of the proof, anyway. I think I do. But I'm no topologist."

Another silence. He looked at me suspiciously.

"Would you like another bowl of soup?"

"No. Is good."

He turned his head suddenly, looking out the door.

Finally, I said, "Brother Fodor, may I ask you something?"

Without turning around, he said, "Yes. Please ask it."

"Do you think my father knew?"

At that very moment the tea arrived. It was poured. Fodor turned and gazed into his cup. Held his hands in the steam. Their backs were lashed with pen marks. Finally he raised his head. "Does he knew *what*?"

"That there was an error. That the logic, at a certain point—that the logic of his proof falters."

He leaned across the table and stared at me. With his hand he moved a piece of meat on the tablecloth: slightly left, slightly left again, slightly right. His eyes were wide, looking through to the back of my skull.

Then, just like that, he composed himself. "Is complicated proof," he said, looking up again. "Mr. Andret. Do you know how complicated?"

"Yes, I think so. I work in probability. As I said, I'm no topologist, but I believe I do understand. What he did and what you did. Both of you."

"Is a very, very complicated proof. You saw this?" He was smiling broadly now. Dark gums shading his molars. "Very. Very. Very. Very. Very. How many would you say?"

"How many what?"

"How many *very*."

"Five is good."

"Yes, agreed! Very. Very. Very. Very. Very complicated." He grinned like a boy now. "Few understand. Few topologist even." Then he bowed from the neck. "I no topologist, either. I think myself as nothing. Not even nothing. Only shadows of nothing." He nodded at me, still amused. "I believe however that you are one really?"

"One what? A topologist? No."

"Yes."

"My question is, Mr. Fodor—may I ask you? I believe you may be one of the few, I believe you may be the only—perhaps in the world—the only one who might be able to answer this." I leaned down and tried to capture his eyes, but they darted away. "Your paper isn't exactly a refutation of my father's proof. I understand that. But nonetheless it alludes to a mistake. A central mistake."

"A problem in the maths."

"Yes, exactly. My question, Mr. Fodor. My question is, do you think my father knew of this problem?"

"Ah." The smile switched off like a lamp. He looked away. "You mean, at *then* moment?"

"Yes, did he know of it at the time it occurred?"

"You will not speak this, please."

"Of course not."

Then he thought. The way another man might have signaled for the bill, or turned his back to place a phone call, or stood to fetch the car, Benedek Fodor sat across the table from me and thought. He closed his eyes, brought his bearing straight, and sat. A pulse showed in his jaw.

After fifteen minutes—I was checking the clock—he made a little nod with his chin. "I will pose question," he said.

"What is it?"

"Do *you* think he knew?"

I closed my own eyes. I pictured him. The boxed-up bottles. The useless drawings.

I opened them again. "Yes," I said. "I believe he probably did."

"Then, yes, Mr. Andret. I say that I agree. Great mathematician always knows."

Contra Deum

DR. GANDAPUR LEANED to the window, half crossing himself. "Does the Lord not work in unexpected ways?"

"He's been like this since they arrived."

With his women around him now, Dad had mustered himself. In the garden, Cle was trickling water from a bucket, and my mother was drawing a rusted hoe through the clods. Dad made the rear, bending forward as he moved up the line, wrapping long weeds in his fist and trying to pull them up. Now and then he succeeded. Sitting alongside the plot was a wheelbarrow, where he'd toss them. When my mother bent to move it a few feet, he lifted his head to watch her.

"And your mother?" said Dr. Gandapur. "She doesn't mind the arrangement?"

"My mother is a saint."

"Ah." He closed his bag and turned to the window. Dad was struggling with a stalk; when it came free, he staggered, then recovered and set it on top of the pile in the wheelbarrow. He pushed himself up the line, his eyes fixed on the back of Mom's legs. After a moment, he turned and looked at Cle's.

"I am afraid I cannot agree," said Dr. Gandapur.

"With what?"

He reddened. "My apologies to the good fathers of Lahore," he said, crossing himself, "but if there is one thing I have learned in this life, it is that there is no such thing as a saint."

"BUT SHE IS," said Paulie. "If she can still care about *him*"—she pointed out at the dock, where he was sitting between Mom and Cle—"anybody who could still care about him—oh, God, look at that—she's more than a saint. She could be *deified*."

We were in our old bedroom upstairs, watching from the window.

"You look good, by the way," I said. Her outfit was divided by two sets of matched creases, as though the skirt and blouse had been pulled a few minutes ago from the same packet of dry cleaning. She was wearing heels, too, which was new for my sister, and her hair had been pinned back in a bun. "You look like the lord mayor of Zanzibar, Paulie."

"Well, Hansie, you look like one of my savages."

We hugged.

"I'm glad you decided to come."

"Well," she said, "we'll see about that." Her gaze dropped to my hand.

"Grapefruit juice." I raised the glass. "Scurvy, you know."

She laughed. Then she moved to the wall, where her bed was still made under the old yellow blanket. Next to it, under the old green one, was my own. She picked up the goldfish bowl from the table between them. "I used to keep my crayfish in here," she said.

"I remember. Mom used to have to throw the water out whenever we got the call from the department of public health."

She looked over at me. "What?"

"You knew that, Paulie. They stunk so bad, we had to hold our noses with clothespins when she brought them down to the lake."

She set down the bowl. "I guess I had a dream once that they just climbed out. Maybe that's why I forgot. I used to be afraid of stepping on them when I had to go to the bathroom."

She leaned down and peeked under the bed.

"Any still under there?"

She rose, allowing herself a small smile. "It's amazing what a child will believe, Hans. I remember thinking that maybe I hadn't been a good-enough mother."

"To raise crayfish?"

"Don't laugh."

"Paulie," I said. "You'd be an excellent mother. You'd *still* be one."

"Thank you." She lowered herself to the mattress and closed her eyes. "Can I ask you something? Are you sleeping in here?"

"I'm in Mom and Dad's room."

She looked over. "Then where's Dad?"

"On the porch. I don't want him climbing stairs."

"Oh. Then where—"

She stopped.

"She's in the other room, Paulie. The downstairs bedroom. By herself."

She raised her eyebrows.

"I don't think so," I said.

"Well, that's good news, anyway. Count your blessings." She stood up and went to the closet. "This whole place, though—don't you smell it? It's being taken over by some kind of fungus."

"Well, I cleaned it as well as I could."

"And all that furniture. Did you buy all that for him, too?"

"As a matter of fact, Paulie, I didn't."

She glanced over.

"Cle did," I said.

"That's what I thought."

"I know. But he didn't seem to mind."

"And if there's anything *she* won't do for him, then *Mom* will? Is that the idea?"

"Oh, come on, now—look at him. You don't expect him to have the energy to keep this up all by himself, do you?"

"Well, what about when we were young?"

"He had other things to think about."

She smirked.

"Oh, come on, Paulie. You can't fight him all your life."

"I know that. But you can't *glorify* him all of yours." She turned and lifted the shade again. Outside, the three of them were still together on the dock, but they were laughing now. Cle's shoulders shook. Even Mom was grinning. Dad bent sideways, reaching for a glass.

"God," she said. "He got everything he wanted, didn't he?"

She let the shade drop, then reached under her hair and placed one tiny earring, then the other, onto the dresser. When she sat again on the mattress, the springs creaked. She shimmied against the headboard and folded a pillow beneath her back. Then she closed her eyes and said, "How's he doing, Hans—*really?*"

"He's looking a lot better than when I got here." I handed her the pillow from my bed. "But the truth is that he's not in very good shape at all."

"Is he in pain?"

"I'd say he's in *some.* But I think what's really bothering him is watching it all happen. I think he's pretending to be fascinated by it."

"That's the way he always was."

"Well, not exactly." I sat down next to her. "I think he *knows* now, Paulie."

She looked up. "Oh, God," she said. She reached behind her neck, and the bun unwound onto her shoulders. Then, as though the hairpins had been a dam, she began to cry. "Oh, God," she said. "I knew it. I knew it would happen like this."

She still cried the way she had as a girl, the tears beading like drops of solder at the corners of her eyes. She leaned back against the headboard, shuddering. One at a time, the tiny pearls budded, grew, and wandered down her cheeks.

"Well," I said to my mother that night. "You came after all."

"Of course I did."

In the dark, I heard the rising pitch of the wine filling her glass; then the squeak as she fitted back the cork. "It's hard not to help when he's suffering."

"It must be particularly hard for *you*."

She looked over.

I pointed up at the house, where Cle was standing in the flicker of the kitchen bulb, drying the pots with a towel. "I mean, with *her* here."

"Oh, please. I couldn't care less about your father as a husband." The bottle clanked against the boards. "And I already have my grandchildren. Do I look like the kind of woman who'd be jealous of another man's wife?"

She tilted up her profile.

"I don't know, Mom. There's not enough moon to see."

Her laugh sounded like one of Paulie's. In a moment, her footsteps moved away from me. When they returned, she set something down. I heard a grating sound. Then I saw the glow: the old dynamo lantern. "Well," she said, "how about now?" She pumped the handle and tilted her face into the light. "Do I look like the kind of woman who'd be jealous of some tycoon's wife?"

"No, Mom. You don't."

"Thank you." She stopped pumping, and the bulb flickered for a few seconds before it went out.

"Paulie's upset," I said.

"Of course she is." Then she added, "That's why we came." She moved up next to me. "And that's why we didn't call. She wasn't sure she could actually go through with it."

"She's still mad about things that happened when we were kids."

"That's just grief."

"Well, she was mad about them *then*, too."

"And that was the same thing, honey." She touched my hand. "It was always just grief."

Up at the cabin, another light went on, and my sister appeared behind Cle at the kitchen sink. Cle reached up and closed the blinds.

"Mom," I said. "Were you ever in love with him?"

"Was I ever in love with your father?" She let out a sigh. "I was in love with what he'd done, I suppose. I was in love with his mind. I mean, think of what he brought into the world. Think of what he built from nothing." She sighed again. "I never know what to make of all the rest. Half the time he was unendurable. But the other half—"

"I know."

She lowered the lantern over the lake and pumped it again. In the ring of light, a pack of water striders froze like thieves. "I suppose it might have been a mistake. But how can you ever be sure? I don't know—for better or worse—he was an extraordinary person." Up at the house, the lamp came on in the downstairs bedroom now, and Cle opened the curtains there. Then it went off again, and when she reappeared at the glass, a candle was flickering in her hands.

"What do you think about *her*?" I said.

"I guess I don't know what to say to that."

After a while, I said, "You're right, Mom. I'm sorry I asked."

We sat there, listening to the water tapping the dock posts.

"Hans," she said, "did he ever tell you about her?"

"He did, Mom."

"Well, I suppose I don't want to know."

"You probably don't."

She looked up at me then with an expression I didn't recognize. "She's fancy," she said. "She's educated. She seems to have a bit more money than she knows what to do with." She sipped her wine. "And I gather she has a *staff*." Then she said, "Bah."

"You're more elegant."

"Bah again."

"Well, you *are*."

"Don't worry, Hans. I know what I am."

But she moved closer to me then, and on her skin I smelled the faint bitter-grass scent that she sometimes emitted. Up at the house, the curtain was still open, and in the wobble of the candle I could see Cle standing back from the glass. Mom rose to her feet.

I reached for the dynamo, and when I found it, I started to pump. Light rose on the filament, like a glowworm climbing a string. Before us, a small halo of cove came into being: the moths, the minnows, the tracts of celery weed swaying in the undercurrent, like rows of hands waving from the bottom. "You're more beautiful," I said.

"*Oh, please,* Hans." Then, after a moment: "Well, thank you."

She set the glass at her feet now and stepped out into the ring of light. Before me, in its lunar brightness, she straightened her skirt and blouse. I kept the dynamo going, and in its glow the ivory of her skin began to luminesce. She placed her hands on her hips and brought her neck straight. She arched her spine and tilted back her head so that her hair fell across her shoulders. She held that pose, like an actress under a klieg lamp. For a long, white-lit moment, she was a young woman again, standing on a brass-railed pier, looking over a rocky New England lake.

Then there was a pop, and behind her, the stars came back into the sky.

"THE MAGIC BULLET," Dad said, pointing through the trees to where the three of them were sitting by the shore. Paulie was dressed in a pleated skirt and Mom in her patched-up overalls, but their likeness was striking. The same drawn-up posture. The same long limbs, despite neither being tall. And Cle, strangely, who sat sideways in her chair, could have been the sister of either of them. "Look at that," he said. "Who wouldn't be cured by that?"

He took a drink and set the glass on the desk. The shed smelled even more like mildew than the house had before I'd cleaned it. The roof must have been leaking.

"I know what you're thinking," he said. "Evidently, your father is a monster. I've been told this fact by your mother. And by your mother's lawyer. And by your sister, many times. But you should know—neither your mother nor your sister believes it. What they actually believe is that they're my salvation." He swirled his drink. "And that I'm theirs."

"Okay."

"You see?" He pointed. "They don't even mind each other."

"I think Mom might."

"You mean she minds that she doesn't hold the monopoly anymore?"

"That's one way to put it."

"Well, she's the one who came up. I didn't invite her."

I stood and moved to where a pile of journals lay on the rug. I hadn't cleaned out here, and he obviously hadn't bothered to pick them up himself—for years, it seemed. Above them on the shelves stood a line of volumes from an old library set. Leather bindings and gold-lettered titles. I ran my fingers over the spines: Augustine, Descartes, Hume, Locke, Russell. A row of philosophers arranged in alphabetical order. "Is this what you've been doing all this time?" I said. "Reading philosophy?"

"I've been attempting to understand the human being, Hans, if that's what you're asking."

"And this is the method you've adopted?"

"I'm waiting to hear a better one."

"Well, you could just walk outside and talk to a few real ones."

"Your generation is so predictable," he said. "It's all about the connection, isn't it? The connectors have gained the upper hand. We isolationists languish in the caves. Take my word for it, Hans, I've tried." He turned and regarded me frankly. "The monster isn't very good at chitchat."

"No one ever said you were a monster."

"Your mother and sister did." He filled his glass again. "And I imagine they've convinced you."

"I believe you don't have much control over it."

He spit, laughing. "Is that the brainwashing they gave you?"

"It wasn't a brainwashing. I had a problem."

"Ah—step one."

When he saw my face, he said, "Oh, come on, Hans. Relax. It's not so dire. Have a drink with your old man." He swirled the bottle. Then he probed beneath the desk until he managed to wrangle out another glass. "Come on, it's your dad offering. I'm feeling better today." He tipped the bottle at me. "Have a drink with your old man, to celebrate. I mean, booze wasn't your problem, anyway, was it? Your problem was those drugs."

"The drugs were the symptom."

"And the problem?"

"I'm working on it."

He raised an eyebrow. "And this is the method you've adopted?"

"Funny, Dad."

"Look," he said, filling the other glass, "you can go round and round with it, but in the end the proofs are worthless. All you're left with is first principles." He pointed at the shelves. "Augustine versus Pelagius. I'm with Augustine. Every one of us is flawed."

He wiped the glass with his shirt and held it forward. In those days, I didn't much like the taste of bourbon; but after a moment, I took it.

"Thank you, Hans."

"You're not welcome."

He turned and looked out the window then, to where the three of them had risen from the chairs. They were picking their way up the path toward the house, like a trio of deer on a hill. I watched him watch them.

"Dad," I said, "do you really think you wasted your career?"

His eyes came back.

"When I told you I'd wasted *mine*," I said, "I mean, *wasted the mathematics,* you said that that made two of us."

"Look. I don't even know what that means." He shook his head and took another swallow. "A mathematician is a mathematician not because of anything he's done, Hans. In fact, most mathematicians understand that in the end they've done nothing at all."

"But you did a lot."

"Did I? You could say that the only thing we ever really figure out is that the thing we want to know next is just one rung up on the ladder of ignorance." His gaze drifted to the window. "A mathematician is constantly aware of having *no understanding at all*. He does what he does mostly because such ignorance rankles him. That's the thing he seeks to remedy. Otherwise, there are a thousand more suitable pursuits." He turned the bottle in his hand. "There's no answer that ends the search, you know. Obviously, there never will be. The artist seeks to capture the world because the nature of every single object is a mystery to him. The philosopher addresses human nature because he's a stranger to every part of it. It's the same for mathematicians. It's all ignorance, Hans. Ignorance and wounded shrieking." He took another drink. "But it's all irresistible, too, isn't it? That's how we're made. We want what won't have us."

"Fuck you, Dad."

He smiled—with real pleasure, it seemed, for the first time in years. "Fuck you, Son."

After a few moments, I raised my glass. "It's true, Dad. You can still talk."

"Ah, yes, Hans. I always could."

I CAME ACROSS the notepad one morning when I was straightening the kitchen. It had been buried under a cluster of bills and retirement magazines. Dark rings on the cover. There were other drawings in it, too, quick sketches of the trees and the cove and the view across the lake, all of them arresting in their own right, even in their simplicity. I took my time leafing through the pages, though I knew exactly what I was looking for. I found it a few down from the top.

There she was. Slender. Her profile turned against the banks of a river. This was a different kind of drawing. Each strand of hair had been individually drawn. Each shadow on the face brought out with a web of fine lines. Dad had reproduced the folds of her skirt exactly, and the rush of water beyond it so perfectly, with nothing but the hatching of his pen.

Still, it took me several moments before I understood what I was looking at: it was Cle Wells, as a young woman.

"MAY I ASK you something?"

"Depends what it is," said Cle. We were in her Citroën, heading back with groceries. She was driving fast, and the bags were rattling in the trunk.

"Did Dad use to visit you in Manhattan?"

For a moment, she didn't answer. Then she said, "A couple of times, yes."

"So when he broke the mirrors in that restaurant, it had something to do with you."

"Well, it had more to do with the fact that he was drunk."

"And what about here, then? Did you ever come up *here* to see him?"

"Once, yes—stupidly. A few years ago."

"May I ask you something else?"

She looked over. "I think so."

"What does Earl think of all this?"

"It's complicated."

"Do you love him?"

"You're talking about your dad, I presume?"

"Yes."

"Well, at my age, it doesn't mean much."

"So you do."

"I mean the *word* doesn't mean much. Not that it did when we were young, either—not for me, anyway. Do I love your father? I suppose I do. Love at this stage is all kinds of things, not the least of which is pity."

"So you pity him."

"Of course I do. But I love him, also. And I feel a duty to him. I feel pity and duty for both of them." She turned the mirror to look at herself, at her narrow features that were still, to me, strikingly lovely. "That probably sounds cruel," she said.

"Do you pity *yourself*?"

"For what?"

"For marrying the wrong man?"

She laughed. "Earl and I do fine."

"Earl told me he doesn't believe in pity."

"He did? Well, that's because he wouldn't know where to start."

On the curves of the cove now she pressed the accelerator, and a man in a driveway shook his head as we passed. "You're always in a hurry," I said.

"Life is short."

"Then why are you staying up here like this?"

"To help out. To be of use."

"But isn't that a little weird with my mother around? Isn't it painful for *both* of you?"

She glanced at me again, slowing the car finally as we turned in at the drive. "You know, it probably makes it easier, actually. For both of us. A young man might not understand that. But your mother's very helpful."

"And you?"

"I'm very helpful, too. You learn it, obviously. I *had* to."

When we stopped in front, she popped the trunk but didn't make a move to get out. Instead, she turned and looked out at the lake. "Your father once did something for me, Hans."

"Oh? What was that?"

"Well, it's a long story. But at this age, I finally understand what I can do for him in return."

"Which is what?"

She put her hand on the door latch. "Let him long for me again," she said.

. . .

"It used to be like rock," Dad said, "right up here, in front. Now it's soft." He poked at his ribs. "There's room now—look, Hans. And I hardly itch anymore." He brought my hand to his flank.

"What am I touching?"

"My liver. Feel how small it's gotten."

He pulled my fingers under the ribs and pressed them against what felt like a purse full of gravel.

"I've always known," he said. "Haven't I? I've always, always known."

"What have you always known?"

"When I'm on the edge of something." He let go of my hand. "Diet and exercise, Hans. And the body itself. The blood tests are going to show it now, too."

"What are they going to show, Dad?"

"That I'm getting better." He pointed up at the cabin, where Cle and my mother were cooking in the kitchen. "I can feel it, Hans. Those two—they're what's going to cure me."

The Lord's Daughter

My first morning back at work, I went in early; but by the time I walked into my office, one of the senior partners in risk was already standing at my desk. This must have been standard practice. I'd told them I'd be out for a week; I'd been gone for a little more than six.

When I shut the door, he moved to the row of windows that looked over the river. The first light of day was just showing behind the bridges.

"You're back," he said, not unkindly. "You were on family leave, right? I'm assuming everything's okay."

"Yes, it is. Thanks for asking." I slid into the chair and powered on my row of monitors. "I'm back now."

"Well, they'll want to have a word with you when they get in."

"Who will?"

"HR."

"I was going to take a look at London."

He kept his eyes on me. "I believe you'll need a password for that," he said.

What I hadn't realized was that by then there were dozens of mathematicians who could do what I was doing—all of them, in one way or another, having learned it from me. You'd have thought, at least, that this would have given the partners pause.

It hadn't.

And so here we are now, Audra and I and the kids, with money in the bank to outlast *their* kids (and their kids' kids), living in a town—Lasserville, New York, population 5,813—where a good part of the citizenry doesn't have enough money to last out the month. We're two hours closer to Kingston, Ontario, than to Lower Manhattan. We're also fifteen minutes from the Aldrich Gap River, which is fast enough along the Narrows south of the house to hold rainbow trout and slow enough along the Wides north of it for the lily pads to grow shore to shore, like a well-tacked carpet.

That carpet is the exact color of pool-table felt, which Emmy likes, because the rug in her room is of precisely the same shade. Like many devotees of group theory, she's excited by all demonstrations of symmetry. She can stand on the shore of that river for an hour while Audra and Niels and I eat lunch under the maples.

We do that quite a bit these days.

I think Emmy likes the mystery of the spot, too, the way she knows from the undulation of the green that the water is there but never actually sees it. The feeling is much like the joy of mathematics itself, the original secret of the guild: that the miracle of the universe can be worshipped without actually witnessing the divine.

I also think she might be counting the lily pads.

THE OTHER NIGHT at dinner, I gave the kids a puzzle. This was on our screened porch. I set a pair of quarters on the table and pushed them against each other so that their ridges meshed like gears. "If you hold one still," I said, "and roll the other one around it, how many revolutions will George Washington make?"

Audra looked up. "Hans," she said.

My wife doesn't like me quizzing the kids like this, particularly if we follow my father's rule that the younger one gets to go first. I suspect she worries that Niels might never get his chance.

"Either of you may answer," I added.

Contrary to what many people think, by the way, Niels is not named after Niels Bohr, the great Danish physicist, but after Niels Abel, the great Norwegian mathematician. I named him after Abel because Abel had improved on Euler's work and had been educated, not coincidentally, by his own father. Emmy's name, on the other hand—Emmy Lovelace Andret—was chosen by Audra, in honor of two great women of mathematics: Emmy Noether, whose brilliance has long been the province of the cognoscenti, and Ada Lovelace, who most likely wrote the world's first computer algorithm, and who also—again, not coincidentally—was the daughter of a poet.

That particular evening, however, Niels was quicker than his sister. Without even having to think, he said, "One."

"Why do you say that?"

"Because they have the same circumference. The gear teeth mesh. George Washington just makes a single turn around himself." He glanced at Emmy. "Isn't it obvious?"

Most mathematically inclined adults, after some thought, will arrive at this very answer—the one that Niels, at ten years old, came up with in an instant. But Emmy was silent.

Her brother laughed—a bit meanly, I thought. "See?" he said, reaching for the coins.

But I held back his hand. "You can't actually *do* it for her," I said. "You have to let her think about it herself."

His hands came back to his sides. "Come on, Em, don't you see?"

I waited for my daughter. Audra had cooked her spicy stew, a holdover from her Texas days, and had seasoned it like the Hill Country girl that she still is—the first bite tastes like a rattlesnake has gotten loose in your mouth. I poured water around. As we waited for Audra to sit down, I watched Emmy think.

She does it the way my father used to—as though it's physical exercise.

It was only after Niels and Audra had taken their first bites, wiped their mouths, and sipped their ice water, that Emmy said, "Wow."

"What is it, honey?"

"It's kind of amazing." She smiled, just slightly, in my direction.

I smiled back, just slightly, in hers.

"He doesn't go around once," she said. "He goes around twice."

LASSERVILLE IS A lot like Tapington, actually. Tapington had the rusted Ford plant; Lasserville has the rusted Maytag plant. A washing machine isn't a pickup truck, but the assembly-line workers who used to bolt the tub rotor to the spin shaft aren't that different from the assembly-line workers who used to bolt the transmission to the drivetrain. The distinction is that in Tapington I lived among the aftereffects of ingenuity. Those midwestern kids who'd grown up rebuilding hot rods in their garages had moved to the Ford plant, and when the Ford plant closed they moved back to their garages— customizing engines and fabricating body parts for the aftermarket. And Fabricus College was there, too, of course.

All this kept something alive in that town. When I was a kid, Tapington had a swimming pool and a public library that were both open seven days a week. Up here in Lasserville, the men and women who no longer make washing machines no longer make much of anything. We have tanning parlors and nail salons and pet-grooming establishments now, the signs planted in the front lawns of people's houses. The pride up here has been fraying for a while. The pool's open all summer, but the library only opens on Saturdays.

Mostly for this reason, our family is talked about around town. The Wall Street kingpin on the run from the feds. The hedge-fund magnate who ditched it all for his wife. The adviser to the Rockefellers. The adviser to the advisers. The savant who gave up a fortune to solve one of the great problems in mathematics.

That's the one I get asked about the most.

Like the others, of course, there's not a shred of truth to it.

. . .

I NEVER DID let them fire me. And, in fact, I'm not even sure they would have. I walked outside that morning, ate a cart breakfast on the piers, and for several minutes enjoyed the underbridge light show that you see from that part of Manhattan at that hour of the day. By the time I took the elevator back upstairs, HR had arrived. I brought two cups of coffee down to the sixty-fifth floor and explained to the rep what I'd decided to do.

Our life up here:

Emmy is the earliest out of bed in the morning. She rises at dawn and performs a check of the house, glancing into all our rooms, then heading downstairs to look out through the kitchen window into the barley field beyond our backyard fence, where deer in impressive numbers congregate at first light. On some mornings there are twenty-five of them. Emmy watches them while she does what she calls her *meditating*.

"What's your meditating *about*?" I asked her one day.

"Oh," she said, smiling patiently at me. "I don't know. About life."

Sometimes the deer will come close to the fence to nibble the branches of the cedars. In the yard they stare back at the spot where Emmy stands behind the glass. She's told me about one of them in particular, a gangly white-spotted yearling who wanders into the mowed area next to the kitchen and lowers her head to eat, despite my daughter's presence in the window. Emmy believes that this particular fawn has learned to trust her.

My wife likes the fact that Emmy believes this. She thinks it shows that she's decided to move outward into the world.

Both kids have changed, I have to say.

Emmy's in sixth grade now, with all the eleven-year-olds, though she's just turned nine. When I drop her off at school in the morning, she lets go of my hand and glances up at the building, then walks halfway up the path before she turns around to look at me. I nod, like a coach sending in a new player. Not that she needs it, of course—not for her schoolwork, anyway. I imagine, actually, that she's already capable of doing the problem sets for most of the math majors at Cornell, a campus not that far from here. But she wears this fact low, like a rabbit's foot in her pocket. In class, she hardly speaks and on the playground she favors the boys' games. She's not the only girl who favors them, though, and she spends her time on the weekends with a couple of like-minded allies—shy, oily-haired, front-of-the-class girls who nonetheless like to reach barehanded into the muddy stream behind the house and pull out frogs and tadpoles and even turtles. Emmy's what my sister used to be.

She can also multiply three six-digit numbers in her head and, from twenty-five miles away, point without hesitation straight at our house. If I ask her what she wants to be when she grows up, she'll look at me, smile, and say, "Older." If someone else asks, she'll answer, "A veterinarian." And if they press, "Small animal."

I'd like to believe it. Though I also believe she's saying it to reassure me.

If Emmy has something to tell either of us, she'll behave like one of her deer, sidling up alongside her mother or father the way a yearling sidles up alongside a cedar. Warily, but for the duration. Standing next to me at the sink while I rinse dishes for the washer, she'll tell me about the bad dream she had the night before or ask what to do about the boy who called her a name at school. I, in turn, must behave like the man watching the deer. No sharp movements. No quick answers.

About Emmy's night habits, Audra is at her wit's end. After dinner, Emmy will dispatch her homework in fifteen minutes, then bake cookies with Audra or sit out on the porch with me until it's time to go upstairs for her bath. Then she'll get into bed. On her night table is a stack of books, and she'll think very deliberately about which one she wants to read. One of us will go upstairs to kiss her good night, and later, at 2:00 a.m., that same one will generally have to rise from bed, go into her room again, and take the book from her hands. For good measure, we'll unplug the bedside light and move the rest of the stack, too, all the way to the far side of the room. The book in her hand, by the way, is as likely to be *White Fang* by Jack London, as *Rational Points on Elliptic Curves* by Silverman and Tate. Sometimes I think Emmy has to read simply because she doesn't know how to extinguish her thoughts. Exceed. Discover. Outdo. That's our daughter.

As for Niels—well, he too could probably do the homework for the math major at Cornell. But it would take him longer than Emmy, and he'd emerge with a red face and a pencil broken two or three times at the tip, then in half. Niels has always been our emoter, and now the emotion he's becoming acquainted with is frustration. He's learned to handle it by running forward into everything—into birthday parties, into the student-council meetings, into his scout hikes, into the spelling bees and science fairs that he's won a couple of times now.

A significant part of his success is due to the single capacity that he's developed into something far beyond his sister's. That is, his capacity to *work*. My son is a powerhouse that way—as was my father, for a time. (I also think that Niels runs so eagerly forward because he must hear the soft, quick footsteps behind him.) Niels might be able to multiply two of those six-digit numbers in his head, but I doubt he could do the third, like Emmy. But he's learning not to let this bother him. Connect. Advance. Contribute. That's Niels. He's always been our social one, and now he's turning out to be our striver, too. When I ask him what he wants to be when he grows up, he smiles winningly and says "A named professor of mechanical or electrical engineering." When pressed further, he'll expand: "At a Research One University." And further still, "At Caltech, maybe, like Aunt Paulie."

Audra, God bless her, doesn't miss Manhattan at all. Or at least, not that she tells me. She prefers the life up here, where the biggest event of the fall is the Wildcats' homecoming parade, and the biggest moment of the homecoming parade is the rambling, overwide turn that our local corn farmer takes onto Main Street (yes) in his half-million-dollar John Deere combine, an S-Series that he banners in

Wildcats purple, pulling behind it a flatbed on which stand all the junior and senior members of the football team. They shake their purple helmets and cheer. Audra reaches up her purple sleeves and cheers them back. I know that the players appreciate her. Everybody does at school. She still has that frank South Texas charm. At Westinghouse, she teaches part-time—remedial English three afternoons a week—a schedule that allows her to spend the rest of the days at home, raising two kids who can solve Korteweg–de Vries equations in their heads but still have a hard time making their beds in the morning.

As for me, I teach my two sections of geometry, my two of trigonometry, and my one of senior calculus. I sit on the Curriculum Committee and codirect the annual PTA garage-sale fundraiser (I'm also its largest buyer). My other jobs: cross-country assistant coach; freshman counselor; Math Club adviser. The Math Club, by the way, meets five mornings a week, by request of the membership.

Do I like it? Well, yes.

Mostly.

If you're looking for the Wall Street profiteer turned Good Samaritan in the small-town classroom—well, it hasn't worked out that way, exactly. The truth is, I still miss Physico. Sometimes badly. It's not so much the money (which I still have) as—I don't know what else to call it: The Game maybe? The Juice? There was a sameness to that life, just as there's a sameness to this one, but the sameness at Physico came with a lot more fist thumping.

I miss the fist thumping.

But we're here in Lasserville now. And my gut tells me we're staying. When I watch Emmy and her friends saunter into the house in their creek-soaked overalls, I feel something that I never felt in my days on the seventieth floor of the Trump Building. When I watch Niels hoisted up onto the hay cart by the middle-school principal during the Fourth of July parade—well, what can I say? I like to believe I'm giving them a little shot of something. A vaccination against the future. Or perhaps against the past, about which they still know almost nothing. Sometimes I think that my own father, who probably had no intention about such things but no doubt remembered his own childhood, might actually have been hoping to do the same for Paulie and me, with his place up in the woods.

Anyway, I do miss the fist thumping.

In Manhattan, I should add, I used to thump my fist no more than 60 percent of the time (the Shores-Durbans, of course, were only probabilities). But 60 percent was enough to put me at the top of my profession by a substantial and probably unassailable margin—unassailable because legions have since joined the game. Out here in Lasserville, on the other hand, I don't get to thump my fist very much at all. Once a semester, maybe. Last winter I landed a kid in the New England mathematics Olympiad. *Thump.* And this fall I discovered that the pouty emo in a faded frowny shirt at the back of my honors trig class wasn't listening to Fall Out Boy through the bright blue earbuds in his bright blue hair but to Yakov Eliashberg's Roever Lecture on affine complex manifolds.

Yes, this happened.

Thump. Thump.

I don't mind that my own children, when they reach high school, will probably not even sign up for Math Club. It's something of an unsaid warrant among us—the overcourteous step of the battle hardened—that we steer shy of one another when it comes to *the field*. Truthfully, both Emmy and Niels are already miles ahead of anyone else around here—and probably miles ahead, even, of where I was at their age—and I do wonder what will happen when they arrive at Westinghouse. The two of them in Math Club would pretty much ruin it for the others, even for the kid who made it to the Olympiad.

I know that Audra, too, is wary. Not of their talents, perhaps, the way I am, but of their other legacies. She probably wouldn't say so, but that night in the living room of our Perry Street brownstone can't be that far back in her mind. When I get home from work these days, she and I will drink a cup of tea together on the kitchen stools, looking out at the fields. She'll tell me about her day. I'll tell her about mine. Sometimes, though, as I talk about a new kid in Math Club or a nice moment in my classroom, she'll look at me so intently that I wonder if what she's actually doing is remembering.

When we're finished with our tea, she'll go outside to the garden for an hour before it's time to make dinner, and I'll go upstairs to the sleeping porch, where I've set up my desk. I take out the homework I need to correct. But for a few minutes, I don't even pick it up. I just sit there behind the screens, doing nothing, moving ahead with nothing, just watching my wife dig in the soil or, beyond her, the hills of barley sway in the wine-colored light, which at that hour looks enough like the sea. I think about the kids. I think about all of us. On my desk, I keep a single finely polished fragment of wood, a charm of well-rubbed beech whose curve slides smoothly against my thumb. Before I start my work each day, I rub it for luck.

Ignorance is the thing we seek to remedy.

I SHOULD ADD: I have fun with the kids.

The reason I mention this is that I remember only one time in my life when my own father actually seemed to have fun with us. Dad wasn't interested in fun. And generally speaking, neither am I. But every Saturday now, Audra and the kids and I do something together as a family, usually in the abundance of woods and streams and meadows that provide our solace up here in Lasserville.

Most of the time we have fun.

One thing we like to do is picnic on the shore of the Aldrich Gap River, in our spot above the Wides. Along a half mile of bank there, the water moves from narrow and swift to broad and still, and the bank changes from steep granite to gentle meadow. That meadow is graced with every sort of sedge, fern, and wildflower, and the bank is alive with beetles, dragonflies, and a dodging air show of brightly winged moths. We use the distant shore to practice our elliptical geometry. I admit that I was the one who started it; but Emmy's taken to it, too, now, and of course Niels has made it into a competition.

I tie a length of surgical tubing to an old pair of copper grounding rods, which Niels pounds into the soil about his own height apart. Now we have a slingshot. With a strong-enough pullback, we can send a baseball-sized projectile a hundred yards across the river into the trees. The sound it makes on release is like a sword being pulled swiftly from its sheath. Then a whiz that slices back across the river. On the far bank, there's a slap, followed by a rustle, and then a puff of leaves floating down. Audra won't let us use rocks anymore because she's afraid we'll hit a bird or a squirrel, so we use water balloons. For a while we experimented with dirt clods, which tended to vaporize, and then with spheres of our own chewed-up sandwiches, which generally burst apart straight out of the slot. Yes, we know that balloons aren't biodegradable—on the way home we stop and look around for the shreds.

Why mention this? One reason is that the kids love it. They shout and whoop. So do I. Niels can shoot farther than Emmy, but I've tried to even it up by declaring the goal to be accuracy. There's usually a stiff breeze over the river, and it varies with its height above the surface, so it's no trick to see that there's a mathematical component to the game, and a spatial one as well. And it's not hard to imagine just how good both our kids might be at it. They pretty much split the victories.

Really, though, in the end there's no more purpose to it than having a good time. I guess the other reason I mention this is that I like to think that I'm a different sort of man than my father was.

As for Mom—well, of course we thought she'd come along with us to our new life upstate. But she stayed in Manhattan. She's alone again, going on three years now. She's still as spry as ever, though, and a spry sixty-seven-year-old divorcee who's longed for most of her life to live in an East Coast metropolis can hardly give up the chance. Especially now that she's unencumbered.

She attends concerts and gallery openings and museum luncheons, and in the park she takes long, unmapped walks with her cronies. She has a Twitter account and a Facebook page and a little plastic card that gives her access to a car whenever she needs one, through some online enterprise that aims to democratize, not to mention monetize, the world's carbon-hungry resources. She's not afraid to drive, either, even in New York City.

She still lives in the place we bought her and still checks on the renters in the brownstone (yes, we keep it—though I sometimes doubt for long), mostly by pulling up a stool at the Starbucks down the block, at the hour when the children return from aftercare and the harried father picks them up for a meal at one of the upscale spots in the neighborhood. "They don't even eat at home most nights," Mom says. "And they never eat together." A pause. "That family."

"Things are different now, Mom."

"We always ate with you kids. And always at home."

"I know."

"And *no cellphones*."

But the surprising thing is that she herself eats in those same up-scale places now, and she's bought herself a phone. A nice one, too. She plays Scrabble on it with Paulie on the other side of the country. If you send her a text you get an answer before your phone's back in your pocket, and her Facebook page has overwhelmed my capacity to follow it. I don't think there's a man in her life, but I've never actually asked.

As I mentioned, she surprises us. Last fall, she spent Labor Day up here. The weather was chilly in Lasserville, and when we went out to a movie together, she put on her new sweater, a luxurious-looking cardigan with what appeared to be ermine-fur edging. On the ride out to the theater, I could tell that Audra was eyeing it.

Later in bed, Audra said, "That was a Loro Piana."

"What was?"

"The sweater your mom had on. It was a Loro Piana. I'm sure of it. Your mother's wearing Loro Piana cashmere."

"I'm sure it's imitation."

"It's not."

"Well, then I'm sure she got it secondhand."

"There was a Neiman Marcus tag in the pocket. A clean one, with the little plastic thingie still on it."

"How do you know?"

"She hung it in the front closet."

We were silent.

"That's a three-thousand-dollar sweater," she said. Then she added, "At *least*."

The next morning, at the breakfast table, I mentioned it to Mom. She set down her coffee and looked across at me. "You want to know if it's real, don't you?"

"Well, I guess I do, Mom."

"Yes, it is."

"Wow."

She buttered a slice of toast. "And you want to know if I bought it at a thrift store."

"Have you been talking to Audra?"

"Of course."

"Well," I said. "I'm sure you got a deal on it."

"I didn't. I bought it new. But yes, at least it was a little bit on sale." She smiled. "People change, Hans."

"I know they do."

"And you can, too."

"Thanks, Mom."

"You're welcome." She slid a piece of buttered toast across the table.

"I was just wondering," I said, "about the sweater."

"I know. I know you were. It was *your* money, if that's something else you were wondering. Mostly, anyway."

"Of course, Mom. It's fine. That's why I earned it."

For a time, then, we ate in silence. When I finished the toast, she buttered another slice for me.

"By the way," I said. "What did you mean by I can change, too?"

"Just because your father couldn't—that doesn't mean that you can't. You've got *me* in you, too, you know." She smiled again. "That's another reason I did it. To show you that it can be done."

"Really?"

"Sort of, really."

"Well," I said. "Thank you."

"You're welcome, again."

"But Mom, what about the things you used to tell us? About thrift and discipline? About being frugal? I *believed* you."

"And now you're all grown, aren't you?"

ONE LAST THING: it happened a few weeks ago, at the Wides. A warm mid-September afternoon when we were out there for another picnic. There was a steady wind from the south, and the moths and butterflies were bumping around on it. We'd been aiming the slingshot at a stump of a beech, probably 125 yards to the north, and letting the balloons ride the wind for the extra distance. The high sun was heating the day, which added to our reach.

It was Emmy's turn to shoot. On the round before, Niels had come within four or five yards of the target, and he was eager to go again. But Emmy took her time. In these types of affairs, she knows how to agitate her competition. She tossed a blade of sedge into the air, checking the wind. She looked across the water into the trees, which were rustling at their crowns. She looked up into the sky, doing whatever she does. She's always been an efficient calculator, but there's something in her character that also relies on intuition, especially at moments like these. I don't know exactly what she sees when she looks out into the world, or even what she's looking for; but she always appears to gather some inscrutable shade of information to which the rest of us aren't privy. The same way my father used to.

When she finally did let it fly, the water balloon vaulted out of its sheath like a missile from its launchpad, instantly transforming its trigonometric fate into a glinting leftward-canted ellipse that elongated obliquely in the breeze. I knew, the moment it peaked, that it would hit the target.

But that's not why I mention it.

Both kids can get off impressive shots—I hardly even remark on them anymore. But on this particular afternoon, as Emmy's balloon climbed swiftly to the river's midpoint and transcended its own apex, I saw it explode into a thousand glittering pieces that shot off in every direction into the sky.

The strange thing is that a moment later I heard it hit the tree on the far side. When I turned, the leaves of the beech were rustling. A few of them floated down. I blinked. I looked back into the air above the river. In my eye, the fireworks continued. Shimmering translucencies of white ember arcing within an oscilloptic polygon, still poised at the apogee. Then they began organizing themselves into a wavering, sinusoidal curve—first dully, then brightly—like an old TV coming on. Finally they peaked. For those who wish it described mathematically—and I still remember it mathematically—I then observed, for perhaps a second and a half, a mobile Lissajous figure continually transforming itself, first homotopically, then homeomorphically, then entirely, into a strange, scattering set of flaming runes, the entire white-hot conflagration sparkling and growing brighter as it fell.

It persisted until I turned my head.

WE CALL IT intuition because we don't have a better word for it.

A few days after I quit Physico, when I was still wandering Manhattan during the daylight hours like a man let out of prison, Audra suggested I go back to see my father. At that point, I'd been home from my second visit for less than a week. I couldn't decide whether I felt the way I did because of Dad or because I didn't have a job anymore.

"Well," she said, "why don't you just go out there again and find out?"

Two days later, when I pulled into the cove, I could see Cle and Paulie and Mom inside the cabin, preparing the feast they'd promised me if I came back. All three of them were in the kitchen, sidestepping one another as they gathered the dishes. Dad was outside, standing in a haze of smoke at the end of the dock, waving a pair of barbecue tongs at the car. When I walked down to him, he raised his glass. "The prodigal son returns."

"Yes he does."

He took a polite-sized swallow of bourbon. "Here's to you, then."

"And to you, Dad."

A longer swallow. "And here's to our singularities!"

"Which singularities would those be?"

"Well," he said. "You quit your job, didn't you? And your old man still feels like a million bucks."

In mathematics, singularities are reversals—the points at which the graph makes a sharp turn.

"To our health," he said. One more gulp. "And to our new free-dom."

Not a half hour later, as I was loading silverware into the picnic basket in the kitchen, I watched him hurry along the dock to help Cle and my mother, who were walking down with their platters. At the stairs, he reached forward and guided them up. (Mom first, then Cle—the order all of them always acknowledged.) He didn't know I was watching—or maybe he did—and as they moved out toward the grill, he stayed at the top of the steps, gazing after them. I have to say, he did look well again, eyeing the women who'd just waltzed him back into his life.

Paulie left the house then, carrying a pitcher of lemonade, and as she came up the beach, Dad waited for her, too, at the top of the stairs. She didn't look happy, exactly, but I remember that she looked optimistic. I hadn't seen her like that in a while. She'd been out here now without me for the week, and she and Dad seemed to be friendly in a way that they hadn't ever been before. She climbed a couple of steps, and he reached forward from the edge of the dock and held out his hand. She looked up for a moment, then grinned shyly and took it. Something about the expression on her face—the hopefulness in it—made me look back down into the picnic basket. That's why I didn't see it happen.

I wish it hadn't been Paulie.

The sound was like a branch breaking off somewhere in the woods. Then the smash of the pitcher. When I looked up, Paulie had fallen onto the sand. On the dock, Dad was staggering backward. He looked down at his hand, which stuck out strangely from his sleeve. For a moment he seemed confused. Then he let out a howl. My mother came running. Dad grabbed his elbow, bellowing now, and careened forward to the top of the stairs, where he stumbled, missed the railing, and fell sidelong onto the beach.

Proof by Exhaustion

THE SCAN CAME up covered with blots: metastases too numerous to count. In the emergency room, Dr. Gandapur steadied my mother with his hand.

The arm had snapped when he'd tried to help my sister up the stairs, then shattered when he'd landed on the ground.

They didn't operate. Instead, he was put in a cast that went all the way over his shoulder. Only his fingertips showed at the end. They were purple. The doctor hadn't even been able to straighten the bones, so the cast bent a second time, midway up the forearm, as though he'd been given another elbow.

But the next day, when we brought him back to the cabin, he sat down on the couch with a cigarette and a glass and used his good hand to light the cigarette. He dragged on it, set it down, and lifted the glass.

IN THE DRIVEWAY, Dr. Gandapur reached out the window of the old Mercedes and handed me a bag. "He'll need this now. As you know, I cannot return every day."

I looked at the label. "He won't like it."

"I know he won't. But I will keep the dose to a minimum."

"Thank you, Doctor."

Glancing back at the cabin, he said, "Pardon me for asking, but are Mr. and Mrs. Biettermann still visiting?"

"Mrs. is."

"And Mr.—is he around at all?"

"He's back in New York."

The doctor remained still for a moment, looking carefully up at my face. Then he said, "Just make sure you keep it upstairs."

AUDRA, I KNOW, thinks I have a hard time speaking about the things that matter to me. And Matthew, at Stillwater, thought the same. I know they both believe that I don't want to reveal myself, or perhaps that I don't know what my feelings truly are.

Well, they're right: I don't.

But not because I don't think about them. I do. A mathematician goes to great lengths to define things. A plane in mathematics is not merely a flat surface but a flat surface of infinite thinness and size. Trivial? Not to us. When I say *plane,* I'm not thinking of a tabletop or sheet of glass or a piece of paper. You might point to any one of these objects; but all of them are precisely that: *objects.* They exist in the world. And because they do, they are defined by their breadth and reach. To a mathematician, a tabletop is no more a plane than a slice of rum cake is. In the world we know, in fact, the only thing that can actually be called a plane—or a portion of one, anyhow—is a shadow.

You see?

Words fail us. Even the world fails us.

Are there not a thousand forms of sorrow? Is the sorrow of death the same as the sorrow of knowing the pain in a child's future? What about the melancholy of music? Is it the same as the melancholy of a summer dusk? Is the loss I was feeling for my father the same I would have felt for a man better-fit to the world, a man who might have thrown a baseball with me or taken me out in the mornings to fish? Both we call grief. I don't think we have words for our feelings any more than we have words for our thoughts. I don't even believe that we actually do the things we call *thinking* and *feeling*. We do something, but it is only out of crudeness that we call it thinking; and when we do the other thing, we call it feeling. But I can tell you, if you asked Archimedes in the third century B.C., or Brahmagupta in the seventh A.D., or Hilbert in the twentieth, when they'd first known that they'd solved their great problem, I suspect they'd all say they had a *feeling*.

Maybe that's why mathematicians like blackboards. Words steer, while equations mostly follow. When the terms of mathematics fail, we invent new ones. Euclid. Diophantus. Viète. Descartes.

What I've often believed about people like my father—and like me, and my sister, and my daughter, and quite possibly my son—is that we'll always be in chase. In chase of the next question, which we're usually familiar with because it was the answer to the previous one. Everything builds. Increment upon increment. There's no proof in mathematics that can't be broken down into steps basic enough for a child of reasoning age to follow. The trick is accumulating the steps, each one so trivial that it can be comprehended by the crippled thing we call the mind. Concentration, if you will. This is all we have. Desire creates the concentration.

I've often thought that the remarkable thing about problems like Fermat's or Poincaré's—or even Malosz's—is not that they were eventually solved but that for so long they were not. Really, each one is nothing but grains of sand. The length of time it took to solve them was in good part dependent on probability: there are so many more wrong ways to stack the grains than there are right ways.

Under our old mulberry tree, when my father was first showing me differential calculus, he once said that the discovery that shapes can be described with incrementally smaller shapes, that anything at all could be approximated in such a simple manner, had guided him in much of his thinking.

The thought comes back to me now.

Does one grow wise in increments? By fractioning a life and then summing it? By stacking sand? An infant, in his first sleepiness, must let go of the world; a man must learn to die. What comes between are the grains of sand. Ambition. Loss. Envy. Desire. Hatred. Love. Tenderness. Joy. Shame. Loneliness. Ecstasy. Ache. Surrender.

Live long enough and you will solve them all.

But how to solve the grief I felt for my father in those last days? We think that our sorrow, like the planes we know in this world, has borders. But does it? When he came home from the hospital that evening, he sat back on the leather couch, his expression dull, his one undamaged hand set loosely around a glass. He was the same man I'd always known. The same shadowed eyes. The same slightly bent features. Yet I also knew that in some frame of time that already existed and had almost been reached he was already gone. So what? If you go out along another dimension, you can come back at any other point in time. For a long while by then, when I looked at him on the couch, I'd been seeing him no longer there, seeing not my father but the empty space in which he'd once lived as though I were looking into the future. Well, was I? Does the soul, like the plane, have only a truncated representation in our world? Do we give it edges and dimension only so that we may say we understand it?

As soon as we conform anything to language, we've changed it. Use a word and you've altered the world. The poets know this. It's what they try so hard to avoid.

I don't have much patience with religion, or even with what at Stillwater they liked to call the spiritual life; but nonetheless, it is part of a mathematician's job to not rule out a possibility until it's disproven. Could the thing I felt when I thought about living on this earth without my father merely have been the first scald that one feels when at long last one lays one's hand upon the infinite? Not the bounded thing whose edges we see but the other thing, the thing whose truth can only be approached if we ignore what we think we know?

Would my father have laughed at such an idea? I actually don't think so. He thought as much about life's verities as any other man; it was simply that he was loath to speak of any of them until he understood.

I myself had realized long ago that he was dying. I'd realized it on the day I found out he wasn't coming back from the cabin to live with us in Tapington. It was a cool afternoon in September, only a couple of weeks before I went off to college myself, and out the window of our house the leaves of the mulberry were already beginning to wither. I was upstairs in my bedroom, looking at a yellow pill in my fingers, when the phone rang in the kitchen. A few minutes later, I heard my mother's slow step on the stairs, and in memory I suddenly saw my father's face, grayed at its edges, newly marked— unmistakably so, in my mind's eye—as it looked up at me from the desk in his shed. It seems strange to say that I knew then that he was lost to us. But I did. I hadn't seen my way to the end of any proof, but for a moment, before it vanished, I'd glimpsed a path.

The day he came back from the hospital in his cast and took his place on the cabin's new leather couch, I walked down to the water, then along the beach to the cluster of rocks at the end of the cove. Those rocks are bigger than most of the others on that shore, and there's a remnant of order in their arrangement that reveals to me some figure out of the past, patiently digging them from the fields or wedging them up from the lake bottom for a long-forgotten reason of custom or beauty. I sat down on one and looked out at the water.

It was evening, and before long a pair of minks emerged. The minks appreciate those rocks because they're a good place to hunt for the crayfish and ducklings that they feed on, but also because they're big enough to play on. Minks are alert animals, and they seem to like to play. A mink's face is vigilant—short ears canted forward and dark, attentive eyes—and a mink always seems to look at the world with an expression of surprise. There's something about this that speaks to me of intelligence.

The pair of them chased each other through the riprap, both of them looping madly up and down in the crags, like a pair of dark-furred Slinkys bouncing along the shore. The sun had already set, but the western sky still showed color, and in the quieting cove I sat watching the two of them play in the boulders. When they realized I was there, one of them hid, but the other stepped to the top of a rock and looked straight at me. I don't know why I saw sympathy in that face, but I did; and it was then, as the wind calmed and the sky darkened gradually from deep violet to indigo, that I finally wept.

DAD WOULD HAVE to eat early—a piece of toast just after dawn—or he'd throw up the first pill. A little past midday, I'd give him the second, with a cup of soup. The third came between dinner and bedtime. Once he'd been asleep, he couldn't keep anything down, so for the nighttime dose I learned to inject him. Dr. Gandapur showed me how. I set the alarm for 2:00 a.m. and in the dark made my way down the hall to the bathroom. The sudden light and the silvery bubbles crowding the syringe—their weirdly jubilant chaos: it was a powerful feeling, knowing I could ease his pain.

Even at that hour, the air on the porch was warm, and he'd have kicked away the blankets. I'd lift the sheets, moving as quietly as I could, but his eyes always opened. He'd roll over, sighing, onto his back.

"Night nurse."

"Leave me alone."

The thin meat of the hip. The brief resistance, then the slip of the needle, as though through silk. When I pulled it out he'd grunt and roll back onto his side. That dose would take him through to breakfast. From then until nightfall, he could manage with the pills.

Sometimes they wore off early, but I learned to recognize the signs. If he was standing, he'd press his hand to the cast and lean back to breathe. Speaking, the words would begin to space themselves. Sitting, he'd shift his neck and rub his hand along the plaster, as though petting a cat that lay in the crook of it.

Now and then, as he sat on the couch, he'd wince.

Still, he was on his feet every day. To the kitchen for bourbon or coffee. To the edge of the cove for air. He didn't eat much at meals, but Paulie was making a custard for him in the evenings that he took to bed and spooned extravagantly into his mouth.

One morning, he walked all the way to the end of the dock, where he sat down on the bench, propped a pad into the bend of his cast, and attempted for a few minutes to draw the view. At one point, I watched him lower himself to the deck, then lean slowly over the side until he could splash water onto his face.

That evening, a parcel arrived—a wheelchair, folded into a box. He watched Cle unwrap it, assemble the parts, and stand it in the corner by the door. Then he got up and walked over to it. "Who's this for?" he said.

THE TIME AFTER dinner was still his most lucid—that stretch between the last meal of the day and the final mercy of his bedtime pill. He'd emerge from his nap and begin to talk. Cle would pull her seat close, not speaking but placing herself in his sight. Mom would stand in the doorway. Even Paulie liked to be near. She didn't say so; but I saw her lingering. Some evenings, as the light grew amber through the screens, then gray-blue, he'd rise from the daybed on the porch and make his way into the living room, where he'd take a place on the sofa and tap out a cigarette. Paulie had thrown away a case of them, but Dr. Gandapur had brought over another, smiling his courteous smile.

If Dad was in the right mood, he'd lean back heavily against the cushions and light one. He could still talk. The words never left him.

One evening, he told the story of a trip to Helsinki for a conference. The crossing of the Atlantic on the *Queen Mary*. The nighttime brightness as they steamed through the Gulf of Finland. Cle was leaving the next morning for Chicago—she wanted to give our family a few days alone—and I could see her watching him in a different way, as though to fix him in her mind. On the couch next to him she sat blinking. Mom was in the doorway, and Paulie was at the table across the room, working her laptop; I leaned in alongside my sister as she pretended to read her email. The sun was low, and the chop on the water made it look as though, all across the cove, matches were being struck and extinguished.

"A Spanish girl," Dad said, leaning back against the cushions. "Married to a millionaire. I met them both at dinner. The captain's table—I'd already won the Fields, you see. The husband was a raw capitalist and a thoroughly ignorant man, and I could see that his beautiful bride was bored. I was sitting between them." He glanced from my mother to Cle. "Beauty prefers truth," he said.

Cle guffawed.

"To riches, that is," said Dad.

"You misunderstand beauty then," said Cle.

He glanced at her, his smile excited. "In her own stateroom, between dessert—"

Paulie slammed shut her laptop. "Disgusting!"

"It's okay, Paulie," I said. "It was before they were married."

"We don't want to hear it! Don't you understand that? Either of you? Don't you know the first thing about any of us!"

When the door banged shut, one of the framed pictures that Cle had so carefully hung dropped off the wall.

4656534

Two days later, on a clear, windless morning, a rental car pulled up the drive, and Niels stepped out of it, followed by Audra. Then, after a moment, Emmy. Emmy seemed puzzled, staying close to the car and looking down at the sand. She'd been in woods like these before, but she'd never in her life seen her grandfather.

He stood leaning against the doorframe at the top of the stairs, waving.

Niels had never seen him, either. But he trotted forward and climbed the steps. At the top, he held out his hand. "You're my grandpa," he said.

"Looks like I am."

"I'm your grandson, Niels."

"I figured as much. And who's this?" Dad moved to the edge of the porch and looked down at the car. "Is this the other young person I've been hearing a little about?"

"That's my sister. We're late because she forgot her toothbrush and we couldn't find one at the hardware store."

"I'd imagine not."

"It was a *general* store," said Emmy. "Not just a hardware store. And I did not *forget* it. I needed a new one the whole time."

"Do you have one for her, Grandpa?"

"Well, I might, young man. I might."

When Audra reached the stairs, Dad bowed and kissed her on the back of the hand. Audra doesn't blush, but when he did that, her other hand rose to her neck.

Emmy had remained in the driveway, and Audra beckoned her now. But it was only when my mother appeared in the doorway that Emmy finally moved, running quickly up the stairs and sidestepping Audra and Dad to bury her head in her grandmother's blouse. "Little Miss," said Mom, "it's so nice to see you here. Now please say hello to your grandpa."

But Emmy wouldn't. She merely looked down, bending and straightening her knees.

THAT EVENING, WHEN Dad woke in a bright mood and leaned back on the cushions to talk, Emmy watched him from the kitchen door, twirling a pretzel ring around her finger. Niels was sitting next to him on the couch. Dad beckoned to Emmy, but she still wouldn't come. He lit a cigarette and smiled through the smoke at her.

"Milo," said my mother from across the room. "Please put that thing out."

He drew luxuriously on the end, then slowly lifted his cast to lay it across Niels's knee. "Why? Does smoke not agree with you, young man?"

"Actually," Niels said, "I find the smell kind of interesting."

Paulie laughed from the porch, then glanced at me. "Such an agreeable young gentleman."

"What about this, young man?" said Dad. He lifted his glass from the table.

"That's okay with me, too, Grandpa. It smells like cough medicine."

He chuckled. "Well, actually, it's a pretty good bourbon whiskey."

Mom marched across the room then, snapped the glass from his hand, and carried it to the kitchen. A moment later, she came back for the cigarette.

"SOME PEOPLE MIGHT say she was a little late with that," whispered Audra.

"Well, I'm not one of them."

We were whispering because we were in a room at the Lakeland Suites, and on the other side of the wall, Niels and Emmy were pretending to be asleep. Through the sheetrock I could hear every crack of the bat from what must have been a Yankees highlights reel on TV. This was Niels, of course; but I also knew that Emmy would be going along with it. Sometimes I think that even with all her talents, she'll always be following him.

"Mom had enough to think about when we were kids," I said. "She did what she could."

"Yes, you're right. I guess she did." Audra was next to me in the bed, staring up at the ceiling fan. "Still—she might have done *something* about it. At a time when it could have made a difference."

At that moment, the Yankees must have pulled off something impressive, because Niels let out a shout, and a second later Emmy followed with a whoop. I tapped the wall. I needed to sleep: in a few hours I'd have to get up in the dark and drive to the cabin to give Dad his shot. Then I'd spend the last half of the night there.

The sound of the TV went off, and we lay there in silence for a while, looking up at the fan.

"It was hard for *me,* too, you know," said Audra. "But I did it. I stopped you."

"Well, you were in a different situation."

"Was I?"

"Of course you were."

"I don't know," she said. "I still didn't have any idea what was going to happen. To you or to me or to any of us."

"What do you mean, what was going to happen? What did you think I'd do—just leave you all and never come back?"

She didn't answer, just turned over onto her side and closed her eyes.

LATER THAT NIGHT, at the cabin, I was jostled awake.

"Did you see?" he rasped.

"What?" I sat up in my parents' bed: 3:58 a.m. I'd given him the shot an hour ago. "What are you doing up here, Dad?"

"He's here."

"Who is?"

"You know."

"No, I don't. Jesus, Dad—you climbed up here in the dark?"

"You forgot to lock the door."

"We always leave it unlocked."

He leaned down. "Well, he got in."

"Who, Dad?"

"Erdős."

"What?" I rose and wrapped him in my blanket. "Let's get you back down to bed. Here, come on now. I'll help."

"He won't leave."

"Let's go take care of him together then. Come on, Dad. He's a good guy."

"He took the bed, Hans. He won't leave." Dad was shivering. "You go tell him. I'm staying up here. You go down and tell him *no*."

BUT THE NEXT morning, he was fine again. He slept late, and by the time he woke, he seemed to have forgotten whatever it was. At breakfast, he was cheerful even, and after an egg and bacon, he got up and walked to the window, where he leaned down to look out at Emmy and Niels playing along the shore and said, "How about we take the kids up to the creek?"

"You mean walk up there, Dad? It might be a little far."

He turned. "For the kids, you mean?"

I glanced at Audra.

It was a beautiful morning. First he led us down the cove to the turn. Then he picked up a branch and turned north into the meadow. I expected the tall grass to tire him, but it didn't. It was higher than his knees, but he just pushed right through it, taking his time and using the branch as a walking stick, never missing a step. When we reached the rutted path at the top, Audra slid in next to him and hooked her arm through the crook of his cast. I saw him puff up like a bird.

By the time we reached the paved part of the road, the sun was trickling through the leaves, and the lake was sparkling. Dad was walking with a straight back. I was at the rear, and I watched him talking to Audra, saying things that made her nod or shake her head or sometimes laugh. Her arm was still in his. Behind them, Niels ran from one side of the path to the other, picking things up to put in his pockets. Emmy followed at a distance.

We made it all the way to the bridge, where he stopped finally and looked out over the slowly moving water. It puckered here and there where the fish were rising. Along the edge, the shore grasses rustled. In the distance, a tiny, dark triangle appeared and began drifting downstream toward us. As it neared, Dad said, "What do you suppose it is, kids?"

"A beaver," said Emmy.

It might have been the first thing she'd said to him since she'd arrived.

Dad smiled. "That's right, young lady. How'd you know?"

But she didn't answer, just shrugged and turned to look back over the creek.

"He likes having you here," I said.

"He just loves women," answered Audra. She set her makeup bag on the counter and leaned down before the hotel's tiny mirror. "I happen to be the youngest legal one in the vicinity."

"That you are, and that he does. And you're a beautiful one, too."

"Well, thank you." She turned from the mirror. "How do you think the kids are taking it, seeing him like this?"

"I think it might be the only chance they'll get."

"That's what Niels said, too." She reached for my hand. "Your dad's trying hard with them, you know. He's trying very hard to be decent."

"I know, Aud. And Em can barely look at him."

"Actually," she said, "I don't think Em can keep her eyes off him. Haven't you noticed? Today, I saw her standing on a stool to watch him out the window."

"Well, he's more interesting than the squirrels."

"She was hiding behind the curtain so he wouldn't see her. He was on the porch about a foot away."

"Did he see her?"

"No. He was concentrating. It's not easy to open a pack of cigarettes with one hand."

I laughed. "Well, at least she keeps her distance. That might be a good thing, in the long run."

"Do you think so?"

"I don't know, actually. I really don't know *what* to think."

"Well, I think she keeps her distance because she's utterly fascinated by him," she said. "There's something so raw about him, Hans. Something so completely raw to the world. I think she recognizes it."

THE NEXT MORNING, Niels came bounding out onto the porch. He opened his fist to Emmy, who hardly looked up from her book; then he came skipping across the floor and opened it to me. "Look what Grandpa made me!" He brought his hand to his mouth and let out a trill. "It works!"

"Apparently so," said Emmy.

"Look, Em! It's got two frequencies!"

"Dork."

"He made two different-sized holes!"

"I'm reading."

When he blew it near her ear, she raised a foot to kick him; but he tore back through the door and down the path. The screen banged shut, and he let out another two-toned blast.

I was watching Emmy. After a time, I said, "What book do you have there, sweetie?"

"Swiss Family Robinson."

"I see."

"Leave me alone."

"You can read what you want, Em. I don't care."

"Thanks."

She turned a page.

"Did your mother say something?"

"Shhh!"

"Well, it's okay, you know. As far as I'm concerned, you can read whatever you want."

She didn't look up. I leaned forward. It was indeed what I thought: Zygmund and Fefferman's *Trigonometric Series.*

"You know," I said, "when *I* was a kid, Aunt Paulie used to think that Grandpa paid more attention to me than her."

She set down the book. "Aunt Paulie used to think that?"

"Yes, she did. I don't happen to believe it myself. I think he paid his own kind of attention to both of us. But that's how your aunt saw it. I wonder if she mentioned anything to you."

She screwed up her face. "It's weird that Aunt Paulie was your sister."

"She still *is* my sister, Ems."

"I know, Dad."

"Aunt Paulie used to be a lot like you, you know. She was great in math."

"I'm not great in math."

"Excuse me?"

"Grandpa's better."

"Oh, I see." I glanced into the house, where Dad was asleep on the living-room sofa, his head thrown back against the cushions. "You could do anything in the world that you wanted to, you know. Mathematical or otherwise."

"Okay, Dad." She picked up the book.

"Your grandfather loves you, Em."

"Thanks."

"Things were different when he was young."

"Mm-hmm."

I reached out and laid my hand over her foot. "He'll whittle one for you, too, Em. You know that, right?"

"You're so weird."

"He will. He'll make one for each of you. I'll make sure he does."

She turned a page. A few moments later, without looking up, she reached into her side pocket and held her hand out in my direction. "He already gave it to me," she said.

"MAY I ASK you something, Dr. Gandapur?"

"Of course."

The two of us were on the dock, waiting for another sunset. Through the broken clouds, the flaming disk was dulling into a copper penny before it dropped into the slot.

"I understand," I said, "that no test is perfect. I know all about specificity and sensitivity. I know all about outcome and probability."

"I'm sure there are few in the world who know it as well," he replied—then added, "Except, perhaps, your father."

"But I have to ask. You didn't send Dad for any tests recently, did you?"

"I could not have, Hans. He would not allow it."

"He wouldn't?"

"Those were not my wishes, you see, they were his. And they have always been. No testing. No treatment. He forbade everything from the beginning. In his situation, I could hardly say I disagreed." He set his hands into his pockets. "Is there a reason you ask?"

"No, no—I was just wondering. That's what I thought."

He turned from the view now, regarding me with his wrinkled eyes. "You're a good son, Hans," he said. "God bless you." Then he lifted his hand to my shoulder. "And God bless your father, too."

ON THE PORCH that night after dinner, Dad was shoveling down one of Paulie's custards. His thready hair was damp with sweat, the ridges of his skull showing through when he sucked at his fingers. "Why don't you all get the hell out of here," he said suddenly. "All you leeches!"

"Milo—" said my mother.

"Get off me!"

"What's the matter, Grandpa?" said Niels.

We'd been gathered on the porch, watching the moon come up over the lake. It had been a fine day.

"I said get out of here. All of you—*out!*"

"What is it, Grandpa?"

He looked straight at Niels. "I want a roll in the hay with your mother, that's what."

Audra burst out laughing. Paulie reddened, then herded Niels and Emmy through the door.

Mom blanched. Then she turned away, blinking.

WHEN I ENTERED the kitchen, the kids looked startled. A Tigers game was on the radio, and Niels jumped from his seat to turn down the volume. Emmy looked away.

"What are you two doing inside on a day like this?"

"Orioles-Tigers," said Niels.

"Well, who's winning?"

"Don't know." He moved quickly to the window and looked out at the water. Behind him on the table, where Emmy was sitting, was a glass that Dad had been using, and alongside it an ashtray crammed with his cigarette butts. I looked at the two of them. "Was Grandpa listening with you?"

"He's asleep," said Emmy. "He's on the couch again."

Niels said, "The president of Harvard tried to make curveballs illegal."

"What was that, Niels?"

"President Eliot. He said a curveball should be against the law for pitchers from Harvard because it was disevil."

"Deceitful," said Emmy.

"Come on, Em." He was at the door already, tapping his fingers. "Let's go swimming."

The door slammed, and a moment later Niels was down at the water; but Emmy didn't follow him. As I cleaned the table, she stayed near me. I tossed away the cigarette butts and wiped down the mats. When the plates were all in the rack, I laid my hand on the top of her head. "Ems," I said. "You didn't try any of that, did you?"

"Any of what?"

"What was in Grandpa's glass."

"Oh, no. Of course not."

"Good."

I picked up the newspaper and straightened the chairs. As I scrubbed the pots, we both watched Niels. He was skipping rocks. He was concentrating, the way he concentrates on everything— searching for each new stone, weighing it in his palm, rehearsing the sidearm flick two or three times before he released. But nonetheless, every few throws he looked up to see if Emmy was still in the house with me.

She was. Standing quietly against my side. Finally she said, "Niels tried a little, though."

. . .

Two A.M. His bed empty. In the dark, I felt through the sheets. Blankets twisting from the mattress. When I turned on the light, his pillow was kicked against the wall.

The bathroom vacant. The wheelchair angled into a corner of the hallway.

"Dad?"

Outside, finally, in the beam of my flashlight, there he was, at the end of the dock. He was kneeling before the water, his pajamas bunched to his knees, his cast hooked around one of the bench posts behind him. He turned. In the other hand was his limp, edemic penis, that arm still vaguely pumping.

"Well, at least the kids didn't see it," said Audra.

"Count your blessings."

She took my hand. "In some ways it's a sign of life, Hans."

"Or the reverse."

Out on the porch, we could see him on the daybed again, struggling to light another cigarette.

"Can I ask you something?" I said. "The other night—when he said that stuff about rolling in the hay—do you think he thought you were my mother?"

"I don't know, actually."

"Or do you think he might have thought that Niels was *me*?"

"I don't know, honey. I really don't."

I looked out at him on the porch. "Or did he actually mean *you*?"

"I don't know, sweetheart." After a moment, she said, "He's not used to having people in his house, either. It must be confusing. It must tire him out."

"I'm sure you're right."

She took my hand. "Hans," she said, "I was thinking—maybe it would be better if I took the kids home early."

I nodded.

She said, "I'm so sorry."

"The thing is, now I wish they'd met him earlier."

"I know," she said. "That's one of the things I'm sorry about."

The Curse of Knowledge

WALKING DOWN TO the water with me one morning, he slipped, his feet shooting out from beneath him. But I caught his shoulder and lifted him back up. Then I guided us the rest of the way down through the trees. At the shore, I held his elbow.

He shook it. "Enough."

In the house now, he moved as though irked by everything. Picked up papers and dropped them. Flipped light switches. From the hallway, we could see him whenever he used the toilet. He no longer bothered to close the door, just propped himself against the wall and waited interminably for relief, his scoliotic back angled over the bowl. Cle had returned from her trip now, but with Audra and the kids gone, Dad had tossed aside all modesty. He'd just stand there in the dull light, turning now and then to shrug. The medicine scorched his bowels, too. Sometimes he would just sit on the toilet and stare, a curl of cigarette smoke rising into the fan. Cle would get up and shut the door.

One morning I watched him try to turn off the hot-water faucet. He leaned against the sink like a being from another galaxy. The knobby fingers clumsily rotating the handles: first one, then the other, then the first again, turning all of them the wrong way in comical succession until finally I stepped in to help.

. . .

IN THE SHED, I found Paulie sitting in his chair. Her hands were at her temples, and she was leaning over the blotter. Without looking up, she said, "You have beautiful children."

"They have their moments, Paulie."

The room smelled the way my sister used to: mud and herbal shampoo. She was in overalls.

"I'm trying to imagine," she said.

"Imagine what?"

"His existence. I'm trying to fathom it. Look at this." With her foot, she pushed the top off one of the file boxes that were on the floor behind her, and I saw the red wax seals on the bottle corks. It was hard to believe they were still out here. "He spent all his time boozing. It's not even a surprise anymore."

"I know, Paulie. It was a symptom."

"*Of?*"

"Of his pain."

She stiffened. Then she said, "All our lives, Hans—all our lives, Mom was the one who did everything."

"Well, that's how it goes sometimes."

"Are you serious? Do you really think that our family was just *how it goes sometimes*? Mom slaved for him. She took care of him. She tried to take care of his career. She took care of everything, so that he could do one great thing. And he had a chance to." She kicked the box. "But all he did was drink. All he did was fucking *drink*." She looked up at me. "Then he abandoned us."

"That's not the whole story."

"And now Mom wants him back."

"What?"

"She does, Hans. I can see it. She can't even help herself."

She dropped her head, and when I looked past her I noticed that the room had been gone through: his papers had been shuffled; books were sideways on the shelves; up in the rafters, the lids had been tipped up on his boxes.

"Paulie?"

"Yes?"

I pointed toward the ceiling. "Didn't you know about all this?"

"About what he was doing out here? Of course I did."

Out the window then, a heron swooped low over the cove and landed in the shallows. We both turned to watch. It pulled its wings in and made itself into a statue.

Paulie kept her eyes on it. "Actually, Hans, I didn't. I had no idea."

"Well, if it makes you feel any better, he fooled *me,* too, Paulie."

"Not the way he fooled *me.*"

Out on the cove, the heron leaned forward, then suddenly speared. When it came up, its gullet was wriggling. The ancient face turned slowly toward us. Then the wings beat, and it lifted away.

"Wow," she said.

"I know. There's not much mercy in the world, is there?"

"I haven't changed my opinion about him, Hans—if that's what you're trying to say. Being sick doesn't change the facts."

"What makes you think you know the facts?"

She blinked.

Then she rose, moved the chair against the wall, and stepped up onto its seat. When she climbed back down, she had another box in her hands, its lid not quite closed. She set it on the floor in front of me. "Go ahead," she said.

When I opened it, the only thing I saw was the top of the burlap sack. Even so, I knew what it was. "My God," I said.

"What *is* it, Hans? I found it up there. It's one of the strangest things I've ever seen."

"I didn't know he kept it."

"Kept what?"

I loosened the ties and pulled out a length of it. "It's a chain he made when he was a kid, Paulie."

"He *made* that?"

"Yes—from a single piece of wood. He carved the whole thing out of the stump of a beech tree. I don't even think he was much older than Niels when he did it."

She blanched. "Oh, God."

Then she turned to me again and composed her expression. I watched the grief move over her face, then gather itself, then pass out of view. "I don't know anything about him, Hans. Do you realize that? Not a single thing."

I WAS UPSTAIRS in the bedroom when the house shook. Then it shook again. I heard running. When I reached the porch, Mom and Paulie and Cle were already out there. He was standing alongside the shelves. With trembling arms, he turned and pushed another row of books onto the floor.

TWO DAYS LATER, on a hot, muggy morning near the end of that month, a taxi pulled into the clearing and the driver got out and set a ramp onto the front stairs. A moment later, Earl Biettermann came rolling up to the door. Cle had packed her things by then, and Earl yanked the first of her suitcases onto his lap and coasted it down to her Citroën. He tossed it into the trunk and turned back for the next one.

I don't think he was really there to pick up his wife, though: she could easily have shipped the car and gone home on a plane.

When the last bag was loaded, he rolled into the house and parked his chair in the living room. My mother and Cle and Paulie were gathered around the table by then, admiring what I'd brought in. "Goodness," said my mother. "What *is* this thing?"

Cle said, "*My God,* Milo—of course you still have it."

My father's eyes lifted. He was making his way out from the kitchen, running his cast against the wall for balance. His hand went to the lamp, then the chairback. At the couch, he lowered himself.

My mother picked up a section in her hands and said, "Oh, my God, Milo."

Dad sank into the cushions. The links were fifty years old, and when they shifted in my mother's fingers they emitted the clink of stone. But the pale grain had hardly darkened.

"Ah," said Dad, "you found it, I guess." He nodded vaguely. "The magnum opus."

His words were slurred, and a moment later his face grew dull. Then he was asleep.

That's when Biettermann rolled closer. "Maniacal," he said quietly. He reached and brought a length of it onto his lap. Each link was the size of his fist, each turn of it cambered into both a twist and loop. He ran his finger around one of the twists. "Born to the field," he said, peering through the gap to the couch. "I have to give him that much."

"Single sided," said Paulie. "Feel it."

"I just did." He dropped it back onto the table and moved toward the couch. "And you know what?" I could see it riling him. "It still comes to nothing—that's the thing. That's the whole problem. Just like everything else he ever did—it all came to nothing."

"Oh, *please*," said Cle.

"Even his Malosz theorem didn't help him in the end."

I looked at Earl. He was in his own pain.

"It was you," I said. "Wasn't it?"

He didn't answer.

"Wasn't it, Earl? *You* sent it to us."

"He couldn't stop himself," Biettermann said. "He was this close. But he fixed on a bad idea. He fixed on bad ideas all his life."

"It was you, Earl, wasn't it? You had to have been ecstatic to find it."

"The whole Malosz thing was luck, you know." He turned the chair. "You all realize that, don't you? It was luck." He tapped his hands against the rails and laughed noisily. "The Fields Medal went to a piece of blind fucking luck."

"Oh, my God," I said.

"Earl," said Cle, "that's enough."

But he rolled closer. "Nobody gets lucky twice, though, do they, Andret?" He shook Dad's shoulder. "Couldn't pull it off with Abendroth, could you?"

Dad's eyes didn't open.

"That's enough, Earl."

In the chair he drew back his shoulders, the way he did before he picked up his weights. "Stuck yourself for a decade on a bad idea. If you hadn't, who knows what you might have done."

"Enough."

"Tossed away your last great chance."

My mother stepped to the center of the room then and said, "My husband changed mathematics. Nothing you've ever done comes close to that."

Biettermann didn't even look up. "He had a good mind," he said, "no doubt about it. But it was crippled. Look at him. You can say what you want. But that's the truth." He pushed all the way to the couch then, where Dad's eyes finally blinked open. "Wasted. Never clear enough to see your way through to the end of anything."

Cle started toward the wheelchair.

"Were you, Milo?"

Dad said quietly, "I don't even see you."

Biettermann bent forward. "Then listen to me. I can smell it. Something's rotten in the state of Denmark."

"And I thought you were coming to say goodbye," said Paulie.

"That's what I *am* doing." He slapped the rails. "Goodbye, Andret."

Cle grabbed the chair then and pulled Earl backward, so quickly that the heels of his shoes bumped along the floor. If she hadn't, I think the chain would have struck him in the head. Paulie had swung it from her hip, so wildly that when it missed him it lashed back around and smacked her on her own knee. "Ouch," she cried and jerked at it.

Like a snake disturbed from its den, the whole slippery thing began sliding off the table then, first slowly, then swiftly, until with a sickening clatter it crashed onto the floor. "Oh, Jesus," Paulie said. She dropped to her knees. "Oh God." She bent over and began pulling at it, passing the loops through her fingers and rubbing them on her skirt. She lifted the burlap sack off the table and started setting the links carefully back inside. "I think it's okay. I think it's—"

Then she whispered, "Oh, God, Dad. I am so sorry."

On the floor lay a single, curved chip.

There was silence.

Biettermann said, "Well, Paulette, that didn't work out quite the way you'd hoped, did it?"

"Fuck you, Earl." She turned on him. "Get the fuck out of here!"

He raised his eyebrows.

My mother said, "Just stay away from my husband."

"To which of us are you referring?" said Earl.

"To *both* of you."

"Well, for one, Helena," he replied, "he's not your husband anymore."

"Please," said Cle. "Please, we came to help."

Paulie wheeled. "To *help*? You came *to help*?"

"Yes. We did."

"Well, you can help by getting the hell out. Both of you. I can't believe you're still here. You *both* disgust me!"

My mother stepped around the table then and pulled Paulie into her arms; then she turned and walked her into the kitchen. When Mom came back in, she was alone. She moved to the center of the room, picked up the broken piece, and laid it on the mantel. It was a crescent, as long and narrow as one of her fingers, still bearing both aspects of its curve.

She approached my father then, who'd fallen back asleep. "Why didn't you tell me?" she said. She leaned down and shook his shoulder. "Milo."

A rough snore.

"You never showed this to me, sweetheart." She reached back and pulled the burlap sack toward her. "You showed *her,* but not me. If you'd loved me, you would have shown this to me." She knelt beside him. "It's extraordinary, Milo. It's so beautiful."

"Helena," Cle said clearly from across the room. "He did love you."

"No, he didn't. I know he never did."

"Yes, yes. He did. He loved you. He loved his children. He loved all of you."

Paulie appeared in the doorway. "He never loved anybody."

"He did," I said.

"Oh, yes," said Cle. "Hans is right. He loved you, Helena. He loved you, Paulie. He loved you, Hans. He loved all of you."

"How could you even say that?" said my sister.

"Because he told me."

My mother flinched.

I stepped across and stood next to her. She was still on her knees alongside Dad, but she drew back her shoulders and said, "All I know is that he never told any of *us* that."

"He never told anyone anything," Cle said. "That's just how he was."

"Then why did he tell *you?*"

"Because he *didn't* really care about me, Helena." She crossed the room, tucking at bits of her hair that had unwound, and when she reached my mother she held out her hands. To my surprise, my mother took them. Without a word then, Cle pulled her gently to standing. She pressed Mom's fingers to her lips and for several moments just held them there.

AT THE REAR of the hotel room, Biettermann looked up. "It was good of you to come," he said. He was sitting in front of the veined mirror, working a cuff link into his sleeve. "Things got out of hand yesterday. I'm sorry it happened."

"Yes, they did."

"I imagine it's the last time I'll speak to you—to *any* of you, probably—but that wasn't my intent. I was here for other reasons. I wanted to say—well, I *did* want to say goodbye to your dad." He nodded at me. "Things got away from us. I've always been a competitor, and so has he. We've known each other a long time."

"I know that."

"My wife and I are going home this afternoon."

"I'm aware of that, too."

The room was the best in the hotel, but the air conditioner was rattling against the wall. He slapped it with his hand. Without turning, he said, "Those pills won't be enough, you know."

"Which pills?"

"The ones the doctor gave him. What that doctor prescribed is pretty much baby aspirin."

"Well, they've worked so far. And he uses something else at night."

He turned from the wall and rolled to the desk. "Well, that won't work forever, either. Not when you need it to, anyway. My wife showed me what you're giving him." He pulled at his sleeve, still finishing the cuff link. "That's all I wanted to say."

"Okay."

"Look," he said, "obviously I'm judicious. I run one of the most profitable divisions in the house. I can't be careless."

"And?"

He rolled closer now, shaking out his sleeve. "And the pain's taught me something, you know? Have you ever been in pain like that? Not everyone can bear it. But if you're strong, it eventually just makes you stronger." He held up his wrists. "That's what I've learned. The stuff they tell you is bullshit. If you're disciplined, you can keep control of anything. That's the only truth." He tilted his chair backward and held it there until his forearms shook. Then he let it down. "Yes, to answer your question, I'm in a *lot* of pain. You've never experienced anything like it. And I hope you never do."

"So what did you want to tell me?"

He rolled to the mini-fridge then and opened the door. "You have to keep it cold," he said. When he returned he was holding the silver cigarette case in his hand. He leaned forward and gave it to me. "This is for your father, Hans."

WHEN I CAME down the stairs that night, he was snoring softly. He'd kicked off part of his sheet, so I lifted it and folded it in around his legs. I wasn't sure he needed his medicine, but I went about preparing a dose anyway, moving quietly and standing at the window so I could use the light of the moon. Through the screens, the lake looked calm, but I could hear it chiming against the pebbles.

"Why am I still here?"

I looked back. I wasn't even sure he was awake.

I waited a moment.

"Hans?"

"Because you're strong, Dad."

A silence.

"You know," he said, "I used to wonder whether I'd be scared."

I switched on the lantern and set it at his feet. I could see his belly now, pushing up the sheet. "Well," I said, "*are* you?"

"Yes."

I pulled the chair closer and took his hand.

"I can't hold anything even. It all falls through. I never know why or when." He lifted one leg, moved it an inch, and set it down. Then he lifted the other. I realized he was trying to roll onto his side so that I could give him his shot. But when I leaned down to help, he shook his head. "I'll do it."

Slowly, he shifted his pelvis. One leg moved a little, then the other. The cast stayed against the wall, and finally, with his good hand, he reached out and brought it close to his side. "But first," he said, "a little ballet."

I let out a small laugh.

He smiled. "Your kids are fine," he said.

"Thanks, Dad."

"They're not the usual."

"I appreciate it."

I realized he was trying to catch his breath, so I sat there quietly. After a time, he said, "Women are the suns, you know. Men are just the moons."

Then his eyes closed. I pulled the blanket over him, and he snored. "All that fucking work," he said suddenly.

The small muscles at the rim of his mouth were quivering. I had that feeling again that I was seeing him in another piece of time. But he was going backward now. Somewhere in the universe, maybe, he was a young man again.

"What did you want to know?" he said, waking. He turned toward me and winced.

"I have your shot."

He thought about it. Then he mumbled, "Okay."

I rolled him over the rest of the way.

"Do you want my advice, Hans?"

"Of course I do." I slid in the needle.

"That burns."

"I know it does. I'm sorry. It's going to feel better in a minute."

His hand reached back and tried to find the syringe.

Another silence. A long one this time, while his fingers moved slowly over the bone. He was feeling for the needle that I'd already pulled out. Finally, he said, "What kind of advice?"

"Whatever you feel like telling me."

He thought about it. Then he said, "You were a lonely boy. So was I."

His eyes closed again.

When they opened, he said, "Life is brutal."

He looked out toward the lake. "I should have just kept walking," he said. His eyes came back to me, then drifted out the window again. "I was deep enough. I should have just kept on going."

. . .

IT WAS THE middle of the night, but Audra picked up on the first ring. "How is he now?" she said.

"Not good."

"Oh, sweetheart, I'll come back out."

"I don't know if it's time yet."

"I'll be there tomorrow."

"Thank you, Aud."

I was on the porch, watching him sleep. Through the screens, the sun was beginning to light the horizon.

"You know," I said, "I think I finally figured something out. Something Matthew said to me once about confession. He might have been right."

I listened to her breathing.

"Tell me what you mean," she said.

"It's a hunch. For a long time, I'd been thinking it was Earl who sent us that journal. But now I realize Earl doesn't know a thing about it. If he did, he would have said something." I looked out the window at the close hills, which were just beginning to be marked out against the day. "I think it was Dad."

"Sweetheart, I'm sorry—I don't understand."

"I think it was Dad who sent me the combinatorics journal, Aud. The one with Benedek Fodor's paper in it. Dad sent it to me himself."

Mysterium Cosmographicum

WHEN IT HAPPENED, the floor hardly shook.

I ran out to the porch, but Paulie was already at his side. Dad was on the rug, the cast pushed up against the wall. His huge belly was splayed beside him like a duffel bag he'd tripped over. I could see the labored heaving of his chest.

"Oh, God," Paulie said, backing away. "He hurt himself."

The cast lifted a fraction of an inch, then fell.

"Oh, God," he murmured.

"Let's get you up, Dad. Come on, Paulie. We're going to lift him. Dad?"

"No, Hans." Paulie had backed all the way to the door.

"Dad," I said, "are you hurt?"

"Up," he said weakly.

"Let's lift him. Paulie, come over here and help!"

She crossed the floor and knelt next to us. I lifted Dad's belly until it flattened over his ribs.

"Jesus," she whispered.

"I know." With the cast I pushed the weight of it over his hips. "Okay, lift."

"Oh, my God," said Paulie. "What was that?"

"It might have been his ribs. Dad, did we hurt you?"

He rasped.

"Set him down, Paulie. Set him down. Take his shoulders. I'll get his legs. Dad, we're going to move you."

She knelt by his head. He was trying to twist onto his side. I used the cast to pin his belly, but when I grabbed his hip my thumb pushed through the bone as though it were a piece of Styrofoam. "Oh, God, Paulie."

"Oh, no. Oh, no." She rose.

"Paulie! Look at me! We have to get him up." I straightened his leg but he pulled it away. "Get the blanket, Paulie! Get the blanket from the bed!"

"Oh, no, Hans. Oh, no. We're going to *hurt* him!"

"He's already hurt! Jesus, Paulie! Get the blanket!"

"No."

"Paulie!"

"No, Hans. We can't *do* this."

I yanked it off the mattress myself, then pushed it under his thighs. When I tried to tug the rest of him up onto it, though, his ribs made a snapping sound, as though I'd yanked open a row of buckles.

Paulie screamed.

I moved to his head and tried his shoulders, but I felt a rip inside the cast. He was shaking now.

"Helena—" he rasped.

Mom was standing in the doorway.

"Oh, God, Milo. Lord help us." She knelt and clasped his hand. "Where does it hurt?"

"Helena—"

"Be strong, my love. Get his shoulders, Hans."

"We tried, Mom. I don't think—"

"Yes, we can." She squatted. "One, two—oh, Lord, what was that?"

"It's his ribs."

"It's going to be all right, Milo."

I heard Paulie vomit.

Mom went to her knees. "Milo!" she said sharply.

He opened his eyes.

"We're going to leave you here. It's going to be okay. We'll leave you right here on the floor. You'll be fine." She was pushing down on his belly now, and the movement seemed to relieve him. He drew a longer breath. "It's all right," she said. He drew another. "It's all right." She was pressing the weight of it to keep it over his hips. "We'll get you comfortable, Milo, just where you are. Just where you are, Milo. Right here."

Then she rose and began pulling pillows from the bed; then cushions from the chairs, sliding them under his head and shoulders and all along his sides. Paulie came back from the living room with more of them from the couch. Dad let Mom move him as she slid them around him. His color was returning now. All the while she kept pressing down on his belly. He was taking longer breaths. "We'll make it okay," she said. "Paulie, sweetheart, it's all right. Hans, you go get his medicine. Paulie, he'll need a glass of water. We'll take care of you right here, my love. Oh, Milo. We'll take care of you right here. It's going to be all right."

AND IT WAS, strangely—it was strangely all right. Over his last days, my father made one final recovery, a recovery that seemed as improbable as all the others; but this time he did it on a makeshift bed, on the floor of that rickety screened porch, in the shifting light of the sun. He slept and woke, ate little, drank in fits, relieved himself without warning or embarrassment, rested his belly on its own pillow and propped the rest of his frame among a raft of cushions and blankets that had been spread around him like the drapery in a harem. My mother pulled his old mattress away from the wall and made it her own bed.

Dr. Gandapur drained him once more, which eased his breathing considerably. As he was packing up the bottles, he turned to Dad and said, "I've made a telephone call, Milo. They would accommodate you quite comfortably at the general hospital where I work in Lansing. And, of course, I would be there, too."

Dad blinked at the ceiling. He ran his tongue over his teeth and said, as loudly as he could, "Fuck off, Danny."

Dr. Gandapur's lips turned up.

The doctor went out to the living room then to make the same offer to my mother, and though they were whispering, I could tell what her answer was.

After that visit, Dad experienced several days of relative comfort. He smoked. He drank a little. He listened to the radio. He talked, quietly and sporadically, but occasionally at length. He even tried to draw again, asking Paulie to bring him the pad—she practically ran to get it—but then letting it fall from his grip a few moments after he'd started. Moths batted the screens. Squirrels shook the branches of the hemlocks. At one point, a doe walked right up to the porch. The world seemed to want to look in.

For hours at a time now, his pain seemed to leave him entirely, as though it had completed its work ahead of schedule and had simply gone on without him. He propped himself up, just slightly, so that he could see out to the water. I don't know how many of his bones were cracked, and he could hardly raise his head. His hand swelled until we couldn't even ease it out of the cast. Inside the hole in the plaster, the fingertips grew dark. But he didn't ask for any more medicine, and sometimes as I was getting his dose ready, he asked me to go light on it or to skip it altogether. I might only be comforting myself, but I think he might have been making one last effort to be present for all of us.

For Paulie, I think, most of all.

After his first day on the floor, she moved her bed down to the sofa in the living room. She would go out to sit with him in the mornings and evenings while my mother took a break.

Mom spent hour after hour with him. She cleaned his face with a washcloth, massaged his feet, held a straw to his lips. She carried out his bedpan and changed his sheets if he soiled them. Even in the middle of the night when I went out to give him his dose, she would wake on the mattress behind him and—not wanting to disturb either of us, I think—watch the commerce in silence.

As for Paulie, I know it must have been a test for her in ways that I can't truly comprehend. I can't imagine what she must have felt, trying to take care of him at last, when it was so obviously too late, or even watching my mother take care of him, as she had for all their years together. The man who'd left us so remorselessly. The man who'd left all of us, obviously; but most grievously, somehow, had left my sister—at an age that now seemed strangely like the age she might remain forever.

ONE EVENING, AS I was cleaning the dishes, Paulie appeared in the kitchen. She was wearing a faded flower-print sundress like the ones she used to put on as a teenager. She seemed more at ease than I'd seen her in days.

"Did you talk to him?" I said.

She turned a quick twirl, and the fabric of the dress flared up. "I did," she said. She moved quickly into my arms and buried her face in my shoulder. When she stepped back, she said, "He asked me about what I do."

"And?"

"I told him. I told him about my work. And my teaching. But, you know—he seemed genuinely *interested*."

"He is, Paulie. I know he is."

"I asked him about his life, too."

"And what did he tell you?"

"He told me a story about when I was a girl. One time when Mom had the flu he had to take us to his office. You weren't even in preschool yet, so I must have been about two or three. He was starting on something new, and I wouldn't be quiet, even when he held me.

So he just lifted me up onto his shoulders. I guess I liked it up there. I sat like that for the whole afternoon, evidently, running my fingers through the hair on the top of his head, while he worked."

"And?"

"And that's all." She was blinking.

"That's a sweet story, Paulie."

"Is it crazy to think that you can remember something that happened when you were two?"

"I don't know, Paulie. Maybe not."

"Because I can. All my life I've had that memory. I've always thought I invented it, that it was some recurring dream about my professional anxiety, or something like that. But I guess I didn't. I guess it's an actual memory. I'm sitting up there, looking at a blackboard, over the top of my dad's head, and I feel so happy."

LATER THAT EVENING, the phone rang, and the next morning a car pulled up the drive.

It was Knudson Hay.

I don't know if Mom had called him or if he'd heard the news some other way. He'd flown in from Florida, then driven up at dawn from Detroit. When he saw Dad propped on the floor among the pillows, he pulled off his suit jacket and sat down on the rug next to him.

"Dad," I said from the doorway, "it's—"

"Chairman Hay," whispered my father. "Punctual as ever."

"Hello, Milo."

Dad was able to reach his hand up a few inches. Hay took it.

"I'll leave you two alone now," I said.

My father glanced at his old boss, then at me, working his lips. "I was right," he said slowly.

I waited at the door.

"About what?" came Hay's temperate voice.

I could hear Dad's lips smacking. "It didn't matter," he said.

"That's okay, Milo."

"No," Dad said. "None of it—I was right. None of it mattered. None of it ever did."

SOMETIME LATER, HAY shuffled into the kitchen. I looked out to the porch and saw Paulie sitting in the chair beside Dad now, reading. He was asleep, his mouth a gash against the pillows.

My mother heated a pot of tea, and Hay sat down with us at the table. My mother seemed strangely comfortable with him, and I must say, sitting between them in that old cabin in Michigan, it took several minutes of conversation before I suddenly recalled that for a decade she'd worked as a secretary in his department. Paulie was right: how ignorant we are of the lives of our parents. In the kitchen now, she poured him a cup of tea and brought out a plate of cookies, then moved to the counter, where, as they spoke, she made a sandwich for him and set it in a paper bag for his flight.

He was doing most of the talking. While my mother listened, first at the counter, then with her hands folded on the tablecloth next to him, he reported in detail about all the people they'd known. In retirement, he'd remained an elegant man, his hair still carefully combed and his summer suit starched in the shoulders. He went through all the old staff, remembering everything: names and dates; illnesses; children; grandchildren. He told her what the faculty had done and where they'd gone. He went on about a few students who'd made reputations in the field. He told her what he'd been doing himself in the years since his retirement.

At one point, from the porch, a snore drifted through the wall. As it did, a look of pain crossed my mother's face.

Hay set down his tea. "There's no use denying it," he said. "He was a difficult man. We both know that." He smiled musingly at her, then looked over at me. "And you, Hans—you know it, too, I'm sure."

I nodded.

"But there was something in him that a few of us responded to, as well. Powerfully. You and I did, anyway, Helena. It was more than just his genius."

"In a strange way," said my mother, "it might have been his honesty."

Hay rubbed his hands slowly together. "I guess I agree with that," he said. "I don't know if many other people would call it that, but I believe that's what it was. Clarity, at least. Incorruptible vision. He had an unwillingness to ease anyone's pain, including his own. No— maybe not an unwillingness. A complete *inability* to ease it. His or anyone else's."

My mother looked down.

Hay broke off a cookie and chewed it, and my mother poured more tea. "I'd always wished—" she said, setting aside her cup. "I'd always wished that when you came all the way out here to help him like that, that he would have had something left of his ambition. Enough to accept the job, anyway." She touched her napkin to her cheek. "Or enough humility. Maybe humility was what he needed at that moment, more than anything else." She smiled faintly, perhaps at the thought of my father being humble. "I know it's long past," she said, "but I've always wished it could have happened differently. I've always meant to thank you for your graciousness, too, Knudson. I imagine there must have been opposition. I should have thanked you years ago." She touched at her lips. "It meant a lot, to all of us."

"It did," I said.

Hay looked up.

"Anyway," she went on. "I suppose things probably wouldn't have been—"

He rose, brought a box of tissue from the counter, and reseated himself next to her.

"Darn it," she said. "I didn't—"

"It's fine, Helena."

Another fitful snore came through the wall.

It was Hay's small chuckle at the sound that allowed my mother, I think, to finally reclaim her poise. I must say, she was of striking beauty as she did. She blinked her eyes, wiped her cheeks, and then produced her familiar, forthright features again, as though they were items she'd merely stowed for a moment in her purse. When she sat straight, she resembled the woman she must have been when she first walked into the mathematics department offices, forty years before. And Hay, too, as he held himself squarely in the chair beside her and touched his pressed cuffs, one then the other, looked like a man of some distant and formal period. It was a visible transformation for both of them.

"I can't help thinking," she went on, "that another chance would have rekindled him. Would have spurred him to accomplish one more thing that would have been worthy of his talent." She raised her chin. "That we all would have been—that we all would have been—even the children—"

She turned to the window.

"I'm sorry, Helena."

"If only he'd been humble enough when he needed to be." She was still looking away.

Hay cleared his throat.

She turned toward him, dabbing again at her eyes. "Thank you for your courage, Knudson. The Andrets will always be grateful."

He reached out then and touched her shoulder, lightly, before withdrawing his hand. Then he leaned back and took a protracted sip of tea—I could see him deliberating. As he set the cup back onto the saucer, he looked up at her with an expression of kindness. "I still don't believe—" he began. "I still don't believe in holding an important conversation on the telephone. And I didn't in those days, either, Helena. That's why I came out here to see him."

Mom was honestly surprised, I think, by the words that followed. He laid them out precisely, as was his unremitting nature, all the while holding out the box of tissues. When he'd finished, his hand went forward briefly again and touched her on the shoulder, then descended to the table, where it closed for a moment, rather tenderly, over her wrist. Then it retreated. Either the gesture or the news seemed to still her—to still her deeply—as if he'd plucked from her shoulders a lifelong cloak of worry.

There were tears in her eyes. Presently she turned to me, a smile emerging almost involuntarily. "Did you know this, too, Hans?"

"No, Mom." I took her hand. "I didn't. But I suppose it doesn't surprise me."

What Hay had told us was that when he'd made the trip up to the cabin all those years ago, he'd done so only to alert my father to a paper he'd heard about, a paper that Benedek Fodor was about to publish. This had been the sole reason for his visit. There had never been any offer to return to Princeton.

Drake

THAT NIGHT, WHEN I bent to give him his medicine, he startled. "They beat me," he said.

He twisted his head, trying to shield it with the cast.

"It's all right, Milo," said Mom.

His body was shaking.

"It's all right, Dad. It's us—it's Hans and Mom. We're not going to hurt you."

IN THE MORNING, Danny Gandapur arrived again. He knelt by the pillows with a tiny electric saw and cut away the cast. Beneath it, Dad's arm was green and yellow, still bent in two places, covered everywhere with a strangely plush layer of hair. The doctor wrapped it in a sling and drew the cinches tight.

That afternoon, the pain returned. He arched his back and moaned. The fist of his good hand, bony and gray, beat the floor.

"Come on, Dad," I said. "It's time for your medicine."

"I don't want any."

He went on writhing. I waited a few moments, then slid in the needle. For a time, I had to grip his fist to keep the bones from breaking on the floor.

. . .

"He and my mom used to lie in this same bed," I said that night. Audra had arrived a few hours before. "They used to lie here worrying about Paulie and me."

She reached over and took my hand. I'd just come upstairs after checking on Dad. There was a breeze outside, and below us, the waves were laying themselves against the pebbles. I didn't feel sorrow, really, just a washing sort of fatigue.

"And one day Emmy will be in *her* own bed," she said, "and Niels will be in his, worrying about *their* kids. It's strange to think about."

The wind was blowing through the big pines, brushing their needles along the roof. "You know," I said, "it's pretty much impossible to define time. Nobody has ever succeeded."

"That's very strange," she said.

"I suppose so. The physicists have been working on it the longest, and I guess they've come the closest."

"Well?"

"They say it's the thing you measure with a clock."

She laughed. "You know who once said that same thing to me?"

"Who?"

"Emmy. That exact thing. She must have read it somewhere."

"Of course she did."

"But you know who thought like that, too, don't you? Your father. Your father and your daughter—they both get absorbed by the same kinds of things."

She turned over on her side then, which is what she does before sleep. I didn't want her to. I felt like I was losing her into the sea.

"Aud?"

"I'm right here."

"I think pain is something like that. I don't think Dad believes it truly exists. Not the way *we* think of it, anyway. Maybe it exists as a measurement of suffering—like a clock does—but not as an essence. I think he truly believes that there's something he hasn't figured out about it yet. If he can think about it long enough, maybe he can define it, and then maybe he'll be able to alter it. I think that's what he's doing down there."

DAD WOKE, BLINKED his eyes, and turned onto his side. He took a sip from his glass, then raised his face. When he saw Audra behind me, he started to smile. She stepped close, knelt beside him, and kissed him on the cheek.

Even now I saw the pleasure on his face.

When I withdrew the needle, he rolled back down and lifted his neck to see her again. Finally, he let his head fall. "Where the wood ducks rest," he said.

He slept for a moment.

"Where they rest," he said. "I lie down on the water."

"It's okay, Dad."

He pointed at the shelves.

"I'm sorry," said Paulie.

She was standing in the doorway.

After a moment, Dad said, "What was that, sweetheart?"

"I wanted to say that, Dad—I wanted to tell you I'm sorry."

Audra rose and left.

Dad gestured to Paulie. She crossed and stood before him.

"Were *you* ever sorry?" she said.

"For what?"

"For everything. For leaving us."

With her fingers, she was worrying her skirt. He raised his arm, and she knelt to let him take her hand. "I was sorry a long time before that," he said.

"*FORETHOUGHT,*" HE SAID the next morning. He turned toward me. "That's the word I was looking for."

"Wow, Dad. You're awake. That's quite a good memory."

"They do not," he said slowly, "tax their lives"—he took a breath—"with *forethought* of grief."

"What is that?"

"I don't know."

"It's a poem," said Audra from the doorway.

He lifted his eyes.

Then he let them fall. I took his hand. The fingers were chilly, and as he drifted, they squeezed mine in a slow rhythm, the way Niels's used to do when he was first walking, his tiny fingers gripping my own—tighter, looser, tighter—as he labored to cross a room. "I should have—" he said, waking.

The eyelids fluttered.

Later in the morning, he turned. We stayed on the porch with him, but he no longer lifted his head. Mom propped him on the pillows. His eyes were open, but they wandered, the pupils darting back and forth as though tiny insects were hovering in the air in front of him. Early in the afternoon, his mouth twisted and his hand went to his belly. It pressed down along the flank.

He moaned. "Tell Earl," he said. "Tell him I'm ready."

"Earl's gone, Dad."

He gritted his teeth, looked up at the ceiling, searched weakly with his hand along the flesh.

Then he rose all the way to his elbows.

"Go get him," he said. "Tell him I'm ready to travel."

THE CIGARETTE CASE was still in the refrigerator, and inside it were the instructions. From the compartment behind the cigarettes, I pulled out two syringes. They were already filled.

That afternoon, I gave Dad the first one. Then I sat down and watched. I, Hans Euler Andret, fellow mathematician, fellow addict, fellow lonely and yet ever-hopeful soul, gave him Earl Biettermann's dose and then lowered myself onto the floor beside him. His face grew quiet. The writhing ceased. The black, withered hand came up and rested in a loose fist along his belly, which in a small bit of mercy had finally shrunk tight. He was at last being allowed to immaterialize.

I could see that behind his eyes he had gone somewhere worthy of his interest. The lids fluttered. They were closed, but he wasn't asleep. He was resting calmly.

I wondered if it was mathematics.

I wondered if that's what he was doing. I hoped, as I sat on the floor beside him, that what he was witnessing behind those lids was the great unbaring of his clue. The way Kekulé, dreaming, had chanced upon his Ouroboros; or Howe, the spears of his cannibals; or Einstein, moving swiftly down the mountain, his transformation of the stars.

On and on he traveled. For the afternoon and into the evening.

Near dusk, clouds moved in, and the wind grew stronger through the screens. My mother and Paulie and Audra came and went. I laid another blanket across him.

At the poles of the earth, time ceases to exist. Or rather, time becomes meaningless because it exists in every form at once. It is always dawn and always dusk. Always noon and always midnight. The reason for this is that, at the poles, every time zone coincides. At those two points—at those *singularities,* as Forsyth would have called them—our construction of the familiar fails.

All through the evening, he lay beneath the blankets, a faint tremor on his face, his bruised fist opening and closing. My mother took long turns with him. Paulie did, too.

Not long after nightfall, his lids opened, and he drew a harsh breath. His back arched and he cried out. My mother took his hand.

After a time, she rose and left the room. When she returned, she was holding all the other vials from upstairs. "This will be enough," she said.

I looked up at her.

"It's okay, sweetheart," she said. "It really is. We're just going to help him now."

. . .

WHEN SHE EMERGED later into the living room, she took hold of Paulie's hand. We all walked together onto the porch and sat down beside him. We stayed there like that, the three of us arranged around him.

I hope he went back to the woods. Back to the great leafy woods of his childhood, where he'd first known solace.

The Battle of Trafalgar

"I SHALL NEVER give up!" I shouted from the bow. "I shall never give up!"

"That's the stuff!" roared my father. "That's my boy!" I saw his glance move to Paulie, who'd turned away at his words.

"That's my girl!"

Now she looked back at him.

We were moored in a muddy cove a quarter mile to the north of the cabin. On their maiden voyage, the *Victory* and the *Royal Sovereign* had proved seaworthy, and now Paulie and I had parked the *Victory* beneath the shade of a weeping willow that arched over the shallows. At the deep end of a rotting dock twenty yards to the east bobbed the *Royal Sovereign*.

"Long live Her Majesty's Navy!" shouted my father.

"Long live Pascal!" I shouted back. "Long live the hydraulic principle!"

"The fate of England rests upon this battle," called my mother. "Every man and woman to their duty. *Dei sub numine viget!*"

Then, from their deck, Dad took aim. His long arm descended, and from the thick barrel of the pipe-cannon came a lopsided yellowish missile, wobbling into view. It arched weakly, tumbling end over end and throwing a halo of drops before it landed with a slap on the water.

I was on the downward slope of a dose: I understood that the misfired potato had been a representation of his care.

"Fire, Hans!" yelled my sister. "Fire!"

"Fuck Princeton University!" shouted Dad. He bent to reload.

My mother glanced back at him. "Well, I don't know—"

"Yes!" I shouted back. "Fuck the Tigers!" I reached into our own supply of potatoes and, with apology, selected the most perfectly spherical. "We shall return!" I called.

"Wrong battle," hissed Paulie.

"I know that, Smallette."

"Wrong century." She looked at me suspiciously.

I dropped the smoothly carved missile into the barrel, fixed my eyes on the target, and thrust my arm down against the piston. Dad, of course, had drilled relief holes to reduce the force of the hydraulics, but somehow my chosen potato had found a way to defeat them. The recoil knocked me sideways. To my astonishment, a pale, buzzing projectile whizzed across the inlet and smacked like a croquet mallet against the stern of their craft. A bottle jumped sideways out of the hull like a fish leaping back into the sea.

"Oh my God!" shouted Paulie. "You did it, Hans! A direct hit! You wounded him!"

"Dear Lord," came my father's shaky voice. "We've been breached."

I reloaded. The next potato had grown a strange curling bud at one end, like the handle of a Klein bottle—it lacked only the connecting dimple—but its central radius seemed, like its predecessor's, to have been grown expressly for the bore of our cannon. Ah, wonders. When I fired, I saw that my bullet had been hurled by God. From the top of the *Royal Sovereign*'s stern came another echoing wallop, this one like a boot kicking a car door, followed by a gurgling dunk as the ordnance careened onward into the channel. My father looked up, frightened now.

"Jesus," he said in a hushed voice. "Two in a row."

"God save the queen!" shouted Paulie.

"We give up!" called my mother from the rear of their boat, laughing and raising her sun-hat on a stick.

"Nonsense," came Dad's measured reply. "One early triumph means nothing. We've just gotten started. We shall never give up!"

"Neither shall we!" yelled Paulie.

"Never give up," I whispered at the sky.

"But we *do*!" called my mother. "We *do* give up!"

"Jesus," I heard my father say. "We're taking on water."

They were. I bent to the potato pail, and when I stood again, I saw that Dad had somehow caught his foot inside the gash in their stern. I slipped the next potato into the barrel—it made a dull *poof* like a dropped sack of flour—and at that moment Dad fell over comically onto his back, his arms shooting up behind him and one leg stabbing through to the other side of the hull, where it kicked lamely at the water. I was aware, briefly, of a rent in time: my shot, though still in the barrel, had already felled him.

A dizzying revelation.

I looked up for a moment at the painted sky, and when I refocused I saw his flailing arms, reaching alternately for one gunwale and then the other. My poor father. The *Royal Sovereign*'s bow jiggered back and forth as though a manatee were bumping past it underwater. He tried to wedge himself up by grabbing the handle of one of the keel jugs. There was a swallowing sound, a row of bottles came out in his hand, and the long deck accordioned around him as though the pins had been pulled from a folding chair.

From the high point of the transom, my mother began crying with laughter.

Dad struggled to his feet. Then he fell again. He pulled himself up and slid back the other way.

That's when I realized it: he was drunk.

Of course.

On the other hand, there was nothing to prove that time had not indeed run backward.

"Fire!" shouted my sister.

"Rudder," I said. "They've lost rudder."

"Fire!"

"Victory is ours, I do believe, Paulie. Superior tactic and preparation—we've prevailed."

"Fire, dopehead!"

"What?"

"Fire!" Then she said, "Oh my God, I believe he's having *fun*."

"Damn all of you," came my father's thick-voiced rebuke. He struggled to his knees and managed to pull his leg back through the breach, lowering his shoulders and shaking his head from side to side like a buffalo fighting a spear. "Man the torpedoes!"

"Honey, honey," said my mother, "we surrender! We surrender!" She moved lightly behind him, still laughing, and pulled him to his feet.

"We shall never—"

"No! No! No!" she said. "We shall right this very minute! Children, we surrender!"

"Never!"

They were halfway submerged now. He twisted around, staggered from her grip, and mounted the slanting transom. There he teetered for a moment on the screeching bottles before, with a bellow, he flung himself sideways like a walrus. The lagoon shattered. A mud-colored polytope of his mass shot glitteringly into the air, where it remained for a moment like a strobe in my eyes. "Lord God," I breathed.

"Victory is ours," whispered Paulie.

"Lord God."

"Hold your fire," called my mother, waving her hat. "We come in peace."

We waited.

I looked up at the unfathomable sky. "We accept in peace," I said.

Then I returned to my battle station. The dark remnant of my father's gravity had by then repaired itself, and all that remained of him

now was a rippling dissipation of the original disturbance. Patiently
it graphed itself toward us. The cove was only a few feet deep where
he'd entered, but it was as brown as coffee. He seemed to have passed
through to the other side of the earth. My mother reclaimed her spot
on the high end of the boat and continued to wave her hat, beaming
her smile across the cove as though we were the next two guests on
her talk show. The plastic pipe of their potato cannon spun numi-
nously in the ripples.

He'd flung himself into the water twenty yards from where Paulie
and I now shaded ourselves beneath the willow, but by the time his
wake reached us there was no sign of him at all. Just the inscrutable
lagoon, meticulously reaveraging its depth. A heron squawked. A
catfish nosed the reeds. His wake returned from the far shore and
passed beneath us again. Still no sign of him. By now, Paulie was
glancing around, and my mother's smile had reversed itself. I looked
up at the horizon, where an airplane's contrail was neatly unzipping
the sky. My sister shaded her eyes and leaned low to the water while
my mother rose to her feet on the now-ebulliently-buoyant deck and
called out, tentatively, "Milo?"

The cattails swayed.

Presently, in a more tremulous voice, she whispered, "Hans?"

"I'm sure he's fine, Mom."

"Mom?" said Paulette. "Hans? What's happened?"

"That is a mystery," I said.

But it wasn't. In fact, I knew exactly where he was. As my mother
raised her eyebrows in alarm and my sister turned her head nervously
to shore, first over one shoulder, then over the other—as though my
father were a leopard waiting for us in the trees—I myself remained
languorously at ease. I pulled another potato from the pail and set it
calmly alongside the barrel, just in case.

"To him I resign myself," I said, glancing to the heavens. "And the
just cause which is entrusted to me."

"*What?*" said Paulie.

"Nelson. On the eve of battle."

The drug gave me one last little shiver then. In its wake, I realized that my father would survive. Would survive this now; would survive whatever came for him, then and for all time. I understood that despite every bit of evidence—despite the ruins of his career and the drunken hurtle of our lives, despite the unremitting quarantine of his own genius and the ever-fateful tick-tock of his calamitous inheritance—he would remain forever invincible, even in memory. Always logical of mind, always forward of intent.

He was merely holding his breath, as he'd been training himself to do all summer.

"It'll be all right," I said. I could sense him advancing toward us through the water, like a torpedo.

"Hans?" Paulette whispered. "Hansie, please—"

"He's fine."

When the torpedo hit, my sister screamed. A scattering cape of weeds flew out behind him as he rocketed from the water, seized her by the waist, and lifted her into the air. She screamed again. His arms shook as he carried her through the churning mud to the shore. When he set her down on the sand, they were both laughing.

I remember being happy.

I watched my mother pole the wreckage of the *Royal Sovereign* to land and step out with a picnic basket in her arms. It had remained miraculously dry. She spread its contents across a pinwheel quilt, which had remained just as miraculously dry. Whistling softly, she began prying rubber tops from containers.

"Wow," said my father, dropping to his knees. "Ribs!"

Untroubled.

That's what we were. Our family, at that moment, was *untroubled*.

"And you even thought to put it in plastic," said my father.

"I'm brilliant," cooed my mother.

"That, you are."

We ate.

After the meal, we all lay back to rest. Presently, the sun's rays grew long. To the east, the trees cast themselves in their silver edging; then in their rose-hued shimmer; then in their inky, purple opulence. Around us on the shore, the evening birds emerged; then the frogs began their song, their melodies disputing the rough shrill of the crickets and the electric roil of the marsh flies that were gathering now above us like a restless foreign crowd in a great public square. The buzzing harmonies laced themselves into an aria. In the shadows of the cove, the temperature of the water at last defeated the temperature of the land, and from the reed beds, a chilly breeze came ambling up to find us. Without thinking, we all moved closer together. I could feel the heat from each of them now, from my mother and father and sister, their limbs splayed all around me on the quilt. And as we lay there, the rhythm of our breathing began to organize itself into the rhythm of a single being, rising and falling. In the shelter of that unfamiliar peace, I watched the horizon climb steadily toward the heavens. Higher and higher it rose, until at last, as it neared the sun, the world seemed suddenly to quiet. A shorebird called out. The clouds darkened, then flared brightly at their rims, and for a few moments, as dusk began to spread, the sky was lit by nothing but a crowning thread of fire.

If you would be a real seeker after truth, you must at least once in your life doubt, as far as possible, all things.

—René Descartes

Acknowledgments

MANY PEOPLE HELPED with this book. Among the most generous was Jon Simon, topologist, friend, and professor emeritus at the University of Iowa, who read the manuscript with astonishing care and offered an extremely generous set of notes, corrections, and suggestions on the mathematics. Similarly helpful was Chard deNiord, poet, essayist, fiction writer, and longtime friend, whose frankness remains legendary. My agent, Jennifer Rudolph Walsh, provided her usual levelheaded mix of encouragement and clarity, as did Gina Centrello, president and publisher of Random House. Steve Sellers was a great boon, as always. So were Joe Blair and Bill Houser.

At Penguin Random House, my editor, Kate Medina, read the manuscript so many times I've lost count, never failing to push it in the right direction. Her fine and generous reading and constant support were instrumental. Anna Pitoniak was never-endingly intelligent, responsive, and reliable—a delight to work with. I'm grateful to my copy editors as well, Amy Ryan and Susan Betz—secret heroes, both of them—and to Steve Messina, the book's production editor, who was my kind of meticulous. Also at Penguin Random House, Maria Braeckel and Alaina Waagner got things going for the wide world. I'm grateful to Avideh Bashirrad there, too, along with Benjamin Dreyer, Derrill Hagood, Joe Perez, and Simon Sullivan.

A number of other wonderful friends gave particularly generously of their time, including Liaquat Ahamed, Dan Baldwin, Alex Bassuk, Deb Blair, Nate Brady, Po Bronson, Michael Flaum, Alex Gansa, Dan Geller, Dayna Goldfine, Mike Lighty, Jon Maksik, Yannick Meurice, Linda and John Spevacek, Jane VanVoorhis, Lauren White, Judith Wolff, and Anne Ylvisaker. I owe a debt of gratitude to my brother, Aram, and to his wife, Lianne Voelm, for their adroit advice. Kurt Anstreicher introduced me not only to some of history's great mathematical problems but also to Bob Vanderbei of Princeton University, who was kind enough to tour me through that famous department of mathematics. My thanks to all of them.

For some key details, I'm indebted to my friend Commander Thomas Corcoran, U.S. Navy (Retired), a man who knows both naval history and computer programming. For Wall Street trivia, thanks go to two other friends, Scott Lasser and Gray Lorig. Eric Simonoff at William Morris Endeavor was also very generous with his time. Thanks again to Maxine Groffsky, who stood by me for so many years. And a special thank-you to Wendell Berry and David Blackwell.

For advice about various tidbits, ranging from orthopedic casting to the OSU frat scene, a tip of the hat goes to Hadley Calloway, Rebekah Frumkin, Steve Markley, Fatima Mirza, Ali Selim, and Tim Taranto.

My kids deserve many thanks for their years of forbearance. Of course, I'm forever indebted to my parents, too, Stuart and Virginia Canin, who continue to mean so much to me, and to my great-uncle Max Shiffman, who was the genesis of all of this.

My gratitude goes as well to the John Simon Guggenheim Memorial Foundation, to the University of Iowa, and to the public libraries of Iowa City and Coralville, Iowa, and of beautiful Elk Rapids, Michigan.

But at the risk of burying the lede, my most profound thanks—by far—go to my wife, Barbara, whose care, encouragement, discernment, dedication, and generosity made all the difference.

—e.c.

About the Author

ETHAN CANIN is the author of seven books, including the story collections *Emperor of the Air* and *The Palace Thief* and the novels *For Kings and Planets, Carry Me Across the Water,* and *America America.* He is on the faculty of the Iowa Writers' Workshop and divides his time between Iowa and northern Michigan. He is also a physician.

ethancanin.com

About the Type

This book was set in Bembo, a typeface based on an old-style Roman face that was used for Cardinal Pietro Bembo's tract *De Aetna* in 1495. Bembo was cut by Francesco Griffo (1450–1518) in the early sixteenth century for Italian Renaissance printer and publisher Aldus Manutius (1449–1515). The Lanston Monotype Company of Philadelphia brought the well-proportioned letterforms of Bembo to the United States in the 1930s.